"Two hundred years ago there was an emperor in the lands of the Romans who was called Marcus Aurelius," Maderun said. "In his time there was war between Sarmatian peoples beyond the borders of Dacia, and one of the losing tribes, the Iazyges, came to the Danuvius and asked for asylum in the Empire. The emperor replied that he could not take all of them together, but if they were willing to be divided, he would let them in.

"Five hundred warriors were sent here to Britannia and stationed at Bremetennacum, to guard the western shore. When their twenty years of service were up, they settled here in the North and their sons entered the *Auxilla* after them. When the veterans were given citizenship, as the custom was, they took the family name of their commander, Artorius.

"My cousin Argantel bears the name also, and keeps the Sword. It came to us through our great-grandmother, a druid's daughter who married the last of the Sarmatian soldier-priests who guarded it. It is an ancient blade, forged from star-steel by a magic that no smith in our day understands. In the hands of a great king, born of the ancient blood, it will bring victory.

"A god lives in that Sword, who has promised that the Defender of Britannia will come of my cousin's blood. But the druid that helps him will come of mine."

"And you think that *I* will be that Man of Wisdom?" Ambros asked.

"I know that you are."

Other Books in
The Hallowed Isle *Cycle by*
Diana L. Paxson

THE BOOK OF THE CAULDRON

Wodan's Children *Trilogy*

THE DRAGONS OF THE RHINE
THE WOLF AND THE RAVEN
THE LORD OF HORSES

With Adrienne Martine-Barnes

MASTER OF EARTH AND WATER
THE SHIELD BETWEEN THE WORLDS
SWORD OF FIRE AND SHADOW

DIANA L. PAXSON

THE HALLOWED ISLE

BOOKS I & II

THE BOOK OF THE SWORD AND
THE BOOK OF THE SPEAR

This is a work of fiction. Names, characters, places, and incidents either are the product of the author's imagination or are used fictitiously. Any resemblance to actual events, locales, organizations, or persons, living or dead, is entirely coincidental and beyond the intent of either the author or the publisher.

AVON BOOKS, INC.
An Imprint of HarperCollins*Publishers*
10 East 53rd Street
New York, New York 10022-5299

Copyright © 1999 by Diana L. Paxson
Library of Congress Catalog Card Number: 98-49035
ISBN: 0-380-81367-X
www.harpercollins.com

First Avon Eos Mass Market Printing: April 2000
First Avon Eos Trade Printing: April 1999
First Avon Eos Trade Printing: February 1999

AVON EOS TRADEMARK REG. U.S. PAT. OFF. AND IN OTHER COUNTRIES, MARCA REGISTRADA, HECHO EN U.S.A.

Printed in the U.S.A.

WCD   10   9   8   7   6   5   4   3   2   1

In Memoriam
Paul Edwin Zimmer

ACKNOWLEDGMENTS

My special thanks to Heather Rose Jones, who took time off from her doctoral studies in Welsh philosophy to advise me on the mysteries of fifth-century British spelling. I would also like to thank Alexei Kondratiev for his suggestions regarding the origins of the Wild Man legend and Winifred Hodge for her comments and for correcting my Anglo-Saxon.

I direct the reader to the work of C. Scott Littleton and Ann C. Thomas for more information on the Sarmatian origins of Excalibur. For those who would like an excellent historical overview of the Arthurian period, I recommend *The Age of Arthur* by John Morris, recently published by Barnes & Noble. There are many works on the Anglo-Saxons, but I suggest in particular the fine series published by Anglo-Saxon Books, 25 Malpas Dr., Pinner, Middlesex, England.

Through the fields of European literature, the Matter of Britain flows as a broad and noble stream. I offer this tributary with thanks and recognition to all those who have gone before.

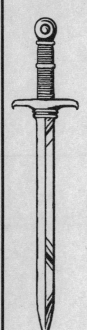

The Book
of the
Sword

PROLOGUE

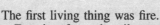 The first living thing was fire.

Erupting from the silent womb of infinite space, it devoured all matter within its reach, grew, raging, and expelled bright showers of sparks to beget new flames. Fire lives still in the glowing heart of the world and in the sun that shines above. All green and growing things feed on that light; it burns in the red blood that pulses through each vein, and in death, all become food and fuel for other things.

Fire is magic.

Above the waving grasses of the steppe, light slashes through the heavens and a solitary tree explodes into flame. Chanting, men carry away the burning branches and fire the coals in their forge. Cunning ironsmiths, their magic is composed equally of skill and spells.

Soon the hearth is ablaze, and in the trough, a lump of rock that fell from heaven begins to glow. It bubbles and cracks, flows out in a river of liquid fire to fill the mold. Once more it grows solid. Sparks fly as hammers beat out the hot iron bar into a shining wire. Again the metal is heated; glowing bundles of wire twining together, fire sparking furiously as the hammer strikes once more.

Twined and twisted, cooled and heated, each particle in each rod is realigned until the mass is no longer iron but something more. As the earth was born out of a spinning star, the steel is born from the forgefire. From the whispering of the flames grow whispered spells; each hammer stroke beats out a complex rhythm; and the steel sings in triumph as its apotheosis nears.

The mage-smiths' chanting compels the steel to hold its shape, slim and deadly and beautiful. Their spells impress upon that shape its nature and its name. They cry out to their god, drawing down his power, precise and anxious lest their work be too weak to contain what comes.

Again the bellows heave and the forge fire furiously glows. Again the blade is heated; the chant marks out the time, wise eyes watch the colors change, and now, with a cry, the steel is lifted. Its shining length seems to ripple as heat-shimmer blurs the air. The mage-smith wraps its tang in leather, and quenches the blade in the heartblood of a captive warrior, chosen for his courage on the field. Sheathed in that throbbing flesh, the sword drinks life. The blade is jerked free, and blood gushes onto the ground. The mage-smith raises it, and lightning sears the sky.

Seven smiths alone know all the spells and secrets to make these blades, the seven mages of the Chalybes. Seven swords they have crafted, forged from star-steel, bearing in their hearts the war-god's name. To seven sacred kings they are given, to deal death in the service of life.

Fire is power.

i

CEREMONY OF THE SWORD

A.D. 424–25

Britannia was burning.

Artoria Argantel pulled her veil half across her face and took a careful breath, staring at the flames. She told herself that this one burning villa was not the world, but even the sun seemed afire in a molten sky, and blue smoke hazed the hills. Her cousin Maderun coughed painfully, then pulled the mantle that covered her bronze-brown hair down as if to shut out the sight of what had once been a prosperous estate. It was a smoldering ruin now, and another column of smoke beyond the hazel wood bore witness to the fate of the next farm along the road.

"Lady, you must come away—" Junius Lupercus reached for her bridle rein. The mare danced nervously as Argantel pulled her back.

"Not yet." He was only doing his duty as captain of her escort, but he did not understand why she had to see.

She stared at the bodies that lay sprawled on the trampled ground. The nearest had been an old man. Blood from a great gash in his crown stained his white hair, but he still clutched

5

a legionary spatha and shield. *A veteran*, she thought, *who had settled near the fort he once defended.* She nudged the mare forward. Junius reached out once more to stop her, but she was already looking at the thing he had not wanted her to see.

Behind the man a little girl, perhaps his granddaughter, stared sightlessly at the sky. The corpse of a red-haired barbarian lay across her bloodied thighs. At least the old soldier had avenged her before he himself was struck down.

"Who did this?" Maderun asked in a shaking voice, putting back her veil.

"Dalriadan raiders, come over from Hibernia," Junius said grimly, pointing at the bloodstained length of checkered cloth. "They will have landed at Bremetennacum and raided northward."

"That's where we met your ship—" said Argantel, her gaze moving from her cousin to the body of the little girl and back again. Maderun nodded, her eyes widening in comprehension.

The captain grimaced. "You were lucky, my lady. Their ships have no comforts, but they are agile and swift. The boat that brought you here would have had no chance if they had caught her at sea." He had evidently given up trying to spare them knowledge of danger.

Maderun grew, if possible, more pale, and Argantel swallowed. At that moment, her cousin's white face and gray eyes must be a mirror of her own. Barbarian raiders, whether from the Scottii or the tribes of Alba who had never come under the yoke of Rome, had been a fact of their lives for as long as they could remember. But for Argantel, learning her lessons among the priestesses of the Isle of Maidens, and for Maderun, safe in her father's court at Maridunum, the attacks had been only a tale of terror.

Until now.

"They must be punished!" she exclaimed. "They cannot be more than a half day ahead of us! Go after them, Junius!"

"And leave you undefended? I will not betray my oath to protect the Lady of the Lake, even at her command. Come, my lady, let me take you home—" He gestured northward. "There is nothing we can do here."

Home. . . . She peered through the smoke as if she could

see through its filthy veils to the green mountains that rose beyond. No enemy had ever penetrated those forests and fells. Even the Romans had built no more than a guardpost there, and soon abandoned it. She closed her eyes, remembering the silver lake within its circle of sheltering heights and the tree-clad island it protected. No raider would ever breach the Isle of Maidens' sanctity. Then she looked at Junius once more and shook her head.

"These people trusted us to defend them and we failed. I will not leave them for the wild beasts to devour." Argantel straightened in the saddle, drawing about her the aura of the high priestess as she held his gaze. "Lay them in the ashes of their home and pile more wood over them. If it can no longer shelter them, let it be their pyre."

She could feel his resistance, but her will compelled him. Even Maderun, watching at her side, eyed her uneasily, as if she could see that invisible mantling of power. It would not be surprising, thought Argantel. Maderun was untrained, but their mothers had been twins, the elder bound to become Lady of the Lake and carry on the family tradition on the druid isle, the younger married off to Carmelidus, the lord of Maridunum. Argantel's hair was more red, and she was seven years older, but they looked enough alike to be sisters. She turned her awareness from the residue of fury and fear that hung like smoke in the air and fixed it on the girl.

"*Don't fear,*" she sent the thought on a wave of reassurance, "*the ones who did this are nowhere near. I would know.*" From Maderun she sensed astonishment, and then relief.

"How could this happen?" her cousin said aloud. "How could God allow it?"

Of course, thought Argantel, Maderun had been raised a Christian. But her question went beyond theology.

"God, or the gods?" she said bitterly. "Your clerics say that these disasters are a punishment for our sins. But whatever evils the old man might have done, I cannot believe that little girl deserved such agony. The god of the Christians does not protect his worshippers, and the gods of Rome fled with the legions."

"Then who will you pray to?" exclaimed Maderun. "Who will give us justice now?"

"I am sworn to serve the Lady who is the soul of this land," said Argantel slowly. "But I think the time has come to wake a different power. By oath I am a priestess of the Goddess, but by blood I have the right to call on the God in the Sword. It is dangerous, but I will dare it. You have the right as well as I, Maderun. Will you stand with me?"

Maderun gazed at the flames of the villa where the bodies of the folk who had lived there were burning. The firelight lent color to her cheeks, and glittered in the tears that filled her eyes. After a few moments she shivered and turned to Argantel again.

"I have no training in such arts as you have learned, but I hope my courage is the equal of yours. In God's name I swear that I will stand behind you, cousin, and do whatever I can to help defend our land."

Maderun reached out and Argantel took her hand. Where their flesh touched she felt a tingling, and then that odd shift in awareness that came when she directed her attention to the gods.

"May the Holy Mother bless us," she whispered, feeling Maderun's wordless assent like an echo, "and bless Britannia!"

The Sword stood upright in the altar stone. Sometimes, as a shift in the air fanned the flames of the tall torches set to either side, it would catch their light and refract a fiery flicker across the stone floor, as if something that lived within had momentarily awakened. Then it would become plain steel, a third of its length sunk into the stone, once more.

With the patience of long practice, Argantel stood before it, as motionless as the Sword. Behind her, footsteps whispered on granite as the others filed in, the black-robed priestesses with their hair unbound, the girls they were training with heads wrapped tightly to protect them from the power. At her back she could feel the cold weight of Ebrdila's glare, as if the older priestess would continue their argument by sheer weight of will.

"You must not do this! Your mother was a greater priestess than you will ever be, and even she did not dare to awaken the Power that sleeps in this Sword! If I were High

Priestess, I would never allow you to risk yourself, and the rest of us, this way!"

"But you are not," Argantel had replied. Not for want of trying—but when their Lady died, the priestesses had chosen her daughter to lead them. *"And even if you were, by birth I am the Keeper of this blade."*

"At least leave your cousin out of this. If he knew about this, her father's wrath would strike us all!" It was capitulation, even if Ebrdila did not want to admit it.

"Maderun has the right to be here. The Sword will recognize her and do her no harm. . . ."

Looking across the stone at the younger woman, Argantel hoped that was true. Maderun had been garbed, like herself, in red. Beneath the fall of shining hair her features were pinched with strain, and her eyes flicked uneasily as each newcomer entered the House of the Sword. It was barely large enough for all of them, round, in the ancient fashion, but built of native granite instead of daub and wattle. The walls were low, but the roof timbers met almost thirty feet above her head.

Argantel sent the other girl a pulse of wordless reassurance. Maderun's gray gaze shifted from the Sword to her cousin, and she tried to smile.

The priestess felt a pang of misgiving. She did not doubt her cousin's courage, but she was increasingly aware of the girl's vulnerability. Yet Maderun would have been shamed if Argantel had tried to exclude her now. And it had seemed to her that the God in the Sword might hear the voices of two who came of the blood of its keepers more clearly than one.

As the women entered they moved deosil around the room, and that constant sunwise circling was altering the sense of watchful expectance which Argantel usually felt in this place to an active anticipation. This chamber needed no warding. Five centuries before, it had been hallowed by priestesses more powerful than any that she would ever know, when Roman legions destroyed the sanctuary on the isle of Mona and the last of the druid priesthood fled northward.

In her grandmother's time it had become something more than a ritual chamber. Her grandmother had brought them the Sword. And what, the priestess wondered, would the

Sword bring to them? For fifty years the druids of the Isle of Maidens had preserved it. Each year they had dutifully honored the god who dwelt within. But this ritual was different. This was the first time Argantel had taken it upon herself to ask His aid.

The torches flickered wildly as the great doors were closed. When they had stilled, the priestess nodded to Maderun, who began to sprinkle herbs from her basket across the coals in the brazier before her. In moments their pungent scent filled the room. Smoke spiraled lazily toward the thatching. Argantel took a deep breath, feeling the familiar lift and swing of awareness, as if her ordinary self were being pushed aside to let the persona of the priestess take control.

Maderun's eyes were already unfocused. The priestess smiled a little and reached out with her own awareness until she sensed the younger woman like a blaze of light before her. A little further, and she felt her cousin's spirit awaken within her own. It was not the steady support of a trained priestess, but it was familiar, as though a forgotten piece of herself had just been found.

She let her breath out slowly, releasing her own tension, listening as the other women began to sing. There were no words to it, only tones that built a bridge of ascending harmonies. Slowly she lifted her arms, compelling their attention.

"Behold the Sword of War!" she cried. "God-steel, star-steel, cast flaming down from heaven to bury itself in earth's womb. Spell-steel, forged by Kurdalagon, master of Chalybes's magic. Neither breaking nor bending, neither rusting nor tarnished, this immortal blade we honor!"

"By what right?" called Ebrdila from across the circle, her voice ringing with a sincerity that was more than ritual.

"By right of birth and blood," together, Argantel and Maderun replied. "We are the granddaughters of Rigantona daughter of Gutuator, who came to be high priestess on this holy isle, and of Artorius Hamicus Sarmatius, who was the last priest of the Sword. From the land of the Royal Scyths his fathers brought it, to guard as a holy trust until the time comes when it shall be wielded by a king once more."

"And when shall that king come?" asked one of the other priestesses.

"The God of the Sword shall raise up a king to serve him when his people are in their greatest need," Argantel answered. "And who can doubt our need now? The Eagles have flown, and Britannia's enemies beset her from every side." For a moment she smelled the reek of the burning villa in the smoke from the brazier and her breath caught in her throat.

"It is so—" came the murmured answer. "Call upon the God of the Sword, and we will abide His will."

Maderun, who had been warned, shut her eyes. Argantel swallowed. The next part she did not like, but she had learned to do it. The high gods needed no sacrifice, but the power that lived in the Sword came from an older time. In a wicker cage at the base of the stone a red cock was waiting, victor of many a battle with other champions bred by the men whose fathers had defended Hadrian's Wall. The priestess bent, murmuring, and slid open the door to the cage.

The bird stared about fiercely, but it did not struggle as she drew it forth and held it high. A good sign, for its tattered comb bore witness to the cock's fighting spirit, and the men who handled these birds were accustomed to wear gloves to protect them from sharp beaks and spurs.

"So, my warrior, be still," she murmured, stroking its feathers and feeling the rapid heartbeat gallop beneath her hand. "Here is a more noble death than the cock pit. You shall go undefeated to the god."

The cock's beady eyes fixed on her own, and then, slowly, closed. Her own eyes stung with mingled exultation and pity, and for a moment she could not move. It would be sacrilege to bungle this, but the cook had made her kill chickens for the pot until she could do it with a merciful efficiency, saying no one should be allowed to eat meat who was not willing to take responsibility for the act that transformed it from living flesh to food. Then she took a quick breath, and twisted, holding tight to the twitching body as the hot blood sprayed across the gray stone.

As the blood flowed she could feel the life leaving, first awareness, and then the energies of the body, and finally an indefinable change that left the cock lighter by more than the weight of its blood. But as the bird became a dead husk in her hands, the stone before her began to pulse with energy.

She laid the body of the cock at the base of the stone, straightened, and lifted her hands; and Maderun, feeling the pulse of power, opened her eyes and raised hers as well.

"Sword-God, War-God, God of Justice, we call you. Cocidius, Red Lord, and Shining Belutacadros we call, as the folk in this land hailed you before the Romans came. Mars of the Soldiers, hear us, and forgive us that we have no knowledge of your other names." She stretched out her hands and set them about the hilt, and Maderun covered them with her own.

Argantel had been taught the secret twist by which the Sword might be withdrawn, but though a woman could guard the blade, it was not for her to wield it. And indeed, as she felt the power focused in the Sword growing, she would not have dared. It was hard enough simply to hold onto it, and she was glad of the strength of Maderun's hands enclosing hers.

"Hear us!" she cried, "as you heard your servants in years of old. Grant us a vision! Show us the Defender who will restore peace to this land!"

She felt Maderun's clasp loosen, freed one hand and gripped her cousin's hard over her own. The younger woman's eyes had closed; she swayed, tremors shaking her body. Argantel suppressed a surge of panic. This wasn't supposed to be happening! Maderun's role was to support, to add her energy, her need, to that of the priestess to whom the God would send His words.

Fool that she was, to think that because her cousin was untrained she had no ability. They shared the same blood and the same potential—and without the disciplines of a priestess, Maderun had no defenses against the force that lived in the Sword.

She moved again, this time trying to detach Maderun's fingers from the hilt. But now it was the other girl who clung with a grip she could not break. Argantel straightened, fighting to control her own breathing as Maderun twitched and moaned.

"Belutacadros!" she cried, choosing the most beneficent of the aspects she knew. "We have called you, and given you honor. Go gently with this woman, daughter of your priests of old. Speak through her, that we may hear, and leave her without harm!"

Very carefully she let go of the Sword and edged backward, lifting her hands in salutation. For a moment longer Maderun jerked, gasping, like a horse that fights the rein. Then she stilled, and the tension went out of her in a long sigh. When the girl drew breath once more, Argantel could *see* how, with the air, something else was flowing into her. Or rather Someone Else, for the figure that held the Sword now stood like a warrior, tall and grim.

"Long . . . it has been long since I wore flesh. . . ." The first words were a whisper, then the voice strengthened. It was deep, with a faintly gutteral accent.

Argantel blinked, for laid like a veil above the form of her cousin she saw a man's shape, clad in a hauberk of overlapping scales, features half-hidden by a helm. For a moment he gazed around the chamber, and the priestesses flinched and bowed their heads, afraid to meet his gaze. Trembling, Argantel held her own head high, praying she would have the courage to face the power she had invoked.

The dark gaze turned to her at last. "Why have you called Me here?"

"My people perish, beset on every side. The Romans forbade us to bear arms, and now they have abandoned us. Send us a Duke of War." He looked at her and suddenly he laughed. It was not a comforting sound.

"You have asked for War and War you shall have. The enemies of whom you now complain are children compared to those who shall come after them."

"What do you mean? Is there nothing we can do?"

"I am a god of Justice. What you ask for you shall receive. If your leaders act in honor, they may yet be saved, but if they are ruled by greed they will lose all. I do not ordain this fate; I only read men's hearts and tell you what I see."

"Then I ask you to give us a King who will rule with honor, a King who will be worthy to wield this Sword!"

For a long moment he looked at her, and the pressure of his gaze forced her to her knees. "He will come," he said softly at last, "not from your womb, but from your blood. You will ally yourself with a husband who is skilled in war and true in heart, and sworn to shed his blood for this land. He will defend the North by force of arms, and you will defend it by the force of the spirit. Tigernissa, High Queen, you shall never be, but *Branuen* I name you, the White Raven of Britannia who rules the hidden realm. You have the will. It remains to be seen whether you have the wisdom. Use your power well."

Argantel felt the color leave her cheeks and then flood back again.

"And what of my cousin, whose body now serves you. What will her fate be?"

"She is an empty vessel, that any power that passes can fill. A wilder power than my own will possess her, nor can you protect her. But from wildness shall come wisdom, and the child she bears must live, for by his magic you shall gain your king."

Once more he glanced around him, and as she heard his voice ringing across the room Argantel realized that his previous words had been for her alone to hear.

"Endure, resist, meet honor with honor, and your Duke of War shall become a Peace-King whose name will live as long as this land lasts."

He looked back at the Sword, fingering the hilt regretfully. Then, with a little sigh, his eyes closed. For a moment Argantel was not sure who she was seeing. Then it was only Maderun who stood there, dazed and pale, and as Argantel realized that the god had left her, the girl swayed and crumpled to the floor.

"You will ally yourself with a husband who is skilled in war, and true in heart, and sworn to shed his blood for this land."

Beneath her lashes Argantel considered the husband the Sword-God had given her. At least she supposed it must be the work of some god, from the rapidity with which the marriage negotiations had been concluded. Amlodius Licinius, Protector of Brigantia, had the height of his barbarian ancestors, tribesmen from the north coast of Germania who .had crossed the Rhenus to enter the service of Rome. His fair skin was reddened by exposure to wind and weather, his pale hair thinning, as if the pressure of a helmet had worn it away. His blunt features bore the marks of a decided character, but she did not yet know if he was kind.

To those who had argued out the marriage contract, that had not been important. What mattered to them was that he represented the last legitimate government established by Rome. As for Amlodius, he recognized that the times were changing, and wished to found a dynasty that would endure in the North by allying himself to the oldest blood in the land. He would respect her birth, and if he did not, she was Lady of the Lake, with her own defenses.

She mopped up some of the meat sauce with a bit of bread and chewed it slowly. She had thoroughly considered all the aspects of this alliance. Amlodius needed her link to the land, and the Old Faith needed a protector. The marriage had the blessing of the gods. The table was strewn with the remains of the wedding feast, and soon it would be time for the bedding. Only now, confronted with the physical reality of her new husband, did she wonder if among all the reasons of state that bound them there might be room for love.

The great hall which had once been the basilica of the Roman magistrates of Luguvalium was garlanded with greenery and crowded with all those who had come to honor the occasion. She supposed she should be flattered, although they had come as much to win favor with Amlodius as to honor her.

Coroticus, newly come to his grandfather's high seat at Dun Breatann in Altacluta, had been given a place at the high table. Flushed with wine, he was debating policy with Vitalinus of Glevum. Vitalinus was as wily, it was said, as the fox from whose pelt he might have taken the color of his hair. Antonius Donatus, Protector of the Novantae country, watched them sourly. He was an old man now, appointed to his post by Theodosius, the last ruler of a united Empire. He had fought the Picts and the Scotii most of his long life, and seen the power of Rome drain away from Britannia like blood from a wound.

At one of the lower tables her cousin Maderun sat with some of the princes' wives. As if she had felt the thought, Maderun looked up and smiled. Smiling back at her, Argantel realized that most of those here were friends to her husband, not to her. Abruptly she found herself wishing she could go down to sit with the other women, and wondering whether anyone at the high table would miss her if she did.

But then she would have had to talk to Ebrdila, who could not quite hide her satisfaction. Argantel remained High Priestess and Lady of the Lake, but at least until Amlodius had got her with child, she must remain in Luguvalium, and the older woman would rule the priestesses in fact, if not in name.

"They say that Ambrosius is dying—"

A sudden tension in the man beside her recalled Argantel's attention. It was Coroticus who had spoken, but everyone was looking at Vitalinus.

"Who will wear the purple after him?" Argantel said then, since no one else seemed willing to ask.

"Does it matter?" asked Coroticus. "The time of the emperors is ended. It was ever the way of our people for each tribe to choose a king, as we do in Alba. Even in Britannia the authority of Ambrosius and the House of Constantine was not everywhere accepted, is that not so?" He looked at Vitalinus again, and Argantel remembered hearing that the Lord of Glevum had opposed Ambrosius to the point of civil war.

"Emperor or overking, the name does not matter," said Vitalinus, pushing away his platter. "But someone must exercise supreme authority. If our people had stood together, Rome would never have conquered us at all." He lifted his goblet, found it empty, and set it down again. Argantel gestured to one of the serving lads to go around the table refilling them.

"I agree," rumbled Amlodius. "Today, Britannia is more than just the British tribes, and the Picts and the Scotii threaten us all. What use is it for me to fight them off here if they then turn their keels northward to attack you, Coroticus, in Dun Breatann? When wolves attack a herd, they separate the weakest animal from the rest and bring it down, but if the others make a ring of defense around it, the attackers can do nothing. We must stand together or they will gobble us up piecemeal."

It was the longest speech she had yet heard from him, thought Argantel. Clearly he was articulate enough in court or camp. She would have to teach him that women were capable of sensible discourse as well.

"My thought exactly!" Vitalinus looked at him gratefully.

"Perhaps such measures are required in the south," objected Coroticus, "where for generations the men of the tribes have been forbidden to bear arms. But the men of the north still know how to use their swords, and we need no emperor who will take more in taxes than the enemy takes in spoils!"

Amlodius shook his head. "There are strong arms in the south—twenty-year men of the Legions who have retired near the old fortresses. They are not British, but this is their home, and they can teach their skills to the sons they have bred up in this land."

"Will you seek to be emperor if Ambrosius dies?" asked old Antonius Donatus.

"I will!" Vitalinus answered, his gaze continuing on to the other men. "Will you support me?"

Amlodius nodded. "I will uphold you, so that you confirm me in my lordship here—" His glance went to Argantel, as if that had reminded him of the other source of his authority.

"I will swear alliance," Coroticus said then, "but my people were never ruled by the South, and will not accept an overlord."

Antonius Donatus nodded his agreement. "But it is not the men of the North that you must convince to help you defend them, Vitalinus. We love our independence, but the Pictish wolf is always at our door. Your task will be to persuade the great folk of southern Britain, who have lived in peace for so long they cannot believe anyone would dare to do them harm."

"I will persuade them," Vitalinus said soberly. "And I will rule."

Amlodius lifted his goblet in salutation. A silence fell as the others drained their own. Then Antonius Donatus looked at Argantel and laughed.

"Well, this is fine talk for a wedding feast! I wonder that your bride has not fallen asleep waiting for you to pay her some attention."

"I am not sleepy, I assure you," said Argantel tartly. "I saw the ruin the Scotii leave behind them only a few months ago. We women may not take up a sword, but we can die on one. Should we not be as concerned with what plans are being made for our defense as you?"

"Ho, you have married a fire-eater!" Coroticus laughed. "Take care lest you set the bed aflame!"

Argantel was interested to see a flush of embarrassment redden Amlodius's neck and ears.

Some of the other guests, overhearing, were beginning to shout that it was time for the bedding of the bride. Argantel felt her own cheeks grow warm, and wondered if her face were as crimson as her veil. Ebrdila was advancing toward her with Maderun and the other women close behind.

"We will escort the Lady to the bridal chamber," she said grandly, "and inform you when she is ready."

It was like a ritual, thought Argantel as she rose to her feet. All the decisions had been made, and it only remained to go through the ceremonial motions. Wordless, she allowed the other women to lead her out of the hall.

Argantel sat wrapped in a nightrobe in front of the hearth, her waist-length hair spread out across her shoulders like a veil. The other women were busy turning back the bed and arranging the greenery with which they had adorned the room. Maderun drew the brush through the last strand of hair and stepped back, head tipped to admire her handiwork.

"Look how it gleams!" Maderun lifted it so that her cousin could see. Argantel nodded. As Maderun laid the lock back again it shimmered with little fiery glints from the flame on the hearth, reminding her abruptly of the Sword.

"Lord, I consented to this marriage because of your words," she prayed silently, *"grant it your blessing . . ."*

Maderun, misinterpreting her stillness, laid a hand on her shoulder.

"Argantel, are you afraid?"

She shook her head. "I have served the Goddess in the holy rites, and I am not a virgin. It is only that this life will be such a change from all I have known."

Maderun sighed. "That is true for all of us. I used to dream of entering a holy sisterhood, but if what spoke to you in the Sword-rite was a divine being and no demon, we must bear the children Britannia needs. No doubt my father will be arranging a match for me when I get home."

"I suppose so—" Argantel looked up at her cousin, and saw something vulnerable, almost fey, in her expression. The other women were already moving toward the door. Filled with sudden tenderness, she took the other girl's hand and kissed it. "Thank you, Maderun, for staying to support me on this day. May your god bless and protect you on your journey home."

Maderun caught Argantel's hand to her cheek and smiled. "And may your goddess fill your new husband with love for you." She smiled tremulously and, turning, followed the others from the room.

Argantel was not left long alone.

Barely a moment had passed, it seemed, when the door was flung open again and the men, laughing, thrust Amlodius into the room.

"Be off with you, now! You have seen us put together in the bridal chamber. Go get drunk or something, and leave us alone!"

Propelled by a volley of bawdy commentary, the door slammed shut. Amlodius drew a deep breath, some of the high color leaving his face. Clutching her robe closed, Argantel rose. She was a tall woman, but he towered over her.

He cleared his throat. "We have not had much time to become acquainted, but I will try to be a good husband to you. You must tell me if there is something you need."

She nodded. "Most of all I will need you to talk to me. I have been used to ruling the priestesses on the Isle of Maidens, as you rule your warriors here. Do not treat me like a woman who knows no more than her distaff and her cookfire, Amlodius. Like you, I serve this land. Do we have an agreement?" She paused. "You are looking at me as if you were surveying a battlefield."

Amusement sparked in his blue eyes, and as he shrugged off his robe, she saw that if this was a combat, his forces were ready. Argantel felt a slow fire kindling beneath her skin.

"That bed is our field, lady, and you shall be my fellow-warrior. . . ."

With a swift step he bore down upon her, and letting her own garment fall, she readied herself for the fray.

ii

†he Wild Man

A.D. 425–29

The road from Luguvalium to Deva ran south through the hills and then straight across the levels beside the sea. In these times no route could be said to be completely secure, but after what she had seen the preceding autumn, Maderun feared to return to Maridunum by sea.

The weather grew warmer as Beltain neared. Creamy primroses clustered beneath the hedges and the first starry blooms of the hawthorne appeared. As each day came to a peaceful close, the fear that had made Maderun tense against each jolt of the horse-litter faded and she began to enjoy the journey. She had never, she thought, known the land to be so beautiful. She laughed at the antics of the new lambs on the hillsides, and plaited the flowers that the men of her escort picked for her into wreaths for their hair. Maderun listened to their singing and laughed, for it was the tune that the lads and lasses sang when they went out to gather greenery for Beltain.

Two weeks of journeying brought them in sight of the northern coast of the old Deceangli lands that curved west into the sea. Here the road ran between the water and the forest. Another long day's journey would bring them to Deva, and a bath, thought Maderun longingly, and a soft bed.

Looking around their campsite, no one would guess that a major center of Roman civilization lay so near. Tonight she would lack even the poor comforts of a shepherd's shelter. Since noon they had passed only one ruined farmstead. The men were already busy cutting branches to build her a leafy bower. However, they had water and firewood, and the evening was calm and beautiful. She watched the sun go down across the Hibernian Sea and knew herself at peace with the world.

Peace there might be in field and forest, but it was otherwise in the world of men. Just before dawn, Maderun found herself sitting up in her blankets, wondering what had awakened her. She looked around for the warrior on watch and could not see him. Alarm burned the last of the sleep from her brain and she drew breath to call out a warning, and in that instant the darkness exploded.

Sword blades flared red as someone kicked the coals and the banked fire burst into new flame. Maderun heard a grunt and one of the struggling bodies fell; warm blood splattered her hand. She gasped and struggled to her feet. *Scottii raiders . . .* the thought came through the gibbering in her brain. *But the sea had been empty. Where had they come from?*

Clutching the blanket around her, she tried to distinguish friend from foe. In the growing light she saw that several of her escort were down. The others were too few to hold all of the raiders, some of whom were already beginning to paw through the piles of gear.

One of them caught sight of her and grinned, and Maderun remembered with appalling clarity the burned villa and the body of the little girl. As the Scot started toward her the horror that had frozen her limbs became a hot tide of terror and she ran.

She fled like a frightened doe, blundering into branches and stumbling over roots and stones. When she came to a halt at last, breathless and bleeding from a dozen scratches, she heard crashing in the undergrowth behind her, and compelled her trembling legs to carry her onward.

When fear-begotten strength finally failed, Maderun forced

her slim body through a hole some creature had made in the tangled lower branches of a hazel copse and lay still. Whether she fainted then or only slept she did not know. But when she became aware once more it was full daylight, and in the forest there were no sounds but the musical gurgle of a nearby stream and the cheerful morning song of the birds.

She had lost the blanket, and the undergown in which she had slept was dirty and torn. But at least no one was pursuing her. Slowly, for overstressed muscles had stiffened and she ached in every limb, she crawled out of the hazels and down to the stream. The cool water eased her thirst, and bathed some of the hurt from her face and arms. She sat up then, looking around her, and realized that she had no idea where she might be.

Argantel would know how to find her way out of the forest, she told herself, looking around her. *What would she do now?* Water ran toward the ocean, she thought, and the road ran beside it. She had only to follow the stream.

But perhaps in her panic she had run south instead of east, or perhaps it was only that the forest brook meandered where it chose, in no hurry to reach the sea. Maderun was still lost when darkness fell on the forest—and hungry, for aside from a few greens whose leaves she recognized, she had found nothing to eat all day. Weeping a little from fatigue and hunger, she curled up between the gnarled roots of a great oak tree.

Maderun woke once in the night, whimpering from a dream of terror; finding herself safe and warm, she dropped swiftly into sleep once more. When she woke again she sensed light through her closed eyelids. She started to move and winced. What had she been doing yesterday to get so sore? She remembered men fighting, and a terrified flight through the forest, but surely that had been in her nightmare, because now she lay in a warm bed. . . .

Her eyes opened. Above her light filtered through green leaves. But the air was quite still. She listened, and realized that what she had taken for the wind was the sound of someone breathing. Her groping fingers closed on fur. She jerked upright, turning, and found herself staring down into a flat, wide-nostriled face. Brown hair thick as a bear's pelt grew low above a pair of dark eyes.

Maderun gasped and started to scramble away. A long-fingered hand, attached to a sinewy arm which was also covered with hair, reached out and grasped her ankle. The grip was not tight enough to hurt, but quite secure. She could not get away.

Swallowing her fear, Maderun looked at her captor. If the beast had meant to eat her she would be dead already. She saw long legs, and feet very like those of a man, a thick barrel, and—she looked quickly away. He—not it—was unmistakably male, but not quite a beast. Seeing him whole, she recognized the original of the distorted masks and tunics of tufted wool in which men cavorted at festivals. It was a Wild Man.

She had been told they were all dead, or at least withdrawn to the far northern lands. What was one doing here? Around his face white hairs sprinkled the dark fur. Was he the last in Britannia?

She searched her memory for the old tales. The Wildfolk were shy creatures, but could fight fiercely if captured. At times they had rescued lost children and cared for them until they were found. That gave her hope. She licked dry lips and pointed to the stream.

The Wild Man chuffed deep in his throat and released her ankle. Carefully she made her way to the brookside and cupped water in her hands to drink. Then she made her way behind a clump of sallow to relieve herself, still uncomfortably aware of his watchful gaze. But when she tried to go further he half rose, growling deep in his throat until she turned back.

Later that morning the Wild Man left her and she tried to escape once more, but he found her when she was scarcely out of sight of the oak tree and carried her back under his arm. Some tender roots and new greens lay on the ground beside the tree root, and a piece of honeycomb. Still weeping, Maderun ate greedily.

The infant moon began to wax with little change in Maderun's captivity. By day she followed the Wild Man, learning which plants could be eaten. By night she slept warm in his arms. She grew thin on a diet of tubers and raw greens, and wept again when the grubs and raw birds' eggs the Wild Man brought began to look good to her. She tried to pray for deliverance, but prayers to the Christian god seemed irrelevant here in the wildwood, and she had never learned how to address the old gods of her tribe. Argantel would have known. "Cousin, help me!" she cried, but her only answer was the wind in the trees.

To think about her situation brought pain, and so as the days passed she avoided thought and banished memory, taking refuge in the forest's eternal *now.* To live was to feel the warmth of the sun or the cool wind, the satisfaction of food in the belly and the sweetness of water on the tongue. Wordless, she seemed to sense the life that flowed through all the green world around her in a way she had only glimpsed when she was part of the world of men.

Bright eyes gleamed through the sparkle of a waterfall; willowy maidens emerged from the trunks of their trees to dance in the moonlight, and once, just at sunset, she glimpsed the turf of a forgotten mound opening like a door, and saw a radiant figure that beckoned to her to come in. She might have gone, but her captor, growling deep in his throat, had grasped her arm and dragged her away.

The Wild Man had a territory through which he ranged, gathering the sweet onion in one place, mustard in another, fish from a forest pool, grubs from beneath a fallen log. It took most of his time and energy just to find enough food to support his giant frame. Maderun tore off the ragged hem of her skirt, and clad now in what was no more than a short tunic, followed him. They slept sometimes in a hollow tree and at others in a kind of nest lined with soft grasses, but always they returned to the oak tree by the stream.

The moon grew full and round, blessing the woodlands with her silver light. In the world of men, if Maderun had had any way to calculate the calendar, it was the moon when men and women danced together around the Beltain fires. In the forest, Maderun lay curled beneath her captor's hand as once she had curled around her pet kitten. The Wild Man stroked her as she had touched her cat, drawing his long, lightly furred fingers through her hair and humming tunelessly as he often did at such times. She held still when he sniffed along her body, nostrils flaring. Sometimes he licked her skin and she shivered, simultaneously repulsed and pleasured. In this state of mindless endurance, it seemed inevitable that one day his touch should grow more intimate, and when he thrust her down and dog-fashion, entered her, she did not try to pull away.

While the moon remained full this usage continued. In that corner of her mind that still could think Maderun knew that reason was her enemy. If she allowed herself to understand what was happening, she would be reduced to gibbering hysteria. And if she recognized that she had come to welcome it her mind would snap entirely.

When the silver round began to thin, the Wild Man seemed to lose interest, though he fed and protected her as before. One night, when the moon was only a thin sickle in the sky, Maderun dreamed. She was looking in a mirror, and then she realized it was not a mirror but Argantel who was facing her, calling her name. And when she replied, the other woman cried, *"Remember the hope of Britannia! Remember the Sword!"*

When she woke, Maderun knew herself as human for the first time in many days. But she scarcely recognized the gaunt features that stared back at her from the forest pool. *If I stay here, I will die*, she thought, and then, *Better to die than to live as an animal. . . .*

The Wild Man was watching her, his dark eyes sorrowful as if he sensed her unhappiness, but Maderun refused to pity him. She no longer feared him, nor did their strange life together disgust her, but from that time she began to actively try to recover her humanity.

It was three days later that she heard in the distance the melancholy belling of a hunter's horn. The Wild Man was off somewhere, seeking food. Heart pounding, Maderun set off toward the sound of the horn. For a time she waded in the stream, hoping to throw him off the scent if he should follow her. Then she took to the bank once more, moving as swiftly as she dared.

The horns grew louder, and she heard the yapping of hounds. But closer still she heard a familiar deep chuffing and knew that the Wild Man was coming after her. Her first cry was a squawk, and for one panicked moment she wondered if she had forgotten how to form human words. Then she filled her lungs and tried again.

"Help—help me!"

For a moment there was silence, then she heard a change in the calling of the hounds. Rapidly they drew closer, but the Wild Man was gaining too. Panting, Maderun leaped for the lower branches of a gnarled apple tree, survivor of some forgotten orchard, and began to climb, seeking the topmost branches that would bear her slender weight but not that of her pursuer. Clinging to the bough she cried out again and again.

The Wild Man splashed through the stream and paused at the foot of Maderun's tree. For a long, wordless moment she stared into his eyes. Then the yammering of the dogs grew deafening and he crouched to meet them, the rough hair over neck and shoulders rising to a crest as he bared his teeth.

"Run!" cried Maderun, gesturing toward the undergrowth. "Run, or they will kill you!"

Once more the Wild Man looked up, jaws opening in a very human moan. Then, as the first of the dogs leaped through the undergrowth, he whirled away into the forest and was gone.

Let the hunters think that the dogs had treed her, thought Maderun as they milled around the base of the beech, whining. Let them think that her tears were from fear of them, and not because now, when she was sure of rescue, she could at last afford to pity the creature that was more than a beast, if less than a man, and who in his way had loved her.

To her rescuers, Maderun would say only that she had wandered in the wildwood, living on roots and greens, meeting no man. Her father received her with astonished joy, for her marriage had figured in his plans. But she continued to weep, and so he sent her for healing to the quiet confines of the convent next to the church of Saint Peter in the town.

The nuns were kind to her, and if their garden was not quite so peaceful as the forest, it was far better than the smoky clamor of her father's hall. Maderun sank gratefully into the routine of song and prayer, and her memories of the wildwood became as faint and disjointed as images in a dream.

When her bleeding did not come at the change of the moon, the Infirmary sister patted her hand kindly and assured her that when a woman had suffered a shock or was as thin as Maderun had become, it was often so. With good food and rest, surely she would grow healthy once more. And indeed, as the summer passed, she began to fill out a little, though her face was still gaunt and pale. But her moon blood did not return.

She dreamed, sometimes, that she was back in the forest. Sometimes she relived the terror of that first flight from the raiders, and would wake in a cold sweat, babbling of blood and monsters among the trees. But sometimes her dreams returned her to the oak tree, and she smiled, thinking she still slept cradled in the Wild Man's arms. Those were the times when she reached out to him, and writhing on her narrow bed, touched herself as *he* had touched her, until she passed into peaceful sleep once more. The other girls in the novices' dormitory would ask her what she had been dreaming, but Maderun could not answer them.

On a warm autumn day just after the Feast of St. Michael, Maderun went out with a few of the older nuns and the three novices to gather apples.

"Have you heard?" said little Felicia as they searched for windfalls among the tall grass, "Ambrosius the Emperor is dead and Vitalinus of Glevum has proclaimed himself Vor-Tigernus—High King!"

"And how would you know that?" asked Thea, the brown-skinned daughter of a legionary from Numidia who had married a British woman and settled in Demetia when his term of service was done. "Did an angel announce it to you in a dream?" The folklore of the convent was rich in tales of supernatural visitors.

"I heard it in Maridunum, of course," retorted Felicia, "when I accompanied Sister Ildeg to market last Saturday."

"God prosper him," put in the third girl. "For well He knows how much we need a strong lord. But I do not think that the chieftains of the West Country will accept Vitalinus's rule."

The others nodded. They were all, if not the daughters of princes, girls of good family. And in the West, even the poorest hill farmer felt free to criticize the doings of those who claimed authority over him.

Thea laughed. "Of course not—it is Ambrosius Aurelianus who has the right to claim his father's honors."

"But he is still in Armorica with his brother. My father says we need a king who will care for Britannia first and foremost," Felicia replied. "Vitalinus doesn't want to be emperor. He titles himself in our own language, *'over king.'*"

Maderun nodded. "I met him at the wedding of my cousin in Luguvalium. He seemed a very determined man."

The others looked at her in surprise, unaccustomed to hearing her speak and remembering now that she outranked them all.

"He will need to be," Felicia said finally. "He is trying to raise an army, and our men will not want to fight for people at the other end of the country when the Dalriadan warriors are at our door."

Maderun shuddered, remembering the raiders, and the others fell abruptly silent.

"They say that is why Vitalinus claimed the power—" Felicia added softly. "Because of what happened to you. He has said it is a disgrace that a princess of a royal house cannot travel safely through the land, and Britannia needs a defender."

"A Defender . . ." Maderun spoke softly in the cadence of prophecy, recalling fragments of the knowledge that had passed through her awareness, it seemed a lifetime ago, "but it will not be the Vor-Tigernus, but another, who shall come after him."

"What?" asked Thea, but Maderun shook her head, losing the memory. This had happened to her often since her ordeal. She lived in the present; all her memories were like fragments of dream, and as easily whirled away.

"We have gathered all the windfalls," Felicia said brightly into the silence. "And for all our shaking, no more apples will fall out of this tree. But there are still some clinging to the upper branches. They are almost ripe, and it seems a shame to leave them there."

Maderun looked up, dimly remembering that trees meant safety. "I will go after them. I am the lightest of you all." Kirtling up her skirts, she began to clamber upward.

From the top of the tree she could see over the convent walls. She could see the roofs of Maridunum, and beyond them a patchwork of field and forest. But inevitably her gaze turned northward, where the land disappeared into a blue haze, and the wind dried the tears that sprang beneath her eyelids before she could wipe them away.

"Can you reach the apples?" the call came from below.

Recalled to the present, Maderun stretched to grasp the fruit, and the wind flattened her gown against her body and blew back her hair.

There was a stifled exclamation from below. Maderun plucked an apple and settled back, turning to look down. Felicia was staring up at her wide-eyed.

"What is wrong?"

"Daughter of Carmelidus, I think you go with child!"

The apple slipped from Maderun's grasp, missed the basket, and rolled across the grass. Only a convulsive tightening of her arms saved her from falling as well. She shook her head and reached for another apple, then picked a third and two more.

By the time she climbed back down the tree, Maderun could almost believe she had not heard it. But the flushed faces and avid eyes of the other girls forced her to remember Felicia's words.

"It is not so—" she said quietly. "I have never lain with a man."

"But your breasts are so round, and your belly—"

"Hush!" said Thea, taking pity on her. "If she is a maiden, then time will proclaim her innocence, and time will accuse her more harshly than any man if it is not so. It is not for us to judge."

It is not true. . . . Maderun repeated to herself as they carried their baskets back to the convent. *I have never loved a man.*

But as Thea had said, time did indeed accuse her—time, and the wagging tongues of two dozen cloistered women, who began to watch Maderun's belly as a farmer scans his newly sown field. And by Samhain it was apparent to everyone that the princess was expecting a child.

Then the questioning began.

"It is a great sorrow, but no shame to you, child, if one of the Scottii raiders who attacked your camp caught and raped you before you fled," said Mother Paterna.

"They were still busy fighting. I got away."

And indeed, the evidence of Maderun's maidservant, who had rolled under a pile of luggage and watched till the fight was over, did seem to confirm that when Maderun ran, the men who followed returned quickly, complaining that she had gotten away.

"Escaped slaves and outlawed men take refuge in the wilderness. If it was one of these who abused you, tell me, and we will hunt him down!" said her father.

"I ate at no hearth and met no human soul from the time I fled to the day that I was found," answered Maderun, and it was true, said some, that even outlaws would not have allowed the girl to live in such a condition as she had been found.

"Why will you not believe me?" she cried. "Put me to the ordeal, let me swear on holy relics that I have not lied to you!"

And she swore, and was not blasted, and so her accusers were no closer to the truth than before. In the convent they whispered that if she had lain with no man in the wilderness perhaps something worse had come to her then, or even— and here the voices of the novices grew faint with excitement—within the convent walls.

"We will wait until the child is born," they said then. "Whether its father be man or devil, the babe itself will proclaim its paternity."

And so Maderun's pregnancy continued through the winter. Her belly grew ever larger, and the older women counted the months, nodding wisely. But the ninth month since Maderun's rescue passed, and there was no child. The whispers changed then, to talk of the incubus who lies with women in their sleep, or the Devil himself, seeking to beget an Anti-Christ into the world.

"Perhaps it is so," said Maderun wearily above the great round of her belly, "for indeed I sometimes have strange dreams. . . ." But the next day she was talking of a prince of the faerie folk whom she had met in the forest, who had fed her on cakes made from sunbeams and moonlight wine. And that might be so as well, the gossip ran, for the girl had been starving when they found her and surely faerie food, like faerie gold, would vanish in the ordinary light of day.

The bishop heard of the case and sent one of his priests, a Father Blaise, to question her, but if Maderun told the truth to him, the seal of the confessional protected it.

Maderun's child was born at Beltain, when the folk of faerie come forth from their mounds and move from winter quarters to their summer homes. But it was no faerie child she gave birth to, for when he arrived, after a nightlong labor in which the midwives almost despaired of saving either mother or child, he was large, lusty, and covered with a fine pelt of dark down.

"The Devil's child," said one of the midwives, listening to him squall.

"*My* child—" whispered Maderun. "Give him to me!"

They exchanged worried glances, for they had meant to carry the babe away to the forest and leave it there. Exposure of unwanted children was forbidden to Christians, but this, surely, was no Christian babe.

But Maderun was a king's daughter, and though she had babbled strangely during the labor, she spoke with authority now, and so they shrugged and gave her the child. But the rumors did not cease from flying, and when storms ruined the harvest that summer, and gave way to a freezing winter, and the next two years were seasons of little rain, folk began to murmur that it was because the King of Demetia was harboring a witch-daughter and her demon child.

Maderun sat in the convent garden watching her boy playing in the sun. From the little church came the sound of chanting; Maderun leaned back against the cool stone and let the sound carry her spirit upward. After Ambros's birth she had asked to be admitted as a novice, but although she was still welcome to dwell among the nuns, the bishop had forbidden formal vows to the mother of such a dubious child. Perhaps it was for the best, she thought dreamily. She had recovered her health, but she found it hard to concentrate, and could never seem to remember the prayers.

Ambros was squatting on the path, making patterns with

the pebbles he found there, his dark hair, coarse as a horse's mane, hanging over his eyes. After his birth most of the fuzz that covered his body had fallen out, except for a line of black down that followed his spine. Carefully he made a circle, and then a square, and other figures, over and over again.

Sometimes he raged, and raced in circles until he was exhausted, but on other days he could play such games for hours. Though he was nearly three, he had never yet spoken a word, but as he worked he hummed softly. The sound made her feel soft and sleepy, and she found it familiar, but could never think where she had heard such humming before.

A winged shadow flickered across the path. The child looked up at the wren that had made it and laughed. Maderun watched in astonishment as the bird fluttered down to alight on his outstretched hand. The wren chirped, and Ambros chirped back at it. Then it took fright suddenly and flew away.

Ambros sat up, dark eyes fixed on the path. Only then did Maderun hear the footsteps and see Father Blaise approaching them. His hair, as always, stood half on end, so that he reminded one of a startled bird, and his step hesitated as he peered nearsightedly around him. But his face was uncharacteristically grim.

"What has happened?" She rose to meet him.

"Three landowners whose hayfields were washed out last summer have brought suit to try you for a witch and sorceress because of the child!"

Maderun made a hushing motion. Because Ambros did not speak, people often did not realize how much he could understand. Then the sense of what the priest had said sank in and she sat down.

"Why?" she whispered. "What harm have I done to them? Surely I am as good a Christian as any woman in this land."

"You will not name the father of your child."

"I cannot—" Sometimes Maderun remembered him as a shining youth and sometimes as a comforting presence in the dark, but she knew that he had no human name.

"God send they will believe it. They have brought the case before their kindred court and the *caput gentis* has chosen Uethen son of Maclovius to judge it, so your father has no

power to gainsay them. You must think of something to tell
them, Maderun. They have the power to drown you, do you
understand?"

She looked at Ambros, and for a moment saw in her
mind's eye moonlight sparkling on a forest stream. Then the
picture darkened. "I don't remember. . . ."

Ambros, who was having one of his quiet days, sat on his
mother's lap, surveying the scene with eyes as bright and
dark as a young bird's. Even though the sky was cloudy, the
court had been convened in the meadow beyond the king's
hall, the only place large enough to hold so many. The people made a circle, chattering. On the isle of Mona, they whispered, a cow had dropped a two-headed calf. In Londinium,
Vitalinus, despairing of building a fighting force from the
men of the South and East of Britannia, had followed the
ancient tradition of Rome and hired Saxon mercenaries from
across the sea.

A damp wind fluttered veils and mantles. Maderun shivered. Once, she thought, there had been someone who would
have protected her—a mighty presence who had kept her
safe and warm.

Uethen son of Maclovius settled himself on a bench on
the hill. His robes were white, but his cloak was woven in
many colors, his right as a man who knew the law. He draped
the folds more majestically and cleared his throat.

"I call Maderun daughter of Carmelidus into this court—"
His voice, trained and resonant, carried clearly, and Maderun
felt a changing tension in Ambros's body as he stilled, listening.

She tried to speak, and could not. She knew this feeling
of being helpless—the other time, it had been no use to
struggle. She shook her head, feeling awareness begin to slip
away like an unmoored boat that the current will carry down-
stream.

Father Blaise, beside her, responded, "She is here."

Uethen nodded. "Who brings suit against her?"

One of the farmers stepped forward. "I bring suit against
the daughter of Carmelidus on the charge of *maleficium*, in
that she willingly gave herself to the Devil in order to bring
his child into the world, who has tampered with the order of

nature and brought us nothing but disaster since that day!"

A murmur of interest swept the crowd and all eyes turned toward Maderun.

"That is two accusations!" exclaimed Father Blaise. "I can bring witnesses to testify that the child was born in a normal manner, and duly baptised when he was three days old. The good nuns of Saint Peter's have watched him grow, and seen him do no magic. If the weather has been bad, it is not his doing. Have you known no other seasons of disaster, when there was no babe to blame? It is for your sins that God has brought this upon you, not his!"

The babble this time was louder, and once or twice she heard laughter.

"It may be so," said the second farmer. "But it does not absolve Maderun of *her* crime. Whether the father be demon or mortal, she has brought dishonor on her kindred by having a nameless child."

"He has the name with which he was baptised," said Father Blaise, "which is Ambrosius, after the emperor."

"And where is the rest of it? Of whom is he the son?"

"He is the child of the nun. And that would be enough among the northern folk from whom this girl's mother came."

"But this is Demetia, and we hold by our own law," said the judge. "If the whoredom of a girl of the kindred dishonors her people, then that of the daughter of a king brings shame upon the whole kingdom, and she must pay the penalty."

"Will you kill *your* mother?"

The question was voiced in a clear and piping tone that carried to the edge of the crowd. Only slowly did men realize that its source was the child who sat in his mother's arms.

"What did you say?" Uethen was staring as if he thought Maderun had played some trick, but in truth she was as surprised as anyone. Could Ambros know what he was saying? Certainly the case had been discussed in his hearing, but how could he understand?

"Your mother doesn't say who *your* father was," Ambros repeated with patient clarity. "Do you drown her too?"

"My father was my mother's husband!" the judge exclaimed.

"How do you know? Do you ask her?"

The first shocked astonishment was giving way to laughter. Somehow, Ambros's question had turned the temper of the crowd toward sympathy.

"That's so, Uethen—it's not fair to condemn the boy's mother until you know about your own! Send for her, man, and let us all hear."

Uethen was flushing angrily, but he could interpret the murmurs around him. People respected his learning, but he was not a popular man. Someone had already gone to fetch his mother. Glowering, he agreed to wait until she should come.

When the woman arrived, escorted by a grinning warrior, Ambros straightened.

"I do not know my father. I know my mother, and they want to kill her. Does your son know his father?" The tone was clear, wistful. The old woman looked at the child and all saw her eyes fill with tears.

"Ah, little one, there's no man born that can be certain of more." She sighed, and looked up at her son. "It is glad I am that my husband is not here this day, for I came to love him. But he was not the father of my child."

The face of the judge set like stone, and the people whispered, divided between shock and glee. His mother looked at him once, and then away.

"It is our law that a stranger who lies with a girl of the kindred must stay and marry her. But my lover was thirsty for learning, and when he had learned all there was to know of Maridunum, he went away. When I knew that he had left me with child I gave myself to Maclovius, who had long courted me, and so I got a husband." She sighed. "If I may speak in your Assembly I counsel mercy, for Maderun at least has practiced no deception."

There was a long silence, while all eyes turned back to the judge, who had drawn his mantle over his head in mourning.

"I cannot judge this case," he said harshly. "The king is your father, woman. Let him deal with your shame!"

King Carmelidus pushed through the crowd, followed by his house-guard, the high color returning to his face as the tension left it.

"My daughter shall have a husband, and her child a father, as good as yours! Matauc Morobrin has consented to wed her." One of the warriors came forward to stand beside him.

Maderun looked at him, ordinary as bread and solid as stone, and felt the last of her bright dreams mist away. But her child had been saved, for whatever future God, or the old gods, had in mind. Ambros tugged at her gown. With a sigh, she put him to the breast. Upon her head, like a blessing, she felt the first drops of rain.

iii

The Red Dragon
and the White

A.D. 433

 The ball, made from a calf stomach stuffed with hay, hurtled through the air. Ambros, who was faster than the others though he was only seven, darted beneath Dinabu's arm and whacked it with his hurley stick as it fell. He straightened to watch as it arced over the other boy's head toward the goal.

"Curse you, that was *my* ball!" cried Dinabu.

"But it is a point for *our* team—" answered Ambros, watching the other boy warily. He had attempted to play with the boys before. It usually ended in a quarrel, but he knew how much it mattered to his mother that he be accepted, and so he continued to try.

The others began to yell as the ball smacked into the bush that was serving as goal, and the horsemen who had paused to watch them play set up a cheer.

Ambros hung back as the ball was put in play once more, aware with all his senses of the pattern that was emerging, the energy of the other players, even the life in the grass. He had learned, painfully, that other people did not sense these things, and so he tried to hide his knowledge. Sometimes he

37

thought his mother felt things also, but she did not seem to be aware of what she knew.

The ball spun toward him. He could see Dinabu running, and knew in the same moment that the older boy would not get there in time. The others were shrieking encouragement. Dinabu would be angry if Ambros hit the ball, but *they* would be pleased. Before he had completed the thought he was moving, placing himself in the correct relationship to ball and goal. Muscles flexed as the stick swung; he felt the vibration all the way up his arm as it struck the ball, the sweet "rightness" as he continued to turn, and the ball soared straight for the goal.

Dinabu turned on him, features contorting. Ambros saw the hurley stick whip toward his head and ducked. Fury reddened his own vision; like a thing foreordained, he could sense how his own blow would strike the other boy's head. With a final effort at control he let go of the stick and saw it whirl away. Dinabu struck again; Ambros plucked the wooden shaft from his grasp and sent it after his own. Dinabu grabbed for his arm, and Ambros danced away, knowing that if they came to grips his own anger would overwhelm him.

"Bastard . . ." panted the older boy, stumbling after him. "No-fathered, demon begotten—"

Ambros avoided his attacks and shut out his words. He had heard it all before. But the other boys, with the pack-mentality of their kind, were taking up the chant, even those on his own team.

"Go away," they cried. "We'll have no devil-child on our side!" Someone picked up a clod of earth and threw.

Ambros knew it would hit him, but held his ground. The tears that smarted in his eyes were of rage.

"You'll ask me—you'll beg me for my help one day!" he growled.

Then, ignoring the insults and the clods that followed him, Ambros stalked away. At the edge of the field a stand of hazels marked the beginning of the woodlands. There was no one in Maridunum who could follow him once he was among the trees.

His rage carried him farther than he had intended. He came to rest at last where water from an unfailing spring trickled down over rock to form a small pool. He bent over it to drink and remained, watching his image take shape as the ripples stilled. Eyes as dark and watchful as a beast's gazed back at him beneath the fall of coarse hair. His brows were heavy, his forehead low. He tried to smile, and large teeth snarled back at him from a heavy jaw. Only in his high arched nose did he resemble his mother's kin.

But I am no child of the Devil, for the priests say that when he comes to tempt humankind his face is fair, and I am as ugly as a hobgoblin. But the hobgoblin was a little fellow, and it was clear already that Ambros was going to be a very big man. *Whatever I am, it is nothing human,* he thought unhappily. *Perhaps I should run away and live in the forest. I am happy here.*

He had considered this before, many times, and always it was the thought of his mother's pain that prevented him from running away. Morobrin was not unkind, but there was no love between them. Maderun and little Ganeda, the girl-child she had borne her new husband, were the only human creatures Ambros loved.

He gazed around him, looking for the other being that cared for him. He used to think she was the spirit of the waterfall, for he had first seen her here. But he had found that if he unfocused his eyes in a certain way he could see her elsewhere, just as he saw the beings that lived in rock and bush and tree. And sometimes, just lately, he would hear her talking to him even when he could not see.

"Girl . . ." he whispered, "will I ever find friends?"

And in the silence of his spirit he heard, faint but clear, *"I am your friend, and I am always here. . . ."*

He lay back upon the bracken and then for a little while he must have slept, lulled by the sweet singing of the waterfall, for when he sat up again, the sky was growing gold.

When he set out for home it was already dark beneath the trees. But Ambros seemed to have eyes in his feet, so swiftly did he go. He was never clumsy in the forest, only in the hall.

Ambros came over the hill to Lys Morobrin as the first stars were kindling in a purple sky. His nostrils flared at the scents of woodsmoke and roasting meat. He began to run, slowing only when he noticed the three strange horses in the pen. They were fine beasts; he frowned, memory supplying an image of them saddled and mounted. They belonged to the men who had been watching the hurley game. What were they doing here?

He doused his head in the horse-trough, combing back his hair with his fingers in an attempt to bring it to some kind of order, but as he thrust aside the spotted cowhide that curtained the doorway he had an unhappy feeling that he had only succeeded in making it stand up in spikes like a bogle's. And his tunic was torn; he had not noticed that before.

Something stirred in the shadows of the entry. Ambros whirled, then relaxed, sensing, even as his eyes adjusted, that it was little Ganeda who was hiding there. He bent and took her into his arms.

"Guests, with pretty clothes!" She pointed into the hall.

"Who are they, sweetling?" Her soft hair, pale as duckling's down, tickled his nose and he set her down again.

"They asked for you," she said, "to bring you honor! Come and see!" She took his hand and pulled him into the center of the hall.

His stepfather and the strangers lay at their ease on dining-couches on the other side of the fire. His mother looked up from her embroidery as he entered, as if that breath of air had alerted her. Maderun was vague about many things, but surprisingly alert where her son was concerned. With one glance she took in his appearance and shook her head with a sigh. In another moment she would try to hustle him out to put on his good tunic, but before she could rise, Morobrin spied him and pointed.

Ambros, still standing in the doorway, found himself the target of all eyes. Flushing, he stood his ground.

"That is the boy?" asked one of the strangers, a tall man with a grizzled beard.

"Ambros," said Morobrin, "child of the nun."

"She will have to come with him," said the other man, "to tell her story."

"Where?" Ambros found his voice at last. "Where are we going?"

"To Vitalinus, to the Over-King."

*   *   *

"The king has promised gold and a bull from his own herds if you can help him," said Maderun as they rode northward. "Your father is very pleased. . . ."

He is not my father, thought Ambros, *and he is pleased to be rid of me. You are chattering, mother—what is the knowledge you are trying to hide?*

He knew already that the Over-King's messengers had not told the whole truth to him. They said that a fatherless child was required to bless the king's new fortress, but what if he failed? Ambros did not believe that his mother would knowingly lead him into danger, but she was very good at seeing only those parts of a picture that fitted her vision of reality.

She even thought *he* was handsome, and Ambros knew full well he was as ugly as Imacdub who was the ugliest boy ever born. The goddess Cerituend had brewed up a cauldron of magic to make her son wise if he could not be beautiful, but the serving-lad Viaun had drunk it all instead.

Perhaps my mother's cousin Argantel could teach me wisdom—I have heard she is a mistress of magic, but I think I will have to be Imacdub and Viaun both if I am to survive.

But whatever happened to him in the Over-King's hall, it would be a change from listening to the taunts of the lads at Maridunum, and the little girl who talked to him in his head had told him he should go. He turned to look at the road behind him. The town was already hidden behind a wooded ridge, and they were passing through the last of the farmsteads.

"I met Vitalinus once, you know," his mother chattered on.

"Who?" Lost in his own thoughts Ambros tried to pick up the thread again.

"That is his name. Vor-Tigernus is only the title he has taken, though I suppose it might be courteous to use it when you address him." She frowned. "He did not seem overweeningly proud, as I remember, but he did have a great many opinions. . . . Great lords do not like to be contradicted—" She turned to Ambros again. "Be careful how you speak to him, but remember that your blood is as good as his."

On one side, thought Ambros unhappily, but he nodded.

"And perhaps," she went on, "it would be better not to tell him about the Sword."

He turned to her. "That will be easy. You have never more than mentioned it to me!"

His mother's face brightened. She liked to tell stories about the past—it was safely over and done. Sometimes, though, the past was like an adder that seems dead until it rolls over and bites you.

"Two hundred years ago there was an emperor in the lands of the Romans who was called Marcus Aurelius." Maderun glanced up and down the road and decided that the riders in their escort were out of earshot. "In his time there was war between the Sarmatian peoples beyond the borders of Dacia, and one of the losing tribes, the Iazyges, came to the Danuvius and asked for asylum in the Empire. The emperor replied that he could not take all of them together, but if they were willing to be divided, he would let them in.

"Five hundred warriors were sent here to Britannia and stationed at Bremetennacum, to guard the western shore. When their twenty years of service were up, they settled here in the North and their sons entered the *Auxilla* after them. When the veterans were given citizenship, as the custom was, they took the family name of their commander, Artorius."

Ambros nodded. "Wasn't your grandmother named Artoria?"

"Just so. My cousin Argantel bears the name also, and keeps the Sword. It came to us through our great-grandmother, a druid's daughter who married the last of the Sarmatian soldier-priests who guarded it," Maderun went on. "It is an ancient blade, forged from star-steel by a magic that no smith in our day understands. In the hands of a great king, born of the ancient blood, it will bring victory."

"You are telling me that Vitalinus wants to be a great king, and would take the Sword?"

"He would," she said softly, "but he is not destined to wield it." She moved her mare up beside Ambros's hill pony. "A god lives in that Sword, who has promised that the Defender of Britannia will come of my cousin's blood. But the druid who must help him will come of mine."

Ambros's pony started to trot at the involuntary touch of his heels. He hauled back on the reins, abruptly making sense of a number of comments his mother had made in the past.

"And you think that *I* will be that Man of Wisdom?"

"I know that you are—" she said serenely. "And you must remember it when you go before this king."

Ambros felt his heart beat as if he had been running. "But what if I say the wrong thing?"

"Say what your heart tells you, and trust in God."

Which one? he wondered grimly. *The god of the Christians, or the one in the Sword, or whatever power my unknown father served?* He had been christened as a babe, but he thought sometimes that his alien blood had somehow repelled the Christian blessing. He attended mass with his mother, but he felt the mystery of the Spirit more strongly in the depths of the forest than he ever had within the chapel's walls.

Ambros grew very silent as the journey continued, for he had much to think about. Two days' travel brought them to the western coast. From there they rode northward, into the old Ordovici lands. Presently the way became more traveled. Boats were drawn up on the shore, and sacks and bales lay stacked under rude shelters.

They camped overnight by the water, and Ambros ran about talking to the sailors and workmen. If he was to grow up into a man of wisdom he would need to know about everything. And so he asked the sailors how they knew when a storm was coming, and the builders how they laid a foundation, and noted not only what they said but the pitying looks they thought he did not see.

Three more days of travel brought them to the Over-King.

Ambros sensed the hill almost before he saw it. A round summit, separate from the surrounding hills, it commanded the vale. The eastern face rose steeply, but their escort led them around to the southwest, where a path meandered slantwise across the slope. From here, one could see to the peak, where the trees had been felled to make way for the building. But there were no walls, only a great deal of tumbled stone.

The royal encampment sprawled over the meadows by the lake. A roundhouse had been erected to shelter the king; a gaggle of rudely thatched lesser buildings clustered around it, leaning a little drunkenly as if they had been built for a temporary use that had extended well beyond its term. The men were as motley as the dwellings.

Many were native British of types he recognized—horse-faced and redheaded Celts from the south or midlands, or the smaller, darker folk of the west. He saw men with the brown skins of legionary forebears from every corner of the Empire who spoke the British tongue with as pure an accent as any tribesman. But there were others, big, heavily muscled warriors with brown or ash-blond hair who exclaimed in deep-voiced gutturals. He knew these must be Saxons, hired mercenaries from across the sea.

A new language, Ambros thought with interest. He was quick at such things, and could read Latin from the church books almost as well as the priest already. He wondered how hard the Saxon tongue would be to learn.

Their escort brought them through the camp and drew up before the big roundhouse. Ambros felt his heart thumping heavily as he slid stiff-legged off his pony.

"The Vor-Tigernus is down by the lakeside," said the warrior who guarded the door. He was a big man called Hengest, the leader of the Saxon mercenaries. "He said you should take the boy to him when you came in."

Ambros was glad for the chance to walk some feeling back into his legs. He did not want them to think they were trembling because he was afraid. Still, as they made their way through the camp and down to the waterside he could not help holding very tightly to his mother's hand.

A group of older men stood on the lakeshore, watching another, who stood thigh deep in the water, holding a slender pole.

"He is fishing," said one of the men as Ambros looked up inquiringly, "we must keep still."

At home people generally used nets, which were more efficient both in time and results, but Ambros had sometimes caught fish in his hands, and knew how silent and attuned to the flow of the water one must be. The man who stood in the water did not move, but his mind was unquiet. And if Ambros could feel that, surely the fish would too. But maybe he did not care if he caught anything, so long as he could get away from other people for awhile.

Maderun was speaking in low tones to a tall man, richly dressed, with silver in his fair hair.

"This is Amlodius, your cousin by marriage. It seems a long time ago that we met—" She turned to the big man again. "Is Argantel well?"

"She is well in body. We had hopes of a child earlier this year, but it was not to be."

"That is always hard for a woman," Maderun sighed. "Take my love to her, when you return."

Amlodius started to reply, then stilled. The fisherman was coming in. The skin on his head was sunburnt beneath the thinning ginger hair, and the skirts of his tunic flapped wetly around his legs, but no one laughed. Instead of the kind of majesty Ambros had expected, he moved with a driving purpose that was in its own way just as compelling. A slave brought up a stool for him to sit on and took his fishing pole. Ambros stiffened as the Over-King's gaze swept the little group and fixed upon him.

"This is the boy, sir," said one of the messengers. Vitalinus beckoned him forward.

"Do you know why you were brought here?" His voice was an even tenor, neither warm nor cold.

"You are building a fortress and it keeps falling down. Your wise men said I could help you, and you will reward my family if I do—" Ambros shrugged and glanced at the two men in the multi-checkered mantles of druids who stood nearby.

"Perhaps, if you are the right boy," said Vitalinus. "Lady Maderun, I understand this is your son. You must tell me truthfully how he was begotten."

Maderun came forward to stand beside Ambros and he took her hand.

"I can say this, my lord, and may God be my witness. Until I was married, after this boy's birth, I never lay with a man. They will have told you that on my journey home from my cousin's wedding I was lost for a time in the forest. What happened to me there I do not remember, but my son was born a full twelve-month afterward, so I do not think he was gotten then. When I lay recovering in the convent I dreamed often of a man as fair as the dawn who came to me. Be he angel or demon I do not know, but that he was my child's father I believe, and no earthly man."

Ambros looked up at his mother with interest. *Does she have an invisible friend too?*

"Maugantius, is this possible?" The king turned to his house-priest, who was looking thoughtful.

"As you know, I have studied the writings of the Romans as well as the Church fathers," he said at last. "And it may be so. In *De Deo Socratis*, Apuleus tells us of beings that live between the earth and the moon which have partly the nature of men and partly that of angels. The ancients called them *daimons*, but we know that they are *incubi*, or *succubi* if they come in female form. It is said that they delight in tempting mortals to impurity. Perhaps one of these appeared to this woman and begot the lad."

"He does not look like the son of an angel," said Vitalinus thoughtfully. "But he does seem to fulfill the terms of the prophecy. My druids have told me that the blood of a fatherless boy is needed to bless the foundations of my fortress. What have you to say to that, Ambros who is no man's son?" he said suddenly.

Maderun gasped and gripped his shoulders protectively.

They did not tell my mother why they wanted me, but I think they told Morobrin! Ambros felt terror shock through him and then drain away, leaving him very still. Neither of the two druids would meet his gaze.

"They are fools," said a still, sweet voice in his head. *"Go to the hilltop and the spirits in the earth will tell you what is wrong."*

"I think that they are stupid," he said in a voice he did not recognize. "You need me with my blood in my veins, not on the ground. The earth speaks to me. Take me to the top of your hill, and I will tell you what she says." Saying the words opened his awareness to the voices in the wind and water. He could feel the flow of energy beneath his feet as he did sometimes in the forest at home.

"It is true that death is very final," said the Vor-Tigernus. "But you must understand that this fortress is an essential link in the chain of strongholds I am building to defend this land. I will do whatever is needful to establish it."

Ambros met the Over-King's eyes and saw something,

perhaps a spark of recognition, kindle in that amber gaze. "You act from need . . ." he said, "but I, from necessity. . . ."

Ambros felt as if he was two people, the one who was climbing the hill, answering questions as if he were a spirit himself, and the other, who was only a little boy, and afraid. But there was a third within him, and it was she who comforted the one who feared and counseled the one who climbed. Perhaps, he thought, she was a *daimon* like the one who had come to his mother. It was a long climb, but Ambros noted with some satisfaction that the adults tired before he did.

Except for the Over-King. Agile as a fox, Vitalinus mounted the path ahead of him, and when they arrived at the summit he was not even winded.

"Behold Britannia spread out before you," said the Vor-Tigernus. "Is it not a fair prospect?" Below them the lake shone bright as blue enamelwork in the sun, surrounded by folded green hills.

"Is that why you want to build a fortress here?"

"I will be remembered. I will defend this land!"

Ambros looked at him, and echoing the voice within, replied, "It is true. You will be remembered."

Vitalinus, sensing something sardonic in the boy's tone, turned to him with narrowed eyes. "And what do you say now that you are here? Your life hangs on it, boy, so speak to me."

At the center of the summit was a hollow, where coarse marsh grasses grew. Ambros made his way to the center, squatted down, and laid his two palms against the ground. With his eyes closed his hearing sharpened, and it seemed to him he could hear running water. His awareness expanded, and he felt two streams of energy, one coming all the way from the farthest point on the holy isle of Mona to the northwest and the other from the Isle of the Dead to the southwest, winding through the earth like serpents to cross beneath the peak.

"The Dragon Path . . ." he whispered, looking up at the king. "You are building on the Dragon Path. Why have your druids not told you?" Once more he sent his awareness downward where the forces churned uneasily, disturbed by the digging.

"Tell the Vor-Tigernus he must dig down until he reaches the water—" came his inner voice. Ambros did not realize he had repeated the words aloud until Vitalinus began to shout for his builders.

"Your head is not safe yet, boy," he said as men ran off to do his bidding, "but if you are right about this I will begin to believe."

For the rest of that day and the next every man who could hold a shovel was set to digging, stopping only when darkness fell. Ambros and his mother were treated well, but they were carefully guarded. The boy slept fitfully, dreaming of warring dragons.

On the third day the mud the workmen had been digging gave way to a bubbling spring, which rapidly washed away the remaining earth around it until they were looking down at a clear pool.

"Your druids could not even tell you what was underneath the ground," said Ambros. "They were wrong about me as well."

"Perhaps. But I still must make the foundations for my fortress."

Ambros eyed him uncertainly, but the Over-King was smiling. A little wind ruffled the surface of the water; or was it something from below? The boy looked upward and saw clouds moving in from the northwest, but the disturbance he felt came from somewhere deep in the hill.

The two druids watched him, muttering, and he turned to them.

"If you are so wise, tell the king what is underneath the pool!"

"Earth and stone are underneath the water," said one, but the other kept silent.

"And what do you say is underneath the pool, oh fatherless child?" asked the Vor-Tigernus.

"Dragons . . ." whispered Ambros. "I would tell you to leave this place, but you will not do it. Command your men to drain this pool, and you will see."

Once more the laborers were summoned. Working with pick and drill, they made a channel through the side of the hill. As the work proceeded the wind grew stronger, blowing now from one direction and now from the other. Overhead, clouds were gathering. Light from the westering sun slanted golden beneath them, gilding the metal of the shovels and turning the grass a vivid green.

Ambros sat on the ground, frowning beneath his heavy brows. He could hear men marveling at how swiftly the wind was driving the storm, but he knew it was not the wind, but an echo of the disturbance in the hill. As the level of the channel neared that of the pool, he got up and edged backward. When he approached the oak trees that grew at the rim of the hill, two warriors barred his way.

"Very well, I will stay—" He sat down again. "But take my mother a little ways down the hill. Tell her it is because of the storm."

The man's grim expression softened a little and he turned to do as Ambros had asked. Vitalinus had been eyeing them suspiciously, but when the boy sat down he resumed his watch on the pool. The last cut was made, well below the level of the pool, and the water began to sink rapidly, swirling in a widdershins vortex toward the hidden hole. So swiftly did it spin that a fine spray flew up from it, continuing to whirl in the wind. In another moment it seemed as if the clouds themselves had caught the motion. Wind whipped at men's mantles and blew anything lightweight away.

Ambros hunkered down where he was, fingers digging into the grass. Leaning against the wind, Vitalinus stumbled toward him.

"What is it?" he cried, staring up at the storm. "What is happening?"

Ambros looked up at the clouds shot with lightnings, partly a dirty white, and partly tinged red by the setting sun. Then his focus changed and he allowed himself to see the energies that other senses had shown him.

"The Dragons are fighting!" Ambros shouted back, waving upward. "The Red Dragon, and the White!" Storm-white and crimson, the sinuous forms roiled; now the white one taking the ascendant and then the other claiming victory. "Don't you see them? Can't you *see*?" He gripped the Vor-Tigernus's shoulder and felt the man stiffen and knew that at least for that moment he *did* see.

The White Dragon had risen from the path that came up from the southeast toward Mona; the Crimson from the line of power that crossed it. The earth trembled with the force of their conflict. But gradually, as he watched he could see that the White Dragon was forcing its opponent downward. Lightning flared, and in the next instant they were deafened by a clap of thunder. Blinking, Ambros saw the Crimson Dragon sink into the earth and disappear. But the White circled upward on the storm, spiraled three times widdershins around the hill, then sped away in the direction it had come.

The great wind died away as suddenly as it had appeared, and the hilltop stood silent. The last light of the sun picked out the wreckage strewn across the grass and the empty hole in the ground. Men picked themselves up, staring about them. One by one, they gathered around the Vor-Tigernus and the boy.

"What does it mean? Why did they come?" Vitalinus picked Ambros up and stood him on his feet. The boy rubbed his eyes. He felt dizzy, and his vision was still seared by that last lightning flash, so that he saw in shadows speckled with little sparks of light.

He started to say that he did not know, but in his head his invisible friend was speaking. As he listened he began to weep, because he was very tired, and what she was saying filled him with fear. He shook his head, but the terrible knowledge would not go away, and in the end, it was easier to close his eyes and let her use his voice to say the words.

"The Red Dragon belongs to the tribes. It is part of this land."

"And the White?" The question seemed to come from a long ways away.

"The White comes from over the sea. It follows the path of the conquerors, the way the first Romans came. The White Dragon belongs to the Saxon folk that you have called into this land. In blood and fire they will rise against you, and only in these mountains will the Red Dragon find refuge from the foe. . . ."

With the words came images: burning cities, dead children lying sprawled like abandoned dolls, fleeing families pursued by fair-haired men with bloody swords. It was too much for him—consciousness fled inward, while from his lips the dreadful prophecies rolled on and on.

When Ambros awakened he knew it had been a long time because it was dark. Beside the empty pool a bonfire was blazing. He lay with his head in his mother's lap, wrapped warmly. He felt empty, as if only his mother's touch anchored him to earth. He stirred a little, and one of the people who had been watching over him ran off. Presently a shadow came between him and the fire, and he looked up and saw the Over-King.

"So, Ambros, you have confounded my men of wisdom," said Vitalinus.

"They were fools. . . . Will you give my mother the gold?" Ambros swallowed. His voice was hoarse, as if he had been shouting. Maderun offered him some warmed milk in a panniken and he drank it gratefully.

"I will keep my word," said the king. "But if my druids are fools I must send them away. Stay with me, Ambros, and be my prophet."

"But he is only a boy!" exclaimed Maderun.

"Is he?" Their gazes locked above Ambros's head.

If I go home, thought Ambros, *Dinabu will tease me and my stepfather will glower and wish me gone. Here, where so many men come and go, maybe I can find out who I am. . . .*

"I will stay," the boy said into the tense silence, and Vitalinus turned back to look at him. Ambros gazed up into those yellow eyes, and in the end, it was the Vor-Tigernus of Britannia who looked away.

Ĭv

ʈHE FORGE

A.D. 437

The Wise Men of Britannia were debating in the Over-King's hall. In the portico of what had once been the palace of the Roman governor of Britannia, the philosopher and priest Maugantius, who studied the stars; a druid from the lands of the Votadini called Maglicun and another from Guenet named Melerius; and Godwulf, the Saxon thyle, argued beneath the dispassionate gaze of painted gods. With them sat Father Felix, who had been a student of Pelagius, and Martinus, come over from Gaul to preach the new theology by which Augustinus of Hippo explained the disasters that had overtaken the empire. And just beyond the circle of light cast by the brazier, the king's prophet, Ambros son of Maderun, sat listening, with his back against a marble pillar and his arms around his knees.

Some of the Vor-Tigernus's wise men viewed Ambros as a mindless vehicle for prophecy. Such creatures were born from time to time—unable to speak properly or care for themselves, but capable of great feats of calculation, or of repeating back lists of names and lore. But Ambros was something else, a wild child with an endless thirst for knowledge. Remembering his mother's teaching, he kept quiet and made himself useful, and they condescended to let him listen to their discussions, though they did not suspect how much he had learned.

At eleven, he had the growth of a boy of fourteen, all long legs and clumsy feet with a head that seemed too large for his body and teeth too big for his jaws. It had been some time since Vitalinus had called on him for prophecy. *Maybe*, thought Ambros as he listened to the men's voices, *when I grow up the gift will leave me, and I will be an ordinary man.*

"It does not matter how hard you strive," said the new priest, Martinus. "You will still fall so short of God's perfection that only His grace can save you, as He has predestined."

Ambros did not yet know what Martinus might have to teach him, for the Gaulish priest still crossed himself and muttered charms against the devil when the boy came too near. Now, he saw Ambros watching him and his fiery gaze flinched away.

"And I call that a heresy!" exclaimed Felix. "I believe in a God of justice, who will reward good works done in His name. Will you tell our lord that all his labor to protect this land meant nothing? For twelve years the wolves have been kept from our borders, and Britannia has prospered as never before."

Felix was a priest in the civilized tradition of the later empire, able to argue philosophy as well as theology, viewing other faiths with an easy tolerance so long as they prayed for Britannia. He had taught Ambros to work hard and to value the wonderful variety of humankind. The boy smiled as Felix continued, for he had heard all this before.

"The Vor-Tigernus has pacified the men of Eriu by marrying his daughter to their king, and the Irish who remained in Guenet are being cast out by the Votadini. Those who tried to take Dumnonia were defeated by the Cornovii whom he has settled there. Coelius and the Army defend the lands around Eburacum, and Amlodius those of Luguvalium, and our allies in Dun Breatann and Dun Eidyn are a further bulwark against the painted people of the North. In the South and East we are protected from the Saxon wolves who formerly savaged these shores by Hengest and his men! All these forces are commanded by the Vor-Tigernus!"

"Praise ice when you have crossed over it, and a king when he is on the funeral pyre . . ." rumbled Godwulf. "Hengest guards you now, but he cannot do so if Vitalinus does not pay his men."

"Let the men of the South and East who have grown rich in these times of peace pay them!" exclaimed Maglicun. "The North must support its own defenders."

It had taken some time for the druids' suspicions of Ambros to ease, but in the end they had remembered his mother's connection to the Isle of Maidens and accepted the boy. Perhaps the alacrity with which he learned from the other sages had something to do with it also, for as Maglicun said, it was not fitting that a child of the ancient priestly line of Britannia should grow up knowing nothing of his true heritage.

"I do not think they will," Father Felix said unhappily. "They complain about the Vor-Tigernus's taxes and talk of calling the sons of Ambrosius Augustus back from Armorica to rule them."

"It is not Justice that Vitalinus needs, but Mercy," put in Martinus. "If all his labors are in vain, will not that prove the truth of Bishop Augustinus's teaching?"

"The stars show that a time of changes is coming, but whether for good or ill I do not know." Maugantius pulled at his beard thoughtfully.

Ambros had found Maugantius more approachable than most of the others, and through many long nights had kept him company as the philosopher watched the constellations wheel across the sky. Maugantius was a follower of Plato and his later disciples, Iamblichus and Porphyry, an initiate of Greek mysteries and Egyptian magic dedicated to the Great Work by which a man might re-forge himself into a god.

Maglicun snorted. "Of course there will be changes. Night gives birth to day and winter to spring. It is the way of the world to turn in a circle, not in a straight line as you Christians say. The end of one thing is the beginning of another.

The wise man learns to interpret these cycles, and moves with them rather than fighting the flow."

Ambros nodded. This was the wisdom of his mother's people, and it nourished something in his soul. But all this talk of change was making him uneasy. Would Vitalinus ask him to prophesy? Could he still do it? At the thought, he felt the familiar wave of dizziness and the presence of his invisible friend, awakening suddenly in his mind like an old tune.

He shook his head and pinched himself to reconnect with his body. *No! I don't want to see what is coming! I don't want to know.*

"That is so," Godwulf was saying, "but the little priest says truly that those threads the Norns have spun may not be broken. In the end, it is not the outcome that matters, but the way a man meets his wyrd. Still, one may face what is to be all the better for some warning. I will cast the runes and see what they say."

From the thyle, Ambros had learned some of the runelore of the Eruli, and found it powerful but strange. Godwulf turned, as if he had felt Ambros staring at him, and the boy felt that premonitory dizziness brush his mind once more.

"We must speak to the men on the Council, and to the Over-King," Melerius said then. "We must make them understand."

These were wise men, thought Ambros, and they would speak with wisdom. But in the end he knew that the Vor-Tigernus would call on the wild power that spoke through the boy without a father, and Ambros could not predict what that power might say.

The river Ictis meandered gently through reedbed and meadow, its quiet belying the proximity of Venta Belgarum, whose tiled roofs could just be glimpsed beyond the trees. The spring had been wet, and the water ran high and strong, but its surface was calm, veiling its power. With the warmer days of summer, vegetation had grown lushly green, at times almost blocking the path beside the stream. But Ambros pushed determinedly onward, looking over his shoulder from time to time at the roof of the basilica where the Vor-Tigernus sat in Council with the lords of Britannia. He was well out of earshot, but it seemed to him that the sound of angry voices still echoed inside his skull.

The day had the sultry stillness that heralded a storm, though there was no cloud in the sky. He paused, looking down into the brown waters, his sharp eyes catching the sinuous movement of the speckled bass and silver-scaled bream, but although he might for a moment touch the slow, quiet thoughts of the fish that hid in those depths he could not forget the passions of humankind. Maugantius had tried to teach him the skill by which a man can barrier his soul from the emotions of others, but Ambros had not yet mastered it. He wondered if even Maugantius had the power to shut out awareness of what was happening today.

For three days they had been arguing, Vitalinus insisting that the rich landowners of the Midlands and the West should contribute to the defense of their eastern neighbors. And for three days the magnates of Britannia had countered that the danger from which the mercenaries had been hired to protect them was past, and it was foolishness to maintain an army when there was no enemy. And throughout it all Hengest, Vitalinus's *magister militum*, stood at his master's right hand and said nothing at all.

Ambros turned his back on the city and kept walking. From above, the musical "ke-ar" of a hawk came drifting down on the wind. He peered upward, shading his eyes with one hand, and glimpsed a tiny speck against the blue. From such a height the doings of men must seem without significance, he told himself. And yet the hawk's sharp eyes caught the tiniest movements of the small scurrying creatures that moved through the grass. *Is that how the gods see us?* he wondered. It was an uncomfortable thought, and he moved on.

Presently, over the gentle murmur of the stream he heard a musical "tink, tink." In another moment a shift in the wind brought him the scent of charcoal and scorched metal, and he knew he was nearing a forge.

The noise grew louder. Ambros saw a path leading away from the river and followed it. Beneath an ancient oak tree stood an unhitched wagon. Nearby, the cart-horse was cropping the grass, while the smith, barrel-chested and bandy-legged, with arms like gnarled trees, hammered at a horseshoe for a dappled mare. He was a freedman, Ambros saw from the Phrygian cap he wore; probably one of those who traveled from farm to villa, plying his trade. Two more horses awaited his attention, tied to trees.

As Ambros neared, the smith finished hammering, took the shoe from the anvil and lifted the horse's hoof to try it, then swore softly and laid it back on the coals of the forge. As he did so, he saw Ambros watching.

"You, boy—come give me a hand with the bellows. You look strong, and my own lad's run off to gawk at the great ones in the town."

Amused, for even the Vor-Tigernus did not order him about in quite so peremptory a tone, Ambros set his hand to the work and quickly got the knack of it.

"Fire's like a man, you see," said the smith, "that will die if you don't give him air."

"And the iron?" asked Ambros.

"Ah, that's like a man too, a strong man who's hardened and shaped by the blows life deals him. But sometimes you'll find a piece of metal, or a man, with a hidden flaw. You strike him wrong and he'll shatter." The horseshoe glowed a dull red when he plucked it from the fire, but the color faded quickly as he began to hammer it once more.

"Are the best pieces the purest?" asked Ambros as the smith got the horse's leg between his knees and set the shoe against the hoof once more. The metal was still hot enough to singe, and the boy wrinkled his nose at the scent of hot horn. This time the shoe fit, and the smith changed hammers and began to nail it down with swift, precise taps.

"Not always." He let go and the horse stamped, unused to the weight of the shoe. "For some things, like swords, you want to melt a little of something else, nickel, for instance, into the iron. If you forge rods whose metal is different together, the sword has the strength of all of them, not just one. Do you understand?"

Ambros nodded, and the smith took up another shoe blank and laid it on the fire. The boy had sometimes watched the smiths who traveled with the Vor-Tigernus, but his ambiguous position in the court constrained communication. To this man, he was only a boy. Ambros applied himself to the bellows once more, watching with satisfaction as the coals began to pulse and glow.

"You work well," said the smith. "Have your people set you to a trade?"

"I'm only eleven."

"That's not too soon to begin, if you're strong. What do your folk mean you to be?"

A Man of Wisdom, thought Ambros, but that was his mother's saying, not his own. And there were many kinds of wisdom.

"I don't know what metal I'm made of . . ." he answered, "or who's to have the forging of me." A flock of rooks flew overhead, calling raucously; he looked up to follow their flight and saw the sun disappearing behind the trees. He let go of the bellows and straightened. The work had freed him from his worries for most of the afternoon.

"I have to go. I'm sorry—" he added, "I liked helping you."

"Did you?" The smith's laughter echoed from the trees and the horses tossed their heads nervously. "Do not grieve then, for we will meet again, and when we do, perhaps you will know what you are."

Ambros's steps dragged as he headed homeward, watching the white swans sail the quiet stream. But as he neared the bridge the echo of the smith's laughter was drowned out by a great clamor from the town. He stopped, staring, as riders clattered over the bridge and set their mounts at a gallop down the road—they belonged to Gerontius of Dumnonia, by the emblem. A few moments later they were followed by a horse-litter surrounded by guards. That was Sulpicius from Deva. What was going on?

He crossed the bridge between cavalcades and tugged at a shopkeeper's sleeve.

"Vitalinus has dismissed the Council!" came the answer. "Or they've dismissed him, it's hard to say. But the great ones are off to their own lands, and talk goes that they've sworn to bring Ambrosius Aurelianus and his brother back from Armorica to be our emperors!"

Vitalinus moved swiftly, marshalling the forces that were left to him. But with the warriors of Dumnonia and Guenet turned against him, and Coelius protesting that the Painted Peoples would attack if he weakened the Army of the North, they were few. Even Amlodius, protesting that after so many years of marriage his wife was about to give birth to a living child at last, refused to come, though he sent a subcommander with some of his men.

From his own lands around Glevum the Vor-Tigernus had the men he had trained, and some from the south coast, but for the most part his strength lay in the barbarian troops who for the past ten seasons had guarded the land. And where they had come from there were many more.

While the sons of Ambrosius gathered forces in the west country, Hengest sent swift ships across the channel to bring more warriors from the German lands. While he waited for them to arrive the Over-King evaded Aurelianus's attempts to bring him to battle, knowing that if he could delay long enough, many of the rebels would go home to help get the harvest in.

The two forces came together at last just before the festival of Lugos at a place called Uollopum, north of Venta Belgarum. Not all of the Vor-Tigernus's reinforcements had arrived, but Aurelianus forced the issue, for he was beginning to lose men. Through all one bloody day they struggled, while Ambros and the other noncombatants watched from a hill nearby. And because their numbers were almost even, when darkness fell neither side could claim the victory. The Ambrosian forces withdrew to Dumnonia to lick their wounds, and Vitalinus and his men fell back toward Glevum.

The sword flares down, slicing through leather armor, cleaving flesh and bone. A man screams as his arm is torn from his body; then blood sprays crimson and the voice is stilled. Others fill the silence, crying out in pain or rage. The clangor of weapons assaults the senses. The smell of blood and sweat and shit fouls the air.

He whimpers, trying to find a way out of the carnage, but everywhere he turns he finds faces contorted in rage, and the swift flare of bloodied swords. . . . He curls in a ball, trying to get away, away. . . .

"Ambros!"

He flinched as a hand gripped his shoulder and jerked

upright on the bench, flailing. The fingers let go and someone laughed. Ambros blinked, saw Hengest looming over him and behind the Saxon, Vitalinus.

"Wake up, boy. Your master needs music to sweeten his mood!" The Saxon laughed again and turned away.

Ambros rubbed his eyes. The only fighting he could see was the battle between the Greeks and the centaurs painted on the wall of the villa where they had stopped for the night, and the angry voice he heard belonged to the Vor-Tigernus.

A slave scurried in with a pitcher of spiced wine. Vitalinus took it before the slave could set it down and refilled his cup, drank deeply, coughed, and drank again.

"Emperor! He dares to take the purple on the strength of one battle which he did not win!" Vitalinus glared around the room.

As his senses returned, Ambros remembered the messenger who had ridden in just before suppertime. That was what had sent the great ones to council. From the sound of it, nothing had been resolved.

"Neither did you," Hengest said drily. "Nor will you, unless you get more men." Despite the guttural accent, he spoke Latin fluently and could make himself understood in the British tongue. He stood with his back to the fire, his face hidden, but his shadow stretched dark across the room.

The Vor-Tigernus poured more wine and began to pace up and down. As he passed Ambros he paused.

"You heard him, child. Take up your harp and see if music will soothe the savage heart of your king!"

Eyeing his master warily, Ambros reached for the harp, a simple crescent of oakwood joined to a soundbox, with five horsehair strings.

"Go on—or do you think yourself a David to my Saul? I will not throw a lance at you!" He jerked into motion once more, slopping wine upon the floor.

No, Ambros thought, *I am not David, for I will never be a king. . . .*

He settled the harp against his shoulder. He had learned to play simple chords and accompany the bards when they chanted the old songs, but he did not think that singing was wanted just now. Softly he began to pluck the thirds and fifths of harmony.

Perhaps the sound did have a soothing effect, for he saw Vitalinus's high color recede and presently the king sat down. He looked at his *magister militum* and sighed.

"You are right. I need more men. Can you conjure them out of the air?"

"Out of the air?" Hengest's deep laughter rumbled in his chest. "That I cannot do. But I can bring them out of the water—over the sea—"

There was a long silence. Ambros clutched the harp, scarcely daring to touch the strings.

"I know. In your country there are many warriors. But they will not fight for love of me," Vitalinus said at last. "If I had the gold to pay them—to pay *you*—I would not be sitting here now."

Hengest sat down before the hearth, clasping his knees. Sitting so, his head was still as high as the king's shoulder, but he no longer loomed over him.

"When I give the gold you pay me to my men, they send it home so that their kindred can buy food that their sea-soaked land will no longer bear. If you have no gold, you possess what my people hold dearer—black earth from which grows the golden corn."

The Vor-Tigernus started, staring down at the other man, but he made no sound. After a moment the soft rumble of Hengest's voice resumed.

"Hirelings must be paid, but there is no question of payment between allies. Give us land, Lord of Britannia, as the emperors of Rome gave Germania Prima to the Burgunds, and Aquitanica to the Visigoths. As guest with host we shall dwell, and take our living from the produce of the land."

"As *feoderati*—" said Vitalinus.

"As allies," repeated Hengest. "And to seal the bargain I will give you a hostage from my own family. You have seen my daughter—"

She had come over from Germania just this year, Ambros remembered, a tall woman, with red-gold hair, and beautiful.

"Reginwynna . . ." breathed Vitalinus.

"You have no woman. Take Reginwynna as your wife, and give us Cantium."

"It cannot work!" Vitalinus jerked out of his chair and

began to pace about the room. "The lords of Britannia will never stand for it."

"It has worked for the Romans," Hengest objected. "Are you not the emperor?"

Vitalinus shrugged. "My fathers were magistrates under Rome, but I do not come of the old princely lines. Aurelianus is kin to the old kings of Demetia and Guenet. If I had something—some symbol of sovereignty that might command men's allegiance, I could rule as I willed." For a long moment he stared into the fire. Then he turned.

Ambros felt the hairs rise on the back of his neck as he realized that the Vor-Tigernus was looking at *him*.

"Your mother comes of the old blood of the North, is it not so? I have heard tales of a Sword. . . ."

Ambros was shaking his head, but he could feel the pressure of Vitalinus's will like a fire.

"Put down your harp, son of Maderun, and speak to me words of truth and prophecy—" the Vor-Tigernus's words sparked through his awareness.

I cannot. . . . I will not. . . . I swore not to speak of the Sword! thought Ambros, but already his vision was blurring. His will was a fraying tether, and his consciousness a wild thing eager to break free.

"In the name of God and his holy angels I command you, and in the name of the Old Powers of this land. Four winters I have fed and clothed you, and I am your lord."

He was a king, and accustomed to be obeyed. Against the authority in that tone Ambros had no defenses. Desperate, he sought his inner *daimon*, and as the inrush of her presence released him from himself, faintly he heard a voice that was not quite his own begin to answer the king.

"Woe to the lord who summons powers he cannot command!" An eerie, tinkling laughter made Vitalinus step back. "You have asked, oh King, but can you understand the answer? I see the White Dragon growing strong; his children flourish in the land. The Red Dragon rises to fight against them, and blood covers the ground. The children of the Red Dragon are slain."

"And what of the Sword?" As from a great distance, he heard the Vor-Tigernus ask.

"The Boar of Dumnonia rages and the White Dragon is

brought to bay; but he in turn shall be brought low and his brother shall rule. But the Sword of the God of War is not for him, for he shall be slain. After him shall come the young bear, begotten by a man who is dead upon a secret queen. No man but he may draw the Sword from the Stone."

"And what of me? How shall I save this land?"

"You have sown the teeth of the dragon and you must reap the harvest. . . ."

The voice came to Ambros like a whisper on the wind. His body was falling, but his spirit fell further, descending forever down a tunnel of night until he knew no more.

Ambros opened his eyes to darkness. He lay on the bench, and someone had covered him with a cloak, but he was alone in the room. He sat up, rubbing his forehead to relieve the dull ache behind his eyes, and pulled the wool around him. A dim glow from the hearth enabled him to make out his surroundings; from somewhere nearby came a faint snoring.

What had the daimon that lived within him said to the king? Nothing good, for he could remember someone shouting. If he was still alive and free it must be because the king thought him too weakened by his trance to be worth guarding. But tomorrow the Vor-Tigernus would certainly punish him.

At the thought, volition came back to his limbs. Ambros wrapped the cloak around him, took a partly eaten loaf of bread from the Vor-Tigernus's plate and stuffed it down the front of his tunic, and poked his head out the door.

He heard snores and harsh breathing, but nothing stirred.

The gods of his people must be protecting him, thought Ambros as he passed through the gate of the villa, for the one guard he had seen had been sleeping. A waning moon showed him his way, and soon he was on the Londinium road. No one would expect him to flee that way, but from there he could double around to the north and then head west to Demetia.

Though the road was not so well maintained as it had been under the Romans, Ambros made good time, and by dawn he was approaching the White Horse Vale. He paused, gazing southward in wonder, as the first light revealed first the noble curve of the downs against the eastern sky, and then, as the sun rose, the attenuated curves of white that revealed the Horse shape carved into the chalk of the hills.

Ambros's breath caught. He remembered suddenly the sculptured curves of bone in the skull of the White Mare that led the procession at Samhain. Swathed in a white horsehide, the Mare was at once the face of Death and the promise of life to come, for she brought the spirits of the ancestors in her train to take flesh once more in the wombs of the women of the tribe. The blood of his mother's people beat in his temples as he gazed upon that mighty form, bound into the very bones of the land.

"White Mare, protect me—" he whispered, then glanced behind him. There was nothing there now, but soon, folk would be stirring, and might remember a strange lad hurrying down the road. But if he struck out across country here, he should strike the Ridgeway, that ancient trail that followed the top of the downs east and north. From there he could spot any pursuers long before he could be seen.

The Vale was bigger than it had looked in the deceptive light of dawn. All that day, the boy struggled to cross it, detouring around meadows whose green hid marshland still soggy from the spring rains. Farm roads petered out in woodlots or pastures, and sometimes he had to hide from men working in the fields. Thus, by the time he began the long climb up to the Ridgeway, dusk was drawing a veil of shadow across the land.

Ambros found the ancient track more by touch than by eyesight, stumbling even when he reached the summit and the smoother ground. He flinched from a flicker of motion, then saw it was a hunting owl, gliding by on noiseless wings. With nightfall, the downs became a different country. He was acutely aware of the mighty swell of the chalk, as if the bones of the earth were pushing through the soil. And the longer he followed the Ridgeway, the more conscious he became of the many feet that had trod that path before.

This was an ancient land, where any stone might be an elf-bolt lost before the fathers of the British tribes ever came over the sea. Some said that the little dark hunters, or their spirits, wandered here still. Ambros glanced over his shoulder, wondering if they hunted by night or by day. The open expanse that had attracted him in the morning seemed now to impose a terrible vulnerability. Uplifted on the shoulders of the downs, he cowered beneath the huge expanse of sky, seeking, like some small scurrying animal benighted far from its burrow, a place to hide.

And so, when he saw a stand of beech trees in dark silhouette against the southern sky, he turned off the path.

Almost at once an odd scent stopped him. Ambros sniffed cautiously, and his nostrils flared at the harsh reek of a charcoal fire. He took a step forward, fancying he saw the glow of flames behind the trees, and then, unmistakably, came the chink of metal on metal, and he recognized the music of the forge.

"Come warm yourself—" a deep voice called him forth from among the beeches. "I have stew to fill your belly as well."

Amazement warred with caution, for this was the same man Ambros had met beside the river at Venta Belgarum. But more powerful still was hunger, for besides the bread he had eaten nothing that day. Licking his lips, he stepped into the light of the blacksmith's fire.

The flickering flames showed him the horse and wagon, and behind them a tumble of stone like a fallen wall. But four mighty uprights still stood among them, flanking a dark passage that led into the mound.

"What are you doing here?" He heard his own voice, stupid with fatigue.

"Shoeing horses—what else?" The smith grinned. "In this country there are many fine ones. The people will bring them to me when they gather in the old fortress for the fair."

There is a fine white mare on the hillside, thought Ambros. *Will you set shoes on Her as well?*

But more important than fear or fancy was hunger, and he dug into the bowl of stewed pork which the smith handed him. There was ale as well, stronger than he was used to, with an aftertaste of honey. The smith continued to tap away with his hammer, talking of the fair with its horse races and peddlers from many lands, when the people scoured away the grass that encroached around the edges of the Horse's limbs. Ambros could not quite see what he was making, and after a time his eyes grew heavy and he forgot to look.

The chink of the hammer came regular as a pulsebeat, but as Ambros began to drowse, it seemed to him that what the smith was beating out was not metal but memories, a sequence of bright images that passed before him until he walked among them. The dark hunters of the hills chipped skillfully at the flint to make their arrowheads and axes. They were followed by a bigger, brown-haired folk who tilled the land and dragged great stones from the mountains to entomb their dead, using hand axes to peck cups and spirals into the rock. Ambros saw the first mound made beneath the beech trees, and then the building of the barrow of stones.

He was sitting in a place of ghosts, he thought dimly, but he sensed a circle of safety in the light of the blacksmith's fire. In dream he saw the leaves of countless seasons drift down across the stones. A new tribe came who drank their ale from beakers of fired clay banded with patterns made by cord or comb, and after them people whose smiths crafted fine weapons of polished bronze, who brought more stones to set in careful alignments where the dragon power flowed through the land. Circles of shaped stone marked the movements of sun and moon with more precision than any of Maugantius's formulae. The makers of the old tombs were forgotten, and bronze-smiths plied their craft before the mound.

And yet these tribes also passed into memory. The weather grew colder, with more rain, and the upland farms were abandoned. Men used new and better weapons of bronze to fight for what arable land remained, and built earth-walled fortresses to defend their territory. Ambros did not understand all that he saw, but he could see a pattern, in which one people succeeded another in lordship of the land.

And presently there came tall, bright-haired folk from across the sea who carried swords of iron, and worked their ornaments in sinuous spirals varied with palmettes and scrolls. He knew them for British, his mother's people, but in his dream they seemed no more than another layering of leaves on the mound. The click of stone axe on stone became the ring of bronze, and then the heavy clangor of iron as, generation after generation, the smiths worked their magic, compelling the inert elements of earth to the service of man.

His head throbbed to the ring of those hammers until he

could no longer see, and then it seemed to Ambros that he himself was lifted and laid upon the anvil. The hammer swung, shattering his old form and shaping him anew. He understood at last what the atoms of which the old Greek magi had written must be, for he could feel each atom in his body realigning beneath the blows. And as he looked up, he saw that somehow the gnarled blacksmith had become a radiant goddess, with hair of flame.

"You were a raw lump, but I have made of you a mighty weapon for the hand of the destined king. But let the lord who makes use of you remember that truth is a two-edged sword. . . ."

Then he was taken from the anvil and sheathed in something soft and warm, and sank into a sleep of darkness too deep for dreams.

Ambros woke slowly. He ached as if he had been beaten all over, but at least he was warm. One eye opened, and then the other. He lay wrapped in the cloak on a bed of sweet-smelling grasses, but above and to either side of him he saw stone. With a shiver he realized that he was lying inside the mound. Still, the light had to be coming from somewhere. Wincing, he turned over, and saw at the end of the passage-way a pale square of sky. He caught a whiff of woodsmoke and then the scent of meat, and his stomach rumbled.

After a struggle, he freed himself from the cloak and crawled toward the daylight.

There was the fire, as he remembered. But there was no wagon, only a muddy horse cropping the grass. Blinking, he peered at the man who sat toasting strips of venison over the flames. The broad shoulders were familiar, but they did not belong to the smith. It was Hengest who was sitting there.

The Saxon lifted a strip of meat and handed the end of the skewer to Ambros. It was hot, but perhaps his encounter with the smith had been a dream, for he was furiously hungry.

"How did you find me?" he asked when he had finished the first piece and was working on a second one.

"I followed the White Horse," came the reply. "For my people, the white stallion is holy. The way he runs tells the priests what is to be. Sometimes when a tribe must move, they loose the stallion, and where he goes they follow. You also see the future—I knew he would lead me to you."

"Did the Vor-Tigernus send you after me?"

"My lord is not happy—" Beneath the grizzled mustache Hengest's lips twitched. "But in this he does not command me." His blue gaze fixed the boy. "Our wise men teach that Woden, who gives the ecstasy that carries men to victory in battle, gives also staves of verse to the shope, and the spirit speech of the *witega*, the wise-man. I think that you belong to the god."

He frowned, and gripped a hank of grass. Earth crumbled dark between his fingers as he lifted the clod. "This is a good land, and my people are hungry for a home. You said that the White Dragon would conquer."

"I do not remember—" Ambros whispered.

"Then the god gave you the words. This land will belong to us, and we to this land."

Ambros shook his head, denying it, but the stones of the barrow, that had seen so many peoples pass, told him that it was true.

Ambros did not protest when Hengest took him back to Vitalinus, nor did he repeat what the Saxon leader had told him. The Vor-Tigernus had heard the prophecy; if he did not heed Ambros when he was inspired, he was unlikely to believe what the boy said in his ordinary senses. But from that day, Ambros avoided the Saxons.

For a time, Ambros dared to hope he had been mistaken. He was growing fast now, as if the hammering he had received from the blacksmith—from Govannon himself, and Brigantia, if he had not been dreaming—had unbound his limbs, which seemed to lengthen day by day. Hengest's son Octha and a chieftain called Ebissa, who was his nephew, were sent to garrison the lands below the wall, and the Picts kept close to their own hearthfires. Ambrosius did not dare to challenge the Vor-Tigernus again.

But while Ambros gained in height, Hengest gained men. Keel after keel rowed past Tanatus to beach their boats where Caesar had landed. Others ran ashore below the white cliffs at Dubris, and their crews marched overland to Durovernum.

Prince Gorangonus lived a prisoner in his own city, but the Over-King would not hear his complaints.

In the year that Ambros turned sixteen, the distant storm whose lightnings had played upon the horizon for so long broke upon the British in all its terrible power.

Cantium had been more than sufficient for Hengest's original war-band, but it could not support the horde that had followed them. Hengest no longer came to Londinium; it was Godwulf who presented his demands for more gold. But the Vor-Tigernus had already given the Saxons all the gold he had.

And so the Saxon wolves turned at last upon the poor sheep they had guarded, and all the south and east of Britannia were engulfed in blood and fire. Venta Icenorum vanished, Camulodunum was overrun; the gate of Lindum was burnt down. And if walled towns fell, how much more vulnerable were the isolated villas and farms. Where the Saxons did not strike, fear of them wielded a keen-edged sword. Everywhere folk fled, and even when the first fury of the revolt ebbed, they did not return.

But in Londinium, the Vor-Tigernus clung grimly to his imperium. The barbarians were not invincible. Even the terrible Attila had been defeated by Aetius at the Catalaunian fields. Vitalinus had sons, Vortimer and Categirnus, who were now come to manhood, and together they set out to reconquer Brittannia.

V

THE NIGHT OF
THE LONG KNIVES

A.D. 458

"Ambros son of Maderun, you are welcome to Luguvalium—" Amlodius led the guest toward the hearth. "We have not seen you here in the north for far too long."

Igierne resisted the temptation to whirl around to look at him. At twenty, a married woman with a child of her own, she was surely too mature to leap up because the Vor-Tigernus's prophet had come. Then her father and his guest moved into her line of sight and her eyes widened; kinsman though he might be, she had never seen anyone like Ambros before.

His height was not so surprising—her own father was tall. But she had never encountered so hairy a man. The hair of his head had been trimmed, but his eyebrows bristled, and the short beard merged with the dark hair that grew thickly on neck and his arms below the embroidered borders of his sleeves. No doubt his legs, covered by loose breeches of fine wool, were furry as well. Then his swift, evaluating glance, moving over the assembly, crossed hers. For a moment black eyes stared into blue.

He is proud, she thought, marshalling her own self-respect to withstand that scrutiny. *He has reason to be.* All men had heard how even as a child Ambros had confounded the wise. During the Saxon wars he had become the Vor-Tigernus's most valued counselor. He wore the garments of a prince, and around his neck hung a pendant of a running stag on a chain of gold. Then his gaze passed on, and she let out her breath in a long sigh.

"Sit—" said Argantel, gesturing to a servant to bring food. "You have had a long ride."

"I have, but my lord wished to honor you by sending his message through one who is kin."

Ambros's voice was deep, with a curiously husky timbre. They said his father had not been human, and Igierne could believe it, for the red glints in his hair were the only feature he shared with his mother's kin.

"The proclamation states that we have defeated the Saxons. Horsa was killed at Rithergabail, but Hengest holds Cantium, and his son, Octha, the old Iceni lands. Is that a victory?" Amlodius asked as they sat down.

"It is all the victory we will have in this generation." Ambros threw back the folds of his mantle, a druid's cloak, checkered in many colors and held by a silver pin, and took his own seat. "He has given both his sons to defend Britannia. If the princes of the West and North would fight under his banner, the Saxons might be swept from our shores, but they will not do so, and he will not submit himself to Aurelianus. Therefore this treaty that Hengest has offered is the best outcome we are likely to achieve."

"But a partition!" exclaimed one of the other men. "It is a recognition that they will never go away."

"This Wall that you guard so carefully is a partition, but the religion and culture of Rome are found in Dun Breatann as well as in Luguvalium. Men from every part of the world have become good sons of Britannia. We will trade back and forth across that border, and in time they will learn our ways."

Amlodius laughed. "I suppose you are right. My own grandfather came from the same lands as Hengest, but I am a Roman."

"And you are one of the masters of the North. Vitalinus

summons all the great lords who are sworn to him to come to Sorviodunum by the first day of May. His sons may be gone, but it will be well for the Saxons to know what strength is united against them when the treaty is made."

Amlodius frowned. Igierne had been surprised, when she arrived for this visit, to realize that his fair hair was now all turned to silver and the massive shoulders a little bowed. In contrast, her mother, despite a sprinkling of silver at the temples, seemed young. It would be a long trip for an old man, but he was nodding in agreement.

"It has been many years since I visited the South. I would like to see what the Saxons have done to the land."

"They have destroyed it," said one of the men who had come with Ambros's escort, "as the wolf who gains entry to the sheepfold in his bloodlust rends and slays far more than he can devour."

"We drove them back, but we cannot force those who fled before them to return," said another. "Good farms lie abandoned, and the towns that remain are dying, for there is no way to get the goods made in one place to market in another. And the weather has been so bad these past years it seems that even God has turned against us, and is giving the coastlands back to the sea."

The servant brought round a tray of silver cups and Argantel poured wine from a pitcher made of Roman glass. Igierne sipped appreciatively. In Dumnonia, they had wine often, brought over by the ships that traded with Gaul, but this was an old vintage, hoarded in the cellars of the Roman fort.

One of Ambros's men asked where the wine had come from, and Amlodius began to talk about the vintages he had known as a young man. With a start, she realized that Ambros was watching her. Argantel followed the direction of his gaze and smiled.

"I forget that you will not have met my daughter, Igierne."

"You are the wife of the Prince of the Dumnonii—" he stated, as if, she thought with a spurt of irritation, he were labeling her. But she smiled sweetly in return.

Igierne had grown accustomed to being viewed as an appendage of Gorlosius when she was in Dumnonia, but returning to the North, she had begun to think of herself in the singular once more. What was he seeing, she wondered, beyond a tall woman with her father's fair hair?

"I was married three years past, and have a little daughter who is just a year old."

Morgause was auburn-haired and strong-willed like her grandmother, and Igierne loved her dearly, but it had been a relief to get away from her for a little while.

"It is well that you are both here at the same time," Argantel said softly. "You two are the only heirs in the next generation of the line of Artorius Hamicus, and it is in my mind to take this opportunity to teach you the rites of the Sword."

Ambros's eyes widened. "My mother told me its history, but I thought the priestesses—"

"On the Isle of Maidens it is guarded, but it can be touched only by those of our line. Will you come, son of Maderun, and take up the priesthood that is your heritage?"

For a moment something unfathomable stirred in his dark eyes; then they became opaque once more. He nodded, and Igierne felt her heart bound in her breast and did not know if it beat with anticipation or fear.

It was inevitable, as they rode south from Luguvalium, that Igierne should find herself often in the company of her cousin. Argantel rode in a horse-litter, but Igierne was mounted on a sturdy hill-pony, and Ambros on a bigger mount of the old cavalry breed. He was interested in her impressions of Ambrosius Aurelianus, who had guested with them several times at Bannhedos, and she, of course, was curious about Vitalinus and the Saxon woman he had married.

"She went back to her father when Hengest broke faith with the king. Among her people it is a woman's right to leave a marriage, and though they were wed in a Christian ceremony, I think in her heart she was a heathen still. But it is true that she was very beautiful."

He frowned, and Igierne wondered if that beauty had stirred him. She had observed that he did not look at women with lust, as some men did, but rather as if they were a puzzle to be solved.

"To be pagan is not so great a sin in the North," said

Igierne. "I was raised to be a priestess and my mother's heir, though it proved necessary for us to make an alliance with Dumnonia. Perhaps when I have given Gorlosius a son I will take my daughter and return here."

He looked at her curiously. "Do you not love your husband?"

The undertone of bitterness in her answer surprised her. "Love has little to do with the matings of princes. From me he expects fertility and faithfulness, and he gives me support and protection. Like most of the Dumnonian lords he has interests in Armorica. He may have a concubine there—I have never asked."

She kept her eyes on the road ahead, where the great crouching shapes of the hills guarded what lay within. The country around Luguvalium was rolling, and in Dumnonia one always felt exposed to the immensity of sky. But the Lake country was a land set apart; those whom it called to itself might find a path through the wooded dales, but the way could not be forced by an enemy.

"Among our people it was not always so," he said softly at last. "The druids teach that the king serves the land and if need be, dies for it. But it is through the queen that he touches its power. But not since the days of Brannos, I think, have we had a High King of all Britannia, and even he had no Tigernissa, no High Queen."

"My mother is Branuen, the hidden queen who performs the rites for the sake of the land, and I suppose that I will bear that mantle after her."

"But what if Branuen and Tigernissa were the same woman, a priestess-queen? Might not the king then become Brannos as well as Vor-Tigernus, a sacred king who would rule over a golden age?" His voice trembled, and turning, she saw that he too was staring at the holy hills.

"Have you seen this in a vision?" she asked softly.

"A vision?" He shook his head. "I have learned more certain ways to foretell what the future holds, and the magic, if need be, to change it."

As their journey continued, Igierne continued to consider his words. He sounded very confident, but Ambros was by his very nature a creature half of myth and magic. If he seemed arrogant perhaps he had reason. As for herself, the latest, and it seemed to her the least, in a long line of priest-esses, what power could she have in a world where priest-esses were becoming as legendary as the gods they had served? If men honored her it was only because she was the daughter of one great lord and the wife of another.

And yet, as they wound their way into the hills, Igierne felt herself slipping backward in time. Her mother, also, seemed to become younger as the Lake grew near. But Am-bros grew strange, as if the veneer of sophistication which he had acquired in the Vor-Tigernus's court was peeling away to reveal some other being, more ancient and elemen-tal, that lived within. He spoke less and looked around him more, and when they paused to rest the horses he would dismount and move to the edge of the forest with a grace so alien and still that she half-expected him to disappear into a tree.

On the fourth day of travel they reached the top of the pass. From here they could look down into the vale whose center was the blue lake with its tree-crowned islands.

"There lies the Holy Isle—" Igierne pointed to the largest, which lay close to the eastern shore. Here and there the gold of thatched roofs gleamed from among the trees; the long feasting hall, the roundhouses where the priestesses lived, and a little apart from the others, the House of the Sword. "We will be there by the time night falls."

"I will be glad of it," he answered harshly. "This wilder-ness makes me afraid."

Igierne looked at him in surprise.

"—Not of the mountains," he added then, "but of myself. When I gaze at these hills the great prophet and learned counselor of Vitalinus seems a crawling insect that one shiver of the ground could knock away. And if I am not the Vor-Tigernus's mage, what am I?"

She nodded. "I have sensed that strangeness in you. It is different for me. Here, I come into my own power."

He considered her curiously. "Is it because you are a woman, I wonder, or because—" He did not finish the thought, but turned to gaze down at the Isle of Maidens as if it could give him his answer.

*   *   *

As soon as he stepped through the door Ambros could scent the power. He stared around the House of the Sword, hair lifting along his spine at the growing sense that something that had been patiently waiting was now awakening. Light flickered madly across the floor as Igierne fixed torches in the sockets, and the draperies that shrouded the altar flared suddenly crimson. He found himself watching her as he had ever since he came to the North: a swift glance, swiftly turned away, lest she should see. Was it because she was a woman of his own blood that he felt drawn to her, or was there some other reason, that he was not yet ready to understand?

He heard Argantel draw a careful breath, then she pulled the cloth away from the Sword, murmuring words of praise and salutation to the spirit that lived within.

The blade stood upright in a block of stone. Perhaps half its length was free; its surface, of some polished metal that had neither tarnished nor rusted during all these years, gleamed red in the light of the fires. Ambros did not use weapons, but he had learned to judge them. The cross-guard was plain, but the hilt had been wound with gold wire. It was a sword sturdy enough to serve a warrior, with a stark elegance worthy of a king.

"I will teach you the prayers later," said the priestess. "Tonight I will do no more than introduce you. . . ." She lifted the cage which held the cockerel. "But it is for you to make the offering. Daughter, you must assist him."

Biting her lip with concentration, Igierne extracted the fowl from the cage. Ambros looked from her to her mother in confusion.

"What, have you never killed a chicken for the pot?" Argantel laughed. "Well it is time you learned!"

He blinked back vertigo. Eating at the king's table, he had never killed anything before, but he could not admit that while the women were watching him so expectantly. He took a firm grip, feeling the fowl's frantic heartbeat. Then he twisted its neck, and gasped as he *felt* the life departing. Hot blood gushed over his hands.

In the next moment his revulsion gave way to an appalling surge of hunger. Then the priestess guided his arm so that the fowl's blood dripped onto the altar stone. His own sensations paled before the approach of the god as the light of a candle dims in the sun.

Argantel was saying something, but he could not understand the words. He saw Igierne reach out, saw her face change as she grasped the hilt of the Sword. Argantel set her own hand over that of her daughter, and together they pulled the blade a handsbreadth further from the stone. Another twist, and the Sword was thrust back. Then the priestess grasped his wrist and pressed his own hand, still red with the blood of the rooster, around the hilt of the Sword.

"You must twist as you withdraw the blade . . ." her words seemed to come from a great distance, "or it will not move." Her grip tightened on his hand, but he did not need the instruction, for the blood of his great-great-grandfather was awake within him. Smoothly he turned the blade and felt it slide freely through the stone.

"Not too far—" said Argantel. "The time to draw it has not yet come."

He stared at her through eyes that he knew were rimmed white with the effort of keeping control. A voice that was louder than the drumming in his blood began to speak in his soul.

"Not yet, man of the ancient blood. You are not the King who shall wield this blade, but the time will come when you shall enable him to claim it. Lift up your eyes, for she in whose womb he shall be cradled stands before you. . . ."

Ambros looked up, blinking as if he had been staring into the light, and saw Igierne. Her face was shining, and her pale hair flared out around her head like rays of gold, and in that moment she was beautiful beyond mortal imagining. He stared at her, and understood at last that for him she was the Goddess, and that what he felt for her was love. What she heard he did not know, but she stretched out her hand and set it upon the pommel of the Sword, and together, they thrust it home.

Radiance flared around them. Dazzled, Ambros tried to look back at Igierne, but it was the face of a boy he saw, brown-haired and intent, with Igierne's blue eyes.

The treaty talks took place at a shrine north of Sorviodunum, on the edge of the broad central plain. Ambros supposed it must qualify as neutral ground, having belonged to both British and Saxons in turn during the past few years. The Saxons had built a shelter for the meetings—no more than a framework with a thatched roof to keep off the rain. Between the posts one could look out past the last sheltering swales of grass to the broad sweep of the plain. It was an empty land, haunted by memories of peoples so ancient no one even remembered their names. Perhaps that accounted for the unease that had troubled him since the meetings began.

They had feasted on beef and pork, a raider's menu. The rich scent of roast meat still hung in the air. But now, at last, the eating was over. When the drinking horns had gone round a few times for men to toast the new treaty, it would be done.

They sat at long trestle tables covered with an assortment of cloths. Hengest, to emphasize the peaceful nature of this festival, had forbidden the usual barbarian custom in which men came armed to a feast and hung sword and shield behind them on the wallposts. But the Saxons still looked like savages. Ambros sighed, remembering the last time he had come to Sorviodunum with the Vor-Tigernus, when he was still a child. They had dined in one of the great houses of the town, and eaten off the elegant table service that had once belonged to the Roman magistrates. Its pieces were probably scattered through half the Saxon army by now.

Not, strictly speaking, that it was all Saxon any more. The chieftain sitting next to Amlodius was Aelle, whose Saxons had settled into the coastal lands to the east of Noviomagus. But Hengest himself had peopled Cantium with Jutes and Frisians. There were Franks as well, and others whose names he did not know. The ravens who feasted on the carcass of Britannia were drawn from half a dozen northern tribes, paired one by one with the British councilors.

Ambros pushed the meat on his platter distastefully aside. *Ah Vortimer*, he thought, *we should have honored your dying wish and buried you on the eastern shore. Then, perhaps, your spirit would have saved us from this day . . .*

His own dinner partner was Godwulf, who had once taught him the Eruli lore. The Saxon thyle had always been hard to read, but tonight he seemed as impenetrable as Hadrian's wall. In the days when he had cast runes for Vitalinus, Ambros had thought him old. But by now Godwulf must be in his eighties, a truly remarkable age.

"You are in health, I see. Your gods have been good to you," Ambros said politely.

Godwulf smiled. He was missing some of his teeth, and could only eat his food chopped fine. It gave him a more sinister appearance than Ambros remembered.

"It is so," the old man answered. "Woden gives victory in the battles of the mind as well as those of the body, and he likes this land. You should make him an offering."

Ambros lifted one eyebrow. Powerful the god might be, but all his help had no more than won his people a toehold in Britannia.

"You may offer to your demon, and I will honor mine," he said wryly, for the Christian priests would characterize the heathen god and the spirit that spoke to him in his soul alike as devils.

Or that used to speak to him. These days, he commanded spirits rather than praying to them. He tried to remember how long it had been since his inner voice had counseled him.

"If different peoples are to live in peace, their gods must make peace as well," unfazed, Godwulf was answering. "So it was when Woden and the Ase-gods fought with the Wanes. Neither side could conquer, and so they became allies."

"Do you mean to put an eyepatch on Lugos and call him Woden-Lugos, as the Romans used to honor Mars-Belutacadros and many another, proclaiming that all the deities of the peoples they conquered were only faces of their own? They are not the same!"

"Your Lugos is not Woden, not as we encounter him, though they both carry a sacred spear," agreed the thyle, "but there is a place where they meet. Those who can come there will understand how disparate peoples can become one."

"Is Hengest such a man?" asked Ambros, looking at the high table. The Saxon leader sat next to Vitalinus, like an old stallion, scarred and gaunt, looming over a grizzled fox. He sat at his ease, but his eyes were watchful, like a man awaiting the beginning of battle, not one who sighs relief at its ending. Once more, Ambros felt that little prickle of unease.

"Hengest loves this land . . ." Godwulf said ambiguously.

"Will he honor the treaty, now that we have given him what he asked?"

"He will keep the oaths he swears on the sacred ring." The thyle touched the silver arm-ring, graven over with runes, that he wore.

Ambros nodded. It was the oath-taking, not the writing of words on parchment, that would bind the Saxon.

A serving lad bore the mead pitcher past the benches and refilled his beaker. Ordinarily Ambros did not drink deeply, but he had felt the strain of this long war more deeply than he realized, and drinking brought release. He looked at the other British lords and saw that for them it was the same. Faces grew flushed and voices louder; laughter filled the air. The Saxons, eyes bright with excitement, were laughing too, but they were accustomed to deep drinking. Indeed, they were being remarkably temperate this evening, as if they feared to shame themselves.

The platters of roasted meat were taken away, and the ill-assorted collection of plates. Did the fact that nothing matched matter to the Saxons? Ambros thought of a Saxon warrior he had seen emerging from a burning village, wearing a Roman helmet and a woman's gown. Perhaps they liked the variety. Perhaps they were naturally perverse. . . . He realized that the mead was affecting him and set down his beaker.

"It is good mead," said Godwulf.

"It is indeed, but do not your own shopes warn against allowing the heron of heedlessness to steal a man's wits away?"

"You are, as always, wise," said Godwulf with a peculiar smile. He swung himself around and eased off the bench. At the high table, Vitalinus had risen to face the man who had been first his greatest servant and then his greatest foe. A priest stood behind him, holiding a reliquary. Gradually a hush spread through the crowd.

The Vor-Tigernus set one hand upon the casket. He looked sour, but determined, as befitted a man who was about to swear part of his native land away.

"We have labored as hard to frame this treaty as ever we fought on the battlefield," he said. "And all the harder, because our goal was not victory, but a settlement that would be fair to both sides. The details are written, but to this I will now take oath: that the lands which were formerly those of the Iceni and the Cantiaci shall belong to the Saxons and Angles who now dwell therein, and such other smaller enclaves as are specified in the treaty. I pledge that my people will honor their tenure and recognize their borders. In the name of the Father, Son, and Holy Spirit." He crossed himself, a gesture which was echoed by most of the British lords.

Godwulf drew the oath-ring from his arm and held it out to Hengest.

"On the ring of Thunor I swear, and in the name of Woden—this land that we have taken, we shall hold—and as much more as the gods shall give into our hand!"

He released the arm-ring, and turning, held out his arms to Vitalinus as if to embrace him. *"Nimet oure seaxes!"* he cried.

Vitalinus recoiled, but with another step the Saxon swept him into a bear hug that carried him away from the high table and toward the end of the hall.

Staring in amazement, Ambros caught the first flicker of movement only from the corner of his eye. Then someone screamed. Steel flashed in the light of the torches—a dagger, when by agreement all men had come unweaponed to this feast. Coelius of Eburacum and three others lay sprawled in their blood already. But the Saxons were not having it all their own way. Those who had not been felled in the first moments still struggled with the men who by chance or design had been placed to partner them, who had shared the same meat and mead, making missiles of their drinking horns or laying about them with benches. Eldaul of Glevum had pulled up a tent stake and was using it like a club.

Following his example, Ambros wrenched a post from the ground and started toward the nearest Saxons, but Godwulf was before him. As Ambros started to swing, the thyle pulled a short wand from his belt and swiftly drew several symbols in the air.

"Eees—" The thyle drew out the syllables of the bind-rune in a pulsing drone. *"Nyd—"*

Ambros felt the air congeal around him; he could still

move, but slowly, far too slowly, like a man struggling through a storm.

Why not kill me? Ambros's mind raced. Did the old man hesitate to murder one who had been his pupil; or did he lack the power? With that thought, Ambros summoned his own energies, drawing on earth and air as Maugantius had taught him, and where they met in his solar plexus, kindling a fire that shocked through every limb.

In another moment he could move again, but in those few minutes the British princes had passed beyond his aid. Men lay sprawled all about him, silent in death or groaning while their murderers stood panting above them, still clutching the dripping daggers they had brought hidden beneath their leggings when they came to the hall.

Ambros forced stiff limbs to carry him across the ground to Amlodius. His cousin's husband still breathed, but life was ebbing out of him from many wounds, and blood frothed at his lips with every gasp. An animal moan of dismay passed Ambros's own lips as he bent over him, pressing a corner of the older man's mantle over the worst of the wounds.

"No use . . ." The whisper was almost too faint to hear. "Tell Argantel . . . choose Caidiau to rule in . . . Lugu—"

If Amlodius completed the word, it was too softly for Ambros to hear. His gaze became fixed, and then the soul-light faded like a dying flame and was gone.

Slowly, Ambros lifted the old man's body in his arms and got to his feet. The air vibrated with the passage of spirits reft untimely from the flesh that had housed them; they made a roaring in his ears that drowned out all other sound. Where his gaze fell men flinched, but he had no interest in lesser murderers, even Aelle. It was Hengest whom his eyes sought, standing like a deity of carnage in the midst of the slain. Vitalinus, his arms pinioned by a grinning warrior, stood beside him, weeping and shouting words that Ambros could not hear.

He drew breath, and Godwulf, eyes widening, lifted his staff and began to draw runes of protection. But the spells of the thyle could no longer hold him. Ambros opened his mouth and released the words that all those wailing spirits no longer had breath to say—

"In the name of Britannia's gods I curse you, and by the

power of all the spirits of this land!" Power shuddered through him and he recognized the oncoming Presence he had sensed when Argantel showed him the Sword. This was not the gentle wisdom of his daimon, but a force that expanded his aura beyond even his own great height.

"Hear Me, men of the forests and fens and hear Me, you who lead them." The voice of the god boomed through the hall. "As you have been false to your trust, so shall you be betrayed by those you trusted. As you have usurped the lordship of this land, the leadership of those peoples you have brought here shall be given to another! You have slain the flower of Britannia, but from their bones a host shall rise up to confront you. I will raise up a Defender, and he will strike you with a Sword of Fire!"

Ambros could not hear the sound of his own words, but Hengest heard them. Yet if some of the triumph left his face, it was replaced by a stubborn pride that would neither defend nor deny what he had done.

The warrior who was holding Vitalinus let him go, and the old man sank weeping to the floor, a dead man who still moved and breathed. Ambros wondered if the god would curse him too, but there was no point to it; the man who had been the Vor-Tigernus had destroyed himself, the White Dragon savaging the Red as Ambros himself had foretold so long ago. His very name would be a curse so long as Britannia endured.

He swayed as the power of the god began to leave him, but enough strength remained for him to bear the body of his kinsman through the door, and no man sought to bar his way.

"Ambros, what has happened? They told me you had come to the Lake, but not your errand. Is my lord—"

Argantel's brisk greeting faltered. Something in Ambros's face must be conveying the message for which he could not yet find words.

"You have had no news?" he asked hoarsely.

"Neither enemies nor news of them can find their way to this holy place without my will." Her words were proud, but he could see the beginnings of a stricken look in her eyes. His mother had said once that Argantel's marriage had been a political arrangement. But the priestess had come to care for her Roman commander.

"I have brought your husband home."

Once more his throat closed. His memories of that journey were confused. In Sorviodunum he had found a man who would build him a coffin, and a wagon to bear it, and up the Great North Road he had driven, pausing only to rest and feed the horse, neither knowing nor caring what tales might follow him. It occurred to him now that the goal of bringing Amlodius back to his people was the only thing that had kept him sane.

But Argantel was a priestess, accustomed to reading men's souls.

"He is dead?" Her voice cracked on the words. She must be guessing already that no simple illness or stopping of the heart would have made Ambros bring him here himself, and in such a state as this.

"They are all dead—" Ambros whispered. "The Saxons killed—" he gasped, and then, like water breaking through a dam, all the dreadful tale poured out of him at last.

He was weeping by the time he finished. Argantel remained calm, but her stillness seemed the quiet of an autumn forest silvered by a sudden frost. She gave orders for the coffin to be brought into the sanctuary and the horse to be cared for. Hot spiced ale was offered and Ambros drank it gratefully, but when she showed him a bed he shook his head.

"I cannot rest, not yet. I have pushed too hard and long. Perhaps if I walk along the shore I will find peace. . . ."

Argantel nodded. "If there is peace anywhere it is here. Thank you for bringing Amlodius back to me."

Ambros stared at her. Didn't she understand? If not for him, her husband would never have gone into danger. She lifted her hand in blessing and left him, and he saw that in those few moments she had become old.

He took up his cloak and went out, turning down the path that led to the shore. The Isle of Maidens was no more than a few boat-lengths from the mainland. The flat-bottomed barge that had brought over his wagon lay drawn up on shore. He turned away from it and began to pick his way among the rocks that edged the water.

Hills rose sheer to the south and west and north, dark shapes humped like sleeping beasts against the starlit sky. By habit his gaze found the pole star and he marked the constellations around it. He could name the fixed stars and those that wandered, foretell their conjunctions and oppositions, but he had failed to read Hengest's heart. He was a fraud and a failure, all his vaunted wisdom worth nothing. He had been a better prophet when he was seven years old!

Ambros looked back at the clustered buildings. By morning they would all have heard the news and know how he had failed. Indeed, by now all Britannia must know how the Vor-Tigernus's prophet had walked into the trap and stood gaping while the princes of Britannia were slain.

How could he face them? How could he face *anyone* now?

Before him the dark waters lapped quietly at the shore. Let them swallow him, he thought numbly, and drown his shame. . . .

Ambros let his cloak fall to the ground and moved forward. The water was very cold, but it did not stop him. Steadily he continued as the water rose to his knees, his waist, his chest. In another moment it would close over his head and he would be at peace.

But instead it receded to his waist again. The lake bottom was rising. For a moment he stood undecided, but if he returned to the island now he would appear not only a failure but a fool. Perhaps the shadows of the forest would be deep enough to engulf him. Shivering, he pushed forward, and when he reached the shore he kept going, blundering blindly on.

Several times during that night he fell, and lay for a time in mindless exhaustion. But always a moment would come when self-awareness returned, and the voices in his head would begin to accuse him once more. Then he would stagger to his feet and push onward. By the time dawn banished the darkness he had covered many miles. He burrowed into a tangle of vines then and sleep delivered him from his accusers at last.

When he awoke, he was aware only of hunger. A heedless squirrel came within his reach, and he, who in all his life had killed only the cockerel he had offered to the god in the Sword, pounced on it and tore it to pieces, ripping off the pelt, crunching up flesh and bone. Wild onion grew nearby and he ate that too, and lapped water, wolf-fashion, from the stream. Then he began to move once more, south and westward, ever deeper into the hills.

As day followed day, the voices grew fainter, and after a time he ceased to think in words at all. His body hardened and he no longer noticed the cold. The strange flapping things that covered his limbs became encumbrances, and he tore them off and threw them away. He became more clever at foraging for food, though he never found quite enough to satisfy his large frame.

He saw deer, and once a thrown rock even brought one down. He smelled bear and avoided them, and became acquainted with beaver and badger and the wild pig and wolf that roamed these hills. One day he came upon a new creature, furred like a beast but standing upright in the rapids to snatch fish from the stream. As he approached it took fright and ran off, still on two legs, and he came down to the waterside to drink.

The backwater was still. As he bent, something moved in its depths and he jumped back. Then, more cautious, he leaned over the water, and saw a creature covered with bristling hair. It strongly resembled the one that had run away.

Wild Man. . . . A distant memory stirred of men dressed in garments tufted with colored yarn who ran shouting through the streets at festivals. And in that moment of clarity he understood of what blood he himself was come.

Were there more than the one he had seen, and would they accept him among them? He sat back on his haunches, the realization that he was himself a beast making it possible, for the first time in weeks, to think like a man.

Sunlight glanced blindingly from the water; he blinked and stilled, for someone was standing there. Not a Wild Man; it was a human woman's form, veiled in shining hair. She turned and he saw a face he remembered from dreams. When she spoke it was the voice he had so often heard in his soul. Among human women, only Igierne had ever stirred his heart. But this being touched a place that lay deeper still.

"It is so—you stand between the worlds of beast and man, and you can choose what you will be. You are a mule, and will have no offspring of your body, but if you return to humankind you will have a child of the spirit, and he will be the greatest of Britannia's kings."

His throat worked as he struggled to form human words. "If I go, will you be with me?"

"If you will open your heart," she answered, "for I am the Bride of your Soul, and in truth I have never been far away."

The angle of the sun changed and the vision vanished. But he could still feel her presence. He waded into the river and began to scrub the dirt away. Then, when he was as clean as he could manage, he started out again, not back to the Isle of Maidens, but south, to Ambrosius Aurelianus and his brother Uthir, who were now the undisputed leaders of Britannia.

THE DRAGON STAR

A.D. 459

"You have sinned against the Lord of Hosts, and the Devil has sent his legions to chastise you!" The tattered sleeves of a robe that had once been white fluttered as the priest shook his fists against the sunset sky. "For your greed you are punished; for your faithlessness you are cast down. You have followed the heretic Pelagius, and thought that your own deeds could save you, and this is the result—rivers running with blood and a land in flames!" Spittle flew from parched lips as the priest brought down his arms.

"It is true!" wailed the people. "We have sinned! We must flee this accursed land!"

The tall figure at the edge of the crowd moved forward, leaning on his rowan staff. These days he called himself Merlin, the name that "son of Maderun," misheard, had become. He did not trouble to correct it. Ambros had been a human name, and that man had died in the forest. It seemed fitting that he, who was not really a man, should bear what was not a real name.

Merlin had come into the wayfarers' encampment hoping

88

for food and fire—this close to midsummer a day's journey was long. Instead, he had found this haranguing cleric, whose whine made him want to turn back to the quiet of the hills.

"You sought to cast out the devil Hengest, and as happened to the man from whom they cast out the devil, seven demons worse than the first one have invaded our land!" the priest was continuing.

And that was true enough, for the German tribesmen who had hung back when Vortimer was battling Hengest to a standstill had come howling like wolves to tear at the poor bleeding carcass of Britannia once the way was opened by treachery. Aelle and his sons held the lands east of Sorviodunum, and the Jutes and Frisians had taken back all their old lands in Cantium and more. The walled cities of Londinium, Verulamium, Regnum and many others still held, but throughout the eastern half of the country the enemy ranged freely.

"Should we have welcomed the Saxon?" asked someone, and a few people grimaced with what might have been laughter if they had not forgotten how.

In truth, they were a sorry lot; even those who had fled with some of their wealth were worn and dirty. The skin on the priest's face hung in folds, as if he had once been a much heavier man. Those whom Merlin passed edged aside, crossing themselves. He had become accustomed to that, for if they were tattered caricatures of their former prosperity, he had abandoned all its trappings, and now went barefoot, in a garment of deerskin, mantled with a wolf's hide that he pinned with the curving tusk of a wild boar. But he knew how to veil his presence so that even those men who had been startled by his appearance in another moment forgot what they had seen.

"Leave the land to the sea wolves, and may they have joy of it," answered another. "We'll make a new home in Armorica."

Many of his countrymen had done so already, following the men whom the Emperor Maximian had led away two generations before. War and plague had left Armorica nearly empty, and Riothamus, who ruled there now, welcomed the men of Britannia.

"Will you leave the land to the wolves, or to those who

still have the balls to fight for it?" A new voice cut through the babble of agreement.

Merlin turned. Several horsemen had pulled up at the edge of the firelight. The speaker urged his mount a few steps forward, and they saw a big man with mouse-brown hair cut short in the Roman manner, a weatherstained crimson cavalry cloak wrapped over his mail.

"Where are your sentries?" snapped the officer, or rather, the prince, for as he moved Merlin glimpsed at his throat a torc of gold. Three of the men at the outskirts of the crowd hung their heads. "We'd have caught you with your breeches down had we been Saxons!"

"My lord, you have no right to talk to us this way!" the priest exclaimed.

"Do I not?" The prince urged his horse through the crowd until he was almost on top of the cleric. "My brother and I were already safe *in* Armorica! You called us back to Britannia, promised to stand behind us if we would lead you. And now we are here, and when *we* start to plough a furrow, we don't leave the job half done!" He made an obscene gesture that left no doubt of his meaning.

Some of the men looked shamefaced, but others faced the prince with a mutinous glare.

"God Himself has cursed this land. Who are we to fight against the will of God?"

The prince glared in frustration. Clearly, if calling men cowards did not move them, he was at a loss for persuasions. Merlin smiled. He had met neither Aurelianus nor Uthir, but this must be the younger brother, for the emperor was said to be a man of some subtlety. One virtue they both had was energy. They had hunted Vitalinus down already and burned him in his tower.

Then Uthir turned, and Merlin's breath caught as memory overlaid that face with another, seen once in vision, with Igierne's blue eyes.

This was the man who would beget the Defender.

Merlin surveyed him with new interest, searching for lines of character in the pleasant face, for a strength of will to match the powerful body. He saw endurance and determination there; it was the face of a good commander. But was there greatness? He could not tell, but then he had not seen the treachery in Hengest's soul. His own judgment had proved lacking, and he could only trust the gods.

"Blame God for the storm that drowns your crops, but not for the fear that makes you flee." He allowed the power of his personality to blaze forth so that to the people, noticing him for the first time, it was as if he had appeared among them by magic. Even Uthir's horse tossed its head in surprise and had to be reined down.

"Rome protected you as a parent protects a growing child. But now Mother Rome is gone. Will you cling to her skirts when she can no longer even guard herself, or will you defend yourselves like men? Fleeing to Armorica will not save you—the barbarians are everywhere. If you do not stand together to fight them here you will have to do it later, in a foreign land."

"Who are you to condemn us?" someone cried.

"I am no man's son and no man's father..." Merlin's voice rang out through the darkness. "I have been a wolf on the hills and a stag in the meadow.... I soar with the eagle and root with the wild boar beneath the ground. I am the Wild Man of the woods and the prophet of Britannia, and my spirits tell me what is to come...."

"Prophesy the future, then!"

"Why should I prophesy what logic can reveal?" Merlin asked contemptuously. "The mysteries of heaven cannot be revealed except where there is the most pressing need for them. If I were to utter them as an entertainment or where there is no necessity, the spirit which controls me would forsake me in the moment of need."

But as he drew breath to continue, he felt the dizzying shift in awareness that told him his daimon was awakening. His face must have changed then, for the man stood openmouthed as Merlin put the knowledge that was coming to him into words.

"You would do better to search your own heart than to question me. Confess yourself to this whining priest while you can, for this much is given to me to say—neither here nor in Armorica can you evade your doom. This very night you shall stand before your God!"

"You dare to curse—" the priest began, but Merlin's gesture silenced him.

"I neither curse nor bless. I only say what I see." He turned back toward the prince.

Sputtering, the heckler started toward him, fist raised. No man could say precisely what happened after, whether the fellow tripped and hit his head, or if he was felled by some invisible foe. But it was certain that when they lifted him up again he was dead and staring.

"Sorcery!" came the whisper, but it was not a loud one, and no one raised a hand to stop Merlin as he continued to Uthir's side.

The prince had gone pale beneath his tan, but he was not one to waste an opportunity.

"Death can strike you anywhere—" he said in a strong voice. "March with me, and if you die, at least it will be *for* something, not running away. Any man who can stiffen his rod to beget a child should be able to stiffen his spine enough to defend it. March with me, and your sons and your daughters will grow up free in their own land!"

Uthir's gaze met Merlin's as the whispers became a babble of discussion. "I know you now. You were Vitalinus's prophet. You will come with me to the emperor."

"I offer you my service."

"I hope you serve us better than you did him," said Uthir, but mingled with the trouble in his eyes was a hope that had not been there before.

North of Sorviodunum, the land rose to a broad plain. Even in more peaceful times it had been sparsely populated, and now it was nearly empty. But ghosts whispered on the wind. There were more ghosts now, thought Merlin, looking at the covered carts that the emperor's men were driving up the track from the shrine. He could sense the spirits of the British princes hovering over those mingled fragments of ash and bone.

Did Aurelianus understand what fulfilling this task, the first the emperor had asked, would cost Merlin? To other men, Sorviodunum, battle-scarred but bravely flaunting a few remnants of past glory, might be no different than any other place recaptured from the enemy; but for him, its population of dead was more numerous than the living, and more vivid, and the ghost of the man he himself had been was the most terrible of all.

To come before the emperor in Sorviodunum was hard. To ride with him to the shrine on the edge of the plain where Hengest had slain the princes was harder still. About the round huts where the monks lived, a military camp was growing. They called it Ambrosiacum now, or Ambrosius's hill.

The Saxons had burned the thatched shelter above the bodies, and though the monks had chanted prayers over them, they had no cemetery. And so Aurelianus had decreed that the princes must have a monument. To create it was Merlin's penance, and the first test of his wisdom.

One of the riders in the lead lifted his lance, pointing. Uthir kicked his horse alongside Merlin's.

"Where is the place?"

The shallow valley that the Abona had carved through the plain was falling away behind them. Ahead of them, grass and heath stretched away toward a line of hills, broken with occasional clumps of trees. Merlin pointed.

"Do you see that lump, perhaps a mile from here? That is the first mound, though indeed, such ancient burials are scattered throughout the plain. But these form a line that points back to Sorviodunum, and extends northward up the backbone of Britannia. East to West, another line passes through the Giant's Dance, and links it to the Isle of Glass, which is also a place of ancient power."

He had first come here with Maugantius during one of the Vor-Tigernus's visits to Sorviodunum, when he was a child. The wide plain had frightened and exalted him then; it continued to do so now.

"What did you tell my brother to get him to come here?" asked Uthir.

Both of them glanced back at the horse-litter in which Ambrosius Aurelianus was following. The emperor was considerably older than his brother, and at times his joints pained him too greatly for riding to be easy. But there was nothing wrong with his mind.

"I told him that this is the most important focus of power in this part of the island," said Merlin. "The spirits whose bones are laid to rest in this place will join with those who were buried here in ancient days."

"Now, this is the border of Britannia," said Uthir with a sigh. "We don't even call ourselves Britons any longer, but *Combrogi*, the countrymen." He was an interesting contrast to his brother. Both had been educated by Greek tutors, but Uthir, perhaps to distinguish himself from the emperor, had adopted the rough language of the soldiers he commanded.

They rode on a little further, and Uthir stiffened in the saddle, pointing. "What is that?"

Out of the grass dark shapes were rising. A few more steps and they became a circle of standing stones, linked uprights surrounding grouped trilithons. The Romans had built works of greater height and complexity, but never with such massive blocks of stone. Stark against the empty plain, the henge waited with a brooding power.

"That is the Giant's Dance."

As the days shortened toward Samhain the men labored, and when they were finished, the line of barrows was longer by one. Beneath it lay the remains of the leaders of Britannia. On the eve of the Festival, Merlin commanded the workmen to build a circle of fires around the barrow and then to withdraw to the river, leaving the fires to burn through the night.

"I will go to the stone circle and make the magic that will bind these spirits to the land."

"Do you have to go alone?" asked Uthir, and Merlin raised one eyebrow, for on such a night any other man would have covered himself with protective charms and huddled by the fire. "If not, I'll go with you."

"As will I," the emperor echoed him.

Merlin bowed. He had not yet had much chance to know Aurelianus, but though the emperor's body was not strong, it was from him that Uthir had gotten his strength of will. He could see already that if Vitalinus had possessed such a purity of purpose, and such ability to make men follow him, the Saxons would never have gained a foothold in Britannia.

"For lesser men it would not be safe. But it is fitting that the kings who rule now should stand where the chieftains of ancient times held sway."

"Was this a druid temple?" Uthir had asked as they passed beneath the portal of stone.

"A temple of sorts, but not made by the druids, though they learned some of its secrets. It was built before ever our people came to this land."

"Was it the Trojans, as some have said, or wise men from Egypt who taught the people how to raise these stones?" asked Aurelianus. Well-wrapped in cloaks against the chill, he sat throned on one of the fallen stones.

"The traditions I was taught say it was neither," answered Merlin. "The mages who built the stone circles came from the west, from a land of magic far across the sea. To Eriu they came and then to Britannia. It is from these isles that the knowledge was carried southward, all the way to the lands around the Middle Sea."

It was almost midnight. They looked across the grass to the fires that circled the mound, and then up at the starry radiance of the sky.

"The stars are like the watchfires of a great host encamped in the heavens," said Uthir. "Will those spirit warriors come to help us in our need?"

"They will come if I call them. You must keep silence now, no matter what you see or hear." Merlin drew from his pouch a handful of herbs and sprinkled them in a protective circle around the princes. Then, chanting softly, he paced sunwise around the henge. As he reached each stone, he saluted it, and within the lichened rock he seemed to see the beginnings of an answering glow. The henge was awakening.

He stripped off his own clothing, laid his wolfskin on the ground halfway between the two pairs of trilithons, and sat cross-legged on the hide. He gazed upward, watching as the great round of the sky wheeled toward the sacred hour, and in the moment when the stars stood still in mid-heaven, the spirit awakened within him and he began to sing.

> Bright-shining stars, brilliant above,
> As fires of foemen burn below,
> Silent, you shall tell your story;
> Stones shall sing histories. . . .

He remembered that night he had spent in the barrow with the smith when he was a child. Then the visions had come uncontrolled and unexpected. Now he was a man in the fullness of his power, and he called them. He sang, and slowly the shining shapes began to come forth from the mounds.

He heard the rhythmic chanting of many voices as men strained to pull the massive blocks over the ground. Stone by stone, the circle was completed. He saw the blood of bulls poured out to bless them; he saw kings with gold upon their shoulders, and queens with gold twined in their curling hair. Season by season he saw the ceremonies; the inaugurations and burials and the foot races and chariot races around the mounds.

All these things he saw; these things he sang, and as the stars began to pale with the approach of dawn, he summoned the spirits.

"You who have loved this land, defend it from those who would destroy. You whose bones have become this earth, defend it from the death-bringers. You who have dwelt here in a time before time, welcome the spirits who are newly come to your realm!"

The glow from the stones grew brighter, raying out across the plain. Where it fell, transparent figures rose from the earth, more and more of them with every moment. As the wind lifts the leaves, his song moved them toward the new mound. In the east the sky grew bright with the approach of dawn. The fires were veiled by an opalescent cloud, swirling ever more swiftly until the earth of the barrow opened and the spirits of the newly dead burst free.

In that instant the burning edge of the sun rimmed the horizon. Merlin heard a gasp of awe from behind him; then he blinked at the explosion of radiance above the mound. The sun lifted free of earth's shadow and light flamed in a burning path from the mound across the grass to flare from the stones of the henge.

The living and the dead and the earth itself joined in a great shout of praise. Merlin felt his spirit reft away in a timeless moment of unity. Then he fell back into his body, and sat up, blinking at the morning light of Samhain Day.

"Their sacrifice has been accepted," said a voice behind him. "They are one with the land."

It was Aurelianus, his face still radiant with awe. He looked younger than Merlin had yet seen him, but fragile, as if the spirit within him burned too fiercely for his flesh to bear. He knew then that the emperor would not live long. Uthir stood beside him, steadying his elbow.

This was the king that he would serve, thought Merlin, until the time for the Defender should come.

"They would ask no greater honor," said Uthir, "nor would I."

From that day, Merlin rode with Uthir's band. While Aurelianus traveled back to Venta to direct the defense of Britannia along the new frontier, his brother marched toward Demetia. While the combrogi had been focused on defending their eastern territories, the Picts and Scotii—the ancient enemy—took advantage of the situation to renew their raiding. Their numbers were reinforced by a band of Saxons led by Pascentius, who had been beaten off by Amlodius the year before, and had taken refuge in Eriu.

For a time, the heavens themselves seemed to be fighting on the side of their foes, for clouds rolled in from the west, washing out tracks and slowing the combrogi army. Uthir rallied them with cheerful obscenities and said that the storms had been sent by God to pin the enemy down until they could catch up with him. He was, observed Merlin, a good commander, willing to listen to advice when there was time and decisive when there was not. He asked his men to endure no hardship that he himself did not share.

As the campaign continued, Merlin grew to know the other commanders as well, Caius Turpilius, whose family had a prosperous estate near Venta Silurum and still held to the old Roman ways; Eldaul of Glevum the younger, a distant cousin of Vitalinus who always sought the most dangerous fighting in an attempt to avenge his father, and Gorlosius of the Cornovii, eldest son and heir of Gerontius, who ruled Dumnonia.

Igierne's husband.

Merlin studied him more closely than the others, and found little to like, though there was much to admire. He too fought fiercely, though it seemed sometimes that his ruthlessness came from outrage that anyone would dare to oppose him. If ever Merlin had thought of offering Igierne more than a kinsman's love, recognition of his own origins would have prevented it, but it galled him to think of her bound to this arrogant princeling, when she was herself the equal of a queen.

They had marched all the way through Demetia and were pushing up the coast toward Guenet before the clouds began to break up and they saw the naked heavens once more.

When they made camp that evening, the only remains of the storm were a few tattered banners of flame across the sky. Merlin—whose usual reaction to rain was to bundle his leather clothing into a chest and go clad only in the twist of linen about his loins—was salving a sore where the wet saddle blanket had galled his pony, when he heard a shout. It was not the standard alarm for an approaching enemy. He turned and saw men pointing at the heavens.

Half these men had been shepherds before the wars. Even the farmers among them were accustomed to tell the seasons by searching the skies. Merlin had been making regular observations since Maugantius began to teach him when he was ten years old. It took no more than a moment for him to see what they were looking at—a brilliant point of light in the southeast where there had been no star before. For an hour it was visible in the heavens, then it sank behind the trees.

The next night it was brighter still, and they could see a blur of light behind it. It was a comet, Merlin told them, such as often foretold events of great import. But it was still rising. They must wait until it reached full magnitude before he could attempt to discover what it might mean.

The three nights that followed were overcast. The combrogi pushed northward, eager to come to grips with the foe. Smoke still rose from the burned timbers of the looted farmsteads they were passing now. The enemy army could not be far away.

The next day a wind came up that tossed the treetops and scoured the clouds from the sky. They made camp early that evening, choosing a rise with a clear view to the south. Merlin put on a good tunic of white wool that Aurelianus had given him; it made no difference to the magic, but to look like a druid would inspire confidence. By now, he himself was as anxious to know the comet's meaning as any of the men. But mingled with his anticipation was fear.

As daylight faded the tension grew. Merlin felt their apprehension as a pressure against his awareness and braced his mind against it. His discomfort lessened, but so did his ability to perceive the subtle currents of the universe. Frowning, he chose a good vantage point on the hill and drew the circle of herbs around him. Not even Uthir would dare to cross it, and as he closed it he felt the strain ease.

He took his place upon the wolfhide, breathing deeply and regularly and rooting his soul in the earth below. He sensed the delicate branchings of power that nourished the land; but they were only tributaries, not a mighty river such as he had tapped at the Giant's Dance. Yet even these tiny channels were troubled. Some change was coming, and soon.

The blue of the sky deepened to a luminous cobalt. The first stars gleamed suddenly, but where had the comet gone? A murmur from the men brought his attention upward and he realized that it was traveling more quickly than he had expected, for it was already high. Merlin lay back, gazing upward and, anchored by his link to the earth, allowed his spirit to soar.

The head of the comet blazed more brightly than Venus when she is the morning star, and its tail seemed to stretch halfway across the sky. Transfixed by its beauty, it took Merlin a little while to realize that someone was calling him.

"Prophet, tell me—" Uthir's voice was thin with strain, "what is this wild star?"

Already half-tranced, Merlin responded to the note of command as a horse obeys the rein. Awareness of the outer world faded; he stared up at the comet until it filled his vision. Its head had seemed a ball of light, but now it was pulsing wildly, and suddenly it was the head of a dragon. Distantly he heard his own voice reporting what he saw.

There was a mutter of awe from the men around him. Then the prince spoke again.

"Such marvels don't come by chance. What does this one mean?"

At the question, knowledge cascaded into conscious awareness with an intensity that brought Merlin upright, tears welling in his eyes.

"Woe and sorrow," he whispered, "woe and weeping for

you, my lord, and for all Britannia. Your brother is dead. The noble prince is gone, and the people left without their leader." Blindly he turned toward Uthir and stretched out his hand. "Arise, son of Ambrosius, and hasten to strike your foe. Go now, while the head of the Dragon rules the sky and promises you victory. Destroy your enemy and take Britannia into your keeping."

He gazed upward once more and saw the mouth of the Dragon opening, and from its jaws blazed a tongue of fire. "You will have victory!" he shouted suddenly, "and a son greater even than his father who will save his people and win fame unending!"

Now others were clamoring, asking how Aurelianus had died, where the enemy was, what they should do. Merlin shook his head, striving to hear the voice that spoke within.

"You shall find your foes camped on the shore where the Isle of the Dead guards the bay—" he whispered. "March now, and take them as they are sleeping. You must move swiftly, for they mean to sail on the morning tide!"

They marched through the night, and the Dragon blazed above them, showing the way. And just as it was growing ghostly with the approach of dawn, the combrogi army wound down from the hills above Madoc's Bay and saw the enemy encampment sprawled across the sands below. They had sent out scouts, and every man knew what to expect and what he must do.

Except for Merlin. Uthir had made it quite clear that he must not risk himself. In any case he had never learned how men fought with weapons of iron, and he had been taught that to use his other gifts to take life would destroy both those gifts, and him. He waited on the brow of the hill, in the shelter of a thornbush. To an enemy passing by he would have been invisible, but his prophecy had brought these men to battle; he owed it to them to watch them fight.

The raiders had thought themselves safe. But they were not stupid. As Uthir's force came sweeping down the hill, guards gave the alarm, and men burst from their rude shelters or struggled free from the cloaks in which they had wrapped themselves to sleep, weapons in hand. Uthir had divided his men into three wings; one to strike from each side and the third to circle round to the shore. In such confusion the horses gave little advantage. After the first wild ride through the encampment, stabbing with lance and spear, most of the riders slid off their mounts and began to lay about them with their swords.

Surprise had evened the odds, but the enemy fought well, and all the more so when the men Uthir had delegated to the task waded out with torches and fired the vessels waiting to carry them away. Most of the plunder had already been loaded into them. Deprived of both escape and reward, the enemy had little to lose, but Uthir was determined that this lot of raiders would not return another day.

The prince had kept his mount. From the hill, Merlin marked him, reining the bay mare in tight circles, stabbing with his lance as if each man he faced was responsible for Aurelianus's loss. It was one way to deal with grief, or at least to put off facing it. The true pain would come later on.

Gorlosius was still mounted as well, on a wiry stallion with a coat as black as his own hair. What he might lack in brute strength he made up in quickness. No sooner had an enemy focused on him than he was gone. Eldaul, on the other hand, was too big a man for most horses. He waded into battle with a sword in each hand, and when one blade shattered, replaced it with an axe he had won from a foe. As he fought his way through the camp the bodies piled up behind him like earth thrown up by the plough.

Then the men who had attacked the ships regrouped at the water's edge and drove those who were trying to escape that way back onto the attackers' swords. The incoming tide ran red above the bloodstained sands.

After that it was soon over. Merlin made his way down the hill. The Frisian, Pascentius, had been killed, and the Irish chieftain, Gillomanus, was captured. But in the battle his leg had been half severed. Even if he were ransomed, he would fight no more against Britannia. Most of the other prisoners were put to the sword.

Merlin moved among their own wounded, cleaning and binding the dreadful gashes, stitching when there was need. Most of these men were scarred already, and they were as healthy as their own ponies. There was good reason to hope they would heal, though he had known a tiny scratch to bring death to a man in his prime. He wondered how Aurelianus had died—for after finding the enemy where he had predicted, he no longer doubted that the first part of his vision was also true. Had some disease stricken the emperor, or had his heart given out at last?

Angry voices roused him from his absorption. He finished securing a bandage and got to his feet. One voice was that of Uthir, clipped and low. The other, louder, belonged to Gorlosius.

"All that those wretches had stolen was on those ships, and you burned them!" exclaimed the Cornovian.

"Would you rather they escaped with it?" Uthir was hanging onto his temper surprisingly well.

"We would have prevented that—" Gorlosius gestured toward the bodies being dragged toward the pyre.

"Perhaps. I had to be sure."

"We should have returned that wealth to its owners, or used it to feed our forces if the owners could not be found. We all bled for this—we deserve a share in the reward!"

"Do you?" Uthir's voice sharpened. "Dumnonia has suffered least of all. If the rest of us can do without, you can afford it as well!"

"Don't use that tone with me!" exclaimed Gorlosius. "You have only the word of this sorcerer that the emperor is dead and yet you are claiming his mantle. Do you think because you're his brother it will automatically go to you? The new High King must be elected from among all the princes when that time comes."

"And so he will be." Uthir's voice shook with the effort he was making to retain control. "But until we return to Venta, the command of this army is mine, and you will obey!"

They took the road south as soon as their wounded could travel. By the time they reached Demetia the messengers had found them. Aurelianus was dead indeed—of illness, said some, while others whispered of poison, though no culprit could be found. The comet had been seen all over the land, and its meaning widely disputed. But by that time, one of Uthir's men had made a banner bearing a red dragon, its head haloed in light. *Pendragon*, "Dragonhead," they hailed him, and the word ran ahead of them so that by the time they reached Venta Belgarum, the whole countryside was calling him by that name.

And it was as Uthir Pendragon that the princes of Britannia hailed him as their High King.

VII

A HERITAGE OF POWER

A.D. 461

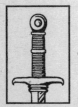The house of the High Priestess smelled of sickness. After the fresh breeze off the lake, it was almost overpowering. Igierne stopped short in the entry, summoning her self-control, and little Morgause bumped into her. The message had said that Argantel was ill and wanted her, but the figure in the bed seemed shrunken, and even the lamplight could not lend a healthy color to her skin. The old woman who sat by her stood up and motioned to them to enter; Igierne recognized Ebrdila, who had served as Argantel's deputy when the High Priestess was away.

Igierne grasped the child's shoulder, holding her tightly, and Morgause, who could never bear to be restrained, struggled to get free.

"Your grandmother is resting, little one—" With an effort she kept her voice steady. "Why don't you run down to the shore to play?"

She felt the girl shake her head. "I want to kiss her."

Igierne looked down at Morgause's ruddy curls with the exasperation her daughter so often aroused in her. This was

104

not how she wished the child to remember her grandmother, but Morgause was almost six, old enough to face the reality of death. With a sigh she released her grip, and followed her inside.

"Mother—"

Argantel's eyelids quivered. For a moment she gazed unseeing, then the blue eyes focused and she smiled. Her hair had just begun to gray before Amlodius died; it was white now. Igierne swallowed. Her parents had always been so matter-of-fact about their marriage. Who would have thought that losing her husband would blight Argantel's autumnal splendor?

"You came . . . and the little one too. . . . It is well that you had a daughter first . . . to inherit . . . the trust."

"I'm not ready," said Igierne.

"Neither was I. . . . Your path lies still in the world . . ." Argantel reached out and grasped her daughter's hand. "You must go back, and be Tigernissa. But a time will come when you will return to be the Lady of the Lake on this Isle. And this one . . . shall rule after you. . . ." She reached out to the child.

Was that a curse, wondered Igierne, or a promise? Morgause's dark eyes grew round, then she bent and kissed the old woman's papery cheek.

"Grandmother, are you a queen?"

Argantel smiled. "In a way I am. . . . Remember, whatever happens in the outer world, so long as the Lady of the Lake . . . rules here . . ." she paused, fighting for breath, "the Goddess still lives . . . in Britannia."

"Not in the South," Igierne said bitterly. "The bishops preach against the old festivals, or change their meaning, and call woman the root of evil. The Saxons are pagans, therefore no loyal Briton can honor our ancient gods!"

"That's enough," said Ebrdila. "You are tiring her." Igierne remembered her mother telling her that the older woman had wanted to be High Priestess once. But she seemed honestly grief-stricken now.

Argantel's features twisted in a grimace that was trying to be a smile. "Let me talk. . . . I will be quiet soon."

"Cannot you do something?" Igierne asked Ebrdila. "You know all the secrets of healing here! Cannot the power of the Cauldron make her whole?" She did not speak of the Sword. Its power was of another kind.

Ebrdila drew herself up. "Do you understand so little? The Hallows can set aright only that which counters the way of nature. But even the Cauldron cannot mend a heart which is outworn!"

Argantel shook her head. "Truly, daughter, if you had not been here, I do not think I would have lived so long. . . . Do not waste the time I have left in mourning. You may weep when I am gone."

Igierne bit her lip and looked down. Morgause had slipped away from the bedside and was wandering about the chamber, fingering the hangings and carved beams, the vessels of silver and bronze, all the odd bits of paraphernalia that had accumulated there.

"You have borne your daughter for the Lake. Now you must bear a son for Britannia."

"How? It has been months since Gorlosius sought my bed. But I was married by Christian rites. I cannot divorce him."

"Gorlosius will not . . . father your child."

"Who, then?"

"You will know. . . ." Argantel's smile faded. "But you must not fail . . . in your trust. Guard the Sword until your son is a man!"

Igierne stared into her mother's blue eyes that were so like her own. Argantel's fingers twitched anxiously, and Ebrdila lifted her hand and set it on her daughter's head.

"Witness!" whispered the High Priestess. "To Igierne I pass the power! May the gods of our people bear witness to what I say!"

She fell back and lay gasping, but Igierne swayed and nearly fell, dizzied by the pulse of energy, as if her mother's life had passed into her through her hand.

"Go. She will sleep now. I will call you if there is need."

There was command in Ebrdila's voice, and Igierne rose, looking down at her mother's closed face. She wanted to throw her arms around her, weeping, but Argantel was already leaving her. She bowed her head and turned, and as she did so, Ebrdila also stood, and made her the obeisance due a High Priestess, or a queen.

That night, after Morgause had been put to bed, Igierne

walked upon the shore. A little after Igierne had left her, Argantel had slipped into sleep as well, a slumber from which she could not be wakened. From the house of the High Priestess Igierne could hear singing as the women of the Isle of Maidens chanted the verses that guide a departing spirit home.

The past few days had been cloudy, but tonight the sky was clear, and the quiet waters of the lake glittered with reflected stars. As she gazed, light seemed to blossom beneath the waters. She looked up and saw the comet, hanging like a firedrake in the sky.

For a long time she watched it, her heart wrenched between anguish and exaltation. When at last she sought her bed, she dreamed of a battle on the sands. In the chill hour just before sunrise, Ebrdila woke her to say that her mother was gone.

Londinium was hot and crowded and full of bad smells. The only thing it did not have in overabundance, thought Igierne, was Saxons. Riding through the empty lands along the Tamesis, she had longed for the safety of the Lake. Now she longed for its peace. Her horse snorted and tried to rear as a peddler waved a tray of glass bangles almost under its nose. She reined the beast down, glancing at her husband in irritation.

"If you were going to ask me again to allow you to return to the Isle of Maidens," said Gorlosius, "the answer is still no. I gave you leave to attend your mother's deathbed, not to become the High Priestess of a pagan cult. You will not speak of that while we are in Londinium, do you understand? The princes will not choose a man who would bring them a pagan queen!"

Since the death of his father, she thought angrily, he had become even more autocratic.

"Do you think my silence will make any difference?" asked Igierne. "They all know who I am. I thought it was for an alliance with the powers of the North that you married me."

"The *secular* power of the North," he snapped in reply. "And you should not have left my daughter on the Isle."

"Your message commanded my presence at your side,"

she answered sweetly. "It said nothing of Morgause."

"Well, that is past praying for now, and perhaps it will do no harm. Until she reaches an age for marriage no one will care too much where a girl-child is bestowed."

"I wonder that you men have not found some other method of begetting offspring if you consider females of such little worth."

Gorlosius refused to dignify that sally with an answer. The old governor's palace was before them; the warriors guarding the gate straightened to attention as the Cornovian prince rode in, and returned Igierne's smile. It was not their fault that her husband had ordered her to join him, she thought as they continued across the inner courtyard. And she might need friends one day.

The basilica of Londinium was the largest building Igierne had ever seen, and drafty. It was a place for court and council, and so it remained. The altar which had once received incense for the emperor had been taken down, but the flaking portraits of dead Caesars still watched from the walls. In Byzantium, she had heard, the emperor was still treated as if he were a god. She sighed as she watched the gesticulating figures below from her place with the other wives. Things were different in Britannia.

"There was a time," Eleutherius of Eburacum was saying as he addressed the other princes, "when our numbers would have been too many even for this hall! Too many of our men of good family have gone to Armorica. It is those of us who have remained, standing fast against the enemy, who should rule, not a man whose family fled."

"Nonsense!" Uthir answered him. "Half the lords of Dumnonia and Demetia rule more lands in lesser Britannia than they do here. My father never ran from the Saxons; my brother and I went only to avoid weakening this island by civil war. And when Britannia called we came back again. *You* summoned the 'sons of Ambrosius' to come and lead you—not Aurelianus alone. You've already chosen me!"

He had not raised his voice, but it carried clearly. He was too far away for Igierne to make out his features, but she wondered if the relaxed lines of his body represented unconcern or an exquisite control.

The woman sitting beside her leaned closer. "He only says the truth. And they say his soldiers love him. If he went outside and appealed to the men, they would raise him on their shields as emperors were made in the old days."

Why was it only the men who were deciding? wondered Igierne. The Saxons killed women as well as warriors. It was said, of course, that a woman influenced the outcome by influencing her husband, but to Gorlosius, she was only a symbol of his status, like the golden torque he wore. Her father, she remembered, had valued her mother's wisdom. In that moment she missed them both acutely. How foolish she had been to expect that her own marriage would be the same.

"Your husband is not a candidate, then?" asked Igierne.

"Oh no. He is Caius Turpilius, a gentleman of good family, but no prince. I am Flavia. But Uthir will have his vote. My husband has served with the prince through several campaigns."

"So has mine," answered Igierne dryly. "But I think I would rather have Uthir as High King."

Flavia, once she had started talking, seemed eager to be friendly. Igierne learned in short order that she had a young son at home and would like more children, but feared it was not to be, for the child was large, and the birth had been a hard one.

"A fine strapping boy is my Cai, but it's hard to bear sons, knowing that as soon as they can hold a blade they'll be off to war. I could almost wish he had been a girl."

"Girls can be a trial too," said Igierne, remembering how Morgause had wept when she rode away. But she was more certain than ever that she had been wise to leave the girl safe in the North.

Eldaul of Glevum was speaking now. His connection with Vitalinus gave him a claim, but was also his greatest liability. Fortunately he seemed to be without ambition, and was supporting his commander.

"Do you think the Protector of Eburacum a serious contender?" asked Flavia.

"He would like to be, but he is young and untried," answered Igierne dispassionately. "The same goes for Agricola of Demetia, and Honorius. Many of the men who might have been contenders died at Sorviodunum. Northerners from beyond the Wall, like Ridarchus, are too far away to be considered, though they make useful allies. I hope that they will choose Uthir."

"You know a great deal about it—" said Flavia.

"Really? You would never think it, to hear my husband...."

Flavia followed the direction of her gaze and understanding dawned suddenly. "You don't want to be queen?"

"I don't particularly want Gorlosius to be High King," Igierne replied.

Flavia raised one eyebrow, then her eyes widened. "And who in the name of Christ and His holy mother is *that*?"

She pointed, and Igierne saw a tall figure that appeared to have formed itself from the shadows behind Uthir. A singularly inappropriate invocation, thought Igierne, recognizing, even at this distance, the slightly stooping posture and the dark hair. But he had changed; his finery had been replaced by a plain white robe and his beard swept his chest. As if he had felt her gaze upon him, he looked up, eyes fierce as a hawk's beneath heavy brows.

"That is my cousin," she said softly, "Merlin...."

She did not encounter Merlin again until the Council was over and the princes and their wives gathered at the church to see Uthir anointed and crowned. Despite the arguments, the choice had been, she thought, inevitable. The Pendragon's name was on every tongue. If the princes had chosen another ruler, no one would have followed him.

During the Council, Igierne had come to value Flavia's simple friendliness. They stood together now outside the little church, mantles wrapped tightly, for a damp wind had come up, promising rain. With the other women and less important chieftains they waited for the princes to emerge, for the little church could not hold them all. Merlin stood apart, appearing rather monkish himself in his white robe. But from what she had heard, he was no longer any kind of Christian at all. From time to time she would find him watching her, but when their eyes met he looked away.

Before we leave here I will find time to talk to him, she thought, *even if Gorlosius disapproves*.

If the bishop sealed the rite by offering communion she

wondered if her husband would receive it. It was a sin, she had been told, to take the sacrament when one's heart was full of anger or envy, and Gorlosius had been festering with fury since the decision was made. She listened with half an ear to Flavia chatter about her eagerness to get back to her child and her home, reflecting that this was what a marriage should be.

I will go home to Dun Tagell with Gorlosius, she told herself, *but when he goes off to fight again, I will leave as well. The Lady of the Lake should not be at any man's beck and call.*

The church doors swung open. From inside came a wave of incense and the sound of voices joined in song. Men began to come out of the sanctuary, blinking in the light. A murmur of anticipation spread through the crowd.

"The Pendragon! The High King comes!"

Igierne felt a wave of dizziness and took a deep breath. Interesting, she thought—his brother had been addressed as emperor, but Uthir obviously favored a British title, accepting that the Roman days were done. More men emerged, a guard of honor, who stood away to either side, drawing their swords. She moved back a little and felt a hand grasp her elbow. It was Merlin.

"You must stay here until they come. . . ."

Before she could ask why, color blazed at the church door. The bishop was coming through, clad in his embroidered cope, and beside him, his brow bound with gold and his shoulders draped in a purple mantle that flowed over a white garment like a priest's gown, came the king.

He looked dazed, thought Igierne, and not because the sun was coming out at last. His gaze was the rapt stare of one who has looked on a holy thing. Two priests guided him between the lines of warriors; he blinked and lifted a hand to acknowledge the cheers.

The crowd surged toward him, shouting, but somehow Merlin was in front of them, still holding Igierne by the arm.

"All hail to the Pendragon of Britannia—" said Merlin. Igierne knew that the people were still shouting, but the noise was muted, as if the three of them stood within a bubble that shut out sound. "I bring you the blessing of the ancient powers, and I bring you the White Raven, the hidden queen!"

Slowly, Uthir's gaze moved from Merlin to Igierne. What was he seeing? She had cast back her hood when the sun came out and with it her veil; she could feel the sun warm on her hair. She felt herself flushing as the dazed wonder in his face became a very focused awe.

Abruptly she understood that he was seeing not an ordinary woman, the wife of one of his chieftains, but the Goddess in mortal form. And understanding, her own awareness became that of the priestess, and looking upon him, she saw not Uthir the man, but the King.

It was Gorlosius who broke the spell.

"Come away, woman!" He took her arm and pulled her after him. "And put on your veil. Our great king has better things to do than stare at you!"

They turned a corner and he let her go, glaring. "What did Uthir say to you?"

Igierne straightened her mantle and drew her veil back over her hair. "He said nothing. Nothing at all," she said coldly.

He had not needed to, she thought as she turned and began to walk toward their lodgings. As king and queen their spirits had touched, and she could not predict what was going to happen now.

Igierne had been taught that the six weeks before the equinox were a time of change, in both the inner worlds and the lands of men. True it was that no sooner had she and Gorlosius arrived at Dun Tagell than the weather grew stormy. From then until the autumnal equinox, the outer coasts of Dumnonia were lashed by violent weather, but the conflicts in the skies were only a mild reflection of the tumults in the affairs of men.

For Gorlosius, overriding by sheer force of will his father's old councilors, had declared Dumnonia a kingdom separate from Britannia, and renounced his oaths to the High King. The rock of Dun Tagell, which had known peace since Vitalinus brought the Cornovii down from the north to drive the men of Eriu away, became a garrison.

The Latin name for the place was Durocornovium, the stronghold of the Cornovii. Its defenses were limited to a wall that enclosed a hall and a barracks built of the native stone, but it needed no more, for it was set on an outcrop at the edge of the sea, with only a narrow bridge of rock to link it to the land. It was not clear to Igierne whether her husband had settled her there to hold it for him, or whether the dozen men assigned to it were there to keep watch on her. Gorlosius himself paid her only an occasional visit. Isca Dumnoniorum and Durnovaria were the first lines of his defense, and to her relief he had little time for his western holdings.

From time to time word came to them of the progress of the war. The new High King, desperate to settle the situation before the Saxons could organize themselves to take advantage of British disunity, had struck swiftly and hard. Gorlosius had fallen back from Durnovaria and made a new frontier at Isca, but Uthir, seeking to besiege him in the city, left a back way open, and instead of driving his enemy down toward Belerion in the toe of the peninsula, had allowed him to escape toward the western coast where Gorlosius had hopes of joining with allies from Eriu.

By the time Uthir caught up with him his enemy had gone to ground once more in an ancient hill-fort called Dimilioc, a few miles south of Dun Tagell. And there they held, as the cold winds blew and the nights lengthened toward winter, until the feast of Samhain, when the dead come home.

Torchflames flickered wildly in the draft, chasing shadows like fleeing bogles into the corners of the hall. Try though they might, thought Igierne, they could never make the building completely proof against the wind. Always before, she had spent the winter in the villa above the sheltered waters of the Fawwyth, on the protected southern coast of Cornovia. In the summer Dun Tagell could be delightful, with the gulls calling as they wheeled above and the sunlight sparkling on the waves. But it was a cold and damp and dismal place to spend the wintertime!

With a silent curse for the husband who had left her here, Igierne set the basket of apples, last of the summer's store, up on the table. It was a poor feast—if they had any sense, those spirits to whom it was offered would return to some table that was better supplied. If there were enough, she reflected, frowning, to go around. In these past years so many had died, and so many of the families who did survive had fled the land. Any ancestors who sought them would have a long way to go.

And so she set out the fruit and the barley bread, and the dishes of boiled meat and cheese. And despite the draft, she fixed the great doorway just a little ajar so that any spirit that might wish to share the hospitality of Dun Tagell could come in.

Certainly the men of her garrison appreciated the break in the monotony of their duty. There was no mead, but when she brought round the ale pitcher they grinned and held out their cups. The drinking went on until late, for there were many toasts to be made, to comrades lost in the recent fighting, to her mother, and to Aurelianus, who lay now in the barrow beside the Giant's Dance with the lords whom Hengest had slain.

By the evening's ending, sorrow had been translated to melancholy on a golden tide of ale. The men went singing to their barracks, and even Igierne's two women were nodding. She herself had drunk enough to feel an unaccustomed detachment, but she was not yet sleepy. When she had helped her women to their beds, she eased out the door and climbed carefully to the lookout post on the wall.

A three-quarter moon glimmered between tattered clouds, touching an occasional glint of silver from the restless waves. And from time to time the water would catch a flicker of light from the torches that burned on the walls, as if the people of the sea were celebrating their own festival. Lights had been kindled over the gates, and at the other end of the arching causeway, to aid any spirit that might be uncertain of the road in finding its way.

Though surely, she thought as she gazed at the shadowed masses of the cliffs beyond it, any spirit that could find a path between the worlds could manage to travel this last little way. She blinked—for a moment she had thought she saw something moving—but when she looked again the land was as dark and featureless as before.

It is the ale, she thought, shaking her head. *I had best seek my bed before I try to walk the moonpath across the sea.*

She made her way down from the wall, choosing her footing with conscious care. The hall seemed warm after the brisk wind outside, and she cast aside her shawl. The pitcher still stood upon the table, half full of ale. It would be flat by morning, and it seemed a pity to waste it when there were so many dead whom she had not yet honored. She filled her cup and raised it high.

"To Amlodius, shield of the North!"

She had barely begun the tally of her father's dead companions when the lamplight flickered wildly and a gust of wind stirred her hair. She looked up. The door to the hall had swung open; three figures were standing there.

"Be you living or dead, I give you greeting—" She held out the beaker. "In the name of the old gods and the new, be welcome to this hall."

They came forward, and the third man closed the door behind them. Igierne blinked, thinking she must have drunk more than she thought, for she found it hard to focus on their features. Then the leader stopped before her and held out his hand to take the cup. He was wearing a checkered mantle she knew only too well, with a golden griffin pin.

"Gorlosius!" she exclaimed, almost dropping the cup. "What are you doing here?"

For a moment he hesitated. "Where else should I be on this holy festival?" His voice seemed strained and hoarse, as if he were very tired. "I gave my army the slip and came here. I couldn't go any longer without seeing you again."

Igierne took a step back and snatched up the lamp, but his features were still in shadow.

"You come here on Samhain Eve, like a spirit from the Otherworld, and you expect me to welcome you?"

"Is it so strange to expect a wife to welcome her husband?"

"It is when I am the wife," she said with a bitter humor, "and the husband is you."

One of his men—she thought his name was Jordanus—hovered anxiously behind him. The third man kept to the shadows by the door. Perhaps they were spirits, she thought, her skin prickling, for surely this was not the Gorlosius she had known.

"Nonetheless," he said harshly, "this night I'll claim a husband's place in your bed!" Before she could react he was beside her, gripping her shoulders with a warrior's callused hands.

But not the hands of Gorlosius. He was a living man—so close, she could feel the warmth of his body; her nostrils flared to the scents of sweat and horse—but her flesh knew that this man had never touched her before.

"I am the Lady of the Lake," she said in a still voice, "and not to be deceived by lesser magics. In the name of the gods my people swear by I conjure your true form back again."

Whether the change was in him or in herself she could not say, but the air seemed to ripple around him, and when it cleared she was looking up into the face of the High King.

"Why?" she said softly. "Why have you sought to dishonor me?"

Uthir shook his head. "The disguise was to protect you. The man at the gate thought I was Gorlosius, and let me in."

"I asked the wrong question," Igierne said then. "Why have you tried to deceive me? It is not the way of a lover to court in the guise of another man, nor is it the way of a king."

"It is the way of a desperate man . . ." he whispered then, glancing toward the man by the door in appeal.

"What is that to me?" exclaimed Igierne. She was slow to wrath, but she was growing angry now. "If this is love, it can learn to wait; if it is lust, then burn!"

"This is the hour in which the Pendragon is destined to beget his son," said the third man, coming at last into the light. "The child which you conceive in this hour, and no other, shall be the Defender of Britannia."

"Merlin . . ." she breathed, remembering how she had faced him across the altar of the Sword. "Is this truly so?"

He bowed his head. "I have seen it in the heavens."

"I will not be coerced . . . even by the stars. . . ."

Uthir stared at her, his desperation gradually giving way to the awe with which he had looked upon her as he came from his crowning.

"Lady—I won't force you." Taking a deep breath, he got down upon one knee. "You are the White Raven of Britannia; you decide." He took her hand and gently kissed the palm.

At the touch of his lips a little shock traveled up her arm.

She bit her lip, feeling a warmth spreading through her despite the chill air. She held out her other hand, and trembled as he kissed it.

"You are so beautiful, Igierne," he said softly. "You haunt my sleep, and I dream you are my queen."

"Truly?" She laughed suddenly, her anger giving way to a fierce exhilaration. "Then as a queen I will claim you! You shall come to my bed, and we will see what ancient soul is hovering in these shadows, waiting to take flesh in my womb!"

One end of the hall had been partitioned off with curtains and woven screens to give the master of the fortress some privacy. A few swift steps brought her to the entrance. Uthir surged to his feet and followed her.

In the dim light that came through the curtain she saw him in silhouette, stripping off his mantle and heavy outer tunic, struggling with the buckles of his commander's belt, and finally letting it drop with a clatter to the floor. She unhooked belt and brooches, pulling first the short-sleeved outer garment and then the long-sleeved undertunic over her head so that she stood shivering in her shift before him.

He had got as far as his braes. Her eyes had adjusted to the dim light, and her breath caught as she took in his breadth of shoulder and the fine modeling of muscle in belly and arm. She knelt to unknot his leg wrappings and he bent, plucking the pins from her coiled hair so that it fell in silken masses about her shoulders.

"Lie down," he whispered. "If you touch me now I will waste the good seed."

She pulled away, looking up at him, and saw that it was true. She wanted to laugh, but her pulse was leaping erratically, and she realized that she had come already to a state of readiness that Gorlosius, with all his efforts, had rarely been able to bring her. She tugged at the neck ties of her shift and as she rose it slid off her shoulders and pooled around her feet. She padded to the bed and lay down upon it, clad only in her hair.

For one moment longer Uthir hesitated, then he surrendered himself to her embrace, and as the embers flare when new fuel is thrust into the hearth, their bodies caught fire. With arms and legs she held fast as the flames rose higher.

Then they exploded in a shower of light, brilliant behind her closed eyelids, and he cried out and arched hard against her and then fell like a slain man back into her arms.

For a few moments they lay gasping. Then Igierne ran her hands down the rippling muscles of his back and felt him come to life again between her thighs. This time their joining had a sweet deliberation that left her panting and helpless in his arms. They made love a third time before they slept, but long afterward, when she thought about that night, it seemed to her that it must have been in the first encounter that she got her son, when all the High King's hoarded passion was released in that great cry.

She felt Uthir's contentment change to the relaxation of sleep, and had time only to draw the blankets over them before oblivion claimed her as well. It was some hours later that she awakened, wondering what had disturbed her, for Uthir lay still beside her and there had been no sound. She opened her eyes, abruptly certain they were not alone.

Beside the curtains a pale shape moved.

She blinked, remembering how a trick of the light on the bedcurtains had been able to frighten her when she was a child. But this image grew ever more distinct until she could make out the tense, wiry shape beneath the mantle, the shock of dark hair and staring eyes. Spectral lips shaped her name.

"Gorlosius . . ." she whispered, answering.

The shape reached toward her. Then from the pen beside the garden came a cock's crow, and its features contorted and began to fade.

Was it Gorlosius's spirit body or his shade? Igierne lay trembling until in the gray hour just after dawn, when the mist lies heavy on the sea, the stillness was broken by someone shouting. She heard the door to the hall slam open and sat up, pulling the blanket around her, as Uthir began to stir by her side.

"My lady, my lady! The High King's men have stormed the fort and struck down Gorlosius. Come quickly, and we will help you to flee!"

The curtains were flung back. She saw two of her husband's men, their armor bloodied, their frantic faces stiffening to astonishment as the torchlight showed them who was sitting there. For a moment Igierne's mind went blank with terror. Then the warrior went down on one knee.

"Lord Gorlosius, I saw you fall!"

"I escaped," said Uthir. As a commander, Igierne thought numbly, he must have developed the ability to sound sensible moments after being awakened by an alarm.

"Then you must flee again, for the Pendragon will surely come here to secure this stronghold!"

"If he's taken Dimilioc then my cause is lost, and I must make peace with him. Go back—tell the men to lay down their arms. The High King won't condemn them for following their prince!"

"Aye, my lord—" said the warrior, sorrow replacing the terror in his eyes. He regained his feet and pushed back out through the curtains.

Igierne let out her pent breath in a long sigh.

Uthir was already pulling on his clothing. "What a tangle—" he muttered. "But with all the rumors that will fly, I suppose no one will know what's true!" He belted his tunic and reached for the checkered mantle.

Igierne still sat with the blanket around her shoulders, watching him. "Does anyone know that?" she said softly.

He stilled, and the warmth came back into his eyes. A swift step brought him to her side and he kissed her.

"I know that you're my queen! Bar the gates after me; and don't let anyone in until I come for you!"

It seemed very quiet when he had gone.

I am a widow . . . thought Igierne, remembering Gorlosius's anguished ghost. Then, deliberately, she thrust the memory away. *I am a queen*, she told herself, and set her hands above her belly, where even now the future Defender of Britannia, planted in her womb like a seed of light, was beginning to glow.

viii

The Sign of the Bear

A.D. 471

"Morgause, your hair is like my mother's, the way it was when I was a child," said Igierne, drawing the comb through the long strands. "It shines like a dark fire."

Through the narrow window of the tower a thin spring sunlight glowed on rich fabric, sparkled from the jewelry waiting in its casket, and struck fiery glints from the girl's long hair. Once, this had been part of the Roman fortress of Eburacum, but Coelius had made it a royal residence. Now his son Eleutherius ruled, and seemed happy to host the wedding of his overlord's daughter to Leudonus of Dun Eidyn.

Morgause shrugged as if she were not convinced, but she stood still as her mother took up the next strand and began to tease the snarls free. Poor child, thought Igierne, at fifteen her hair was almost her only beauty. She herself had been the same at her first marriage, a pudgy adolescent with no graces to charm her new husband. She wished they could have delayed this wedding until Morgause grew into her own looks, but Uthir needed the northern alliance now. She could only hope that Leudonus would have the sensitivity to cherish this flower until it bloomed. Now in his thirties, he had buried one wife already, and was newly come to his grandfather's throne.

She finished the last lock and smoothed it into place. "There now. Put on the jewels and you will look splendid!" She picked up the necklet of Alban gold.

"I look terrible," said Morgause. "I hate this color—"

"Crimson is traditional," Igierne began, although she had to agree that this particular shade did not flatter her daughter's complexion.

"—and I hate this city. You should have left me on the Isle of Maidens to finish my training. The Isle needs a High Priestess, and if you do not want the position, I do not see why it should not go to me."

Igierne stared at her. *I do want it*, she thought, and each time she had visited Morgause she had wanted to stay with her. But Uthir needed her, and when she was with him, her memories of the Lake became a fair dream.

"Perhaps one day it will," she said aloud. "But the Lady of the Lake needs to know the ways of the world as well. And we need you here—"

"Then why are you sending me to Dun Eidyn?" retorted Morgause, sliding the bracelets onto her wrists.

"Would you rather we had wedded you to some southern magnate who thinks the old ways are a sin?" exclaimed Igierne. "At least the Votadini still honor the gods. Leudonus's mother was a Pictish princess. He will know how to value you not only as Uthir's daughter, but as my heir."

Morgause looked thoughtful as she hung the discs of gold filigree in her ears, and Igierne was unhappily reminded that the girl was her only heir, so far as the world knew. In ten years of marriage, she had given Uthir no other child than the one tiny son, born six weeks before his time at Dun Tagell, the Midsummer after his conception, and handed over to Merlin to foster as soon as it became clear that he would live. She had given him her mother's family name, Artorius, but she would not even know him if she saw him now.

"Well, at least Leudonus is not a bad-looking man," Morgause said finally, finishing with the second earring. "And, as you keep reminding me, he is a king." As she held up the bronze mirror Igierne saw them both for a moment reflected—Morgause ruddy with her father's dark eyes, and herself still pale and fair. But the bronze canceled out such differences, revealing the elegant modeling of cheek and brow, the firm line of the jaw, and beyond such surface similarities, their pride.

There was a stir at the doorway. Igierne turned, expecting the women whom she had banished from her chambers, wanting a little time alone with this daughter whom she was about to lose once more. But it was the High King—with Merlin, as usual, behind him.

"Go out now," she said briskly. "The other ladies are waiting with your wreath and veil. In a few moments I will follow you."

Morgause looked from her mother to Uthir with thinly veiled hostility, but she went without arguing.

"I hope this marriage will work," said the king, looking after her.

"That is the chance you take, is it not, when you marry girls off so young, and without consulting their inclination," Igierne replied, a bit more sharply than she had intended. "What's to say they won't find someone that suits them better when they are grown?"

Uthir had the grace to flush, and her frown softened. Since their marriage he had put on flesh, and from time to time he experienced episodes of dizziness and joint pain that worried her, but he still looked at her with the ardent gaze that had won her ten years ago. With Uthir she had the kind of partnership she had dreamed of, and their physical harmony had only increased with the years.

"It will be enough if Leudonus is as brisk in bed as he is in battle, since her children may be my heirs . . ." he said thoughtfully.

"But what about our son? Isn't it time you brought him to court and acknowledged him? How can he be a king if he is not trained up to rule?"

"How can he be a king if he's dead?" Uthir responded. "People tried to poison my brother and me three times before we were fifteen. Aurelianus never did get over it, really. And we were Ambrosius's legitimate sons!"

"Are you saying that Artorius is not?" Her voice shook.

"Not by Church law—we weren't married 'til Midwinter.

A pity the child came early. Curse it, I myself proved how Gorlosius could have visited you six weeks before. The boy's too young to face the whispers that will follow once I claim him. People know you bore me a child, but many think he died, and they don't know where he is now. He is safe, Igierne; let him be!"

"Is he?" Igierne whispered. She turned to Merlin. "He was such a tiny mite when you took him away from me. Have you told me the truth, cousin? Did he live and thrive, or is he only a few tiny bones in an unmarked grave?" It was a nightmare that haunted her—that Gorlosius's ghost had somehow blighted Uthir's seed.

"On your mother's soul I swear, I have seen him every year since he was born," Merlin said quietly.

"Have you seen him this year?" she exclaimed. "You made me Tigernissa, and as High Queen I command you. Go to him, Merlin, and report to me every detail of how he looks and what he does! Then, perhaps, I will believe."

Over her head the two men exchanged a look. Then Merlin nodded. Igierne knew they were humoring her. Perhaps it was seeing Morgause again that made her so desperate to know about her son.

"I will go to him," said the druid, "as soon as the marriage festivities are done."

She drew a trembling breath. "The wedding procession will be forming. You must take your places. Give me a moment to compose myself, and I will come."

On the table there was a flagon with wine. She poured some into a goblet and drank, waiting for her breathing to slow. There was a sound from the entry and she turned. Morgause was standing there, with two spots of color blazing in her cheeks. How long had she been there? wondered her mother. What had she heard?

"It's *him*—it's my brother that you really want, isn't it?" the girl said in a low voice. "But he doesn't even know who you are, and Ebrdila was more of a mother to me than you. You might as well never have had any children at all! If I have babies I swear I will keep them by me! They, at least, will know they had their mother's love!"

She turned in a swirl of draperies and swept out.

After a moment Igierne's fury turned to a laughter that

edged hysteria. She gulped down the rest of the wine and strove to control her breathing. It seemed a long time before she was calm once more. But when she emerged at last, the wedding procession was just getting underway. She took her husband's arm, and the High King and High Queen of Britannia escorted Morgause to meet her destiny.

Always, when Merlin came into the pleasant lands above the Sabrina estuary, he felt he was moving back in time. The Silure tribesmen to whom they had once belonged had long ago embraced the manners and culture of Rome, and though the old tribal capital of Venta Silurum now went by the name of Ker-Venta, on Saturday evenings the gentlemen of the countryside heated their baths, and they rode to visit, in the old fashion, in a carriage and pair.

Merlin traveled on a sturdy gray mule, and he preferred to lie upon a patch of woodland rather than seek shelter with folk he did not know, and to bathe in the cold stream. The silence of the forest eased his spirit, and he blessed Igierne for sending him on this errand. Caius and Flavia would be surprised to see him, but their son Cai and Artor their fosterling knew him only as a wandering druid, and accepted his comings and goings without questioning.

He came to the villa a week before the old festival of the goddess of the harvest and Lugos her defender at the time when the grain begins to ripen in the fields, which the Christians now called the Feast of Mary. To the people it made little difference; as always, they prepared to offer their first fruits to the Lady, and pray to the Lord to protect the harvest. It was not only the wheat that was growing stiff and golden and the barley heads that were beginning to hang low. In the orchards, the topmost apples were blushing red and golden with promise of sweetness to come.

As Merlin turned down the lane from the High Road the branches of one of the trees began to shiver as if agitated by an extremely localized storm. From within the tree came high-pitched shouting. The druid reined in, and after a moment's reflection, spun around himself the sphere of shadow that kept him from being seen.

The branches thrashed again and a small, copper-haired

figure dropped to the ground. Merlin recognized him as one of the villa's Irish slaves.

"I can't get them, Cai, no matter how hard I shake. Those apples may look ripe, but they aren't!"

"I have sworn to offer them to Our Lady tomorrow!" said the boy who was standing by the trunk of the tree. Big-boned and black-haired, he had the look of Caius Turpilius senior already. "Climb back up and pick them if they will not fall."

"The top branches are too little—they will break, and *I* will fall!" objected the slave.

"Well, *I* am certainly too big to climb up there!" said Cai rather smugly. "Try again! I order you!"

"No," put in the third boy, younger and smaller than the other two. His hair was the color of the tree trunk and he seemed nondescript, until you looked at his eyes. "That is an unjust order, and he doesn't have to obey."

"Be quiet, Artor! I am the master's son, and you are only a nameless fosterling! Treni, get up that tree!"

Merlin bit his lip with remembered pain at the old insult. No doubt Caius Turpilius had kept his promise to raise the child as his own, but boys were acutely sensitive to questions of status; they should have anticipated that the other children would mock Artor.

The boy himself did not change expression. Perhaps he was used to it or perhaps, like Merlin, he had become an expert at hiding his wounds.

Cai gripped the slave's arm and dragged him forward, but before they reached the tree, Artor scrambled up the trunk and gained the lowest branch.

"I'll do it—I'm the lightest of us three. Lie down, Cai, so I can land on something soft if I fall!" A sudden grin transformed his rather stiff expression into a look that caught at the heart. The branches shook as he clambered upward.

Merlin nudged his mule forward, rehearsing spells to knit broken limbs. He could see the topmost branches, and as the Irish boy had stated, they were indeed very thin and small. For a few moments the motion ceased. Had Artor decided not to try it after all? A little way down from the crown of the tree he could see a thickening that might be the boy.

Then something poked up through the leaves. It was a branch, with a twig pointing down like a shepherd's crook.

In another moment the branch on which the apple hung was hooked and pulled down into the leaves. *He thinks!* thought Merlin. *He thinks as well as feels.*

"Throw it down, Artor!" came Cai's voice from below. "I'll catch it!"

"You couldn't catch the sun if it fell from the sky," Artor called mockingly. "The apples shall come safe in my tunic, one each for the Virgin, the Mother, and the One who sorrows." Another branch was captured and its fruit disappeared. A third apple went the way of the first two, then the hooked branch dropped and the tree began to shake as the boy started down.

Merlin, who had brought the mule up behind the other two, let out his breath in a long sigh, dropping his concealment, as Artor appeared beneath the leaves and slid to the ground. The boy's gaze traveled past Cai to Merlin and his eyes widened.

"Lord Ambros! Cai—look, the druid has come! Treni, run back to the house and tell Lady Flavia! My lord, we did not expect you until autumn—you've never been here in the summertime!"

He took one of the mule's reins, and Cai took the other, and so escorted, Merlin passed through the orchard and up to the villa where Flavia was waiting.

"You've not come to take him away?" Caius Turpilius asked as they waited for the evening meal. The long porch of the villa faced westward, so they could watch the sun set above the hills.

"Not yet," answered Merlin. "He looks healthy. He is doing well at his studies?"

"Well enough," Caius smiled, "though it is hard to keep the boys to their books on these summer days. His tutor says he asks too many questions."

"And physical exercise?" Merlin already knew that Artor was nimble, but the boys had sworn him to secrecy.

"Cai is better at swordplay—of course he has the advantage of size. Artor is very quick, though, and no quitter. When he has his growth I think he will do well."

A gong announced the imminence of dinner, and they went in. The Turpilius household dined in the old Roman manner, reclining on couches around a central table. The food was simple, but well prepared: the usual hard-boiled eggs; a dish of lentils with cow-parsnips, seasoned with mint and coriander; fried trout from the river with a sauce of herbs and peas from the garden; and a boiled chicken with honey sauce. Merlin had often eaten worse at the table of the High King.

It was more than enough for five adults, for Caius had invited their nearest neighbors as well. Caius and Flavia, of course, knew who and what Merlin was. To their household and neighbors he was merely Ambros, a wandering druid always welcome for his news and his wisdom.

Tonight, they wanted to hear about the wedding. It was surprising, they thought, that the betrothal had not been longer. But perhaps, commented Caius, the High King wanted to secure his northern borders in case Hengest's son Octha returned from Germania.

"What were they about to let him escape?" asked Flavia. "Because the old wolf had lost his teeth, did they think the young one had no fangs?"

Hengest still lived and held his lands in Cantium, but he had not stirred outside his borders in many a year. No one knew whether he was still the leader of the invasion, or barely holding his own. When they were not attacking the British, a new generation of heathens squabbled with each other, and Octha, who had nearly overrun Eburacum some years before, had been among the most successful.

But after several defeats, Uthir had taken him captive, and instead of killing him outright, as many advised, had held him as a hostage.

"Did they think that Brannos's ravens would guard him? They say that the heathen devil, Woden, is the lord of ravens. Perhaps his birds proved stronger than those of our ancient king!"

They all laughed, but in truth, Merlin had wondered. As long as men could remember, there had been ravens on the hill by the Tamesis that was called the White Mount. According to the ancient lore, it was there that the head of the divine king, Brannos, had been buried, with the promise that so long as it stayed there Londinium should never fall.

After the other guests had departed, Merlin took Caius aside.

"It is in my mind to take Artor with me into the mountains after the festival. There are things that I can teach him there."

"Very well. I will instruct Phylox to pack his things."

Merlin shook his head. "No baggage. To live off the land is part of the teaching."

They left the villa before dawn, for the hills were farther off than they seemed. To Artor, Merlin said that he needed help to gather the herbs that grew wild there. At first Artor skipped ahead, exclaiming at the first birdsongs, the swift dart of the awakening swallows, the flicker of motion as a fox disappeared into the hedge. But as the sun climbed higher, he settled to an observant silence, imitating the druid's ground-eating stride as well as his shorter legs could manage.

Merlin had hoped that they could talk during the journey. When he had visited before, they had always been surrounded by the folk of the villa, and in planning for this journey he had realized that although he had been acquainted with Artor since his birth, he knew only the bright surface that the boy presented to the world. Was this reticence a natural characteristic, he wondered, or a response to the boy's ambivalent status in Caius's family?

Merlin had spent his life gathering knowledge. Since the Night of the Long Knives, when he had failed so disastrously to see through Hengest's cordial mask, he had devoted himself to the study of men's souls, seeking to understand what lay behind their surfaces as once he had studied the secrets of the sky. Uthir depended on him to reveal the hidden motives of the men around him; it should not take long for him to learn the secrets of one child.

By midafternoon they reached a band of open pasture, studded with limestone outcroppings, and began to search for herbs. In the deeper soil they found self-heal, paired leaves marching up the stem to the long purple flower head. In an ointment with goldenrod it was good for infected wounds. Among the rocks twined the strands of mountain pea with their paired leaves and tiny blue flowers.

"Say a prayer of thanks to the spirit of the plant," said

Merlin, "and then dig it up and strip off the tubers that cling to the roots."

"What are they good for?" asked the boy.

"Clean one off and chew on it, and you will see. The druids call this *corma*; it will stave off the pangs of hunger and give you energy."

Artor looked dubious, but he did as Merlin asked. In a moment his face changed, and the druid smiled.

"It tastes good . . . sweet. . . ."

"Save the others—you will need them for our journey."

Artor frowned and gazed back across the banding of grass and woodland that fell away toward the valley of the Wae, veiled by blue summer haze.

"It is midafternoon," he said thoughtfully. "Shouldn't we be turning back soon?"

"Not yet. Just beyond this ridge there is an oak wood that has other plants I need."

At the edge of the forest they found bilberries and brambles whose fruit was just ripening. Artor began to pluck and eat with a boy's enthusiasm, moving deeper and deeper into the wood. Even Merlin was not immune to their attraction, though the taste brought back memories of his wanderings.

What am I doing? he asked himself. *I carry the blood of the Wild Men, who live on such things, but this boy is all human. Can he survive? What will he learn by starving here?*

"He will learn what you learned," his daimon replied. *"He will learn what he is made of . . . and so will you—"*

It seemed to Merlin that the answer was somewhat ambiguous, but he could get nothing more. Still, in this smiling weather, the boy could come to no harm wandering in the woods for a day or even two, and so he watched the sun dip toward the hilltop and kept silence.

The sudden chill as the sun disappeared brought Artor back to awareness of the passage of time. He straightened, looking at Merlin accusingly. "It will be dark long before we get home!"

"That is true," said the druid. "Perhaps we should make camp here and start back in the morning. It will be an adventure—" He added, as Artor looked dubious, "It is something Cai has never done."

As he had expected, that argument had power, and the boy began to look about him with a new interest.

"But what if we get lost?"

"So long as the sky does not fall and the earth stands solid you cannot be truly lost," said the druid, leading the way down the hill. "Have I not taught you how to observe the sun and judge the lie of the land, and what herbs will serve as food?"

"Where will we sleep?" asked Artor.

"Farther down the hill we'll find water, and the trees will shelter us from the wind. Wrap yourself in your cloak and burrow into the leaves and you will sleep warm."

Artor nodded. "Soldiers camp out like this when they're on campaign."

"Do you want to be a soldier?"

"I have to know how to fight. We all do. My foster-father says that if we British had not forgotten how to be warriors, the Saxons would never have come."

"That's so," said Merlin. "That is why Vitalinus hired Hengest in the first place. He begged the magistrates and the chieftains to raise armies, but they were too accustomed to being defended by Rome."

"That was years and years ago—" Artor looked at him skeptically.

"Ah well," said the druid evasively, "that is what I have heard."

Beneath the trees it was growing dark already. They followed the sound of water until they found a grass-grown mudflat above a little stream.

"Are the Saxons truly devils, as Father Paternus says?" asked Artor as they heaped up bracken for bedding and gathered sticks that the spring floods had lodged against the tree-trunks to build a fire.

"There are Saxon slaves in Caius Turpilius's household," answered Merlin. "Are they demons?"

"No . . . but they have been baptized."

"The priests make great claims for that holy water of theirs, but I have never noticed that it stopped any man from doing evil if he saw some great advantage in it, or that its lack prevented men from doing good if that was their will.

No doubt those same Saxon devils are loving husbands and fathers when they are at home."

"But this isn't their home!" exclaimed Artor.

"The Wild Men might say the same to you. . . ."

Merlin shut his mouth, wondering why he had said that. Even his mother, before she died, had managed to persuade herself that her child was the offspring of an angelic visitor. He rubbed his arms, with their telltale covering of hair. He had never spoken to anyone of his time in the forest and what he had learned there.

"Wild Men are a legend . . . aren't they?" Artor gave him an odd look, and Merlin wondered what the boy was seeing in the flickering light of their little fire.

"This whole wide earth is a matter of legend. The water is holy, and the stones, and the fire. The wind whispers tales of times that are gone. Maybe you and I will be legends one day."

Artor laughed, and somewhere within, the druid felt a pang. He had plotted and planned for this boy's birth since he first set his hands upon the Sword of Kings. Only by raising up the Defender could he expiate his failure to avert the massacre at Sorviodunum. Only now, gazing into those clear eyes, did it occur to him to question his right to cast Artor in that role.

His mother had cast *him* in the role of Prophet of Britannia. Did it matter that his childhood would have been even more unhappy if he had grown up in Maridunum? Her words, and the Vor-Tigernus's need, had set his feet upon the path, and now he could not choose but follow.

But Artor still had a choice. Igierne wanted to bring him up as a prince, but the dangers that had forced his guardians to raise him in ignorance of his destiny had also protected him from its stresses. Unlike Merlin, Artor had been allowed to be a child before he was forced to become a man.

I will teach him all I can, thought the druid, *but in the end, it is the spirit within him that must seek this fate. He must be allowed to choose.*

But that spirit must be tested. A young raven spent many days clinging to the edge of the nest, stretching and beating his wings against the air. Only if he did so would his wings be strong enough to bear him when his spirit finally compelled him to fly.

"You are a good climber," he said aloud. "Perhaps tomorrow we will find some mistletoe. In the lore of the druids it is called all-heal, and the powdered berries have great power against fever and diseases of the heart. But it must be used sparingly, for like many herbs, in the wrong dose it can be a poison."

As the fire burned down he continued to speak of the herbs of the forest and their lore, and which plants were good for food and where they could be found. Artor's eyelids began to droop, for it had been a strenuous day, and presently he sank down upon his leafy bed.

Merlin rubbed out the remains of the fire, but he did not sleep. The stars pricked through the velvet of the sky and the moon rose, and still he watched over the child.

It was nearing midnight when his senses told him that Artor had passed through the borders of sleep and lay now in the deepest slumber, and he arose. First he stripped off his own clothing and rolled it into a tight bundle to carry, for it would only slow him, and in truth, his own body heat made clothing a formality. Then, murmuring spells to keep the boy dreaming, he lifted him in his arms. Artor was no great burden, for he was small for his age, and Merlin's strength was beyond that of humankind. Moving quietly, the druid bore him away.

His long strides carried him through the forest and into the next valley, over a second ridge and down into woodlands that grew beside another stream that like the first flowed into the Wae, but several miles away. There he found a drift of leaves beneath an oak tree and carefully laid the boy down. Chanting softly, he paced a circle around him and sealed it with a sigil of power.

Then he climbed into the tree and curled his long limbs into a fork where the foliage would prevent him from being easily seen from the ground. His situation did not permit deep slumber, but as the night turned from midnight toward dawn he passed into a state halfway between wakefulness and sleeping, suspended between the earth and the stars.

In that dream his spirit hovered above the clearing. With spirit sight he saw the life-force flow through every tree; each leaf outlined in light. And as he watched, the light grew stronger, resolved itself into forms which his mind interpreted as human as they stepped forth from the trees. Merlin's circle had been meant to repel all evil, but these beings were beyond such considerations, like the land itself. The hazels, the green herbs, even the blades of grass had spirits, and all of them gathered around the sleeping boy.

Were they simply curious, or were they drawn by something within him? As Merlin hovered, wondering, he saw Artor's lifelight pulse, and the spirit of the boy, detaching itself as often happens during dreaming, rose up from his body, connected only by a silver cord. He laughed with delight, seeing those bright beings around him, and they bent—in homage, or in welcome?

The rippling stream made a soft background for the chirring of the crickets as the tree-spirits began to dance. At first Artor simply watched in wonder, but presently they drew him into their round. They continued to dance until the moon disappeared behind the hill. Then, one by one, the bright spirits drifted back to shrub or tree, until only the spirit of the oak remained. She it was who escorted the boy's spirit back to his slumbering body, and then herself merged into the solid trunk of the tree once more.

When Merlin woke, it was a little past dawn, and the pile of leaves that covered Artor was beginning to stir. The druid peered through the branches, watching as the boy sat up, rubbing his eyes. It took him some time to realize that not only was the druid not sleeping on the other side of the fire, but that this clearing and this stream were not the ones beside which he had fallen asleep the night before. Merlin could see the moment when his eyes went still and watchful, count the minutes it took for Artor to decide that though he might be lost, he was in no immediate danger.

He got to his feet, brushing off the leaves, and with an instinctive courtesy whose source his waking mind did not remember, relieved himself against a rock instead of a tree. Then he went to the stream to drink, and stayed there for a time, gazing at the light on the trees.

Good, thought the druid, *he is getting his directions from the angle of the sun.*

Artor had already passed the first test, having neither wept nor run screaming in circles, though his face was rather pale. Now he proceeded to pass another, cutting reeds whose tender inner stems were edible and catching several of the big frogs that hid among them. He gathered tinder and managed to get a spark from his flints to light it, and soon the frogs' legs were sizzling on twigs above the fire. Some rather squishy bilberries from his pouch completed his meal—a better breakfast than the druid was having, still perched in his tree.

Then, when the sun was high enough to cast a good shadow, the boy put out his fire and buried the remains of his meal, rolled up his cloak and tied it across his back. But before he set out he paused, looking around him.

"Green lord of the forest," he whispered, "it is not by my own will that I must pass through your realm. Guard my ways until I come to the lands of men."

From what he remembered of the night, Merlin thought the prayer would be heard. But whether it was or not, he himself, unseen, would keep watch until the boy reached safety. With considerable relief he slipped down from the oak tree as Artor moved off down the stream.

The boy went slowly, and Merlin had time to take care of his own necessities before he followed. Woodland streams could be deceptive, but eventually they all flowed downhill. Artor had correctly judged that this tributary would in time reach the Wae, where he could find the road that would take him southward again and home. It was only a matter of keeping his nerve and keeping on.

Will he thank me for the adventure? wondered the druid, *or will he be angry with me for abandoning him?*

Perhaps it was a little of both, for as the journey continued, Artor's set features relaxed, and he paused more often to watch the glittering dance of the dragonflies over the water, or the swift dart of a swallow above the trees. Once he surprised a lordly stag who had come down to drink, and they stared at each other in mutual astonishment that turned on the boy's part to awe before the deer, deciding this two-legged creature posed no threat to him, stalked away.

This is my gift to you, thought Merlin, watching. *Whatever you may inherit from your father, this is your inheritance from me.*

And so they continued on as the sun rose past her nooning and began to arch westward. The trees were still too thick to see the end of the forest, but Merlin knew that the road was near. He lagged behind to put on his crumpled garments, intending to double around to meet the boy on the road. And so, Artor was out of sight when the wind shifted and Merlin smelled the rank scent of a bear.

For an instant, shock held him immobile. He had encountered bears in the northern hills and avoided them, for their tempers were uncertain, and nothing less than a band of armed men could make them afraid. He had not thought any still roamed in these hills.

Then, skirts flapping, he began to run. Self-castigation could come later, when he had saved the boy, or failed. Even in the tunic he went swiftly, but before the boy was in sight he heard the bear's cough of warning. Moving silently, lest his presence set off the attack he feared, he covered the last few feet to the stream.

The bilberries were thick here, growing nearly to the water, and Artor had stopped to pick them, apparently surprising a bear who had come this way with the same thing in mind. It was still standing half-reared in the midst of the bushes, trying to decide whether this two-legged being was a threat.

It was a young bear, perhaps a season separated from its mother, big enough to be dangerous, but perhaps not old enough to have learned to hate humankind. Artor stood absolutely still, the bilberries he had already picked still cupped in his hand. All the color had left his face, but his eyes were very bright. He looked, thought Merlin, *present*, as if by danger the essence of his being had been focused and revealed. At that moment he saw in Artor a spirit that burned like a flame, and knew that men would follow him.

If he lived.

The bear's wet black nose wrinkled as it sniffed the unfamiliar scent mingled with that of the fruit. Branches crackled as it moved toward Artor. The druid drew breath to cry out, but the boy was stretching out his hand, fingers folded flat as if he were offering grain to a pony. The bear lowered its heavy head, and a rough pink tongue swept the berries from Artor's palm. Its sun-bleached brown fur was exactly the color of the boy's hair.

The bear nosed at his hand, then licked his berry-stained cheek, and Artor lifted his other hand and gently stroked the thick fur. For a few moments they stood, man-cub and bear-cub together, then the bear snorted, dropped to all fours, and moved off through the bushes.

The blood pounded in Merlin's head as he remembered to breathe. Artor blinked a few times, then he turned, eyes widening only a little as if after what had just happened the appearance of the druid was no surprise.

"Did you see?" he whispered.

"I saw—" Years of discipline gave Merlin his voice again. "You are Arktos, the Bear, and your totem has blessed you."

The Birds of Battle

A.D. 473

The command will have to go to Leudonus—" the king's words came out like a curse. "If he can stop ploughing your daughter's field long enough to get into his armor!"

The warm light of a summer's morning on the Tamesis reflected through the window of the old Roman tower and glimmered on the whitewashed ceiling; a clear, pitless light that illuminated his face and showed every line worn there by the past year's pain.

"Uthir!" Igierne shook her head, torn between anxiety and exasperation. He must be feeling particularly bad today, for in general when she was present he guarded his tongue. "Morgause is pregnant with their second child, and Gualchmai is just a year old."

"Two brats in three years is a good yield," growled the king. "Time we made sure there's something for them to inherit. Leudonus is the best of the lot—if I can't take the field he'll have to command."

"That is why you gave him Morgause in marriage," Igierne reminded him.

"Hoped it wouldn't come to this—Damn!" He swore again as he tried to shift position on the bed. It was as comfortable as his household could make it, but the old garrison fort had never been intended for long habitation. Londinium was a commercial city, not a fortress, and the old tower, with the river to the south and a rampart and ditch between it and the city, was the safest place they could find.

In the past three years the episodes of joint pain and muscular weakness had become ever more frequent. At times, when the weather was mild, Uthir would be free of it, but Octha and his warband would not wait on the king's convenience. Hengest's son had kept the oath he swore when he escaped from Londinium, and the army he had raised among the tribes of Germania had made a landfall in the country south of Eburacum.

"My lord, be easy," said Jordanus. "I will send the message by swift riders. If the enemy strikes north, he will be ready."

"And if they move south?" asked Igierne.

Uthir frowned. "Cataur of Dumnonia is energetic, and so are his brothers, but he doesn't have the experience. Catraut is a good fighter, but headstrong. Maybe Eldaul . . . but some still don't trust him. We've worn out our best men in these endless wars! If they come south . . . I'll have to get myself out of this damned bed . . . somehow." He tried to raise himself and fell back again, grunting with pain.

Igierne knelt by his side, wiping the sudden perspiration from his brow. She kept a smile on her lips, but she was weeping within. All his life Uthir had been a warrior—he could have faced death in battle gladly, but not this invisible enemy that was making him a prisoner in his own body. There must be something that would ease this lingering agony!

That night she dreamed of blood and battle, but just as the darkness was about to engulf both friend and foe, light flamed in the west, and she saw riding through the carnage a figure with Uthir's brown hair, grasping in his hand a blazing sword. Where its radiance fell, the Saxons hid their eyes and fled, but the British rose up like souls on the Day of Judgment, crying out in praise of the High King.

"The Sword of Kings. . . ."

She woke in the dawning, whispering its name. Her dream fled away, but the image of that burning blade remained before her. She sat up, drawing the covers around her against the morning chill.

Decision came to her. "I will bring the Sword from the Isle of Maidens. Its power will make the High King whole!"

The House of the Sword had that indefinable air of damp and emptiness that marks a place not often used. Or perhaps not quite empty—Igierne's gaze moved to the shrouded shape in the center of the chamber. Even covered, she could sense the presence of the Hallow it concealed, but the energies of the Chalybe blade were muted, as if it dreamed. Brows bent in concentration, she returned to her sweeping. It had always been her task to clean this chamber when she lived on the Isle. But today would be different. Today, she would unsheath the Sword.

Ebrdila had sought to dissuade her, but she could not stand against the queen's resolve. Morgause might well have argued, for she had never had any great love for Uthir, but Morgause was Leudonus's broodmare now.

Igierne had made her preparations carefully. The old sheath had fallen to dust years ago, but she had prepared a box, bound in iron and lined with crimson silk, to carry the Sword. For a week she had taken no fleshmeat, and today, only water. She could not rival Merlin in knowledge of the stars, but she knew enough to calculate an auspicious configuration, and to perform this rite at the waxing of the moon.

When she had cleansed the chamber, she went back to the lake for her own purification, shivering as the chill water touched her skin. Only the lapping of the little wavelets against the shore disturbed the hush that lay upon the lake. It had often seemed to her that the great hills gave off silence as the sun gives off light. Here, it was very easy to listen to the voice of the soul. Perhaps that was why the priestesses had made it their sanctuary.

She sat back on her heels, letting the cool morning air dry her skin. *I may be a grandmother, but I am still young and strong. And the Sword will restore my beloved!* That was the voice of her will, she knew it. But if her soul had any different wisdom, even in this silence she could not hear.

As the sun was nearing the heights of noon, Igierne put on her crimson robe and entered the House of the Sword. Twelve dark-clad priestesses stood in a circle around her, chanting softly, drawing power from the earth as she drew strength from them.

"Cocidius, Belutacadros, Mars of the Soldiers—" she whispered.

"Hear and bless us . . ." chorused the priestesses.

"Star of Hope, Hand of Justice, Pillar of Power—" And indeed, Igierne could feel the power increasing; she scarcely heard the other women now.

"Sword of the Defender, Sword of Kings, Sword of God!"

She twisted the red cock's neck and the blood flowed over the stone, and then, as in the world outside the sun reached her zenith, grasped the swordhilt, twisted, and pulled the Sword out of the stone.

"For Britannia I draw this blade, and for her lawful king!" With trembling arms she held the weapon high, and the shining steel refracted the light of the torches in red lightnings around the room.

The priestesses recoiled, but Igierne stiffened, shuddering as she tried to control the uprush of power. Behind her closed eyelids cities burned; she saw a crimson sky, swinging swords and bloody spears. In another instant the bloodlust of the blade would overcome her—

—and in that moment of panic the spirit of the sword-priest who was her ancestor spoke within her and she remembered the words that she must say.

"Fortitude binds fury. . . . Strength binds savagery. . . . Right binds rapine. . . . Lord of the Sword I summon Thee; control Thy power!"

For a breath longer the blade's hunger blazed; then something immense and ancient and cold descended from on high to enclose it, and Igierne was left gasping, hanging onto the sword. With her last strength she dragged it into the box, for it had grown heavy with the power it contained. She closed the lid, and then her knees gave way and she sat down beside it on the cold floor.

Igierne had waited almost too long. While she was traveling to the Isle of Maidens and claiming the Sword, Leudonus and his army were halting Octha's northern campaign. Just after Beltain they fought a great battle near Eburacum, and though it ended in victory for the British, Leudonus's forces had been too well savaged to pursue their advantage, and the Saxons retreated unhindered toward Londinium.

Now, the great city's inadequate defenses turned to its advantage, for the enemy wanted a walled town where they could halt and lick their wounds in safety. Just north of Londinium lay Verulamium, and there Octha took refuge.

As Igierne came back down the Roman road, she encountered roving scouts who told her that the army of Southern Britannia was beseiging Verulamium, where the martyr Albanus had his shrine, and that the Pendragon had had himself carried there in a litter so that he could command.

"You should have stayed on the Isle," said Uthir when he saw her. "You'd have been safe there."

"My mother may have been Lady of the Lake, but my father was a warrior who died on the Night of the Long Knives. I hope my courage is no less than his."

Uthir cleared his throat gruffly, but his eyes had kindled when he saw her, and she knew he was glad to have her at his side. Indeed, the excitement seemed to have distracted him from his troubles, and though he looked feverish, he did not seem to be in so much pain as before.

They had found quarters for the king in a partly ruined villa near the town. That evening, the British commanders gathered in what had been the dining chamber for a council of war.

"Another few days of siege and we'll have them!" exclaimed Cataur.

Still young enough to be enthusiastic, there were times when he reminded Igierne painfully of his uncle Gorlosius, but he seemed to bear the High King no enmity for a death which had, after all, put him in line to inherit Dumnonia. His wife had recently borne him a son whom they named Constantine, for they were descended from the grandfather of Uthir in the female line.

"But do we want them—" objected Eldaul, "if it means a house-to-house fight where we can make no use of our cavalry?"

"Do you propose to leave them there unmolested?" Cataur replied.

"Of course not," said Ulfinus. "Give them a good scare on the walls, and perhaps we can winkle them out of there!"

Matauc of Durnovaria, who had created a princedom from the old Durotrige lands, shook his head. "Beseige them long enough and they'll starve to death inside!" Leonorus of the Belgae, who was even more cautious by nature, nodded agreement.

"We don't have that long," exclaimed Ulfinus. "It is high summer now—if there is to be a harvest, our men must be getting away home!"

"There is a way." Merlin, who as usual had been effectively invisible until he wished to be heard, came forward. Several of the commanders jumped, and one of them crossed himself.

"The Saxons are concerned above all with their reputation as warriors. They will pursue glory even to their own disadvantage. You complain, my lord, that your weakness will not allow you to fight—" He turned to Uthir. "Let it work for you. Have them carry you in your litter before the walls, and let your men mock the enemy by saying they are too cowardly to fight even a man who cannot ride."

Uthir flushed angrily. "And what about my honor?"

"Is it dishonor to tell the truth?" Merlin spoke dispassionately, but Igierne could see the sorrow in his eyes.

"It's not, but you're the only man who would dare say it to me—" growled the king.

"And what if it works, and they come out to fight us?" Jordanus said into the silence that followed. "We can use our cavalry then, but they still have the greater numbers. We must not only win, but win so decisively that the Saxons will run away to lick their wounds and not come back again!"

"Merlin . . ." the king said slowly. "In all these years I've never required you to take a role in the fighting. But I'm asking now, for I see no other way. Can't you find a spell to cast madness on the enemy? To call spirits from the earth to fight them?"

Those parts of the druid's face not covered by beard went perfectly white. Igierne realized suddenly how much silver there was in her cousin's hair.

"You don't know . . . the cost of what you're suggesting—"

"Maybe not. But I think you know what it costs me to ask!"

For a long moment dark eyes met gray, and it was the druid who first looked away.

"I do . . ." whispered Merlin. "I will do what I may."

From there, the conversation turned to ways of disposing of their forces if the plan to draw the enemy out should succeed. Merlin went out almost immediately, and presently the others also took their leave and went away.

"They're so hot for the fight," Uthir said painfully. "I'd give my soul to stand with them, but I can hardly hold a sword!"

"There is a Sword that I think you could hold," Igierne said softly, "and it will not require your soul, but only your promise to serve this land."

"I gave that at my anointing—" he began, not understanding.

Igierne shook her head, pulling the long box from beneath the cloak she had laid over it and laying it on the bed beside him. "This belongs to an older mystery." Feeling her own heart beat faster, she opened the box and turned back the cloths that wrapped the Sword.

"Touch it—"

Uthir gripped the hilt and jerked, let go, then carefully grasped it once more. The color came and went in his face as power pulsed through him, then, with an effort of will, he released the hilt and covered it with the silk again.

"By Beli's blazing balls!" he breathed, which if not precisely the same god, at least belonged to the right religion. "That thing will either kill or cure me! Where—"

"It will cure you!" Igierne exclaimed. "It must!" She could not allow herself to contemplate any other possibility, for he had pulled the box closer to his body, and it was clear that he would never now give up the Sword.

And so, as the British prepared for battle around them, Igierne recounted to her king the history of the Chalybe blade.

* * *

Merlin watched, frowning, as Uthir's litter was carried onto the battlefield. Behind him, the British were moving into position before the western gate of Verulamium. Smaller forces had been delegated to watch the other gateways, but it was here, where broad pastures spread out to either side of the road, that the major fighting must be. Overhead the sky was clear, but to the west, gray clouds were building, and a restless wind bent the grass.

The men seemed grim, but determined; there had been little rest for anyone the night before, as warriors sharpened weapons and checked the straps of their armor or simply sat by their campfires, too tense to sleep.

Merlin's preparations had been more complex, if less tangible, as he searched his memory for the appropriate spells and contemplated the ways in which they must be focused and combined. He calculated their interaction as carefully as a master chef making choices from his spice jars. But a cook could only ruin a meal; if Merlin made a mistake, both armies might be destroyed. When he tried to rest, his sleep was troubled by images of destruction from whose midst rose a flaming sword.

Uthir had given them their instructions with a kind of febrile gaiety that Merlin found disturbing. Was he fey, or had the prospect of battle simply made him forget his pain? Either way, he should not be out there. Merlin had only meant to suggest that Uthir have himself carried before the walls to taunt the Saxons, not station himself in the midst of the battle line. Even if the British did not win this battle, their cause would not be lost while the High King lived. He had to survive long enough for Artor to grow up.

Thus the druid in him had reasoned, but as he watched the king go by, the tears on his cheeks were those of the man.

He turned his attention inward, seeking solace from that invisible companion who had been his inspiration and comfort for so long.

"I give life—I do not take it. I cannot help you here. What you do today will be done on your own. . . ."

"So be it—" whispered Merlin, but there was a knot of unease in his belly that would not go away.

"Hai, you Saxon dogs!" cried the British warriors, "why are you hiding behind those walls? Are you afraid to face us? Even our sick are a match for you! Come out and play!"

From beyond the wall they heard shouting, then above the gate a Saxon head appeared.

"We have no need for children's games," came the guttural answer. "We are men!"

Another helmed head appeared beside him. "What honor is there in killing a man who is half-dead already? Take your king home and let him die in peace!"

Merlin looked up and saw a buzzard circling hopefully. He climbed into one of the wagons where no one would trip over him, lay down, and sent his awareness arrowing upward to seize the mind of the bird, then directed it to fly toward the town.

"Skulk inside there and starve if you want to," called the British, "but we give you a chance to settle this now. The only peace between us will be in the grave. See, we will withdraw to give you room!"

The escort surrounding Uthir's litter began to retreat. The buzzard soared over the walls. Through the bird's eyes, Merlin could see Saxon warriors crowding toward the walls, knots of men tangling and separating as they argued.

"Pee-oo," called the buzzard, *"Fight, kill, win—"* Carried by the force of his will, the message arrowed down. *"Charge, strike, destroy! Pee-oo, pee-oo, pee-oo. . . ."*

This time the noise from inside the town was louder. The fair-haired man who had first replied seemed to be arguing with the others. It was Octha, Hengest's son. Merlin guided the buzzard closer.

"Pee-oo, pee-oo, blood will flow and I will feast! Go out and win glory!" Three times widdershins he circled the Saxon leader, then winged out past the gateway, and Octha's disputation became a battle cry.

The gate trembled as men hurried to draw the bar, then swung open. The Saxon warriors began to form up into their battle array.

Soaring back toward the British, Merlin saw their spearmen ready, the cavalry wings waiting to either side. Uthir's litter was still in the center, but the High King was sitting up now, speaking to his men.

"The Saxons called me the half-dead king," Uthir burst out laughing, "because I lay flat in my litter, felled by illness.

And it was true, but I'd rather fight them half-dead than live healthy as a horse and have them think me afraid! Better to die with honor than live disgraced!"

From the gateway came the thunder of spear-shafts beating on shields.

"Do you hear them, lads? They are coming out—will you show them how rough the men of Britannia can play?"

The British replied with an ululation of defiance whose echoes left a mist of brightness in the air. Merlin released the buzzard and sank back into his body. Even with his eyes closed, he could sense the High King's presence as a radiant sphere of power. Had the exultation of the moment released some potential the druid had never noticed before, as Artor had been transfigured by meeting the bear? Or was it something else—

There was no time to wonder. Octha and his warriors were coming out of Verulamium. More and more of them poured through the gate. The mournful call of a cowhorn sounded above the noise and the drumming of spear on shield gave way to the thunder of feet on sod as they began to run.

From the British side trumpets blared. The sound of thunder was abruptly amplified as from one side, Cataur of Dumnonia and his horsemen, and from the other, Eldaul and his cavalry, began their own charge. The wood of the wagon shivered to the vibration. Merlin got to his feet, holding to the side for balance, just as the charge hit, and the separate groups of combatants became a single struggling mass.

In moments, Uthir was surrounded, as in the game of *tabula* the enemy pieces attack the warriors guarding the king. The clangor of clashing weapons smote the ear, pierced by the cries of those who were struck down. Merlin had been present at other battles, but before, he had always waited with the physicians. Now he forced himself to really look at the carnage, striving to understand what was happening.

The Saxons were experienced fighters. Once the British had charged, they lost their main advantage. Horsemen skirmished around the edge of the battle, picking off foes with their lances, but they could not affect the fighting farther in. The British were going on the defensive. This, then, was why Uthir had insisted that the druid help them; without Merlin's magic to tip the balance, the British might well lose.

Once more he sat down. This time, he could not merely ride a passing raptor; he must *become* it. Focusing inward, he formed the image of the raven, Cathubodva's bird.

Goddess, it is your people who are suffering—come to us, blast our foes!

His breathing grew deeper; awareness of his body faded, to be replaced by an alien sense of taut strength, of lightness, of the air. Spirit borne by the raven, he opened his eyes, spread wings to catch the wind, and beat heavily into the sky.

To spirit sight, the forms of the men locked in that mortal struggle were no more than shadows. What he saw was their spirit bodies, flaring brightly as courage spurred them against the foe or fading as they were overcome. Those whose lives were severed floated free, gazing down in confusion at the battle in which they could no longer join.

The raven dove downward, beak opening in the terrible cry with which the Lady of Battles freezes the courage of her foes. Glossy feathers flared white in the light of the sun. And though fleshly ears might hear nothing, the souls of the Saxons heard, and quailed. That moment of hesitation put heart into the British warriors, who drove with renewed vigor at their enemies.

The raven, flapping skyward once more, saw a knot of combatants at whose center swayed Octha's fair head. They were perilously close to the High King; Octha could reach him in a moment if he broke free. The raven circled, gathering momentum, but before he could dive, two dark shapes sped between her and her goal—two other ravens, cawing defiance, which Merlin heard as words.

"This man is my kin through many sons . . . I remember!" called the first raven, and Merlin recalled that Hengest's family believed themselves to be descended from one of their gods.

"I protect him, for he plans wisely and well—" the other echoed.

"What is that to me?" Cathubodva's voice came through her bird. *"He has attacked my land and killed my people! He must die!"*

There were two of the enemy ravens, but the one who was Cathubodva was bigger. Wheeling and slashing, they joined in a battle as furious as the one below, the German god and the Celtic goddess confronting one another.

Even the overflow of power from that conflict of forces was enough to madden the human warriors. Shrieking and grunting, they dropped their weapons and went for each other with teeth and fingernails. The impact of that violence reverberated from one plane of existence to the next. Merlin felt his own mind disintegrating into a madness in which he had no thought but to rend and slay.

And then the fabric of the world was rent by a Sword of Light, and a great Voice that cried out—

"Stop! If they must fight, they shall do so within the bounds I establish—not as beasts, but as men!"

From the Sword came the shape of a Warrior. To some He seemed the helmed Mars of the old shrines, and to some, red Cocidius of the Wall. To the Saxons, He appeared grim and tall, with only one hand. He lifted the blazing sword and swept it above the battlefield, and everywhere combatants sprang apart, staring about them like men waking from a dream.

But the power of that stroke swept Merlin back to his own body, and for some little while he knew no more.

Merlin opened his eyes and groaned. His head hurt—indeed, every part of his body ached as badly as if he had been out on the battlefield. In a sense, he thought painfully, it was true. He should have anticipated that his astral activities would be reflected in his physical body. He sat up, wincing. Then he remembered.

Fear sent its own anodyne through his body as he jumped down from the wagon, but now there was nothing to distract him from the images that flooded his memory. And there before him was the reality of the battlefield. Where there had been green fields was now a trampled mass of mud and blood and the remains of men. Already the ravens—the real ones—were gathering. With all his senses still open, he felt the agony of the wounded, the confused spirits of the slain.

My fault . . . he thought. *It was I who made this a conflict of forces beyond the nature of humankind.*

In the distance he could see fleeing figures; a few horsemen were chasing them. The British were not running.

From that, he supposed that they must have won. He certainly could not tell from looking at men's faces. They all looked as stunned as he. But they did not carry his guilt. Already he could feel the madness that had driven him to the mountains once before nibbling at his control. Rubbing his forehead, he looked around him. Where was the king?

In the center of the carnage, men were moving. They lifted the litter and bore it slowly toward the villa, stopping often to rest, for all had wounds of their own. Leaning on his staff, Merlin hurried to meet them.

Uthir opened his eyes as the druid bent over him. He was splashed with blood, but none of it seemed to be his own.

"Octha's dead—" he whispered. "We have the field."

Merlin nodded. "My lord, how is it with you?"

"As if I've been ploughed . . . by a red-hot poker." Uthir coughed painfully, and lifted his mantle so that Merlin could see what he had hidden there.

The druid stopped short, appalled recognition making everything suddenly very clear. He had never seen the full length of the Chalybe sword until now, when it gleamed with deadly beauty at the king's side. Now he understood where Igierne had gone, and why she had avoided him when she returned.

"I should have known!" Merlin exclaimed. "I sensed its presence—" It was one more thing in which he had failed.

"I didn't have the strength to wield it. The power . . . burned through me . . . killed everyone around."

"And no matter what Igierne may have said, you did not have the right," the druid replied.

Uthir grimaced. "Don't tell her . . . she'll blame herself. Must . . . keep it safe. . . ."

"I also am of the blood of its keepers. I will guard the Sword for your son, who is its destined lord." He pulled off his cloak, and kneeling beside the litter, wrapped it around the blade.

"I'm sorry I won't see him grown. . . . I always thought there would be time. Give him a father's blessing for me. . . ."

Merlin looked down at that white face and nodded.

The king smiled faintly. "But at least . . . Octha is dead."

Some of the servants who had stayed with Igierne at the

villa came out, saw the litter, and began to run toward them. Merlin stepped back, still watching Uthir, as they took him up and carried him inside.

For a few moments Merlin stood unmoving, the shrouded Sword held close against his breast. Overhead, ravens were flying, calling harshly to their kin. Already he could smell a charnel scent from the battlefield. If he stayed here, with the Sword, he would indeed go mad. He took a deep breath, drawing up a cloak of shadow around him. Then he strode swiftly away.

Merlin had planned, insofar as thinking was possible, to carry the weapon northward, back to the Isle. But three days later, when the daze in which he had been wandering began to lift at last, he found himself many miles to the southwest. The Saxons had raided through this land several times, and many of the villas and farmsteads were in ruins, but there were buildings enough left to shelter him, and food in the gardens that had been left to run wild.

Only Calleva, on the old Roman road, still maintained itself as a center of civilization. Near an abandoned chapel just outside of the town Merlin came to rest.

"Stop here . . ." said his daimon.

"Make me a house," said the god in the Sword.

When Merlin began to rebuild the roof, folk from the town decided he must be a hermit, and some of them started to leave food as an offering. They were not so far wrong, though his devotions were not quite what they might have expected. As the days passed, he fell into a trance of labor in which the task of rebuilding kept his madness away.

He repaired the roof, and thatched it securely. He brought stones and mud with which to repair the shattered wall. While he was gathering them he had noted a boulder half his height, and almost as wide. When all else was done he went out during the night, and chanting to focus his strength, managed to roll it inside. Then, using a chisel and mallet that he had found in an outbuilding, he began to carve into the stone a new channel in which to sheathe the Sword.

It was precise and patient work. Long before he completed it he heard men in the road outside the chapel, talking of the death of the High King. Some whispered of poison, but others said it was only that he had exhausted his last strength in the battle. It was said that his queen was bringing the body to the Giant's Dance to lie with that of his brother and the British lords.

Merlin remembered a Samhain Eve beside the sacred stones and the wonder in Uthir's eyes, and wept, but he did not stop chiseling at the stone.

There were more rumors after that, as first one lord and then another sought support in order to claim the overlordship of Britannia. But there was no one on whom all the princes could agree.

The autumn was well advanced by the time Merlin finished his work at last, and slid the Sword into the channel with the secret twist that prevented anyone who did not know the secret from drawing it out again. And when it was sheathed, he carved into the front of the stone these words—

Quicunque me distringet rex iustus Britanniae est . . .

Then, at last, the compulsion released him. Over Sword and stone he draped his mantle, and walked out of the little chapel for the last time.

A ghost of the man he had been whispered that he should go to Igierne in Londinium, or to Artor in Demetia. But he no longer trusted his own wisdom. Let the men who lusted to rule Britannia and the gods they served do the fighting. He had had enough of humankind.

Merlin's feet carried him northward, traveling by night and speaking to no one. By the time he reached the Wall it was hard to remember human language, and so he passed into the shadows of the Forest of Caledonia and disappeared from the knowledge of men.

X

THE SWORD IN THE STONE

A.D. 475

In her dream, Igierne was sitting in an apple tree.

Cradled in its branches and rocked by the wind, she watched the slow-wheeling stars, yet even as she marveled at their majesty she knew that these visions were not hers but those of another, whose dream she shared.

Her tree was surrounded by oak and ash and stately pines, for the forest had grown over an old orchard and only the single apple tree remained. Hungry, she reached for an apple; the arm that moved was long, sinewy, and covered with coarse hair. Abruptly she realized whose mind she shared.

"Merlin," she called, *"where are you? We feared you dead—Britannia needs you, I need you!"*

"I am the Wild Man of Caledonia. . . . Merlin is a dream. Are you my little lass? I have seen you in a moonbeam, Lady, but you do not speak to me anymore. . . ." Through his eyes she saw leaves that glittered in the moonlight and the pale shapes of distant hills.

"It is Igierne who calls you. Return from your wanderings!"

He bit into the apple, and she felt the swift rush of sweetness on her own tongue.

"Merlin loved Igierne, when he was a man. . . . The Wild Man loves the little pig that roots beneath his tree. . . ."

For a moment surprise and pity held her silent, then need drove her on. *"If you ever loved me, find my son! The princes tear at this poor land like ravens at a carcass, and only he can make it whole—"*

A sudden wave of anguish blurred her vision; she smelled once more the deathly reek of the battlefield. Then the image faded, but the sorrow remained.

"Let the White Raven beware the Raven of Battle. To Calleva come the princes in search of sovereignty. . . . Where you find the Sword you shall find the King. . . ."

Branches tossed as he climbed downward. The ground blurred beneath her vision as he began to run, faster and faster until his awareness dissolved into pure motion and Igierne's consciousness fell away.

She opened her eyes, grasping for memories that were already fast fading, but on her lips the taste of apple remained.

How long had it been, she wondered, since she had awakened with happiness in her heart? Whatever her dream meant, it was better than nightmares in which Uthir died in her arms yet again. She had buried him in the barrow by the Giant's Ring, as he had asked, and then begun the long journey back to the north, staying for a time in one town and then in another, until she came to Isca in Demetia, where Bishop Dubricius had welcomed her.

Igierne was in no hurry to continue on, for what remained for her, even at the Lake, but to live out an empty existence mourning the death of Britannia's joy and her own?

But today she had hope once more, hope, and a fragment of prophecy. Bishop Dubricius was accounted a wise man. Together, perhaps they could make one last attempt to persuade the warring princes to seek unity.

*　　*　　*

In Calleva, one could almost believe that Rome had never departed from the Isle. Its walls were intact, its amphitheater only a little overgrown, its gracious houses, set amidst their gardens and orchards, still the homes of cultured men. It was also convenient in location, far enough to the west to be out of easy reach of Saxon raiders, and connected to the rest of the country by good roads. If summoning the lords of Britannia to this place had been no more than a night fancy, thought Igierne, then it had been a useful one.

For the warlords and chieftains and magistrates were coming in.

During the two years since Uthir's death there had been no central authority. Hengest, recovering from the shock of Octha's loss, had designated his grandson Oesc as heir, and though he no longer took the field, the chieftains he had summoned from Germania were swift to fall upon their British neighbors. In the North, Colgrin and Baldulf had made alliance with the old enemy, the Picts and Scots, and were extending their holdings. In the West the lords of Demetia and Guenet fought the men of Eriu and each other.

But now, when the first winter storms were putting an end to the fighting season, the British had braved bad roads and wild weather to converge on the old *civitas* of the Atrebates. The chieftains and their families were given hospitality in the better homes of the town, while the lesser lords and *gentiles* set up camp, with their men, in the fields outside. Even Leudonus had left the Votadini lands in charge of his clan chiefs and come south to the conclave, and with him came Morgause.

Igierne was sitting in the atrium of the chief magistrate, made pleasant by shrubs in pots and beds of late-blooming flowers, when a light step on the flagstones made her turn and she saw that her daughter had arrived.

Though the atrium was protected from the wind, Morgause's draperies fluttered with supressed motion. Clearly, marriage and motherhood agreed with her. What the girl's face had lost in childish roundness, her breasts had gained, and her complexion was blooming. Igierne frowned in sudden suspicion.

"Morgause, are you breeding again?"

Quick color came and went in the girl's face, then she set her hands over her belly and smiled.

"I shall have three children in four years of marriage. In all your years as a wife, you never managed but the two!"

Igierne's eyes widened a little at the taunt; she had not meant to sound disapproving—well, not very.

"I congratulate you on being one of those women who are built for bearing." She managed an answering smile. "Your husband must be pleased."

"I will give him enough sons to defend the North with the fruit of my own womb! Or perhaps they will rule a greater kingdom. Clearly, Uthir meant Leudonus to be his heir."

"Certainly he respected Leudonus's abilities as a commander," Igierne said evenly. "But the lords of southern Britannia may feel that his strength lies too far away."

Morgause shrugged and paced across the stones. Her mantle was dyed a deep crimson, not the color that had clashed so with her complexion at her wedding, but a shade like Gaulish wine. Heavy earrings of gold and garnet hung in her ears, and her golden pennanular brooch was set with garnets as well. Igierne remembered when she used to adorn herself in jewels. She had worn only black since Uthir died.

With a swirl of her skirts Morgause turned to face her once more.

"That argument might be used against any of them. At least Leudonus *has* strength. I will be Tigernissa, and it will be your turn, mother, to sit on the Isle of Maidens and watch the world go by!"

"Oh, the Lady of the Lake can do a little more than that—" said Igierne tightly. "Did you learn nothing when you were there?"

"I learned a great deal. And I am learning more in the North, where they revere their queens. Leudonus's mother was a princess of the Picts, who trace their descent through the female line. They choose their husbands to defend the land, but they are the source of power."

Igierne picked up her embroidery again and took a stitch or two. What Morgause had said agreed with the secret teaching of the Isle, but southern Britannia had been Roman too long, and the men who ruled it had forgotten many things.

"Neither queen nor king is the source of sovereignty," she said at last, "but the Goddess Herself who is Lady of this land. Do not forget that, daughter. Whatever I have done or you shall do, we are only Her deputies."

Morgause responded with a rather odd smile. "Oh, I have not forgotten. But the Lady sometimes wears a different face in the northern lands. . . ."

Igierne raised one eyebrow, but before she could inquire she heard voices in the entry and another woman, draped in a gown and palla of dusty blue, came into the atrium, followed by a lanky boy.

"*Domina*—" She made a reverence to Igierne, and then, after a moment's hesitation, to Morgause. "I do not know if you will remember me, for it has been many years—"

"Of course I do! You are Flavia, wife of Caius Turpilius." And indeed, though Flavia's figure had become more matronly, she had not really changed. "I am glad that you and your husband have come. They will need his good sense at the Council."

Flavia nodded. "He and young Cai are down at the meadow where the warriors will show off their strength in the games. God send that it does not become a battlefield!"

"Will not your younger son be fighting?"

For a moment Flavia looked troubled, then she smiled. "He is only fifteen, though he is taller than Cai. Time enough for him to be fighting when he has grown into his bones. . . ." She looked fondly at the boy, who flushed red as he realized he was the center of attention.

He reminded Igierne of a young colt, still all legs and neck, but with the promise of grace and speed. At least his skin was not disfigured by the spots that afflicted so many lads that age.

"If he has the time, perhaps you would lend him to me as an escort," she said to Flavia. "I no longer have a real household, and the town has become very crowded as the chieftains come in."

"Too crowded . . ." Morgause said softly, eyeing the newcomers.

Igierne frowned at her. Why should Morgause care if her mother showed some kindness to this gangling boy? But clearly it was so. *She still wants my approval*, thought the queen, *despite all her proud words.*

"I would be honored—" The boy spoke for the first time. If he resented being shuffled off among the ladies he was too well-bred to let it show.

"Come to me tomorrow," said Igierne. "You may be my escort to the warriors' games."

"My children in Christ, to this place I have called you to take counsel for the safety of your own children and the future of this land."

Bishop Dubricius stood on the dais at the end of the basilica, illuminated by light from the upper windows, which picked out the golden embroidery on his robes. He was a humble man, who on ordinary days dressed as simply as any of his monks. But he was not an unworldly one, reflected Igierne, watching from the gallery, and he knew the power of a judicious display of gold.

"The heathen encompass us on every side, and we have been abandoned by the eagles of Rome. Under the authority of our own emperors we have fought them; at times we nearly drove them from our shores. But only when we were united. When each lord cares only for his own lands, the devil's spawn can gobble us piecemeal, like a herd that has been scattered by the wolves!"

From his audience came a murmur of appreciation, if not for his text, at least for his rhetoric. The farther windows lit them as well, glinting on swordhilts and brooches and torques of gold.

The basilica of Calleva was second only to that of Londinium. The nave was seventy feet high, arches supported the upper walls and separated it from the aisle. In happier times, the decurions of the district had met there to conduct the business of government; now the benches were filled by nearly a hundred proud men from all over the Island.

"Indeed, your grace." Cataur of Dumnonia, representing his father and his grandfather, the prince Gerontius, rose from his bench to answer. His brother, Gerontius the younger, was at his side. "If we did not agree with you we would not have come here. But there is no man remaining

of the direct line of Constantine to inherit, and how else shall
we choose?"

His question seemed innocent enough, but every man there
knew that through the female line Cataur was descended
from the British emperor who had challenged Rome. It occurred to Igierne suddenly that Morgause, through her father,
carried that blood as well. Had she thought of that? From
the intent way in which she was watching, her mother felt it
likely, and if so, Leudonus would be considering it as well.

Despite four centuries of Roman emperors, who were as
likely to be raised to the purple for their popularity, or their
power, their competence, or sometimes by pure chance, as
for their heredity, an honored bloodline still carried weight
with these descendents of Celtic kings.

If Uthir had allowed Merlin to bring back their son,
thought Igierne, there would have been an heir in the male
line. Where was he now, her little boy? Did he know of his
heritage? Or was he dead, and had Uthir and Merlin resisted
her pleas to bring him to her because they feared to tell her
so?

It hardly mattered now. Cataur had just proclaimed himself
a candidate. Igierne remembered him as energetic but headstrong, requiring a firm hand. Would he have the self-
discipline to rule?

"Who is that?" asked Flavia as Eleutherius got to his feet.

"The prince of Eburacum. His father ruled the lands from
the Wall to Lindum, but the Anglians are carving out a
homeland there now."

Eleutherius cleared his throat. "Any lord we choose must
care for the peoples of the North as well as the South; the
remnants who hold out in the East, surrounded by Saxons,
as well as the safe western lands. The sons of Ambrosius
came back from Armorica to lead us. We do not want a High
King who will flit oversea to Dumnonia if things go badly
here."

That was close enough to a challenge to make all eyes
turn to Cataur, for the northern coast of Armorica had been
given its name by Britons who fled there from the lands his
father had ruled. But before he could answer, Catraut, who
had established himself in Verulamium after the battle, spoke
in favor of choosing a man with experience on the Saxon

frontier. He was followed by others, as each region proclaimed its importance, or its needs.

Throughout all this, Leudonus had sat in silence. He had put on weight since his marriage to Morgause, but he was still in his prime, broad rather than tall, with thinning reddish hair. His mantle was woven in wool of many colors, in the traditional royal style. Igierne had seen him in Roman dress, which he wore well, and knew that this appeal to Celtic memory must be deliberate.

He will let them talk themselves out before he makes his move, and hope that in their desperation they will accept even a northerner, if he has sufficient power.

The light through the windows was deepening toward sunset when Bishop Dubricius held up his crozier. Reluctantly, the men fell silent.

"We will not decide this issue today, but I think that those who have spoken have set forth the qualities we must seek in our king—strength, wisdom, a care for all parts of this land, a right to rule which can be accepted by everyone here. . . ."

"A miracle . . ." whispered someone nearby.

"Christ Himself in His second coming could not win acceptance from them all!" another voice answered.

One of the local men got to his feet. "We will never agree until God Himself gives us a sign! But in the hermit's chapel just beyond the town there is a sword thrust into a stone which no man can pull free. The writing on the rock says it belongs to the king!"

Igierne sank back against the wall as if she had been struck to the heart by that same blade.

Her dream of Merlin had been true! And this was what had happened to the Sword, and why he had told her to seek Calleva! But why? Only Merlin and she knew the trick of making a slot that would hold the Chalybe blade. Had he meant her to draw it herself and choose her king as a priestess of the Lady of Sovereignty?

"My lady, are you unwell?" asked Flavia, and Igierne realized that her skin had gone clammy and she was perspiring beneath her veil.

She shook her head, though she was trembling with a sudden awareness of great forces building around her. She dared not touch the Sword, she realized then. She had given it to Uthir, and it had killed him. She straightened, striving for calm. She could not interfere, but she would bear witness to what must come.

The combats had already started when Igierne arrived at the amphitheater, accompanied by Flavia's boy. The horse races were scheduled for later in the day. The amphitheater lay to the northeast of the town, where it caught the morning light, but the day had dawned cloudy; now and again a cool breath of mist touched her skin. She had wrapped up warmly, and the people of Calleva had set up a shelter over part of the seating and made it comfortable with rugs and cushions for the benefit of the noble ladies and the older men.

It was the Bishop's idea that a day of martial displays would relax the chieftains as well as enabling them to judge the temper of each other's men. And it was just as well, she thought, that they should have some time to get over last night's embarassment at having tried to draw the Chalybe Sword from the stone—and failed.

Once more she bit back her anger. *Curse you, Merlin, for preparing this test and then disappearing! If you know who is destined to draw the blade, why are you not here to make sure he does so?*

Originally the amphitheater must have seated nearly the entire population of the town. She guessed it was not now much used, for some of the timbers had decayed, but the stands that remained gave a good view of the arena, whose grass had been cropped by the sheep that ordinarily grazed here into a mat of green.

The boy leaned forward as two new combatants strode onto the green, armed as for war, except for the leather bands that wrapped their swords.

"Who are they?"

"One of Cataur's men and a man from Demetia, by the badges," she said. "I don't know their names. Do you want to be a fighter?"

He looked at her in surprise. "Peace is better than war, but nobody will have peace unless some are willing to spend their lives to guard the others. At least it is so in these times."

"Is that what Caius Turpilius told you?"

"It is what I believe."

His gaze returned to the field. The two men saluted the stands, then faced each other, feet braced and weapons raised.

"But don't you dream of winning honor, or hearing people praise your name?"

He colored, and she knew that she had guessed well.

"If I fought for the right things . . ." he said in a low voice, with a quick glance to see if she was laughing at him.

One of the swords slammed against the opposing shield and he looked back to the field to see the exchange of blows. The fighting settled into a pattern of tense pauses and flurried engagement. It was a shock when the Dumnonian's blade slipped past the enemy guard and stopped just touching the Demetian swordsman where the neck and shoulder joined. Igierne admired his control—if the blow had landed with full force it could have broken the man's neck even with a blunted edge. The Cornovians began to cheer and there was a patter of applause from the stands.

"I had a strange dream last night," the boy said as the next pair came out onto the green. "I was standing in a forge, watching a blacksmith at work, except that it was not a man, but a woman, like one of the old goddesses, with hair of flame. She took the fragments she was hammering from the anvil and cast them into a crucible. But they weren't metal, but the limbs of men. And then she turned and spoke to me—"

He fell silent, frowning. Igierne felt her skin pebble. Who was this boy to have a dream of such power?

"Can you remember her words?"

"All that is made will in the end be broken. I gather the shards and try them in the flame. The dross I skim away, but the true metal runs together, all the stronger for its mixing."

"What happened then?" Igierne asked softly.

"The lumps melted and mingled until they were a single glowing mass. The goddess poured the molten metal into a mold, and when it was solid, she laid it on the anvil and began to hammer it. She hammered it into a sword . . . and when she was done," he swallowed, "she asked if I would serve her, and held it out to me. . . ."

Igierne's heart began to bound unevenly in her breast.

"Boy, look at me—" She searched his face, striving to find something familiar in the curly brown hair or the blue eyes. But her own eyes blurred so that it was hard to see. "What is your name?"

"Arktos, because once I met a bear—well, really, it's Artor—"

Or Artorius? If this was her son, clearly he had not been told. She must speak with Flavia!

The boy was still staring at her in amazement when she saw a beefy young man with the Turpilius nose running toward them across the grass.

"Artor, Artor!" He pulled up in front of them, sketched a bow to Igierne, and grasped the rail in front of the boy. "I broke my sword practicing at the post! Run back to the camp and get my good blade—quickly!" He danced from one foot to the other. "I'm due to fight in the next round!"

Igierne looked from Cai to Artor, who was already on his feet, apparently accustomed to being ordered around in this way. "My Lady, do you mind? I will not be long—"

She gestured to him to draw nearer, and said softly, "You will return all the quicker if you stop in the old chapel just beyond the eastern gate and take the sword that is there—"

His face brightened, and he vaulted over the railing and darted away.

Well, Merlin, if that is interference then it is your fault for not being here to stop me, she thought defiantly. *If our blood runs true in him, he will draw the Sword!*

"It was kind of Artor to help you," she said to Cai, who was still standing there.

"Oh, well, he has some funny ideas, but he's a good lad all the same."

Not a bad recommendation from an older brother, she told herself, trying to gauge how long it should take the boy to get to the gate and find the chapel. Was he there already? Could he draw the blade, and if he succeeded, she wondered in sudden fear, what would happen then?

It seemed an eternity before she saw his tall figure across the grass, but Cai seemed surprised at how quickly he had made the journey. Artor was walking, not running, and a bundle, swathed in his cloak, was clasped in his arms. He seemed dazed, as one who has looked on too much light.

Igierne felt her heart begin that heavy beat once more.

"What's wrong? Did you run too fast?" Cai was hurrying toward him. "Here, I'll take it—"

For a moment Artor resisted, then he released the bundle, and Cai fumbled for the hilt.

"Ow! It *burned*!"

The blade slid from his hands and Artor bent to catch it before it could hit the ground. Igierne let out a breath she had not known she held, sudden tears blurring her eyes.

"That's not my sword!" Cai took his smarting fingers out of his mouth to cry. Artor looked at Igierne in appeal.

She got to her feet, pitching her voice to carry, though her vision came and went in waves, as if she looked through fire.

"It is not, nor ever shall be. It is the Sword of Kings that Artor holds, the Chalybe blade that the Defender of Britannia shall bear. By blood he is its rightful heir. Before his birth this destiny was written in the stars!"

Her knees gave way and she sat down again, but she had said enough. From every side, men were gathering. Caius Turpilius came hurrying forward. His face blanched as he saw Artor holding the Sword.

"Arktos, lad, where did you get that blade?"

"I found it in the chapel beside the gate. Father, did I do wrong? *She* said—" He broke off, for Caius, seeing the triumph in Igierne's eyes, had gone down on one knee before him.

"Boy, the druid told me that your birth was good, but I see now that you come of higher blood than ever I dreamed of!"

"Father, get up! I don't understand!"

"What he means is that you are my son, Artor, by Uthir the High King," Igierne said in a shaking voice, "the son that we entrusted to Merlin when you were a babe, that he might find you a safe fosterage."

"The druid came to us in the summer of the year Uthir made the lady Igierne his bride," Caius echoed, "with a boy-child a few weeks old."

The murmur of commentary from the men who had gathered around them became a clamor as word spread. Now the great lords were coming, Cataur and Leudonus and Eleutherius, with their champions behind them.

"What is this tale?" challenged Leudonus, fixing Igierne with his pale gaze.

"This boy is Uthir's son, and he has drawn the Sword!"

Leudonus wheeled round to glare at Artor, who still stood with the Sword clasped against his breast.

"Do you say so? We'll go back to the chapel and if he proves it, then, woman, you can explain!"

The word spread fast. By the time the procession reached the hermit's chapel, most of the chieftains and their men and half the town beside had joined it. Someone had even sent for Bishop Dubricius, who arrived, red-faced and puffing, just as they reached the door. With his usual imperturbable good sense he began to create order out of the confusion, calling on the chieftains to calm their men, and selecting, with an unerring grasp of the politics of the gathering, the witnesses, for it was clear that the chapel would hold barely a dozen men.

In the end, besides the Bishop himself, the group included Leudonus and Cataur, the chief magistrate of Calleva, Eleutherius, Catraut and Eldaul, Ulfinus, who had been Uthir's friend, Igierne, Turpilius, and his son Cai.

And Artor, who looked about him like a beast that scents the hunters closing in. But he was still hanging onto the Sword.

"Don't be afraid, lad," said the Bishop. "The truth will prevail, here on this holy ground."

Artor nodded, and Igierne knew it was not the men he feared, but his destiny.

"Will you swear before God and His holy angels that you drew the Sword you are holding from out this stone?"

All could see that the slot in which it had been fixed was empty. Artor nodded again.

"Then I will ask you to thrust the blade back into the rock, and draw it out once more."

Something grim in the set of the boy's jaw reminded Igierne painfully of Uthir as he moved forward. She heard Ulfinus's breath catch, and knew he saw it too. Artor dropped the swathing cloth, and with a swift turn of the wrist, brought the blade up, positioned it over the slot, and with the twisting movement that Igierne's own muscles remembered, thrust it home.

"There is blood on the stone—" said someone, pointing at the dark stain that had run down into the "r" of the *rex* in the rock surface.

"I cut my hand," said Artor, "when I pulled it out before."

"I have heard that such blades must be blooded when they are drawn," said Eldaul reflectively.

For a moment Artor studied the sheathed Sword, his brows bent in a frown, then he turned to the men. "There it is, as it was before. Try if you will. . . ."

"It has burnt me once already!" exclaimed Cai. "I have no desire to touch it again."

"Well I will try," said Catraut, grinning, "though I have no wish to be High King." He went forward, and though the sword did not burn him, neither could he budge it from the stone.

Cataur tried then, and some of the others, to no avail. And all the while Leudonus watched them, pulling at his beard, his gaze going from the Sword to Igierne and back again.

"I think my wife has told me something about this blade. There is a trick to its sheathing, is there not? Are you so tormented by your grief, my lady, that you have told this poor boy the secret and convinced yourself he is your son?"

"Indeed I know that Sword," Igierne said proudly, "for my family guarded it for many years. But I did not bring it here. And as for the boy—my heart began to whisper to me who he must be, and so I told him where to find the blade. But no more—before Our Lady's throne I swear it. I told him no more! It is not the drawing of the blade, but the wielding that is the test, Leudonus. Let Artor pull it out again for you and see if you can bear its power!"

"Do as she says, my son," Bishop Dubricius said softly. "As you did before . . ."

"I knelt down before the altar and asked God's leave," said Artor, "for I was not quite sure it was right to take something from a shrine." As he spoke, he knelt once more, head bowed in prayer. Then he signed himself and went to the stone. "But I did it all faster, because I was hurrying . . ."

He was not hurrying now. Igierne saw him swallow as he

faced the Sword, this time knowing what pulling it out might mean.

He set his hand on the hilt, and she saw him stiffen at the first uprush of power. Then he set his feet more firmly and pulled, the muscles in his forearm rippling as he turned the blade, and with a faint hiss it came free. Artor took a step backward and swung it high, and no man could say after whether it was the last light of sunset coming through the open door that lit the Sword or some radiance from within.

Seen by that light, Artor's face was transfigured as well, the boy's unformed features overlaid with the stern majesty of a king. He brought the blade down and drew the keen edge across his forearm next to the other gash. Once more, blood dripped upon the stone.

"It is speaking to me . . ." he murmured. "It only whispered before—" He turned the flat of the blade against his wounds, and when he lifted it, there were two white scars. He straightened then, resting the weapon across his two palms.

"My son," said Igierne, "what does it say?"

"It tells me that the power to defend is the same as the power to destroy. One must balance the other. It says . . . it is a Sword of Justice, that will endure no lie." His blue gaze lifted to Leudonus's face, and the older man could not look away. "Stretch out your hand, my lord, and prove the truth or falsehood of your suspicions on this blade."

Leudonus did not lack courage, but as he neared Artor his steps slowed, as if he walked against a wind. Still, he managed to grip the golden hilt for a full minute before his features contorted in pain and he wrenched his hand away.

"Do not try to take the Sword again. From this hour to his life's ending it will bear no touch but that of the Defender," said a new voice.

They all turned. Merlin stood in the doorway, leaning on his staff. His hair and beard had grown longer, and he was clad only in a kilt of hide, but the Wild Man no longer looked out of his eyes.

"I took him from his mother's breast and gave him to Turpilius to foster. He is Igierne's son."

"But is he Uthir's?" asked Leudonus, recovering. "It was Gorlosius who visited her at Dun Tagell, as I have heard."

"It was Uthir, in Gorlosius's guise," said Merlin. "And Gorlosius himself lay dead already when the king came to her."

"Then it was not adultery," someone whispered. "Look at his face—who else could he be but Uthir's true son?"

"He is very young—" Eldaul began.

"Then you will advise him," snapped Igierne. "Does it matter whether he is my son or he dropped out of the sky? For many generations my family guarded this Sword. Now it has chosen its King."

She turned to Artor. "Will you accept the trust the Sword has laid upon you? Will you swear to defend, not one region, or one tribe, or one faith, but all this Hallowed Isle?"

Artor knelt before her, the Sword fixed upright before him. In his face shone exaltation, and terror, and joy.

"By this holy blade I do so swear . . ."

People and Places

A note on pronunciation:

British names are given in fifth-century spelling, which does not yet reflect pronunciation changes. Initial letters should be pronounced as they are in English. Medial letters are as follows.

SPELLED	PRONOUNCED
p	b
t	d
k/c	(soft) g
b	v (approximately)
d	soft "th" (modern Welsh "dd")
g	"yuh"
m	v
initial ue	w

†

PEOPLE IN THE STORY

CAPITALS = major character
* = historical personnage
( ) = dead before story begins
[ ] = name as given in later literature

*Aelle—chief of the South Saxons

*Agricola Longhand—prince of Demetia

AMBROS/MERLIN, son of Maderun and a Wild Man, druid and wizard

(*Ambrosius the Elder)

*AMBROSIUS AURELIANUS

AMLODIUS, Protector of Brigantia, husband of Artoria Argantel

*Antonius Donatus, lord of the Novantae

Artoria Argantel, Lady of the Lake, high priestess of the Old Faith at the Isle of Maidens

ARTORIUS/ARTOR [Arthur], son of Uthir and Igierne

(Artorius Hamicus Sarmaticus, priest of the Sword and Argantel's grandfather)

Baldulf—a Saxon ally of Octha

Belutacadros, ancient British war god

Blaise, priest, confessor to Maderun

(Brannos [Bran the Blessed], a legendary king)

*Cataur [Cador] of Dumnonia, son of Docomaglos

CAI [Kay], son of Caius Turpilius, Artor's foster-brother & companion

Caius Turpilius, Artor's foster father

Carmelidus, king of Moridunon, maternal grandfather of Merlin

*Categirnus, older son of Vitalinus

*Catelius Decianus, lord of the northern Votadini

Cathubodva, ancient British war goddess, analagous to the Morrigan

*Catraut, prince of Verulamium

Cerituend, Viaun, Creirbiu and Imacdub, Ceridwen, Gwion, Creidwy and Afagddu, from the old legend of Ceridwen's cauldron

Cocidius, an ancient British war god

*Coelius [Coel Hen], lord of Eburacum

*Colgrin—a Saxon ally of Octha

*Constantine, son of Cataur

*Coroticus, lord of Strathclyde

*Dumnuall [Dyfnwal], daughter's son of Germanianus and Ridarchus' brother, lord of the Southern Votadini

Docmaglos, prince of Dumnonia, second son of Gerontius the elder

*DUBRICIUS, bishop of Isca and primate of Britannia

*Ebissa—nephew of Hengest

Ebrdila, a priestess on the Isle of Maidens

Eldaul, lord of Glevum

Eleutherius, lord of Eburacum

Felix, a Christian priest in the service of Vitalinus

Flavia—wife of Caius Turpilius, Artor's foster-mother

Ganeda [Ganiedda], Merlin's half-sister, wife of Ridarchus

*Germanianus, lord of the southern Votadini

Gerontius the Elder, prince of Dumnonia

*Gerontius the younger, son of Docomaglos

*Gillomanus—an Irish raider

Godwulf, a Saxon thyle in the service of Vitalinus

Gorangonus, prince of Cantium

GORLOSIUS, his elder son

(*Hadrian, emperor A.D. 117–138, builder of the Wall)

*HENGEST, a mercenary warrior from Anglia

*Horsa, Hengest's brother

IGIERNE [Igraine], Artor's mother, the daughter of Amlodius and Argantel

Junius Lupercus, commander of the the warriors who guard the Isle

Kurdalagon, legendary smith of the Sarmatians

LEUDONUS [Lot], king of the Votadini

MADERUN, princess of Moridunon, Merlin's mother

Maglicun, a druid in the service of Vitalinus

Maglos Leonorus of Venta Belgarum, king of the Belgae

(*Magnus Maximus [Maxen Wledig]—emperor of Britannia 383–387)

Martinus, a Christian priest and follower of Augustinus of Hippo

Matauc of Dorchester—king of the Durotriges

Matauc Morbrin [Madoc Morvrinus], Merlin's stepfather

Maugantius, a philosopher in Vitalinus's service

MORGAUSE, daughter of Igierne and Gorlosius, married to Leudonus

*Octha, son of Hengest

*Oesc, son of Octha and Hengest's heir

Pascentius—a Frisian raider

Peretur [Peredur], son of Eleutherius, lord of Eboracum

Reginwynna [Rowenna], daughter of Hengest, wife of Vitalinus

*Ridarchus [Rhydderch], king at Altacluta

(Rigantona, daughter of Gutuator, Argantel's grandmother)

*Johannes Riothamus—a British warlord in Gallia

Sulpicius—prince of Deva

*VITALINUS of Glevum, the VOR-TIGERNUS

*VORTIMER, second son of Vitalinus

Uthir [Uther Pendragon], brother of Ambrosius

    Jordanus

    Ulfinus   warriors in service to Uthir

† PLACES

Abus Fluvius—R. Humber
Alba—Scotland
Altacluta—Dumbarton Rock
Ambrosiacum—Amesbury
the Barrow on the Ridgeway—Wayland's Smithy
Bannhedos—Castle Dore, Cornwall
Bremetennacum—Ribchester, in Lancashire
Britannia—the island of Great Britain
Calleva—Silchester
Camulodunum—Colchester
Cantium—Kent
Cluta Fluvius—R. Clyde
Cornovia—Cornwall
Dalriada—northern Ireland
Demetia—modern Pembrokeshire
Deva—Chester
Dubris—Dover
Dumnonia—the Cornish peninsula
Dun Ambros—Dynas Emrys, Wales
Dun Breatann—fortress of Dumbarton
Dun Eidyn—Edinborough
Dun Tagell/Durocornovium—Tintagel
Durobrivae—Water Newton
Durolipons—Cambridge
Durovernum Cantiacorum—Canterbury
Durnovaria—Dorchester, Dorset
Eburacum—York
Eriu—Ireland
the Fawwyth—the Fowey river, Cornwall
Gallia—France
Giant's Dance—Stonehenge
Glevum—Gloucester
Guenet—Gwynedd, North Wales

Hibernia, Eriu—Ireland
Isle of Glass or Isle of Apples—Glastonbury, Somerset
Isle of the Dead—Bardsey Isle, Wales
Isle of Maidens—Derwent Water, Lake Country
Isca Dumnoniorum—Exeter
Isca Silurum—Caerleon
Lindum—Lincoln
Londinium—London
Luguvalium—Carlisle
Madoc's Bay—Tremadoc Bay, Wales
Maridunum—Carmarthen
Mona—the Isle of Anglesey
Novantae lands—Dumfriesshire & Galloway
Noviomagus—Chichester
Portus Adurni—Portchester (Portsmouth)
Regnum—Chichester
Rithergabail—Episford, Kent
Rutupiae—Richborough, Kent
Sabrina Fluvia—the Severn River and estuary
Salmaes—the Solway
Sorviodunum—Old Sarum (Salisbury)
Stratcluta—Strathclyde
Tamesis Fluvius—Thames River
Tanatus Insula—Isle of Thanet, Kent
Tava Fluvius—the Tay
Treonte, Trisantona—the Trent
Vecta Insula—Isle of Wight
Venta—later Gwent, modern Monmouthshire
Votadini lands—southeast Scotland, from the firth of Forth
    to the Wall
Venta Belgarum—Winchester
Venta Icenorum—Caistor, Norfolk
Venta Silurum—Caerwent
Verulamium—St. Albans
the Wae—the River Wye
the White Horse—White Horse on Uffington Downs

THE BOOK
OF THE
SPEAR

PROLOGUE

In the beginning was the breath.

When the first Fire met primal Ice there came a wind, released by their meeting, feeding the flame. By virtue of that third element, the breath of life and the spirit that moves through all the worlds, matter and energy interacted.

It moves upon the face of the waters, and life begins to stir; the trees of the forest exhale it; the newborn babe breathes it in and becomes a child of time.

In the beginning was the Word.

Invisible, essential, it moves through all that lives, knowing everything, itself unknown. Aware, it wills the world to change and grow. Conscious, that will is borne on a breath of wind in the form of sound. . . .

In the morning of creation the god who gave men breath hangs on the Worldtree. Nine nights and days he hangs suspended, neither eating nor drinking, until out of his agony comes understanding, and he calls forth the primal energies of the world in sacred sounds. One by one he calls them into manifestation as Runes of might and power. And then he gives them to the world.

The Breath carries the Word.

In a northern forest, a rune-master chants, calling the wind. All through the night the wild storm rages. He stands to face it, hair streaming, garments blown to ribbons, shouting out the names of his god. When dawn breaks and the wind grows gentle, he sees before him the limb of an ash tree that the storm has speared into the ground.

Whispering a prayer of thanks, he pulls it free, finding it exact in weight and balance for his needs. From fallen wood he builds a shelter at the foot of a hill, and there, for nine nights and days he labors, eating nothing, drinking only from the sacred spring.

Carefully the wood is smoothed and polished, all irregularities planed away. As he works, he sings of the sun and rain that nourished the tree, the earth that bore it, the wind that ruffled its leaves. When he is finished, he holds a smooth shaft, almost as long as he is tall.

With his graving tool, he carves into the ashwood the angular shapes of the runes. One by one he carves them, chanting their names so that the wood vibrates with the sound. With the sounds come images, each rune name is a doorway to another realm. With blood and breath and spittle he colors and consecrates them, and as each one is added, the shaft gains power.

On the eighth night he is finished. To his eyes, the rune staff seems to glow. Now, it contains, but does not yet direct the power. In the dawning of the ninth day, he draws forth from its wrappings the one thing he himself has not made. A cleanly polished leaf-shaped blade of translucent, smoky stone, it came to him from his father. But it is far older.

When he holds it images come to him of hide-covered huts beneath a northern sky, and he feels the icy breath of eternal snows. The soul of the shaman who made that blade still guards it, whispering of ice and fire and monstrous enemies. Since the time when the fathers of the fathers of his people first spoke in human words, this blade has warded them; it comes from a time even before they knew the runes.

Handling it with reverence, he eases it into the slot that

he has carved into the shaft, bedded in glue made from the hooves of stallions. With the sinew of wolves he wraps it, and ties two raven feathers so they will flutter in the breeze.

When he is finished, the wood feels different. It is not only that the balance has shifted. The power that was inherent now is focused. As the ninth night falls he climbs the hill. The wind that has sprung up with the coming of darkness is whispering in the trees.

He turns to face the breeze and it blows stronger. With both hands, he holds up the spear. Wind shrills down the shaft.

"Gungnir I name you, to Woden I offer you, to bear his word and his will throughout the world!"

I

The Wild Hunt

A.D. 470

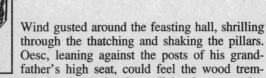 Wind gusted around the feasting hall, shrilling through the thatching and shaking the pillars. Oesc, leaning against the posts of his grandfather's high seat, could feel the wood trembling beneath his hand. *Maybe this will be the storm that destroys us,* he thought with a shiver in which excitement mingled with fear. *The wind will knock down the hall and then the sea will pour in over the fields and wash us away . . .*

Storms were common at this season, when the forces of winter fought a rearguard action against the advance of spring, but in all his nine years Oesc could not remember so mighty a wind. For generations the Myrgings had held this land, stubbornly clinging to their homes when other tribes passed away. Men spoke of gentle winters and good harvests when they sat around the fires, but since his birth, it seemed, the weather had been bad, and this was the worst year of all.

A cold blast whipped up the flames in the long hearth as the door opened. Several drenched figures pushed through and slammed it shut, stamping their feet and shaking themselves like wet dogs. Oesc listened with interest as they swore, testing the forbidden words with a silent tongue.

"The etins are pissing up a storm, curse them!" exclaimed Æthelhere, flinging his cloak at one of the thralls. "I swear the rain is coming in sideways, straight from the sea!"

"—And cold as the milk from Hella's tit, too!" echoed Byrhtwold, following him. Their boots squelched, and water ran down their necks from their wet hair.

"What of the tide?"

Oesc looked up at his grandfather, who had been sitting motionless since noon, listening to the wind.

"It will be high just past sunset, lord," said Æthelhere. "If the wind has not dropped by then—" He grimaced and shook his head.

He did not need to say more. At this season the wind, adding its power to that of the tide, could turn back the Fifeldor in its course. The storm tides and the flooding river between them would drown the newly planted fields.

"The Norns have cast for us an evil fate . . ." muttered Eadguth. "If foes attacked us I would go forth in arms, old as I am, but no man can hold back the sea."

Oesc looked up at his grandfather. Eadguth had always seemed eternal. Now the boy saw the sunken eyes and furrowed brow, the transparent skin on the thin hands, and knew that the Myrging-king was *old*, not as a standing stone is ancient, its rough surfaces weathered by the years, but like an old oak, decaying from within until it has no strength to withstand the storm. Already this wind had torn limbs from several of the trees that had rooted themselves in the wurt-mound on which stood the royal hall. What would it do to the old man? He crept closer and clasped his arms around Eadguth's leg as if his young strength could root him into the ground.

The old man's hooded glance turned downward and his lips twisted.

"Is it a curse on your line, boy, that has doomed you to find rest nowhere? I am glad that your mother did not live to see this day. . . ."

Oesc let go and sat staring. He did not remember his mother, a fair woman with eyes the rich brown of tree bark in the sun, so men said, who had run off with an Anglian adventurer called Octha and crept home again, heavy with

child, when her man went over the sea to join his father in
Britannia. Eadguth's sons had died in battle, and his daughter
had been the apple of her father's eye.

"Or is it you who are the doom-bringer?" The king's gaze
sharpened. "Doom to your mother in child-bed, and now the
doom of my land?"

Oesc edged carefully away. He knew Eadguth's black
moods too well. When he was smaller he had tried to say he
was sorry, though he did not know what for, and only been
beaten harder. He looked like his father, said the women.
Perhaps that was why. But the old man, he could see, was
too weary to strike him now.

Byrhtwold glanced from his king to the boy, pity in his
eyes, and gestured toward the door. The old warrior would
never criticize his lord, but he had showed Oesc what kindness he could. Nodding his thanks, the boy reached the shadows behind the row of pillars and slipped down the aisle
between them and the bed boxes until he reached the door.

His grandfather, king of the Myrgings and lord of their
land, was the supreme power in his small world, but Eadguth
had ever been a chancy protector. Still, he was not the only
power. Oesc slipped through the door, straining to hold it
against the wind, seeking the one person by whom he had
never been betrayed.

Before he had gone three steps he was soaked to the skin.
The storm was driving down from the north, cold as the seas
from which it came, lashing the land with rain. With each
gust the big oak tree beyond the palisade thrashed wildly;
the ground was littered with leaves and branches. Bent nearly
double, Oesc splashed through the puddles, shielding his
eyes with his arm. Even so, the wind slammed him against
the weaving shed and sent him sprawling beside the store-
house before he came under the lee of the log palisade and
crept along it to his goal.

Hæthwæge's hut was partially sheltered by the wall; the
horse's skull on the post before the doorway rattled in the
wind, and the raven feathers tied beneath it flapped wetly,
but here Oesc could stand upright. He took a deep breath
and wiped his eyes before knocking at her door. The moments seemed long before there was an answer. Surely, he

thought, on such a day she would stay indoors, although the wise-folk were not like other men, and if her magic required it, even a woman who was a wicce might brave the storm.

The weight of the spindle drew out the thread, spiraling ever round and round like the turning of the seasons, the lives of humankind. Half-tranced by the motion, Hæthwæge did not at first distinguish the knocking from the sound of the storm. It was the flare of emotion that got her attention, rather than the sound. In another moment she sensed a pain more of the mind than the body, and recognized, as one identifies the pungence of bruised pine needles on the wind, that Oesc was waiting there. She twisted the thread through the notch in the shaft of the spindle, and before the knocking could come again, opened the door.

As the boy started to ease around it, the wind gave him a sudden push that propelled him the rest of the way inside. He fell to his knees, blinking at the darkness.

"Child, you are wet through! Take off your shoes—you are already making a puddle on the floor."

The words were harsh, but the tone was not. Hæthwæge had been Oesc's nurse when he was little, and knew that he was used to her scoldings.

The fire flared in the draft, showing her a boy whose hands and feet seemed too big for his thin frame, his fair hair plastered dark and flat by the rain. She took up a cloak and wrapped it around him. He sank down on the three-legged stool beside the fire, nose wrinkling at the smell of wet wool as its heat began to absorb the moisture from his clothes.

Hæthwæge took up her spindle again and began, humming softly and watching him from the corners of her long eyes, to spin. Oesc eyed her curiously, knowing that a wicce's spinning was sometimes more than yarn.

"It is black wool and white," Hæthwæge answered his unvoiced question, "carded together. Opposites entwined balance the magic."

"What do you use it for?"

"For healing, mostly. I can use this yarn to take a sick man's measure and seal it with a drop of his blood. Then I bring it home and sing over it, and the magic works as well to heal as if the man were here."

To heal, or, of course, to harm. . . . Those hanks of yarn measured trust as well. In the dozen years she had lived with the Myrgings, Hæthwæge had treated almost everyone in the king's household. She glanced at the boxes and sacks crammed into the space above the boxbed and around the room, trying to remember how many twists of grey yarn she had stored there.

"Can you use the measure to change my grandfather's mood?" Oesc said suddenly.

The twirling spindle stilled. "Has he beaten you again?"

Oesc shook his head. "I almost wish he had. He talks like one doom-fated, and blames it on me. Is it true, Hæthwæge? Is that why my father never came back for me?"

For a moment she considered him. She had known that one day he would ask her this question, and understood as well how careful she must be in her reply, so as not to alter the twinings of wyrd and will.

"Doom-fated you are, and so is Eadguth, and so is every man, all the more when they are god-descended, the children of kings. Eadguth traces his line to Ing the son of Mannus, but your father's family comes of Woden himself. When you were born, I cast the runes, and told your grandfather that he must lift you in his arms and give you a name." She fed out more yarn from the distaff and set the spindle to turning once again.

Oesc nodded. No doubt he had heard the maids gossiping when they thought he could not hear. Until the head of the family accepted the child, it had no legal existence. Her throat ached with pity for the boy whom she had taken as an infant from his dying mother's side, sensing his potential, and impelled by her god. She could not leave it there.

"I told him that you were the hope of his house, that if he gave you to the wolves, it was not Octha's, but his own line that would fail. And yet I do not see you sitting in Eadguth's high seat here. You will have a kingdom, but it lies elsewhere. The rune that goes before you is Sigel, the sun-road that leads to victory."

"Does my father know?" Oesc asked sullenly.

"A message was sent, but even I cannot tell if it ever found him. He has been fighting in Britannia. Perhaps he felt you would be safer here. And remember, the wandering shope who sang at last year's Yule feast told us that Uthir the British king had taken him prisoner."

"Perhaps he's dead . . ." muttered the boy.

Hæthwæge shook her head. "I have *seen* the two of you together. Your time will come."

Oesc sighed and let the blanket slip from his shoulders. His damp clothes were beginning to steam in the heat of the fire.

"Well, if it's not my fault, why does the king lay the blame on me?"

"Do not judge him too harshly. He is an old man. Since his own grandfather was slain by Offa of Angeln on the banks of the Fifeldor things have gone badly for the Myrgings. Now he sees his land being eaten away by flood and storm. When he goes to his fathers, the shopes will not sing that the harvests were good in his reign, and no one will lay offerings at his grave. Of all dooms, that one weighs hardest on a king."

As Hæthwæge played out more wool the thread broke suddenly, sending the spindle rolling across the floor toward the rune-carved spear that leaned against the wall, its head shrouded in a piece of cloth.

Hah, Old Man! she thought, *Has the time come for you to take a hand?* For a moment it seemed to her that a faint radiance played about the spear. A dozen years ago it had been entrusted to her, at the same time as her visions had instructed her to take service with the Myrging king.

Oesc bent to retrieve the spindle, his troubled gaze meeting her own, and carefully set it beside her stool.

"My grandfather hates me, and my father doesn't even know my name," he said bitterly. "Who will protect me?"

Hæthwæge twitched, feeling the first brush of power against her mind, subtle as the draught that stirred the fire.

"Look to the father of your fathers," she answered, her own voice sounding strange in her ears. Sight darkened as more words came to her. "Not the god of the land, but the one who hunts on the storm. He is coming—do you hear him?" She pointed northward, head cocked, listening.

The fire hissed, and above that came the sound of the rising wind, gusting through the branches of the trees beyond the palisade with a sound like surf on some distant shore.

And beyond that . . . deep as her own heartbeat, the drumming of hooves.

Oesc's voice came to her as if from a great distance. "I don't understand—"

"Come—" The wicce rose from her stool. Without needing to think about it, she took the spear from its corner and started toward the door.

She could sense the boy's confusion, but to her spirit the hoofbeats were growing ever closer. If the boy's presence had been a scent on the breeze, what was coming now was the wind itself, a storm of terror and delight that could whirl consciousness itself away.

Hæthwæge pulled open the door. Wind swirled around her, insistent as a lover, plucking the pins from her hair. She felt the spearshaft vibrate in her hand and laughed.

I am coming, I am coming, my lord and my love. . . .

Laughing, she walked into the storm to meet the god, in that moment scarcely caring if the boy followed her.

Outside, dusk was falling fast. Oesc splashed through the puddles to catch up with Hæthwæge, raising his arm to shield his eyes from the driving rain. It came in flurries, as if the storm clouds were being broken up by the force of the wind. Head high, her hair streaming out behind her and with every moment growing darker in the rain, the wicce strode across the yard to the eastern gate. Oesc knew her as a woman just past middle life, her shoulders rounded and her body thickened by the years. But now she looked taller, and young, and by that he understood she was already in trance.

Below the mound that raised the village above the floods stretched a level land of wood and marsh and field, dotted and channeled by pond and stream. To the west, a little light shafted below the scudding clouds, touching the Law-Oak and the Field of Assembly where the tribal moots were held with a sickly yellow glow. In the distance he caught the pewter gleam of the sea. That last light gleamed on water that was closer as well, for from here he could see that the slow curve of the river had become a crescent grin of silver water that with every moment nibbled away more of the sodden fields. Monster-gate, they called it, but now it was

not the etins who lived in the North Sea but the waters themselves that were devouring the land.

Beyond the palisade that sheltered the workshops and the
king's hall, the long-houses of the villagers clustered closely
along the slope. Oesc saw Hæthwæge disappearing between
the last two and hurried to follow her. To the east stretched
the home pasture, but on the west side, the marshes came
nearly to the base of the mound. A narrow causeway, in this
season half underwater, led through it. Picking his way carefully, Oesc followed the wisewoman. He could guess where
she was heading now. In the heart of the boglands lay the
dark pool where the Myrgings made their offerings under the
staring eyes of the carven gods. Except at the time of sacrifice, most folk avoided it, but Oesc had gone there once or
twice with Hæthwæge when she was gathering herbs.

Though the rain had diminished, by the time he caught up
with the wicce, water from swinging branches had drenched
him as thoroughly as the storm. Together they pushed
through the screen of alder and willow that edged the pool,
and at that moment the sun set and the clouds closed in once
more, as if the mists of Nibhel had overwhelmed the world.

The wind stilled. Oesc shivered and drew closer to
Hæthwæge. Reason told him that the horse whose hide and
head were suspended on a framework of poles above the
water was quite dead, but the water had risen, and it seemed
now to be standing in the pool.

"What is happening?" Instinctively he dropped his voice
to a whisper.

She turned, and this time she saw him, though her pupils
were still dilated so that her eyes seemed to open on darkness.

"Wait." A tremor ran through her body. "Soon, he comes."
With trembling fingers she unwound the cloth from about
the head of the spear. The smoky stone glimmered in the
shadows as if it shone with its own light.

Faint with distance, he heard a long horn-call. The raven
feathers tied to the shaft fluttered in a sudden wind. Then
came the hoofbeats. Men were riding on the wooden causeway that led through the marshes, he thought, but the sound
grew rapidly louder. No horse could gallop safely on the
rain-slick logs, nor could they cross other than in single file.

What he heard now was the sound of many horses—or was it thunder? Was that the shrieking of the wind or the bitter answer of many horns?

He could not tell, but the sound sent a chill deep into his body. He crouched at Hæthwæge's feet, wishing he could burrow into the earth for protection. The animal heads spiked upon the offering stakes swayed frantically, and the horsehide heaved above the ruffled waters, straining toward the attenuated images of the gods.

In the next moment the tumult he had heard approaching was upon them. The last of the light had gone; he could make out only a confusion of shadows. Was it his imagination that shaped them into skeletal horses and wild riders who brandished spears or swords, or worse still, into wælcyriges, warhags riding slavering wolves with serpents for reins. He bit back a cry as a gust of wind sent the horsehide flapping into the air to join them.

He cowered beneath their keening until Hæthwæge's hand on his shoulder made him look up again. The horrors had passed. The shapes that swept above him now, limned in their own light, were of a nobler kind.

"Behold, son of Octha, your fathers of old—Wihtgils, Witta, Wehta, and their sires before them. . . ."

Shaking, Oesc got to his feet and raised his arm in salute. The names rolled on, but he could not hear them. All his being was focused on those luminous shadows, grim or kindly, that looked on him with a considering gaze as if deciding whether he was worthy to continue their line.

And then, though all around them the trees still bowed to the storm, the air above the pool grew heavy with a sense of presence. Oesc remained standing, but he shut his eyes tightly. Whatever was coming now was something he was not yet ready to see. But he could not keep from hearing, though he never knew, then or thereafter, if the words had come to his mind or his ears.

"*So this is the boy—*" a deep voice seemed to say.

"Since his birth I have warded him," Hæthwæge answered. "When will the future I foretold for him come to be?"

"*That is Verdandi's business. But when that time comes, he will have to choose . . .*"

"What are his choices?"

"To stay here and live long in a dying land, or to risk all across the water. . . ."

"But the runes spoke of victory—" the wicce began. That other voice interrupted her.

"To endure the turning of the seasons is as much a victory as death in battle. The one is the path of Ingvi, but the other is mine. If he chooses Me his name shall be remembered in a new land, and he shall sire kings."

"Is that your will, lord?" Now it was Hæthwæge's voice that trembled.

"I will what shall be, but it is not for me to choose how it shall come to pass—that lies with the boy, and with you."

Oesc had the abrupt sense of being the focus of attention, like a mouse trapped between a wolf's paws. He scrunched his eyes shut even more tightly. For a moment more he was held, then the pressure was released with a hint of laughter.

"I do not force you," came that whisper from within, *"but the Norns will force the choice upon you, my son, and soon."*

"I have chosen you, High One, since I was young—" Hæthwæge said then.

"It is so, nor have I ever been far away."

If there was more, it was not meant for Oesc's ears. He sank down at the woman's feet, and only afterward, when the god and those he led had passed, did he realize that his face was wet, not with rain, but with tears.

The wood seemed very silent. Oesc stood up, wiping his eyes. Then he stiffened, hearing once more the sounds of hoofbeats and horns.

But this was no spectral hunt—he could tell the difference now. Those were mortal horses whose hoofbeats he heard ringing on the wet logs, and mortal lungs behind those plaintive horns.

"There are riders, Hæthwæge! Riders on the causeway!" he exclaimed. "Hurry, we must get back to the hall."

She nodded, shrouding the spearhead once more, and he saw her face still luminous with memory. But as she turned her awareness back to the human world the lines deepened in her skin and she became merely mortal once more.

"So, it has begun. . . ."

* * *

Oesc peered through the door to the great hall, which only this morning had seemed so huge and empty. Now it was filled with men clad in well-worn war-gear and battered finery, with a liberal splashing of mud over all. The folk who served the hall were bustling around them, taking wet cloaks away and bringing beakers of heated ale.

"May Freo bring you blessings," said their leader, accepting a horn of mead from Æbbe, the king's widowed sister, who had ruled his household as long as Oesc could remember. He must have been handsome once, thought the boy, but now one eyelid drooped and the left side of his face was stiffened by a long scar.

"But where is your neice, Æbbe? Should it not be she who gives the welcome?"

"There is no other Lady in this hall," said the woman, taking a step backward. "And what unholy wight has taught you my name?"

The stranger frowned. "Did Hildeguth remarry, then? I suppose she thought I was dead—I've thought I was dead a few times myself, these past years!" His hand moved to touch his scar. "Have I changed so much, Æbbe, that even you don't know me?"

"It is my daughter who is dead," came a harsh voice from the far end of the hall, "killed by the seed you planted in her belly, and if you had not already claimed guest-right I would drive you from my door!" Leaning on his staff, Eadguth limped forward to his high seat and took his place there.

Oesc stared from one to the other, aware of every heartbeat that shook his chest, understanding without quite believing who the newcomer must be.

Octha, son of Hengest . . . his father.

Octha straightened, the muscles of his face stiffening into a battle-mask. "And the child?" he asked in a still voice. "Did it die too?"

"Shall I tell you it died in the womb?" Eadguth spat, "or that I set it out upon the heath for the wolves?"

"You shall tell him the truth, old man," said Hæthwæge, gripping Oesc by the shoulder and pushing him before her into the light of the fire. "Sore though it grieved you, you have reared up his son!"

For a moment longer the warrior's glance clashed with that

of the king. Then Octha turned, his face changing as he looked at the boy.

"Come here—"

With feet that did not seem his own Oesc stepped forward. Octha knelt and gripped the boy's face between callused hands. After a moment he swallowed.

"You have your mother's eyes . . ."

Oesc nodded. Hæthwæge had told him so.

"But I see Hengest in your brow . . . What do they call you?"

"I am Oesc, son of Octha—" His voice wavered only a little.

"My son!"

Powerful arms closed around him; Oesc smelled horse, and wet wool, and the strong scent of the man. It was very strange. Not so long ago, Woden had also called him son— from being fatherless he seemed suddenly over-supplied with kin. He took a deep breath as Octha let him go.

"I am going back to Britannia, where the cows grow fat in green pastures and apples hang heavy on the bough. Will you come with me?"

Soon, Woden had told him, he would have to choose. Oesc looked into his father's storm-grey eyes, but when he spoke, he knew he was answering the god.

"Yes, father, I will come."

Since Octha's arrival three days had passed. The storm had moved on, but on the Field of Assembly scattered pools mirrored the blue sky. Only a few rags of cloud still clung to the southeastern heavens. As the people gathered, the green grass was being trampled to a muddy brown. But perhaps it would not matter, thought Oesc as he watched them from his place at his father's side. If the moot voted to follow Octha over the sea, the cattle would be slaughtered or sold and there would be no need for pastureland.

The thought awakened an anxious flutter in his belly. He knew there were other lands, for he had heard the shopes and gleemen sing of them, but Eadguth's hall was the center of his world. Most of the Myrgings had gathered, women and children forming a larger ring around the chieftains and heads of families. He looked around him for Hæthwæge, then remembered that the wicce had told him she had no need to watch. She had already seen this wyrd when she cast the runes.

Why did she not inform Eadguth, then, and save us all the trouble of deciding? he wondered, but as the wisewoman had often told him, you might predict the sun's rising, but you had to wait for it to happen just the same.

A bench had been placed for the king beneath the oak tree. His *witan,* the tribal elders, sat around him. Sunlight glowing through the young leaves dappled his white hair. Eadguth Gamol, they called him, Eadguth the Old, for of all the kings of the north, only Healfdene of Sillende had reigned longer.

His other grandfather, Hengest, was old too, thought Oesc. But he ruled a confederation of war-bands, like the sea-kings of Frisia. Eadguth was bred and bound through many fathers to his kingship and his land.

A murmur ran through the crowd as Geflaf, leader of the king's sword-thanes, stepped forward. He raised a great silver-mounted horn to his lips and blew, and as its echoes faded, the people also became still.

"Hear, ye chieftains and people of the Myrgings here assembled. A stranger, Octha son of Hengest, has come among us. The witan has called you to hear and consider his words."

"He is an Anglian of royal kin, and our enemy!" cried the chieftain of one of the older Myrging clans.

"He is not of the kin of Offa the king-slayer, but a lesser line, and has never borne arms against us," came the reply.

"Our kin serve in his father's war-band," said one of the Jutes who had settled among the Myrgings, taking up farmsteads left vacant after the Anglian wars. "Let us hear what he has to say."

For a little longer the clamor continued, but eventually it became clear that the mood of the moot was in Octha's favor.

Another murmur arose as he stepped forward, Oesc at his side. By now, of course, everyone had heard the rumors that the mysterious father of their Lady's son had reappeared. Oesc hung back as he realized that they were staring at him as well, but Octha's grip was firm.

He is using me to show them he is not an enemy, the boy realized suddenly, and allowed himself to be pulled along.

For most of his short life he had been at best an embarrassment to his mother's kin; to stand forth before the people as one with a right to honor seemed very strange. For the first time, it came to him that he too might one day be a king.

"Men of the Myrgings!" cried Octha, "and all of you—be you Jute or Saxon or Frank, who by marriage or alliance have become part of this tribe. I come here as your ally, for it was a princess of your people who gave me my son!"

Someone started a cheer, and Oesc felt the hot color rise in his cheeks.

"Then why have you waited till now to claim him?" came another voice.

"There's many a man who goes off to war childless and returns to learn he has an heir. For ten winters I have battled in Britannia; I have slain many princes of their people, and cut down those who thought themselves the heirs of Rome. At first we fought for treasure, but now we fight for land. The British have little strength to resist us—their king is a sick man, and he has no son. The land lies undefended, ripe for the taking. To hold that earth men must till it, and so I come to you.

"Follow me to Britannia—bring your wives and your children. Bring your axes and your ploughs."

"Why should we abandon the hearths of our mothers and the howes where our fathers lie?" came the cry.

"Because this land is drowning!" responded Octha. "Look around you—the fields are blighted by bad weather and your cattle are dying. Each year more of your shores are eaten by the sea. In Britannia there are wide fields, fruitful and flourishing—good harvests of oat crops and broad barley-crops, white fields of wheat-crops and all that grows in Middle Earth."

"But they are not *our* fields. Will they bear for us if we do not know the names of the wights that dwell there?"

"Those fields have borne fruit for all the tribes the Romans settled in that land," said Octha. "Warriors from Iberia and Sarmatia and Gallia and other lands who took up farming after their time in the legions was done. Our cousins the Franks get good crops from the lands they have won in Gallia. Till the fields and make the offerings, and when your time comes, lay your bones in the soil. By blood and toil shall we claim Britannia and make it our own."

"We will go!" said one of the Jutish chieftains, a man called Hæsta. "There are men of my blood already in Hengest's war-band. They have said that Cantuware is a land of good soil and good grazing, where the cows give milk thrice a day at this time of year."

"And it breeds good fighters—" an older man spoke up, lifting an arm scarred and twisted by an old wound. "In my youth I too have been to Britannia, but all I got there was steel. It is well enough for warriors to take such chances, but I will not risk my family in a land whose native folk are awakening at last, determined to get back their own."

"Better to die by steel than starvation!" exclaimed another, and suddenly everyone was arguing.

"What says Eadguth?" someone cried at last. "What is the word of the Myrging king?"

Slowly, silence fell. When it was quite still, the thrall Cubba, who was even older than the king, assisted Eadguth to unfold his gaunt frame from the chair. The king came forward, leaning on his staff. For a few moments he looked around him, and those who had cried the loudest for emigration found it hard to meet his eyes.

"The gods have given me long life. For more than forty winters I have been your king. . . ." His voice did not seem loud, but it carried.

"In those years I have seen many things. I have seen five summers when the rains were so scant that the river sank down till its banks gaped like toothless jaws. That time ended. So will this. I have seen blizzards that heaped snow halfway up the walls and held us prisoner from one moon to the next. That time ended—this will too. And I have seen harvests so plentiful we had not the barns to store it all. And those times also came to an end. You cry out now like children who cannot go out to play because of the rain. And I say to you, neither will this time last."

He spoke slowly, a kindly grandfather chiding willful boys, and here and there a man would hang his head with a shamefaced grin.

"A man's mood changes, sometimes happy and sometimes sorrowful. Our holy mother earth has also her moods and changes. Will you desert her because now she is weeping?

For men who have been uprooted from their homelands perhaps it is true that one land is as good as the next. But the Myrgings have been here since Mannus himself walked the earth. We are a free land and a free people, bound only to this soil."

Carefully, Eadguth bent and grasped a handful of muddy earth. He held it high, and the water squeezed out between his fingers and ran like brown blood down his hand.

My mother's bones lie in this earth, thought Oesc. *If I leave here, I will have lost her entirely.* But his father still stood beside him, and his bones were clad in warm and living flesh.

"Will you leave this holy earth, blessed by the blood of your fathers, for an alien land? Perhaps, as Octha says, in time it will accept you. But I say this—it will not be in your time, nor in that of your children. Stay, men of the Myrgings and those whom we have welcomed here. Stay, and defend the land that has nourished you."

Some of the men knelt in reverence and set their hands on the wet grass, but others were still standing, brows bent in thought.

Geflaf stepped forward once more. "The Myrging-king has spoken. Go now, carls and eorls, free men of our nation. Speak together, and when the sun is sinking toward the sea, return and say what your decision will be."

He turned away, and the men drew into knots and clusters as they began their debate.

"What now?" asked Octha, watching King Eadguth make his way slowly back toward the hall.

"Now we wait," answered Geflaf. He also was watching his king, and Oesc saw sorrow in his gaze.

That day seemed very long to Oesc, longer even than the day before the Midsummer festival. He tried to fill it by showing his father where Hildeguth was buried, and the best place to catch fish below the whirlpool, and even the god-images in the sacred bog, but he could tell that Octha's attention was elsewhere. And as the sun drove her wain across the fields of the sky his distraction grew, until the time came to turn their steps back toward the great oak tree.

Away to the west the sky was glowing in shades of amber

and rose. Broad bands of light rayed out from the setting sun as if showing the way to Britannia. But a great peace lay on the Myrging lands. Even the sea lay still, its waters a lucent blue, and each leaf and blade of grass seemed to have caught the sunset's gold. Did it seem so fair, wondered Oesc, because he might soon be leaving it? Then he looked again and thought, *But perhaps we will not be going. It is too beautiful. On such an evening, no one could make the choice to go.*

Once more King Eadguth came forth and sat in his carven chair, gazing at his people with hooded eyes. Once more the people gathered around the great tree.

"Men of the Myrgings," said Geflaf when they were quiet. "The sun has finished her course and it is time to choose our own. Are you ready to decide?"

"Aye," came the response from many voices.

"Then let the leaders of your clans and families stand forth and say your will."

Hæsta was first to step out from the crowd.

"I speak for the Jutes who dwell along the Fifeldor. For a generation we have guarded your northern border. We do not fear fighting. But the fields will not bear for us. We vote to seek the new lands across the sea."

There was a murmur at that, for the Jutes made up a sizable portion of their fighting men. A Myrging thane came forward next, and said that he would stay by his king. One by one others followed and spoke the will of their clans. And though there were some who swore to stay in the Myrging homeland, it became clear that those who had been convinced by Octha's words were in the majority.

"I would stay, but I see the choice being made for me," said one farmer, whose rich fields lay inland, away from the sea. "We cannot stop those who decide to leave us, and how can we defend ourselves against our enemies if only a tithe remain?"

A mutter of agreement swept through the people, and after that most of the men who stepped forward said that they would follow Octha. Now, only a few chieftains from the oldest families spoke for staying, and Eadguth's sworn sword-thanes, who said that while he lived, they would remain by their king.

Geflaf turned to his lord with troubled gaze.

"My king, the will of the moot is clear. Will you not change your mind and agree to lead us to the new land?"

Eadguth rose from his chair and set his hand against the rough bark of the great tree.

"Will you uproot this oak and carry it over the sea?" His voice grated painfully. "It is too old, too deeply rooted, and so am I. Go if you will—I cannot prevent you. I will remain with my land."

Oesc looked at his grandfather and felt a tremor beneath his heart as if someone had struck him there. *He looks like a dead man.* Suddenly he wanted to run to the old man as he had when he was little, before he understood why Eadguth hated him. But his father's hand was on his shoulder, and he did not move.

Once more Eadguth's dark gaze passed over his people, then he turned and started back toward his hall. His house-thanes fell in behind him, but their faces were grim.

But those who had voted to go with Octha pressed around him, clamoring with questions about the new land.

Oesc woke from a nightmare, fighting for breath. The bed-clothes were strangling him—he fought free and lay gasping. In the hall, his own harsh breaths were the only sound, but outside he could hear birdsong. It must be dawn, he thought, blinking. Through the parted curtains of his bed-closet he glimpsed a faint glow from the long hearth and beyond it a colder light. He pulled back the curtains and looked out into the hall.

Along the hearth he could see the humped shapes of sleeping men. But beyond them, the little side door stood open. What clumsy thrall, he wondered, had left it so? Æbbe, who always rose early to supervise the thralls as they got break-fast, would have a thing or two to say about that when she knew.

But now he was curious. Who had gone out so early? He pulled his tunic over his head and tied on his shoes, and then, because the air was brisk, took his cloak from its peg as well. Silently he made his way between the sleeping men and sought the door.

Beyond the threshold the muddy ground showed many footprints, dusted by a light frost that was already melting in the growing light. But across that sparkling veil two sets of tracks showed clearly, and the larger prints were punctuated by the round mark of a staff. For a long moment Oesc stared, a cold feeling growing in his belly.

"Close the door, boy," came Æbbe's voice behind him. "You are letting in the cold."

"Æbbe—" he said, turning, "why has the king gone out so early?"

"What do you mean, child? Old men sleep late—he is in his bed still!"

"Look, are not those his footprints? Where did he go?"

For a moment she stared over his shoulder at the marked ground, and then, without a word, hurried back into the hall. Oesc sank down on a bench, shivering, but it was not from the cold. In a few moments the old woman returned with Byrhtwold and Æthelhere behind her. When they started out across the yard, Oesc followed.

The trail led toward Hæthwæge's hut, and when they picked it up again, there were three sets of footprints, one of them a woman's. Near the side gate they lost the trace, but the young warrior who guarded it, confronted with his king's senior thanes, confessed that his lord had passed through just as the first pallor that precedes the dawn was brightening the sky. The thrall Cubba was with him, and the wisewoman.

"I thought they were going out to make some offering to the gods. He told me to keep silence and stay at my post," said the warrior, "but my shift is almost over, and surely I do not break my oath to tell *you*. . . ."

"No doubt that is it," said Æbbe with a sigh. "I will go back to the kitchen—the king will be wanting his breakfast when he returns."

"I will go out to meet him," said Æthelhere. "It is not right for the lord of the Myrgings to go about without an escort."

Byrhtwold nodded, and when they passed through the gate, Oesc followed the two thanes down the hill.

Here and there a scar upon the frosted grass marked the trail. It led toward the Law Oak. As they came around the edge of the woods they stopped short, staring, for an untimely fruit was dangling from the oak tree's limbs.

It was King Eadguth's body that was hanging there. Blood from a rent beneath his breast had stained his tunic, and the thrall Cubba lay below him, a knife in his hand and blood from his slashed throat soaking the ground. *"An ætheling can look on anything, even his doom,"* Eadguth had once told him, but after Oesc had taken one look at his grandfather's purpled face and staring eyes, he fixed his gaze firmly upon the ground.

"Ah, my dear lord," said Æthelhere, shaking his head. "This is ill done, to go before me with only this thrall to escort you. Still I think your start is not so great I cannot overtake you."

"Why did he do this?" asked Byrhtwold. "We would have stood by him to his life's end."

"And so you have done—" came another voice. They turned, and saw that Hæthwæge was standing there, leaning on a staff whose top was swathed in a blue cloth. "Do you not understand? He had no son to follow him, and those who vowed to stay here are too few to defend the land. By his death Eadguth has freed them from their oaths and made offering to Woden for their protection. This was a noble sacrifice."

"By the knife of a thrall?" asked Byrhtwold.

Hæthwæge shook her head. "Cubba took his own life, but Eadguth's blood was shed by Woden's own spear." She lifted her staff, and Oesc's skin pebbled as he recognized the rune-carved shaft beneath the wrappings.

"This is the last and greatest act of a king," said Æthelhere, "to give his breath to the god and his blood to the land that his people may live."

ii

Verulamium

A.D. 473

A dead horse lay stiff beside the road. The ravens, busy at their feasting, waited until the approaching riders were upon them before fluttering aside, cawing their mockery. Beyond them the Roman road ran straight southward, where a thin haze of smoke stained the pale morning sky.

"We move from before your feet," they seemed to say, *"but one day you will be our meat!"*

Oesc suppressed a shiver; then his mare, scenting the carrion, tossed her head, and the boy reined her sharply in. His grandfather in the old country had not had the wealth to give him a pony, and in any case it was not the tradition of his people to fight mounted. But Britannia was a large island, and in the three years since Octha had brought him across the sea it seemed to Oesc they had ridden over most of the eastern half that the Angles and the Saxons and the Jutes and tag ends of other tribes were making their own. Through necessity, he had become an adequate horseman. He lifted his chin and straightened his shoulders in unconscious imitation of his father, sitting his big grey easily at the head of the column.

Most of the Myrgings had been settled in Cantuware, along with the Jutes and Frisians and others who had answered Hengest's call. But the best of the warriors had left the rich fields of the south coast, settled for a generation already by men of the tribes, to ride north with Octha, where there were new and perhaps even richer lands to be won.

Hengest had wanted the boy to stay with him in Cantuware, but there had been no question, really, what Oesc would choose. He had spent most of his short life mewed up with one grandfather, and the other was past eighty, so ancient that many assumed he must be dead by now. No boy could resist the chance to ride with the men and share their glory. It was only sometimes in the night that he regretted the well-built hall and the peaceful fields of his homeland, and the gulls soaring over a sea that glittered with a golden treasure no Roman hoard could match in the light of the setting sun.

Oesc wondered now if he had made the right decision. Men of the German tongue held half the south and the fenlands on the eastern shore, and three years of campaigning had made the beginnings of an Anglian realm south of Eboracum. Only the valley of the Tamesis still separated the chEnglish lands. But Leudonus of Alba, having married the British king's daughter, had thrown all his strength into the reconquest of the north, and six days since, had brought the Saxons to battle on the banks of the Abus, and won.

Oesc kicked the mare's stout sides and drew up beside Colgrin, an Anglian who with the Jutish Baldulf was second only to his father in the band.

"Have the scouts come in? Is Leudonus following?" He glanced back, where the Saxon column, dissolving into its own dust, seemed to extend all the way back to Eboracum. Hæthwæge was back there somewhere, in the wagons with the wounded. Beyond them storm-clouds hung heavy in the sky.

Colgrin shook his head, the grey hair hacked short where they had bandaged a slash from a British sword. "Nay, lad, he will not catch us—we gave him too sound a savaging."

"But he is following . . ." Oesc repeated.

"Not yet . . ." the older man admitted. "There's no need to fret. By the time his men can march, we'll be safe behind Verulamium's stout walls."

"How long till we get there?"

Colgrin pointed to a blue smudge that lay across the road on the horizon. "Verulamium lies just beyond those hills."

Oesc squinted ahead, and then, as a breath of cool air touched his cheek, looked back again. The curdled clouds were rolling after them, a visible expression of Leudonus' wrath. If the storm hit before they reached shelter the wounded would suffer. He looked at his father's straight back, frowning.

Colgrin, following his glance, sighed. "Not even the greatest of leaders can make the best decision always. And sometimes all choices are flawed. Octha thinks like a warrior, and takes a warrior's chances. Woden loves a brave man, and will give him victory."

"I know. . . ." Oesc nodded, but for the first time it occurred to him to wonder in what way the choices of a warleader might differ from those of a king. The wind blew once more, ruffling his pale hair, and with it came the first spatterings of rain.

The gates of Verulamium were open. Oesc, watching from the walkway atop the old Roman wall, gazed past the tower of the gatehouse to the British army encamped outside. But it was not Leudonus and his blood-stained veterans who were beseiging them. The forces outside the gate—dark-haired Romans in their grandfathers' breastplates or bright-haired British with checkered mantles over their mail, were men of the south and west, under the command of their dying king.

Octha's face had darkened when he heard that Uthir had come against him. He remembered his captivity in the Tower. And then he had told them to unbar and open the great gates that guarded the western route into the town.

"Why not just send Uthir an invitation to charge through?" Baldulf had exclaimed when Octha gave the order.

"That is what I am doing," answered Octha, grinning through his mustaches. "Or did you fancy spending the winter starving behind these walls? Inside the town they will not be able to use their horses, and we can overwhelm them."

"If they come—" said Colgrin.

"If they do not, it will not matter whether the gates are open or closed!"

And Oesc had heard the sharp silence, and then Colgrin's explosive laugh. But the British army, nestled in tent and brush shelter around the city, neither attacked nor lifted the seige.

As he had every day since the British came, Oesc watched them from the guard tower, curious, after all the stories he had heard, about this enemy. Sometimes the wind carried the swift, lilting gabble of the British speech, or the more sonorous cadences of Latin, but mostly he learned by watching. He had become accustomed to the diversity of the Saxon forces, composed of men from all the tribes of the north. But these Britons were more varied still, and in their faces he saw the mosaic, in miniature, that was the Empire.

To the Saxons, they were an accustomed and worthy enemy, but from time to time Oesc, seeing the British king being carried through the camp, would remember how his other grandfather had clung to his land, and feel ashamed. But when he saw his father again the feeling passed. Octha, his skin ripened to bronze by the weather and his body honed to muscle and sinew by the summer's campaigning, was now at the height of his powers, as great a hero as Sigfrid Fafnarsbane, of whom the shopes liked to sing.

Eadguth had been a landking, bound, blood and bone, to his native soil. Octha son of Hengest was a conqueror.

That night the Saxon chieftains met in the dining room, its walls painted in red ochre edged by a design of twining vines, of the house where once Catraut, the British prince who had been the city's chief magistrate, had entertained his peers. Its owner was fled long since—Oesc, bringing in more ale, wondered if he might be even now in Uthir's camp, gazing longingly toward the walls that hid his home. Most of the notable men of the town had escaped, or been killed when the Saxons marched in. But Octha had the authority to forbid looting, and if the common people had not accepted the warriors billeted among them with gladness, neither did they show active hostility.

"How long will we stay cooped up here?" asked one of

the younger chieftains. "If we wait too long, Leudonus will come to his good-father's aid!"

"If he does so, I will close the gates—" The golden torque around Octha's neck glinted as he laughed. "But I do not think the British will maintain the seige so long."

"It is true. The British king is a sick man," said Baldulf thoughtfully. "And a military camp is no good place for healing."

"And unless you count Leudonus, he has no heir," said one of the others. "When Uthir dies, the British will be easy prey."

"Easy prey?" exclaimed Colgrin. "Is that the word of a warrior? The weaker Uthir becomes, the less honor there will be in defeating him. I say we should attack them now . . ."

But Octha was looking at the doorway, where Hæthwæge had appeared. "I called her—" He answered the question in the chieftains' eyes. "In the old days, the priestesses always went with the warriors. Hæthwæge is alone, but she was trained by the Walkyriun. Sit—" he gestured toward one of the benches, and then to his son, "bring her ale."

Hæthwæge accepted a sip from the cream-colored clay cup, but she did not sit down. Oesc's words of greeting stuck in his throat. He had grown too accustomed to her care for him, he thought, and forgotten what she was. Her eyes were wide and lightless, as if she had fared halfway down the road to the Otherworld already. As always when she worked magic, her face seemed simultaneously ancient and young.

"Wise One," Octha said softly, "our enemies surround us. Speak to the spirits and give us good counsel."

"I must have a high place . . ." she whispered.

Octha nodded soberly. "It shall be so—" He gestured to the others. Silent now, they rose, and as they moved down the empty street Oesc followed them.

Hæthwæge stared up at the dark bulk of the gatehouse of Verulamium, stark against the sky, its towers looming to either side of the arched gateway. The night was very still. It was only within that she sensed the slow stirring of power. Somewhere not too far away someone was working magic— perhaps it was the British witega they called Merlin.

They say you are strong to foretell the future, gealdor

crafty. But I too am witege, and tomorrow you shall see that I too can sing battle spells. She moved into the darkness of the doorway, frowning. For a moment her questing spirit had touched something stronger and sharper, like the mind of a god.

The planks of the stairway rang hollow as they climbed, feeling their way along the curving wall, but when they emerged at the top they breathed freely beneath the starry vault of the heavens. To one side glimmered the lamps of the city and on the other the watchfires of their enemy glowed like red eyes in the darkness. A faint breeze stirred men's hair as if the night were breathing.

Hæthwæge sank down upon the bench beneath the parapet and pulled down her veil. One by one, the warriors sat on the cold stone walkway until only Octha remained standing, his speech becoming the chant of ritual.

"Wicce, hear me . . . to this high place I have brought thee. From here thou mayest soar between the worlds."

"This deed I will dare," her own voice came hoarse to her ears, "but the way is long and weary. It is your prayers I carry—let your power carry me. . . ."

Octha nodded, and began to strike the palms of his hands rhythmically against his thighs. The other men followed his example, swaying gently as the soft vibration pulsed in the air.

> *"Wicce, Woruld-Aesce ymbwend,*
> *Wisdom innan thin hyde gewinn.*
> *Wicce . . . Wicce . . ."*

The word, repeated, became part of the soft susuration of flesh on cloth, a whisper of sound that lifted the hair and the spirit and whirled them away to journey around the World-tree to the worlds it contained and gain access to the wisdom they held. *Wicce, to the Word-Ash win . . . Wisdom, shape-strong, find within. . . .*

Hæthwæge took a deep breath, and then another, letting her limbs relax against the parapet. Awareness extended into the stones, all the way down to the foundations of the tower and then back up again. As her consciousness changed she fancied she could feel it swaying, even though there was only a little wind. She focused on the singing, and with each repetition felt the links between body and spirit loosen, until like a boat that has slipped its mooring, she fell inward and away.

Images whirled past her—the tower and the army encamped around it, the undulating bands of field and forest, still under starshine, with the rivers, black and shining, veining the land. Then these too dimmed, and there was only the great plain of Middle Earth, and in its midst the huge column of the Worldtree, its radiant branches brushing the skies.

But the will that carried her drew her downward, diving into darkness beneath one of the three great roots of the Tree. Around and around her spirit spiraled, past mist and shadows, past the roots of great mountains where rushed the icy streams. Through the heat of Muspel's fires she journeyed, and sped by the cool grey mirror that was the Well of Wyrd. And still her way led downward, around, and deeper within, until she saw the great gorge of the worldriver and the last bridge, and beyond it the land where the Dark Lady rules and the apples of the blessed and the wild hemlock grow.

One final gate remained to pass. She dropped into darkness, and for a time beyond time, knew no more.

A long time later, it seemed, she became aware of a quiet voice calling her name. Unwillingly she forced her mind to focus. It was Octha, using the same calm voice with which he commanded his warriors.

"Wise One, say then, what dost thou see?"

At the words, images began to dislimn from the darkness. She struggled to make her lips form an answer.

"A dark plain, and a dark lake, and a black swan swimming . . ." she murmured, her voice sounding thready with distance. "My raven flies before mè, and around me glimmer the pale faces of those who have gone before."

"Our enemies surround us. How shall we bring them to battle?"

In the pause that followed, her breathing came and went like the wind, fluttering the fabric of the veil. The scene before her blurred. There was still water, but in its midst now she could make out an island. From the woods that surrounded it she could hear the yammering of hounds, and in another moment she saw them, leaping up and down on the shore. What were they barking at? She strained to see, and presently became aware that she was speaking once more.

"I see a wolf brought to bay upon an island. The dogs wait on the shore. They will not swim across to meet the wolf's sharp fangs. He gazes around him and sees where the circle is weakest—where the old pack-leader watches—there he will make his fight." She drew a deep breath. "Wilt thou know more?"

"Will the British king die?"

"All men die!" the answer came to her immediately. "And this one is half-dead already."

"And will our sons inherit the land?" Octha added then.

Hæthwæge took a deep breath, releasing the vision, observing the ebb and flow of image until at last there came something she could put into words.

"I see the wolf and the dog running in one pack . . ." more visions came to her ". . . I see the wheat crop and the barley crop growing in one field . . . his seed shall rule men's hearts, but yours will rule the land. . . ."

While they were still chewing on that answer, another voice, that she recognized as Baldulf's, spoke.

"And what about the battle?"

Hæthwæge shivered violently, her awareness battered and reeling beneath the onrush of vision. Ravens were fighting— not the friendly presence that was her own spirit guide, but feathered forms, huge and terrible, whose cries scored the soul.

"I see the Raven of Battle rising, men die when she screams. But Woden sends Hyge and Mynd against her; men battle as the god and the goddess strive. . . ." Her spirit soared with the battling birds.

Then with a suddenness that seared her vision, the scene was split by a Sword of Light. Hæthwæge stiffened, features contorting. For a moment she glimpsed the figure that gripped it in all His glory. "Tir comes, Tir comes! Beware the Sword of War!"

Light and darkness crashed together around her and with it vision and consciousness were swept away.

When she could hear once more, she realized that she was

lying on the cold stone of the walkway, her head resting on Octha's arm.

"Hæthwæge," he said softly, "do you hear me? Come forth from the dark plain and the dark lake. Return to Middle Earth—in Woden's name I summon you! Your raven will show you the way. Come to my calling until you can feel the night air on your skin and the bench beneath you. Come then . . . come. . . ."

With a murmur of soft speech, as if he were gentling a fractious mare, Octha continued to call her. Hæthwæge forced herself to breathe, to reconstruct the image of the dark lake and to send forth the inner call that would bring her raven to her side. She wanted only to float in the friendly darkness, but Octha's voice was insistent, and so, painfully, she moved to the gate, and image by image, summoned the landmarks of the spirit that would show her the way home.

By the time she had recovered control of her limbs and was able to sit up again, her memories were fading.

"What is it?" she asked, looking at the grim faces around her. "What did I say?"

"You called out to Tir, and told us," said Baldulf, "to beware the Sword of War."

For a moment she closed her eyes. "I remember," she said finally, "it blazed in the sun."

"What does it mean?" Octha asked then.

"I give you vision," answered the wisewoman tartly. "It is for you to find the meaning." Then a fragment of memory came to her. "But in the land of the Huns, I have heard, there were once great smiths who forged seven magic swords for the god of war."

"There are no Huns here," said Colgrin.

"Perhaps not. But there are swords. Make an offering to Tir before you fight, and perhaps he will spare you."

"Tir is a god of justice, not mercy," muttered one of the men, but Hæthwæge shook her head and would say no more.

The earth trembled beneath the tread of the warriors as the Saxon army marched out to meet its foe. Their footsteps rang hollow from the great arch of the gate and pigeons fluttered screaming from the cornices. Then five hundred spear butts smote as many shields, and thunder leaped from earth to heaven. Oesc, a helm drawn down to hide his features and a tattered cloak concealing his lack of armor, felt himself become one with the men who were crowding through the gate. The driving rhythm overwhelmed thought and hearing, and with it, the fear that even now his father might somehow discover he had disobeyed and send him back.

Then they were through the gate, and the crush eased as men began to spread out into the wedge formation called the Boar's Head. Faint through the thunder he could hear the blare of British trumpets, then the irregular drumming of hoofbeats blurred the rhythm of spear and shield. In the next moment the British horsemen struck the Saxon line, and the thunder gave way to the clash of steel.

Oesc was lifted off his feet for a moment as the shock of the charge drove the man on his left against him. Then the Saxons steadied, spears bristling outward, and began to drive forward against the foe. Oesc got his breath back just as a horseman in a scarlet cloak crashed through. He made a clumsy sweep out and heard the horse scream. Then another man thrust upward and the rider fell, blood spraying red around him.

The boy stared, but there was no time to worry about his reaction. Another enemy, dismounted, was slashing wildly with a long Roman cavalry spatha; a Saxon fell, then Oesc jabbed and caught the blade with his spear. The impact jarred down the shaft, almost knocking him over, but in the next moment two warriors speared the Briton through the body and he went down.

A figure in Roman armor loomed up before him and he thrust, then stared in horror as his point sank in and the man's face contorted in agony. Oesc jerked the spear free, shuddering. Again and again his swordmaster had told him that in battle there was no time for thinking. He had never explained that no sane man would want to think about what his blade was doing as it tore through flesh and bone.

Then another figure lurched toward him, and without his will he turned, taking the attack on his shield and jabbing back until his foe fell or the tide of battle tore him away, he never knew which, and the next enemy came on.

Some endless time later, a scream from overhead recalled

him to himself. His spear had broken, and the short seax was in his hand. All around him, Saxon warriors were staring upward, their arms faltering as the raven wheeled above them, alternately black and white as the sunlight flared from its wings. He saw the litter in which the British king had been carried to the battlefield, and near it his father, staring upward with a face as anguished as his own.

But the British returned to the attack with courage renewed. "Cathubodva, Cathubodva, Raven of Battle," they cried.

Oesc yelped at the sting as a spear tip sliced across his shoulder and got his shield back up, striving to shut out that dreadful keening cry. The enemy spear struck again and he felt the wood begin to crack, then two shadows flickered past and it seemed to him he heard a deep voice crying—

"Stand fast, son of Woden, and you shall have the victory!"

Wind swirled in the dust of the battlefield; suddenly the air had a bite that tingled through the veins. Now it was his enemy who paused. Oesc glanced up and saw two smaller, darker, ravens, engaging the first one in a deadly aerial dance. *Hyge and Mynd*—he thought. *Hæthwæge has called on the god!*

The British raven screamed her fury, and the two attackers replied, and as those cries clashed in the heavens, to Oesc's blurred vision his opponent was revealed as a monster, the foulest of etin-kin. The burning in his belly erupted in a scream of fury, and casting away both seax and shield, he leaped upon his foe.

It was a Sword of Light, searing through mind and vision, that separated man from monster and mind from madness. When Oesc came to himself he was on his hands and knees, with the iron taste of blood in his mouth and his chest and arms splattered with gore. Guts roiling, he struggled to his feet. All around him those who could still stand were doing likewise. Only near Uthir's litter were men still fighting, but as Oesc stumbled toward it, an arc of brightness seared his vision once more.

For a moment he saw, red against the radiance, a figure who rose from the ruins of the horse-litter, wielding in his single hand a Sword whose stroke scythed down all foes within a radius of ten yards. Then the light flared beyond his strength to bear it. Sobbing, he sank to his knees, arm raised to shield his eyes from that deadly flame.

And then it was gone.

The plain light of day seemed dim in contrast. But there was enough of it for Oesc's recovering vision to make out the body of his father, blood still pumping from the stump of his neck. The head had fallen a few feet away; its features still bore a look of appalled surprise.

Scarcely knowing what he did, Oesc crawled forward, pulled off the remnant of his cloak, and began, fumbling, to wrap the head. As he did so, one of the stricken figures stirred. It was Baldulf. Groaning, he gained his feet, then stopped short, features contorting with grief as he saw the boy, and the headless body of his lord.

He cast a quick glance around him, then limped forward.

"Tir's judgment fell against us—" he said hoarsely, "the field is lost, but our hope lives so long as you are alive."

Oesc looked up, dimly aware that most of the figures that were beginning to move around them wore British gear. Beyond Octha's body he could see the British king sprawled among his cushions, in his hand a sword whose brightness still hurt the eye. Baldulf took a step toward it, but the British warriors were too close. Swiftly Baldulf gathered up Octha's torque and his seax. Then he hauled Oesc to his feet and hurried him away.

There was no wind.

Oesc was never able to recall much about the journey that followed. His wound went bad, and at times he was fevered, but mostly he simply did not want to remember. At some point Hæthwæge found them. He did recall the foul taste of the herbal teas she brewed to bring down his fever, as her compresses and charms fought the infection in his arm. For three nights, he was told, they had hidden in the forest, waiting for the crisis and muffling his delirious mumblings when British search parties went past.

Of that, the boy had no recollection. All he retained were visions of a dark land and a dark lake beside which he wandered, calling his father's name, until the wisewoman came walking through the shadows, her raven on her shoulder, and led him back to the light of day.

And through all his illness, and the travel that followed, the head of Octha, hid now in a leather sack and packed with leeks to preserve it, stayed by his side.

Travelling mostly by night, they fled to the East Saxon lands, where they found a boat to carry them across the broad mouth of the Tamesis. After that, they were in Hengest's country and could move openly, following the old Roman road between the sea and the North Downs. By then, of course, word of their coming had gone before them, and Hengest had sent an escort and a horse litter in which Oesc could travel like the British king.

But Uthir was dead. Even in hiding, they had heard that news. The High King of the Britons had died after the battle and left no heir. If the Saxons had lost the battle, and with it the greatest of their own leaders, at least that much had been achieved, and they, like the British, would have time to heal before the warring began once more. Better still, the rumor was that Merlin, the witega who had caused such devastation with his magic, had disappeared.

For Oesc, life began once more when they drew up in front of the meadhall Hengest had built in the ruins of Cantuware and he saw his grandfather, tall and weathered as a storm-battered oak, waiting for him there.

Oesc swung at the practice post set into the mud of the yard, wincing as the wooden blade hit the straw that had been bound around it and the impact jarred the weak muscles in his arm. In the three months since Verulamium his flesh had healed, but it still hurt at times. Since he left his bed, he had spent his days in ceaseless motion, hunting, running, even chopping wood for the fires. And whenever Byrhtwold was free, he had pestered the old warrior to give him more work with the sword.

His body was fined down to bone and sinew, and day by day he could feel his arm growing stronger. But no exercise he had tried could make his heart strong enough to deny the pain, and though each night he fell into bed, too tired to move, the hours of darkness brought dreams from which he would wake whimpering, his vision seared by a sword of fire and his cheeks wet with tears. But once awake, though his throat ached with grief, he could not cry.

Only when it grew too dark to see the post did Oesc give up. From inside the hall he could hear voices, but the yard was empty. Above the wall the first stars were glittering in the deepening blue of the sky. A bird flew toward the trees, crying, and then it was still once more. Now that he had stopped moving, fatigue dragged at back and shoulders. Sweat drying cold on his skin, he stumbled toward the hall.

After the brisk air outside, the warmth was welcome. His stomach rumbled at the scent of boiling beef and he realized that he was hungry.

His grandfather was already in the high seat, long legs stretched toward the fire, his gaunt frame as splendid in its ruin as a Roman tower. Once Hengest had fought to master all Britannia, but now he was content to cling to the corner that the Vor-Tigernus had given him. But his son would never inherit it now.

At his feet sat the shope Andulf, head bent as he tuned his harp. Firelight glistened on the silver strands threading his brown hair. As Oesc approached, the shope straightened, and the murmur of conversation began to still. Once, and then again, he struck the strings, then, in a voice with the honey of sweet mead and the bite of its fire, he began to sing.

> *Eormanaric, noblest of Amalings,*
> *Great king of Goths, who got much glory,*
> *Fought many folk and fed his people,*
> *Lost land and life to Hunnish horse-lords.*

Hengest beckoned, and Oesc joined him on the broad bench. In a few moments one of the thralls brought him a wooden bowl filled with savory stew, and he began to gobble it down. The first bowl took the edge off his hunger. He held it out to be refilled, able to listen now to the mingled honey and gall of the tale of the great king who a century earlier had led the Goths to create an empire, and when the Huns invaded, lost it. From the Pontus Euxinus to the Northern Sea he had ruled, and from the Wistla to the great steppes, conquering tribes whose names were lost in legend. He had defeated Alaric, king of the Heruli who had made a kingdom north of the Maiotis, and controlled the trade routes to the western lands.

Mightiest among his warriors, Eormanaric had been a man of evil temper, who had the young wife of a chieftain who had deserted him torn apart by tying her limbs to four wild stallions. Her brothers sought to avenge her, splitting the Gothic forces at the moment when they most needed unity. And so the Huns had rolled over them and the Goths who survived fled westward, some to cross the Danuvius and seek service with Rome, and some to push all the way to Iberia, where now they ruled.

> *Fierce to his foes and to the faithless,*
> *Betrayed by trampled traitors' kin,*
> *In old age he embraced his ending,*
> *His blood in blessing fed the ground. . . .*

In the end, ran the tale, Eormanaric had taken his own life, seeking by the offering of his own blood to placate the gods.

"It is said that one should not praise a day until it is ended," said Hengest, when the last note had faded to silence. "I suppose that the same is true of a king. He lost his empire, but perhaps his blood bought some protection for his people, since they have prospered in their new land. At least his death had meaning. . . ."

"That is what King Gundohar said—" answered the shope.

"You knew him?" exclaimed Oesc. He had been aware that the man was a Burgund, his accent worn smooth by years of wandering, but he had thought that everyone close to the royal clan died when the Huns attacked them a quarter-century before.

"He taught me how to play the harp," said Andulf, his voice tightening with old pain. "It is he who wrote this song."

"But you don't look old enough—" Oesc broke off, flushing, as the men began to laugh.

"I was a boy, younger than you," said Andulf smiling, "serving in his hall."

"And now the Niflungar themselves are becoming a legend," added Hengest, shaking his head. "And yet I myself saw Sigfrid when he was only a child and I scarcely older.

Who, I wonder, will the heroes of this time be?"

"The deeds of your youth are meat for the bards already, lord," said Byrhtwold.

"Do you mean the fight at Finnesburgh?" growled Hengest. "To keep one oath I was forced to break another, but it is not something I remember with pride."

"You will be remembered as the leader who brought our people to this good land!" said one of the other men.

"If we can hold it . . ." someone said softly.

"Does that matter?" asked Byrhtwold. "Hunnish horses pasture now in the land where Eormanaric died, and the heirs of Gundohar have found refuge in Raetia. Sigfrid left only his name behind him. But in death they triumphed, and they are remembered."

"Do you mean that if we succeed in winning all this island it will be Uthir and Ambrosius about whom men make the stories?" Guthlaf, one of the younger warriors, laughed disbelievingly.

"It may be so," said Andulf, frowning, "for the winners will belong not to legend, but to history." He began to slide his harp into its sealskin case.

The conversation turned to other matters, and as the drinking horns were refilled, grew louder. Oesc leaned against the hard back of the high seat, exhaustion dragging like a sea-anchor at his limbs.

"Send the boy to bed, Hengest, before he falls asleep where he sits," Byrhtwold said presently.

"I'm not sleepy!" Oesc jerked upright, rubbing his eyes. "Grandfather, Octha was a hero, was he not?"

The old man nodded, his eyes dark with shared pain, and the boy knew that he too was thinking of the lonely mound just within the wall.

"Do we have to choose?" he said then. "Do we have to choose between a glorious death and living for our people?" He waited, realizing that his grandfather was taking him seriously.

"Many men fall and are not remembered . . ." Hengest said slowly. "It is because they died for a reason that we honor heroes, because they never gave up, but fought to the end. Death is not a failure, Oesc, if a man has truly lived."

"Then he didn't fail . . ." whispered the boy. "We lost the

battle and they killed him, but Octha had his victory. . . ."

"Boy, is that what has troubled you?" Hengest set his gnarled hand on Oesc's shoulder. "Your father waits for us even now in Woden's hall. You must strive to live so that you will be worthy to see him again."

The ache in Oesc's throat made it hard to breathe. He sucked in air with a harsh gasp, and awkwardly, his grandfather began to pat his back, then seeing his face, gathered him against his bony breast. And there, breathing in the scents of leather and horses and the old man's flesh, Oesc found at last the release of tears.

iii

HOLY GROUND

A.D. 475

Every fall, when the raiding season had ended and the crops were gathered in, it was Hengest's custom to travel around the territory that the Vor-Tigernus had given him. At this time of year, when the quarrels of the summer were still fresh in memory, the king heard complaints and rendered judgment, lest resentment, festering through the dark days of winter, should erupt into bloodfeud and destroy the peace of the land. In the second year after Verulamium, Hengest took his grandson Oesc with him on the journey, that he might learn the land and its law.

That fall the first of the winter storms came early, soaking the stubbled fields. But it was succeeded by a season of smiling peace, and the king and his escort rode through a landscape as rich in autumn color as heaped amber, splashed with the vivid scarlet berries of rowan and holly and the varied crimsons of the vine.

Their way first led south to the coast, where the Roman fortress of Lemanis still guarded the Saxon shore. They travelled by short stages, for the king's age would not allow him to do more. In the mornings, when he stretched stiff joints, swearing, he would say that next year, surely, he would let Oesc do it all. But by evening he was smiling, and the cold knot of anxiety in Oesc's belly would disappear.

From Lemanis, they worked their way back north and east along the shoreline to Dubris, where the high chalk cliffs looked out across the sea. Their next stop was Rutupiae, where the Vor-Tigernus's son had once driven Hengest into the sea. The fortress was in ruins now, only the great triumphal arch still proclaiming the vanished glory of Rome. Here, the rich lands by the shore were thickly settled, and the cases being brought for judgment mostly quarrels over boundaries or complaints about strayed stock.

They passed through Durovernum once more and then made their way eastward along the straight line of the Roman road that led to Londinium. To their left the land rose in gentle slopes to the North Downs, scattered with ruined villas and new Saxon farmsteads. To their right the green fields stretched down to the estuary of the Tamesis, sparkling in the sun. Where the ribbon of the road passed, habitations, or their remains, were most thickly clustered, and as they neared Durobrivae, the Roman town that guarded the crossings of the Meduwege and the western half of Cantuware, the land became more populous still.

"The British have got themselves a high king!" Red-faced and perspiring, Hrofe Guthereson shouted out the words even before he greeted his king. He had come out with his houseguard to escort them into the city, but with his news the whole party had come to a halt in the road.

"Who?" barked Hengest. "Has Leudonus finally got the southern princes to accept him?"

"No—" Hrofe shook his head, eyes sparkling. "It's a fifteen-year-old boy! Uthir had a son!"

Fifteen! thought Oesc. *My age. . . .* How strange to think that the battle in which he had lost his own father had so deprived another boy as well.

"Legitimate?" asked Byrhtwold.

Hrofe shrugged. "That's not clear, but Queen Igierne has claimed him as her child by the king."

"I remember hearing talk of a babe," Hengest said, frowning, "but I thought it died. . . ." Slowly they had begun to move forward again.

"They say he was sent away to the west country for safety, so secretly that even the folk that fostered him did not know who he really was."

Hengest smiled sourly. "Well perhaps they had some reason. When you are trying to get rid of a family of bears, you should attack the den."

"Well this one is a bear cub, right enough," said Hrofe. "Arktos, they call him, or Artor."

Artor . . . To Oesc's ears, that name rang like the clash of steel.

"And they accepted him on the queen's say-so?" Hengest said dubiously. "I know the British princes, and they would be hard put to agree that the sun sets in the west without nine days of arguing."

The walls were quite close now.

"It was not the queen's word that convinced them," said Hrofe, with the air of one who has saved the best for last. "It was because the boy could handle the Sword!"

The sword that killed Octha. . . . Oesc's stricken gaze met that of his grandfather, and he saw Hengest's face grow grim.

"I had hoped that accursed weapon would go with Uthir to his grave."

"Oh no—" Hrofe babbled on with hateful cheer.

Unable to bear it any longer, Oesc dug his heels into his mare's flank and pushed past the king and through the shadowed arch of the eastern gate into Durobrivae.

Shaded by an awning of canvas, Hengest sat in judgment in the forum for five long days. Oesc fidgeted beside him, the arguments half-heard, dreaming of the hunting he was missing while the weather held fair. His other grandfather used to spend a lot of time listening to men complain against each other too. Why, he wondered resentfully, would anyone want to be a king? But even the master of a farmstead had to settle disputes among his people, he supposed. The men the king judged were more powerful, that was all.

"And how would you decide this matter, Oesc—" Hengest said suddenly.

Blinking, the boy tried to remember what the man before

them had just said. He was a big, fair, fellow with the lines
of habitual ill-temper graven deeply around his mouth and
on his brow.

"He says," the king repeated, "that his neighbor deliberately burned down his woodlot, and nearly destroyed his
house as well."

"It is not so!" exclaimed the accused, glaring. "I only
meant to burn the stubble from my fields."

"But you burned my woods!"

"Is it my fault if Thunor turns the wind? Blame the gods,
not me!"

Oesc gazed from one man to the other, frowning, as he
tried to remember the law. "Was it a large wood?" he asked
finally. Hengest began to smile, and the boy continued more
boldly. "Were there many big trees?"

"A very fine wood," said the plaintiff, "with noble oak
trees!"

"Untrue! Untrue! There was one tree of some size, and
around it nought but hazels!" The accused pointed at an older
man in the front row of the crowd. "Tell them! You know
the place—tell them what was there!"

Oesc stood up, having remembered the relevant traditions
now. He cast a quick glance at this grandfather, who nodded
reassurance, then held up one hand and waited until silence
fell.

"It is the law of our people that compensation shall be
paid for deeds, not thoughts. It does not matter why you
started the fire," he told the accused man. "If you were so
foolish as to burn stubble on a day of wind, and it did damage to the property of another, you must pay for it. The fine
for damage to a wood is thirty shillings, and five shillings
for every great tree, and five pence for each of the smaller."

"It is his word against mine as to what was there . . ." the
man said sullenly.

"Your word, and that of your witnesses," agreed the boy.
"Let each of you call those who will take oath to support
your assertion, and so the fine shall be set according to the
decision of your peers."

"Unjust!" cried the plaintiff, but the men in the crowd
were nodding and murmuring their approval of the plan.
Clearly the fair-haired man's taste for contention had not

endeared him to his neighbors, for only two men came to his support, while the accused could choose from a dozen or more.

"Did I do right?" asked Oesc when the oaths had been sworn and the fine paid over.

"You did very well," answered the king. "That man is a trouble-maker whom I have seen in court before. A more reasonable man might have settled the matter with his neighbor privately, and not burdened us with it, but he got his recompense, and will not, one hopes, feel compelled to get satisfaction by burning the other man's hall."

"I know it is law that the man who set the fire should be held responsible, but it does seem unfair when he intended no harm," said Oesc thoughtfully.

"Do you think our laws were made to do justice? No, child, if my decisions keep our hot-headed tribesmen from killing each other I will be satisfied. It is each man's wyrd, not I, that will give him the doom that he deserves."

Oesc was glad when they left Durobrivae behind them and took the road once more. Now they moved southward, climbing the tree-clad slopes where the valley of the Meduwege cut through the North Downs. From time to time the trees would part and he could glimpse the river below them, carrying the waters that drained from the Weald, the great forest that covered the central part of the Cantuware lands.

As the day drew to its ending, the road dropped downward into the valley, and he saw the red-tiled roofs of a cluster of Roman buildings set on an oval mound, and beyond them the thatching of a Saxon farmstead amid the water meadows by the stream. Closer still, he realized that the structures on the mound were temples, and that the farm had been built on the foundations of a Roman villa. Here the Meduwege broadened, running chuckling over the stones of a ford.

"Who holds this place?" he asked as they came to a halt in the yard.

"An Anglian called Ægele who sailed in one of the first three keels that came with me across the sea. He lost a leg in the fight at Rutupiae, and I settled him here," his grandfather answered him.

"And who lives up there?" Oesc pointed toward a small

square building with a peaked roof, surrounded by a covered porch on all four sides. Some of the tiles were loose, and in places the white plaster was flaking from the stones of the wall, but someone had recently raked the path.

"Ah—that is the other reason we have stopped here. I am not the only one who will find in this place a friend."

But it was not until the following morning that Oesc found out what Hengest had meant, when together they climbed the temple hill.

She could hear them coming up the pathway, the old man's tread heavy and halting on the gravel and the boy's footsteps a quick brush against the stones, his rapid questions abruptly cut off as they paused in the shadow of the porch. A breath of air set the lamp flames to leaping, lending life to the carven eyes of the figures carved on the altar, and elongating her shadow across the wall. Oesc stopped in the doorway and she put back her shawl, smiling as his eyes adjusted to the dim light and he saw her sitting there.

"Hæthwæge!" The delight on his face was like another lamp in the room. "Where did you come from?"

"Where have I not been?" She patted the bench that ran around the wall and the boy sat down. Hengest eased down on the opposite bench and sat with his veined hands crossed on the head of his staff, watching them. "I have been going up and down, searching out the holy places of this land."

Brought back to awareness of where they were, his eyes flicked uneasily around the small room. He had grown, she thought, since she had last seen him. At fifteen he was leggy as a colt, with the promise of strength in his bony shoulders and character in the line of his jaw, where the first fuzz of manhood was beginning to appear.

"And who did the Romans worship here?"

"That is their image of them—" She gestured toward the altar.

Waist-high, the edges of its flat top were scrolled and fluted, forming a canopy for a bas-relief that showed a seated goddess in a wide sleeved, pleated garment, and three standing figures in cloaks with hoods. The goddess held something, possibly a spindle, in her hand. Below the figures there had been a Latin inscription, but the stone was too worn to make out the words.

"But who *are* they?" he asked again.

"They are not Roman, though they are figured in the Roman style," Hæthwæge said slowly. "This is an old place, where the track that runs along the downs crosses the river. It was here before Rome, maybe even before the British came. I have sat out all night upon a barrow beside that trackway and listened to those whose bones lie there."

She shivered a little, remembering voices in the windy darkness. She still limped where her knee had stiffened after that night's out-sitting, but she did not grudge it. The Romans, she gathered, had not bothered to listen, but had fastened their own names onto the native divinities and confined them in new temples, ignoring the old powers of the hills. The ancient ones had been pleased, she thought, that someone was paying attention to them at last.

"Why?"

"To learn about the spirits of this land so that we can honor them and gain their blessing. I left an offering at the barrow before I came away. You must leave a portion, also, when you go hunting in the Weald."

Oesc took one of the lamps from its niche and squatted, holding the flame so he could see.

"Do you think the Lady could be Frige, and the hooded gods Woden and Willa and Weoh?"

"Little by little our tongue is replacing that of the Romans on the land. I do not think its gods will mind if we call them by our names," Hæthwæge answered, and heard in her head a whisper of approving laughter.

Old Man, be still, she told the god within. *It seems to me you have too many names already! Are you greedy for more?*

"But is that who they really are?"

Hæthwæge shook her head. "Child, there is no name a human tongue could master that would tell you that. In many places, the Britons called their Lady Brigantia. But perhaps these are the names they will bear for us here."

"That is why I have brought the boy," Hengest said then. "So that we may make our offerings."

The wicce nodded and got to her feet. Taking up the second lamp, she moved around the altar and held it high. Light glimmered warm on the worn grey stones of the well coping, and glittered on the dark water within. Enclosed within stone walls, this place was very different from the pool in the marshes of the Myrging lands, and yet the power of its waters was much the same.

"The shrine was built around this spring. It rises from the same waters that feed the river, coming down from the Weald and the Downs. They carry the lifeblood of the Lady of this land."

Hengest had risen as well. Now he took from his belt purse three golden coins that bore the blurred image of some long-dead emperor. Carefully he bent over the well.

"Gyden . . . Frige . . ." he said in a low voice, "I took this land by the sword. But the folk I have brought to live here will tend and till it in love and law. All my days I have been a man of blood, but I have no strength now to force men to my will. Let this land feed my people. . . ." His voice trembled. "And let me leave it in frith to the son of my son."

As he spoke the air inside the temple grew heavy, as if something very ancient and powerful had directed its attention that way. Then the coins splashed into the pool and the tension broke.

It took a few moments for the king to straighten. Then he sat down again, his old eyes moving from Hæthwæge to the boy.

The wicce felt a pang of pity for this ancient warrior who had outlived his own strength and all his companions and now, at his life's ending, sought in a new land the justification for his deeds. For a moment her memory went back to Oesc's other grandfather, Eadguth the Myrging-king, who had been so bound to his land that like an ancient oak, he could not be transplanted from his native soil.

"Now it is for the heir to make his oath and his offering," she said aloud.

Oesc set the lamp he had been holding on the rim of the well and knelt beside it, staring down into the pool. The current, welling slowly from the depths, broke the reflection into a scattering of gold, as if more wealth were breeding already from Hengest's coins.

Rather reluctantly, he unpinned the silver brooch that held his cloak, the only thing of value that he had on. Once more the atmosphere changed, this time to a kind of singing tension that lifted the hair on Hæthwæge's arms and neck. Oesc felt it too. He cast an uneasy look in her direction before turning once more to the well.

"Lady of the spring, this is for you." His voice cracked on the last word and he flushed, swallowing, and swiftly tossed the brooch in. "Let me be worthy of my grandfather's trust. Body and spirit I offer, if you will give me this land as a home for my children and my people. And please, Lady, let me one day know your true name!"

The tension built to an audible hum, like crickets on a day of summer, though the leaves were turning and the air outside had the crisp clarity of fall. It intensified to the edge of pain, then, very slowly, ebbed away, leaving behind it a great peace and the conviction that all would be well.

From Ægele's ford the road cut southward through the Weald, dwindling to a rough track by the time it reached the southern coast. There, the Jute, Hæsta, had settled his clan near the old Roman iron workings where a low ridge ran down to the sea. Just down the coast, the sea-fort of Anderida provided safe harbor, and with a good wind and a pilot who knew the shoals of the coastline, they could return to Lemanis by boat in no more than a long day's sail. Hæsta's other guests had ridden eastward from the South Downs, where Aelle had been lord of his Saxons for almost as long as Hengest had held Cantuware, though he was thirty years younger. The farmstead, where the rich fields sloped down toward the sea, lay on the border between the lands the two leaders ruled.

Hæsta himself had come down to escort his guests from the landing. As they approached his hall, more men came out of it—a thickset, muscular man with grizzled hair and a king's torque who they said was Aelle, and behind him a tall young man with red hair. The child he carried on his shoulder stared at the newcomers with bright, considering eyes.

"He has brought Ceretic, I see," said Byrhtwold, "and that must be Ceretic's young son. That's a man to watch, lad. If he fights half as well as he talks, he'll be calling himself a king too one of these days."

Oesc nodded, understanding that this was one of the men

with whom he would have to deal, in friendship or without it, when his own turn came to rule. Hengest's bid to claim lordship over all the men who had come over from Germania had failed, and Aelle seemed content with his coastal hills. Despite their numbers, the Saxon settlements were scattered, each under its own chieftain—men who had never gone under the yoke of Rome and saw no reason to bow down before one of their own.

Octha might have united them, Oesc thought grimly, until his battle-luck failed. But no—it had not been bad luck that felled him, but the sorcery in Uthir's sword. *I might do it . . .* he thought grimly, *and Artor will be my opponent if I do.* Then they were dismounting, and Hæsta led them into the friendly shelter, its air blue with woodsmoke and the welcome scents of cooking food, of his hall.

That night, new clouds rolled in from the sea. For three days, rain and sleet kept the Saxons inside the hall. They scarcely noticed. Hæsta had been brewing for weeks in preparation for the feasting, and so long as the ale-vats did not run dry, no one would complain.

In a break between the discussions, Oesc sat by the long hearth, carving scraps of wood into crude figures of horses and split twig-men to ride them. As each one was finished, he gave it to the child beside him. Cynric, he was called, with hair as red as his father's, the legacy of the British grandfather who had given Ceretic his name.

"That is a mighty army—" said Ceretic, looking down at his son. Cynric nodded, took the rider that Oesc had just finished and set it in order with the others.

"These with the bark on are Romans, because of their armor, and the peeled ones are Saxons," the child explained. Several of the figures fell over and he set them up again.

"I see you are placing your unmounted warriors in a wedge formation—" commented Ceretic.

"*He* told me—" said Cynric, pointing at Oesc.

"It was what my father used at Verulamium." Oesc swallowed, his stomach knotting as he remembered that day.

"Ah, yes." Ceretic transferred his attention from the child. "You were in that battle, I have heard."

Oesc flushed. "Against my father's orders," he said with

a quelling look at Cynric. "But I brought away his head so that the British should not dishonor it. I have sworn that I will avenge him one day."

"Perhaps we will march to battle together. For now, I am in Aelle's following, but my father rules in Venta, and he refused to acknowledge Ambrosius as his master. It is certain he will not bow before this child the British are calling high king!"

"You are British?" Oesc stared at him. But of course, he thought as he looked at the milky Celtic skin and bright hair, it must be true.

"My father is—" Ceretic's lips twisted wryly. "Maglos took my mother as a second wife when he made alliance with Aelle. I grew up speaking both tongues equally. My father likes Saxons because they are good fighters, and if this new high king tries to recover the lands around Venta, Maglos will need more men to defend them. So he has sent me to Aelle."

"Does Aelle have them?"

"Not enough—hence, this meeting. Your grandfather's people have held Cantuware long enough for there to be a few younger sons who need new holdings. If they come to the Isle of Vecta, my father will make no objections. But I will need to bring more men from Germania to settle the land around Clausentum, along the estuary of the Icene. From there I can drive northward into the heart of Britannia. Maglos thinks he can defend the land with Saxon settlers and still call it British. But when I rule in Venta, I can strike northward to the British heartland!"

Listening to him talk, Oesc understood how it must have been for Hengest and Horsa when they were young. But in Durovernum the scars of warfare had been repaired, the burnt houses scavenged for building material or allowed to go back to the soil. The British who remained there were grateful for the protection of their new masters, and the Saxons were rooting themselves ever more deeply into the soil.

"And what about you?" asked Ceretic, as if Oesc had been thinking aloud. "Will you push westward as well? You are young, with your name yet to win. Have you no ambitions to take Londinium?"

"Londinium and the British lands around it divide us from

the Anglians in the fen country, as Lindum divides them from the north. We would be stronger if we could take it," Oesc added thoughtfully, "but the city was more important when there was trade with the Empire. In itself, it is not so useful now."

"Go around it, then. If I push northward and you move west, our armies can join forces, and who will stop us then?" He threw his head back, laughing. In the flickering light his hair was as red as the fire.

"What armies? Are you Woden, to breathe life into these sticks your son is playing with, and make them men? Let us wait at least until the seed is planted before we sell the tree!" exclaimed Oesc. "When you have brought your warriors from Saxony and I command the men of Cantuware, we may talk of this again."

"It is so! It is so!" shaking his head, Ceretic hunkered down and began to help his son pick up his scattered men. "Always, my dreams have outstripped reality. But it will happen. Among the Saxons a second wife has equal standing, and my mother went willingly to Maglos's bed. But the Christian priests called her a Saxon whore and me a bastard. I had to fight for every scrap of food and nod of approval, but the sons of my father's Christian wife were killed in battle, while I survived and took a wife from my mother's people. Maglos has no choice now but to trust to me and my Saxon kin to defend him. I have come too far already not to believe it is my Wyrd to be a conqueror."

Oesc believed him. Ambition pulsed around Ceretic like heat from the flame. *And what is* my *Wyrd?* he wondered then. But even as he questioned, a memory came to him of lamplight on dark water, and a breath of wind.

My Wyrd is to be a king. . . .

Hæthwæge dipped up a spoonful of broth, tasted it, and decided that she could add a bit more of the infusion of galluc root and mallow without rendering it so bitter the king would refuse to drink it down. As she poured, she bent over the pot, whispering—

> *"Galluc, Galluc, great among herbs,*
> *You have power against three and against thirty,*

Against poison and all infection,
Against the loathsome foe that fares through
    the land. . . ."

In her mind's eye she saw the plant from which that root had come, its broad leaves frosted with prickles, the pale pink-purple flowers trembling like bells in the breeze. *Boneset*, they called it sometimes, but it had great power also to heal internally. The mallow would soothe and smooth it on its way.

Hengest would not admit that he was ill, though the cough he brought home from his visit to Hæsta's hall had hung on throughout the winter, and his frame grew as gaunt as the horsehide hung over the poles at the offering pool. Her more elaborate curing methods were useless if the patient would not admit he needed them. All she could do was to doctor his food and drink as unobtrusively as possible, and sing her charms over her pots as she prepared them.

Eadguth had been much the same in his old age. *Why,* she wondered, *have I spent so much of my life nursing old men?* But the god she served appeared most often in an old man's guise, so perhaps it was not so surprising.

And to balance the old man she had the young one, although these days Oesc spent most of his time outdoors, hunting, exploring the countryside, even helping the farmers with the work of each season as it came. She supposed it was inevitable, after his dedication at the sacred spring. The goddess of the land was speaking to him in each tree and hill, and as time passed, he would learn to understand her.

Oesc came to the wisewoman for liniment for sore muscles, and sometimes to dress a wound, but on the whole he was a healthy young animal, for which she thanked the gods.

She stirred the broth once more, then dipped it carefully into a carved hornbeam bowl, its wooden surface smoothed to a rich patina by the years, and carried it from the cookshed across the yard to the hall. In the years since Hengest had built it in the space adjoining two of the better preserved Roman dwellings, trees had grown up on the western side, screening the weed-covered waste where half-burned houses had been pulled down to serve as building material. Afternoon sunlight slanted through the branches, glowing in the new leaves. A pattern of shadow netted the path.

As she passed, a portion of that shadow solidified into a human shape: a tall man, wrapped in a cloak and leaning on a staff. Hæthwæge stopped, eyes narrowing. *High One,* she queried silently, *is it you?*

As if he had felt the touch of her mind, the stranger straightened, turning toward the light. The wisewoman noted the dark eyes beneath their heavy brows, the brown beard where only a few strands of silver yet showed, and let her breath out in a long sigh. It was not the god. But neither, she thought as other senses picked up the aura that surrounded him, was this entirely a man. And knowing that, she thought she could put a name to him.

"Merlin Witega, wæs hal! Be you welcome to this hall!"

His eyes widened at the greeting, and some indefinable tension in his posture ebbed away.

"A blessing on you also, woman of wisdom. I had heard there was a bean-drui in the house of the king, and I think you must be she."

Hæthwæge bowed her head, accepting the compliment. She should have expected that he would be able to see beyond the old shawl and apron to her own aura of power.

"Come with me, then. The king has been ill, but he is well enough to speak with you. Perhaps he will be ashamed to fuss about drinking this down if you are by."

His broad nostrils flared, though it seemed unlikely he could pick up the scent from there. Then he began to ask if the king's cough had lasted for long, and she realized that he had indeed recognized the herbs.

"We were not certain whether Hengest was still living." His deep voice rumbled up from somewhere near his belly. "I knew him when I was a boy in the Vor-Tigernus's hall."

"He is old, but he still has his wits." Hæthwæge answered the unspoken question.

A swift grin of understanding split the flowing beard. "Then he will remember me. But it might be better if to the rest I were known only as a messenger." He said, and Hæthwæge, remembering how Oesc still blamed Merlin for the magic that had caused his father's death, had to agree. Then he pushed open the door and together they entered the hall.

* * *

He is an old man, Merlin told himself as they made their way past the empty feasting benches toward the high seat. *He cannot hurt you now.* Somewhere inside him there still lived a child who remembered Hengest as a towering force that could break him without even breathing hard. But in the man before him there was nothing of the Vor-Tigernus's war leader but the eagle gaze. *Who would have thought that the terrible Hengest would live to be so old?*

"Am I well?" Hengest echoed his question. "At my age it is enough to be alive. No doubt you seem ancient to Artor." He chuckled grimly. "I have outlived all my enemies, and most of my friends. But I will last until my grandson is old enough to rule. Uthir's son has the name of king already, but is it he or his council who have sent you here?"

"His council—" admitted Merlin. "But the boy is no weakling. In time he will be a powerful leader in peace or in war."

"I don't suppose you have come to say that Artor wants me to give back Cantium. Even the hotheads on his council must recognize that we have sunk our roots too deeply into this soil."

"Nor have I come to ask whether you will try to take advantage of Artor's youth to attack Londinium," Merlin answered pleasantly. "What my king and his council offer is a treaty to confirm your possession of these lands, in return for your support against any of the Saxon kings who would try to expand their territories."

Hengest gave a bark of laughter, took a sip of broth, and grimacing, set it down again. "Why come to me? I am not high king of the Saxon kind. Do you think they will listen to me?"

They may not obey you, old wolf, but they listen, thought Merlin as the old man went on. *What is it that you are not telling me?*

"While I live, the warriors of Cantuware will not march against you. I can give no surety for the others, nor even for what my grandson will do when he has drunk my funeral ale."

He looked up, a warmer light coming into his old eyes, but Merlin had already felt the stir in the air as a youth who stood, like Artor, on the threshold between boy and man, came in. He was taller than Artor, and fair where the other boy was brown, and in his gaze Merlin perceived something watchful, as if he had already learned not to trust the world, where Artor's gaze was still open and unafraid.

"Not for a long time, I hope," he said, sitting down at the old man's feet.

"This is Oesc, Octha's son," said the king. But Merlin had already recognized the set of the shoulders and something of Hengest about the line of brow and jaw. "He is the one who will have to deal with Artor, not I."

"Yes . . ." Merlin shut his eyes, shaken by a sudden inrush of images—Artor and Oesc side by side on a hill where ravens flew, at feast and at hunt, and again, older, striving to meet amid the blood and terror of a battlefield. As foes or as allies? And if they fought, which one would have the victory? That knowledge was not given.

Then the moment of vision faded. When he looked up again, Oesc and his grandfather were still talking, but the witch-woman, Hæthwæge, was watching him with troubled eyes.

"If you wish to keep your anonymity," she told him when the interview was over, "you had better come with me. I will tell the thralls to bring food for us both."

Merlin nodded. He would lose the chance to pick up whatever revealing gossip the men might share in the hall, but it seemed to him that he knew the answer to his question already. Cantium would stay quiet, but the council had better keep a sharp eye on the South Saxons and the Anglians from now on. This wisewoman, on the other hand, clearly had considerable influence with both the old man and the boy. He could not afford to leave her a mystery.

He sensed a prickling beneath his skin as he entered Hæthwæge's house and smiled a little, recognizing in its pure form the feel of the wardings he had noted in the hall. Flame leaped as she built up the fire, and he looked around him with a fellow-professional's curiosity. Since his studies with the Vor-Tigernus's wise men when he was young he had had little to do with other workers of magic.

His nostrils flared at the mingled odors, spicy or musty or sour, that swirled around him, and with them the mingled currents of power. A witch he had called her, and the drying herbs that hung from the rafters, the sacks and baskets and packets ranked neatly on their shelves, confirmed it. What else she might be he could not yet tell.

Hæthwæge poured mead from a Roman flask into a silver-mounted drinking horn. "Do not fear," she said when for a moment he hesitated, "I know better than to set a spell upon it beyond a blessing on the yeast to make it brew, even if I thought such a thing would escape your notice."

"I did not doubt you," he said stiffly. He drank, savoring the fiery sweetness, and handed the horn back to her, then seated himself on the bench beside the fire.

The wisewoman drank in turn and took her place across from him. She was a woman who would look much the same from her middle years to extreme old age, deep-breasted and broad-hipped, with a lacing of silver in her hair—ordinary, in fact, with no claim to beauty, until you met her eyes.

Those eyes held his now, with a silvery glow that hid the depths behind them like light on a pool.

"You ask Hengest what he will do with his warriors, as if those were the only powers at war over this land. Of another messenger I would have expected that, but not of you. Have you come to spy out our defenses, as you did when you rode the body of the bird at Verulamium?"

Merlin suppressed a shudder, remembering that day. Then the sense of what she had said reached him.

"That was you, with the ravens, opposing me?"

"For a little while—until it became a battle between your goddess and my god. You should know that Woden has long been a friend to the goddesses, and he will seek to learn her wisdom. Even then, it was not she who defeated him, but the god in the Sword. Will it kill its new master as it did your king?"

"Artor is its destined master, the Defender of Britannia. When he draws it in a just cause, it will bring him the victory." Remembering the particular pulsation of power the Sword carried, he became abruptly aware that he was sensing something similar here.

He turned, attention fixing on a long shape in the corner, swathed in leather wrappings and spells. Now that it had attracted his attention, its power overwhelmed all the other magics in the room. Behind him, Hæthwæge had gone very still.

"I should have realized that against you, the magics that hide it from other men would be useless . . ." She spoke slowly, as if listening to some voice within. "But perhaps . . . it was meant that you should see it." She moved slowly to the corner and began to unfasten the wrappings, and he saw that it was a spear.

For one moment only Merlin glimpsed the physical form— the wooden, rune-carved shaft and the blade of translucent stone. Then its power swirled through his senses in an explosion of meaning; its shaft a chain of incantations, its blade piercing the heart with pure song. Altered vision perceived it limned in light, as bright as the radiant being who was offering it to him.

"Take it by the shaft. . . ." Through his confusion he realized that Hæthwæge was speaking.

With an effort he managed to answer. "What will happen if I do?"

"You will know the god . . ."

"Woden? He is no god of mine!"

"You may say so, but still you bear a part of his wisdom in this world. You do not know him, but he knows you, and he claims this holy ground. . . ."

"Is it a weapon?" He mumbled, thinking it might be his duty to seize it. "Will your kings bear it against the Sword?"

"It is a weapon, but not for war . . ."

Sound came and went. He was not certain of her meaning, only of his own rejection of what she was telling him. And then the power was muted. Ordinary vision returned, and he saw that she had replaced the wrappings around the spear.

"I have walked this land through the seasons, and Woden went with me," said Hæthwæge. "He likes this country and will stay here. He says to me that you will serve him also, and it will be easier if it is with your will."

Merlin shook his head. "I serve the Lady of the Land."

"Of course," said the wicce, "but in time to come, their purposes may prove to be the same. . . ."

IV

The Ostara Offering

A.D. 477

In the second year after his acclamation, the High King of Britannia kept the feast of the Resurrection at Sorviodunum on the borders of the Dumnonian lands. The Roman town had been burned during the first Saxon rebellion and only partially rebuilt afterward. Merlin, riding in behind Artor's houseguard, had thought the intervening years would have faded his memories, but instead, the ghosts of Ambrosius and Uthir now haunted it along with the shades of those who had been murdered by Hengest's men.

The little church, only lightly scorched, remained. While Artor heard the Pascal mass inside with Docomaglos of Dumnonia and his sons, the rest of the princes and notables waited with more or less patience in the open area around it, nourishing their spirits on the incense that drifted from within, and the earthier scents that drifted from the cauldrons where the feast was being prepared.

Merlin sensed the strength of the mystery that was being celebrated within those whitewashed walls, but the power that he was feeling did not come from the church, but rather flowed through it, drawing him northward through the gate to stand staring across the plain. To the north lay the Giant's Dance. He could not see it, but he could sense its presence. As the Christian ritual built to its climax the power moving along the line between them increased until he could see a pathway of light. Did Uthir's spirit ride that road from his grave by the ring of stones to the church where his son knelt in prayer?

The druid lifted his hands in salutation as the light flared and then began to fade. With its passing, he was aware of the fragile balance of light and darkness as the world stood poised for the explosion of growth that the approaching summer would bring. Always, in the old days, men had propitiated those forces at this time with an offering. The Christian priests said the death of their god was a sufficient sacrifice for all times to come, and from the point of view of the divine powers, that might be so. But it seemed to him that sometimes it was men, like Abraham in the Christians' stories, who needed to make an offering.

Light filtered coldly through the interwoven branches to illuminate the features of the British princes. Brush had been bound over a framework of beams to shelter the council, since there was no building in Sorviodunum that would hold them all. The fire that burned in the center seemed to produce more smoke than heat, which might also be said, thought Merlin, of the arguments.

Artor had a place close to the fire, with Merlin behind him. From habit, the druid cloaked his aura. The British chieftains, at first inclined to be suspicious of his motives, had become accustomed to his silent presence. They did not accept his influence on the boy so much as ignore it.

"Last year they came by the hundreds, and the year before!" exclaimed Catraut, who had fought his way through two ambushes on his way down from Verulamium. "As a dead horse breeds maggots, Germania breeds men. Who knows how many more will arrive when the sailing season begins? There are so many Anglians now they have brought over their King Icel to rule them, with his lady and his sons, while *you*—" he swept an accusatory finger toward the Dumnonian lords, "flit back and forth across the sea to Armorica like migrating birds, preparing cozy nests to which you can flee when by sheer pressure of numbers the Saxons have crowded us into the sea!"

Docomaglos, who had inherited Dumnonia after his brother Gorlosius died, bristled indignantly, while his sons, Cataur and Gerontius, looked uncomfortable. "My home is in Isca of the Dumnonii, and I will defend it to my life's end!"

"That may be so," Catraut continued implacably, "but can you deny there's scarcely one of your lords who does not have a cousin or a brother waiting to welcome him across the narrow sea? You must forgive those of us who do not have such a refuge if we say that your risks and ours are not the same!"

"My lords, my lords—" Eldaul of Glevum extended a placating hand. "We have been hearing these arguments since the days when the Vor-Tigernus strove with Aurelianus. The men of the east protest their sufferings, and those of the west, their loyalty. If we had all been willing to aid each other then, we might not face this threat today. . . ."

There was an uncomfortable silence. Artor, whose eyes had begun to glaze, roused suddenly, looking around the circle. In the past year he had added several inches to his height, and he was beginning to learn how to manage his long limbs.

"It seems to me, my lords, that Eldaul speaks truly, and since it is so, surely we ought to be taking council on how we may meet the threat instead of wasting our energy accusing each other!"

For a moment they stared, as if one of the posts had grown a mouth to speak to them. Then Merlin saw their expressions change as they remembered that it had been their decision to make this boy their king. At this point, one might wonder if they had really meant it, or whether, to paraphrase that bishop Augustinus whose new ideas were upsetting everyone, they had prayed God to give them a king, "but not yet."

"My lord, it is clear that we must mount a campaign in the midlands," answered Catraut finally, "to destroy this Anglian kinglet before he is firmly seated in his power."

"From where you sit, that may be clear," said Matauc, who had ruled the Durotrige lands from Durnovernum on the coast for many years, "but when I look eastward, what I see is that Devil's cub Ceretic in Venta Belgarum!" His tone remained mild, and Catraut, who had begun to frown, sat back again.

"*He* has been bringing in more men from Germania as well," said Cataur, "with their families, so it is clear that these wolves are after more than plunder—they mean to plant themselves on the land."

"Leonorus Maglos has been a traitor since the time of Ambrosius," answered Eldaul, "but he is concerned only with the Belgic lands."

"He is an old man—" Docomaglos's second son, Gerontius, spoke then. "Ceretic speaks for him now in Venta, and Ceretic thinks like a Saxon, for all he bears a British name."

Artor nodded. For the past year Gerontius had captained the men who guarded the king, ate at his table and slept by his door, hunted and played at *tabula* and taught him the art of the sword. It was inevitable that the boy would end by either loving or hating him, and Gerontius was as good-hearted and fair-spoken as he was tall and dark and strong. No wonder, then, if his young king listened with admiration in his eyes.

Cataur, seizing the opening, leaned forward. "The word that we hear from Venta is that Ceretic means to expand northward. Do you want to fight the Anglians with his Jutes and Frisians snapping at your heels? Icel is not yet firmly seated in his power, and he must bring those chieftains who have grown accustomed to living without a lord into line before he can lead them against us."

One or two of those present looked embarrassed at that, for what he had said of the Anglians was surely true of the British as well. But Cataur was continuing—"Ceretic's men are sworn only to him. Your argument for fighting Icel applies to Ceretic as well—let us cut out this canker on our flank before it grows!"

There was a murmur of comment at that. Artor allowed it to continue for several minutes before lifting his hand for silence once more. In two years he had at least learned how to manage a council, even if he did not yet always have the confidence to impose his will. Silently, Merlin projected his aura toward the boy and allowed some of his own energy to flow into it. To the others, there seemed only an intensification of his presence, which focused their attention until everyone was still. At first, the fifteen-year-old king had needed such bolstering constantly, but along with his father's armor, he was growing into his power.

"I think we agree we're going to have to fight somebody—" Artor's grin was reflected in the faces of some of the younger men. "And the choice seems to be between Icel and Ceretic. They are both dangerous. Tell me what we have to fight them with, and maybe that will help us to decide."

If you want to know how the colt will run, look at his breeding, thought Merlin, hearing echoes of Uthir's easy style. It sounded ingenuous, but clearly Gerontius had been talking, for it was obvious, when you looked at the problem, where the men and resources would have to come from if the British intended a spring campaign.

"By the end of this month my people will be done with the spring planting," said Docomaglos. "I can have three thousand men on Ceretic's doorstep before he gets word we are moving. We can hit hard and fast and drive him into the sea by Pentecost."

"That reasoning seems good to me—" answered Artor. "Catraut is right—Icel is a problem, but I think we'll tackle him with more confidence without Ceretic's spears pricking between our shoulder blades."

Merlin suppressed a smile. Uthir would have said ". . . poking up our backsides." But without the crudities, the boy certainly seemed to have inherited his father's knack of putting men at ease. The northern princes not only dropped most of their objections, by the time the council ended, they had even promised to send men.

It was the sound of swordplay that led Merlin to the king. After dinner, most of the princes had gone back to sit and talk and drink by their campfires, watching the daylight fade from the sky. When the druid went to look for Artor, he found that most of the younger men had disappeared.

He hardly needed magic to find them. Just outside the town, where the river flowed quiet through grassy meadows, two figures strove, shadow against shadow, the last of the sunset flickering from their swinging swords. After the first shock Merlin realized that they were doing slow work, bodies moving with the graceful deliberation of dream. But it was still dangerous. He drew breath to stop them, then let it slowly out again. He could not keep the boy swaddled forever; Artor was almost a man.

But it was a boy's voice that protested, laughing—"But how can I touch you, Gerontius, when I can hardly see?" He danced back out of range and stood leaning on his sword, breathing hard.

"If the enemy makes a night attack you won't be able to see, or in the dust of the battlefield, or if you take a head wound and blood blinds you." Gerontius straightened, his voice cool and unstressed.

A third figure, by his voice, Cai, spoke up—"At least in battle you don't have to worry about hurting your enemy."

"If you can see which ones *are* the enemy," said Artor. "Once battle is joined, Gerontius, how do you *know?*"

"If his spear is pointed at your belly, he's an enemy!" said one of the others.

"If he shouts at you in Saxon—"

"If he's facing the opposite direction from your line—"

"Artor is right—" Gerontius cut into the discussion. "In the confusion of battle it can be hard to tell friend from foe, especially now, when our warriors and the Saxons copy each other's gear. What I am trying to do with this exercise is to teach you to perceive your opponent with senses other than sight or even sound."

"Ah . . . Merlin has showed me something of that . . ." said Artor. "He said you have to sense your enemy's energy, to become one with him. But I'm not good enough to risk it with the blade, so—" He stooped suddenly, scooped up something from the grass and flung it.

There was a blur of movement and then a thunk as Gerontius's sword struck the incoming missile and smote it to bits.

"Wretch!" he said, over his students' laughter. "If that was a cow patty, I will make you clean this blade."

"No," Artor caught his breath on a whoop, "only a piece of sod."

"Very well." Gerontius tried to sound stern. "And now it truly *is* dark, so I suppose we must bring this practice to an end. There should be time for some more work tomorrow morning, however, before the *consilium* begins again."

"Not more meetings!" exclaimed Cai over the murmur of talk as they began to gather up their gear.

"Do you think that several thousand men and all their gear are moved into place by magic, as they say Merlin sang up the stones to make your father's monument? There is still a great deal of planning yet to do . . ."

As the group started back toward the buildings, Merlin fell into step beside them. Artor had learned enough to sense *his* presence—Gerontius started and went for his sword when the dark shape appeared at the king's elbow, but Artor only sighed.

"Your teaching is done for the evening, but there is still time for some of mine," Merlin said to the warrior. "Take the others back to camp. I have something to show the king."

"He must be guarded—" objected Gerontius.

"Do you doubt my ability to protect him?" He drew in a breath of power, holding it until even the warrior must be able to see his glow.

"Do you doubt that I will track you down and break every sorcerous bone in your body if you fail?"

"Stop it!" exclaimed Artor. "I feel like the bone, with two dogs growling over it. Go on, Gerontius. I'm sure we will be back soon."

"Yes, my lord—" Gerontius's voice was harsh with reluctance, but he obeyed.

"We *will* be back soon, won't we?" asked Artor when he had gone. "I've worked hard this evening, and I'm tired."

"No. But we will take horses, so you can at least sit down."

Artor stopped short. "Horses? Where are we going at this hour?"

Don't you trust me? thought Merlin, but trust and reason made poor bedfellows. He remembered suddenly something that the Saxon witch had told him about her god, that he sometimes seemed treacherous, betraying men for their own good, or some purpose greater still. Maybe he himself was a little like Woden after all. *If you learn to trust me in small things, that I can explain, perhaps you will obey when the time comes to follow my lead without knowing why. . . .*

"We go to the Giant's Dance. It lies six miles hence. If

we go now we can be there before the moon is high, and I do not know when we will be in this part of the country again."

There was a long silence. "My father is buried there . . ." Artor said at last. "Very well. I will come with you."

The standing stones cast long shadows, stark in the moonlight. In silence Artor and Merlin rode around the circle. The plain stretched away before them to a horizon dim with distance, its pale, moonwashed expanse broken only by the line of mounds.

"Who set up those stones? What are they for?" asked Artor, eyeing the henge circle uneasily.

His father had asked the same thing. Remembering, Merlin began to tell him of the ancient tribes and how they had watched the stars.

"The plain is so empty," Artor whispered when he had finished, "as if we were the only living beings in the world."

Merlin looked around him, seeing with spirit sight the need-fire that danced above the mounds.

"The only ones living, perhaps—but these spaces are thronging with the spirits of those who have gone before. That is what I have brought you here to learn. All things pass, but nothing is lost."

Artor swallowed. "Where is my father's grave?"

Merlin pointed toward the last of the mounds, the one they had raised next to the mound of the lords killed in the Night of the Long Knives.

"He lies there, with Ambrosius his brother."

"I never knew him . . . If I could meet him now, I wonder what wisdom he might have for me?"

"They say that if a man sits out the night on a sacred mound, by morning he will be mad, or dead, or a poet. We must be back at the camp before dawn, but if you wish, you might sit there for a little while."

"Is it dangerous?" Artor's voice, the druid was pleased to note, held not fear, but a healthy caution.

"The dangers are those you bring with you," he answered. "Anger for anger, fear for fear. Remember what I have taught you, and you will do well."

And if he does not, I may as well go back to my northern

forest and stay there, Merlin thought wryly, *for my life will not be worth a denarius here!* But his fear was not for the boy's physical safety. If Artor failed this testing, then everything for which Merlin had worked and suffered would be lost as well. And for the druid, this place held its own dangers; it would be fatally easy to come too close to the nexus of powers that met here, and be drawn through into some other world.

And so, as the young king took his place upon the mound that held his father's bones, Merlin his teacher sat down upon a boulder a little to one side of the line of power that ran from it to the henge of stones, to watch with him while the moon sailed serenely westward and the skies wheeled toward dawn.

When, in the grey hour before sunrise, the druid called his charge to come down from the mound so that they could begin the ride back to Sorviodunum, the boy's face was drawn, his eyes scarcely seeming to focus on the world. It was not until they were nearly back to the encampment and the first streaks of light were awakening the sky that Artor sighed and the bleak look began to leave his eyes.

"Did your father speak to you?"

"Don't you know?" The boy's voice held mixed wonder and bitterness.

"You are a child of prophecy, as am I, but our choices are our own. And this was *your* mystery," Merlin said gently. *I must learn . . .* he told himself, *to let him go.*

"Yes . . . I think he did . . ." Artor answered then. But he would not tell what the spirit of his father had said to him.

Oesc caught the blur of motion against the blue sky and dodged, thrusting up his wooden shield. The stave thwacked home with a force that nearly knocked him from his feet. He stumbled backward, shield-arm throbbing.

"You blocked well, but you were off-balance," said Byrhtwold, resting the oak stave on the ground and leaning on it.

"That hurt." Oesc let the shield slip off and rubbed his shoulder.

"No doubt. But without the shield a blow like that would have broken your arm."

"If I had a weapon I could hit you back," said Oesc. "You act as if I were still twelve winters old!"

"Maybe, but if you lose your blade in battle, only your shield will save you until you can grab another weapon," the old man replied. "Because you have been in a battle you think you are a warrior. I think you have habits which you must unlearn. So we go back to the beginning. When you can hold me off with shield alone you can practice with the blade. In the meantime, keep strengthening your sword arm."

"Chopping wood?" Oesc asked with a sigh. "That's thralls' work, I only did it before to strengthen my arm."

Byrhtwold grinned. "But good practice. And if you cannot master the skills of the folk who serve you, how will you keep them to their work?"

Oesc nodded, recognizing the futility of argument, and Byrhtwold handed him the stave.

"Tomorrow morning we will practice again." Byrhtwold turned away, then paused, relenting. "Be patient, lad—you will be chopping something more than wood soon enough. Ceretic has asked that you come with the men your grandfather is sending to Venta Belgarum. You are going to war."

Oesc stood watching as the warrior walked away, his mind in a whirl. The morning was sunny, though great puffy clouds like hanks of wool were moving in from the west, casting dappled shadows across the wall of the old theatre that dominated the remainder of the city like an old oak, after a storm has blasted all the lesser trees. No doubt there would be rain before evening. When his father first brought him to Cantuware, he had thought the buildings that still stood in Durovernum the work of etins. Then he had seen Eburacum and Verulamium, noble still despite their battle-scars.

But Venta had never been destroyed. Venta had welcomed the Saxons as the rightful heirs to the empire, as Gallia was welcoming the Franks even now, and the Visigoths had been received in Iberia. Even Durovernum was becoming Cantuwaraburh on men's tongues. *We are the future,* he thought, and if he marched with Ceretic, his own name might live in that future as well.

Ceretic assembled his allies in the fields outside of the old naval fortress of Portus Adurni that another German, the admiral Carausius, had built long ago, and there they held the feast of Ostara. It was a tribal celebration, in the old style of Germania, meant to remind men of their common heritage. The penned animals moved anxiously, as if aware of their role in the proceedings, but the rest of the camp hummed with anticipation.

Scouts had confirmed the rumors. The British princes were advancing, led by Docomaglos of Dumnonia with his sons and the boy whom they had made their king. Leonorus Maglos had fled Venta, and Ceretic had no desire to test the enthusiasm of his allies by exposing them to a seige. It would be better to meet the foe in open battle on the flood plain across from the Isle of Vecta, where the estuary of the Icene met the sea.

In the midst of the fields was a fine grove of oak trees. Here, some Roman had set up an offering tablet to Mercurius. It had been abandoned when the Christians came and grown over with vines until Ceretic had claimed the place and raised beside it an altar of heaped stones.

Oesc stood holding the tether of the white ox that Hengest had sent for the sacrifice. Across the field he could see the fyrd of Cantuware, farmers who had left their fields at their king's command, and the professional warriors of Hengest's household who had come to guard his heir. The ox stamped, and rubbed its head against his thigh, rocking him on his feet and leaving a smear of white hairs across the crimson wool of his tunic and knocking off some of the primrose blossoms from the wreath around its horns, then bent and lipped up more of the grain that had been poured out for it. A little of Oesc's anxiety eased. It was holy corn, mixed with sacred herbs and blessed by the priests, and for the ox to eat it signified acceptance of its role as offering.

He could see Hæthwæge standing with the other god-folk who had been assembled to bless the proceedings: the ancient Godwulf, who had once served at the court of Vitalinus, and two witegas who had been brought over from Germania with the most recent shipload of warriors. From the eagerness with which they surveyed the cattle, he guessed it had been some time since they had had sufficient beasts on which to practice their craft.

In the space between the animals and the men of the army

three tumblers were performing, while another beat out a cheerful rhythm on a small hand drum. As the day drew toward its nooning, the clouds began to part, and the bits of metal sewn to the players clothes flashed and glittered in the sun. Then the light broke through completely, and from within the sacred grove came the call of a horn.

The chieftains who held the nine white horses began to lead them forward, followed by the oxen. As the beast next to him moved out, Oesc jerked on the halter of his animal and joined the line. From the sound, the pigs were being brought up behind them; he pitied the men who had to keep *them* under control.

In slow procession, men and beasts moved sunwise around the grove. Aelle's son Cymen was just ahead of him, with another ox, even bigger than his own. Men of the fyrd stepped out from the encircling crowd as they passed, draping the beasts with additional garlands, or simply patting the smooth hides as they murmured their prayers—"Let me fight bravely!" "May I kill many of the enemy!" and sometimes, "May the gods bring me safely home."

As they came around for the second time, each animal was led inside the grove. The beasts were becoming more restive as the blood-scent grew stronger, but when Oesc's turn came the ox followed docilely down the well-trodden path.

The heads and skins of the earlier victims already hung from the trees. Now the ox did plant his feet, nostrils flaring, and though the boy tugged on the rope, refused to stir. As Oesc struggled to make it move, Hæthwæge came forward, singing softly, a spray of ash leaves in her hand. He recognized "Ger" the rune of harvest, and "Sigel" for victory. At the sound, the ox calmed and stood quietly as the wicce moved around him, brushing the leaves across head and back and flanks.

Ceretic came after her, a knife in his hand. He cut a pinch of hair from the curling cowlick on the animal's forehead and stepped back, holding it high.

"Woden, to you this ox is offered, for you made holy. Accept it, War-father, and give us the victory!"

The air around the altar tingled with the energy of the blood that had been spilled already. As the war-leader spoke, wind whispered in the leaves and lifted the hair from Oesc's brow, and as Ceretic opened his fingers, the white hairs whirled away.

Hæthwæge's fingers closed over Oesc's hand on the rope, and the ox followed them to the altar, where the butcher was waiting. He was a huge man, heavily muscled, with a hammer in his hand. As the ox reached the edge of the blood pit, he swung. There was a loud thunk as the hammer hit, and the ox went to its knees.

For a moment Oesc simply stared. Then he remembered to draw his seax, and Hæthwæge guided his hand to the pulsing vein in the throat of the ox and he struck and pulled the blade through.

The animal jerked, but within seconds the gush of blood dropped its internal pressure past the point of pain and the breath sighed out through the sliced windpipe in long gasps. Like everyone, Oesc had helped with the butchering each autumn, and when he was hunting, given the mercy stroke to hares or deer. Death was always serious, but he had never before understood that it was holy.

"Make your prayer now—" whispered the wisewoman, holding a brass bowl underneath the ox and letting it fill with blood.

"Woden, receive this spirit, and fill us with your soul. Father of Victory, bring my men back home to their fields, and me to my grandfather's hall!"

The eyes of the ox were dull already, and he could feel the life of the body ebbing from the flesh beneath his hands like grain from a torn bag. But the grain still existed even when the bag was empty, and he had the sense that the life of the ox had not been extinguished so much as drawn away.

Your flesh will give us power! he thought. *May my own blood, when the time comes, be as good an offering!*

The blood was draining now in spurts. Hæthwæge took Oesc's arm and pulled him to his feet, and as the last of the flow dribbled into the pit, men looped ropes around the ox's feet and hauled it away to be skinned and butchered for the feast that would follow. The wicce dipped the spray of leaves into the blood and sprinkled Oesc, then handed it to the boy and gave him the bowl.

Still dazed, Oesc made his way out of the grove to bless the men whom he hoped to lead to victory.

* * *

The armies came to battle three days later, under weeping skies. The Saxons formed their shieldwall on the shores of one of the streams that came down to the sound, feet planted in the muddy soil, watching the British cavalry sweep toward them across the plain. Rather than creating a solid line, Ceretic had ordered each contingent to form a wedge, so that more of the spears could come into play. It was a saw-edge that would cut the British to pieces, he had told them, riding up and down along the river bank.

Now the commander stood with his hearth-companions at the center, his white horse led off by a thrall to the rear. If he turned his head, Oesc could see the gleam of the gilded boar image that crowned the steel crest of Ceretic's helmet. On the other side, Aelle waited with his sons beside him. Oesc's helm was rounded, with a nasal and side flaps, and ringmail hanging around the back and sides. Beneath tunic and mail shirt he was sweating, but most of his men would fight with no more protection than a leather cap banded in iron, bodies defended only by their shields.

Beyond the reed beds, pewter-colored waters stretched away to a smudge of darker grey that was the island. Above the army, gulls rode the wind, crying like wælcyriges seeking out the slain. Soon they would be able to make their choices. The British were drawing steadily closer, trotting in close formation. Their shields were painted Roman-fashion, each contingent bearing its own device. He could see the glitter of their lance-heads as they came on. Perspiration made his hand slip on the shaft of his own throwing spear. Oesc leaned it against his shield, wiped his palm on the skirts of his tunic and grasped the javelin once more. Hæthwæge had a spear, he thought suddenly, as powerful as Artor's legendary sword. Why, he wondered, had Hengest not ordered her to bring it to war? When they got home he would ask her.

If he got home. . . . The British were cantering now, nearing with appalling speed. Surely the river would slow them, he thought, and then the hooves of the horses were churning the water into arcs of glittering spray. They surged up the bank like a rising wave, lancepoints dipping in deadly unison.

Oesc set his feet in the mud, lifted his left arm and felt

his shield braced by those of Byrhtwold on one side and Eadric on the other, and raised his right arm, spear poised to throw. Wild-eyed horses expanded to fill his vision, the faces of the riders contorted above their shields. He felt a yell leave his throat, lost in the roar of the Saxon battle cry.

A ripple of motion swept the shield wall. Instinctively his arm swung forward, releasing the spear. Here and there the oncoming tide of horsemen faltered, but that first flight of spears was not enough to stop them. Oesc hunched behind his shield, straining to hold it in place between the others as an oncoming horseman struck the line.

The shieldwall rocked backward, and for a moment Oesc was lifted off his feet, but he did not fall. The enemy horse, pierced by spiked shield-bosses, reared, screaming. A lance thrust down at him, passing just above his shoulder. Oesc managed to get his sword free, and glimpsing a mailed body, stabbed upward. For a moment he felt as if he were supporting the entire weight of man and horse, then the foe recoiled and he caught his breath once more.

The British riders had broken the shield hedge in several places, and were in amongst the Saxons, stabbing with lance and sword. Others had swirled off to either side in an attempt to outflank them. Over the tumult Oesc glimpsed a dragon banner that he supposed must belong to Artor. It was being carried by a big man with dark hair. Then a horse loomed suddenly above him; a sword clanged against his shield boss and he gave ground, and for a long time after that was too busy to think about anything at all.

Consciousness returned gradually on a tide of lamentation. *Why are they weeping? Am I dead?* Oesc wondered. But the dead didn't feel pain, and as awareness returned he realized he had a raging headache and was sore everywhere. For a few moments he lay still, trying to remember.

Then a flash of memory showed him Byrhtwold lying sprawled before him with a spear thrust through his chest. After that he had been seized by battle madness. That must be why he felt so awful now. *They must be wailing for Byrhtwold,* he thought then, and felt hot tears on his own cheeks. *He died saving me.*

Oesc opened his eyes. Blurred vision showed him a night

sky and the shapes of men moving back and forth between him and the fires. Then he tried to sit up and discovered that his hands and feet were tied.

Alarm shocked through his body, sharpening his senses. The lamentations he heard were in the British tongue, and the faces and gear of the men around him were British as well. He had been taken by the enemy.

He knew enough of their language to make out the words—

> Before Gerontius, scourge of the foe,
> I saw white horses swiflty go,
> After war cries, bitter the blow . . .

At least, he thought with grim satisfaction, the Saxons had accounted for one hero among their enemies. The British were not rejoicing, and yet he was a prisoner, his mail shirt enough to mark him as worth saving for ransom. Who had won the battle?

He took a deep breath and tried to break his bonds, and at the effort agony slashed through his head, dividing him from consciousness once more.

When Oesc opened his eyes again, it was morning. His other wounds had stiffened painfully, but the headache had subsided to a dull throb.

"Yes, that's him—" said a Saxon voice nearby. "Octha's whelp. I saw him in Venta."

Biting his lip to keep from groaning, Oesc rolled over. Squinting against the sunlight, he looked up at his captors. The Saxon was only a churl, of no importance. He blinked, trying to make out the features of the other two men.

"Let me kill him!" said one of them, a man of about thirty years with curling dark hair. "My brother's blood cries out for vengeance."

"Do you think I don't mourn him too?" said his companion. Oesc couldn't see him properly, but he sounded young, his voice hoarse with unshed tears. "He taught me to fight! He saved my life a dozen times yesterday . . . he was my friend. . . ."

"We all grieve for Gerontius, but this one is worth more to us as a hostage," said an older man.

"How so? He's no kin to Ceretic."

"True, but he is Hengest's grandson, and while we hold him, Cantium will stand surety for Ceretic's good behavior."

There was a long silence. Though his head was throbbing furiously, Oesc struggled to get up, refusing to remain bound like a thrall at his enemies' feet.

"Cut his bonds," said the young voice tiredly.

The older man sawed at the thongs with his knife and hauled Oesc to his feet, supporting him until the dizziness passed and he could stand alone.

Artor... thought Oesc, taking in the rich embroidery on the bloodstained tunic, and the golden torque beneath the thin fringing of brown beard on the jaw. He himself was a bit taller, otherwise there was little to choose between them for size.

"Can you understand me?" Artor asked, waiting for his prisoner's nod. "We didn't win the battle, but neither did you. You will come with us, bound by iron chains in a wagon, or bound not to try escape by oath before your gods, riding free. It's up to you."

Your father killed mine... thought Oesc. There was a dagger at the king's belt. If he could grab it and strike, Octha would be avenged. But at this moment it was taking all his strength just to stand. Once more he met Artor's eyes, and this time he could not look away.

He saw grief in that gaze, and a weariness almost as great as his own, and something else that he did not understand. Oddly, at that moment what he remembered was the trust in the eyes of the ox he had led to sacrifice. He had heard that the Christians of Eriu called it a white martyrdom, when they were exiled from their land. He swallowed, knowing himself self-doomed.

"I swear... in Woden's name. I am the offering."

V

The Raven's Head

A.D. 480

 While Ceretic licked his wounds in the south and Icel gathered strength in the midlands, Britannia lay at peace. Even the Picts and the Scotti were keeping quiet, and Artor's advisors thought the time ripe for him to take possession of his father's city of Londinium. With him went his houseguard and his servants, and Eldaul of Glevum and Catraut of Verulamium, who had become his principal ministers. And with him also went Oesc, his Saxon hostage, riding sad and sullen in the rear.

Oesc's heart ached to think of his grandfather waiting for him in that shadowed hall. Hæthwæge would take care of the old man's health, but who now would play at tabula with him in the long evenings, or bring in venison when the salt beef of winter began to pall?

And more than he could have imagined, Oesc missed Cantuware. When he closed his eyes at night he could see how the waterfowl spiraled down into the marshes, or the wind brushed gentle fingers across the growing grain. He could see sunlight falling through the forest of the Weald in showers of green and gold, and blazing with pitiless clarity on the high shoulders of the Downs.

It was that day in the temple at Ægele's ford that had made the difference, he thought, looking backward. Sometimes he cursed Hæthwæge for having brought him there, and sometimes he took comfort in the memory. He was rooted now in Cantuware as deeply as if he had been born there, and away from it he would never be happy, even if he were free.

He was not badly treated. Rough repairs had made most of the old Governor's Palace habitable, and there was room enough for all of Artor's household there. Merlin had rooms in an old tower, but was rarely in them, being often away to other parts of Britannia, carrying messages, said some, while others whispered that he went off to consort with demons.

Oesc grew accustomed to carven pillars and marble facings and cold tiled floors. He had a whitewashed chamber to himself, with a shuttered window that opened out toward the river. Only sometimes, wandering through an empty passage or a courtyard where a dry fountain accused the sky, he remembered how he had felt once when he dressed up in his father's armor. It was as if he and all the others here were only children, playing at being kings, and soon the adults who had built these halls would reclaim their dwellings. Sometimes, watching Artor as he sat in splendor on the dais of the basilica, he wondered if the high king felt that way too.

But the legions were gone. Odoacer, a warlord among the Saxons whose father had been one of Attila's generals, ruled now in Italia, and unlike the barbarian generals who had gone before him, he refused to nominate a Roman as titular emperor. The Empire of the West was ended, and only in Britannia, and the parts of Gallia where Riothamus led British warriors whose families had fled the island after the Night of the Long Knives, did its memory live on.

On an afternoon in October, Oesc stood with the rest of the household in the basilica, watching as Artor welcomed a delegation from Gallia. He was placed near the front, with Cunorix, the son of an Irish chieftain who had been making trouble in Demetia. All the hostages were on display together, he thought bitterly, like the high king's sight-hounds, who lay panting on the mosaic floor, or the tiercel hawk on its perch by the throne.

With nothing much else on which to spend his energy, Oesc had found a certain interest in watching the young king grow into his power. Artor was now almost twenty, and a man's beard, clipped close, outlined the strong curve of his jaw. He had dressed for the occasion in a dalmatic of crimson silk, with twin bands of embroidery running over his shoulders and down to the hem on either side. Around his neck glinted the golden torque of a Celtic prince, but there was Byzantine enamel work on his diadem.

Oesc, who had become accustomed to seeing his captor lounging by the fire in his favorite tunic of faded green wool, suppressed a smile. But the dark-haired boy who followed the Gaullish envoy was gazing in awe at the marble facings on the walls and the gilding on the coffered beams of the distant ceiling, and most of all at the brilliant figure on the throne. To him, Artor *was* the emperor.

Eldaul stepped forward and read from a scroll, "Johannes Rutilius, Comes Lugdunensis, bears greetings from Riothamus, Dux of the Britons north of the river Liger, to Artorius, Vor-Tigernus of Greater Britannia."

"Let him approach—"

The dark-haired man with the boy bowed.

"My king, I bring the best wishes of my lord Riothamus for the continued good health of yourself and your realm." His British had an odd accent, but by this time Oesc understood the language well.

Someone in the crowd behind Oesc snorted. "About time— were they waiting to see if the lad could hold onto his crown?"

"My lord offers a treaty of trade and alliance. The Franks worry at our borders in Gallia as the Saxons trouble you here. Barbarians sit at their ease in the Holy City, and the Emperor in Constantinople is very far away. You and Riothamus, my lord, are the heirs of the Western Empire, and it is only good sense for you to work together."

"As you say," Eldaul interrupted him, "we are still fighting the Saxons. What help will Riothamus offer us?"

"Nay," growled one of the older men, "we need no help

from men who fled Britannia when the Saxons first rose against us in blood and fire."

Artor frowned at both of them. "I think Gallia needs all her men for her own defense, and our own warriors can defend us here," he put in quickly.

"But the wharves of Londinium are often empty," Catraut added. "Trade has been poor while the Saxon wolves ranged the Narrow Seas. Once Britannia helped to feed the empire. Send us merchant ships, with war galleys to guard them, and we will send you corn from the rich midlands that we still hold."

The flush that had risen in Johannes's face subsided. "That is what I have come to propose, though I would add a provision that either ruler might call for aid to the other if times should change."

"That seems good to me," Artor said while his advisors were still drawing breath to answer.

"In earnest of our sincerity I have brought you my own son, the child of my wife who is sister to Riothamus, to serve you as part of your household." He set his hand on the boy's shoulder and pushed him toward the throne.

"What is your name?" asked Artor, learning forward with his elbows on his knees and the first genuine smile of the afternoon.

"I am Betiver, my lord." The boy spoke softly, but boldly enough—he must be accustomed to courts, thought Oesc.

"Then you shall be my cupbearer. Would you like that, Betiver?"

"I would like it very well—"

Betiver's eyes were shining. Oesc sighed. There was no denying that the British king had charm. All of the younger men were half in love with him. *Except for me . . .* he thought, glowering.

"Then you may stand over there, and tonight, when we feast in honor of your father, you shall serve me." Artor gestured toward the hostages.

As the business of the court continued, Betiver turned to his new companions.

"Who are you?"

"We're the king's hostages. This black-headed lad is Cunorix, an Irishman from Demetia, and I am Oesc from Can-

tium." Now, he thought, the boy would understand what his
status truly was, despite the fine words.

"Do you dislike it?" Betiver asked with surprising percep-
tiveness. "They say that the great Aetius was a hostage with
the Huns, and Attila himself hostage for a time in Rome.
That's how we learn about other peoples and their lands."

For that to be any use, thought Oesc sourly, *you have to
get home again.* But he said no more.

One evening just past Midsummer, when every window
had been opened to let in whatever cooling breath of breeze
might come from the river below, Artor came striding back
from a meeting of the council with a face like thunder and
Cai at his heels.

Oesc and Cunorix, who had been taking turns playing
Round Mill with Betiver, stood up as the king appeared in
the doorway. To try and get three counters in a row on the
diagram was a children's game, but Oesc liked it because
the pattern reminded him of a Germanic protective sigil
called the "helm of awe." He made a grab for the counters
as the board rocked, then straightened again.

"I've spent most of a stifling day listening to old men
argue," said Artor. "They may have no blood in their veins,
but mine needs cooling off. I'm going down to the river for
a swim—would anyone else like to come?"

"I would!" cried Betiver, knocking the board askew as he
pushed past. Cunorix rescued it this time and set it on his
bed. He glanced at Oesc and then nodded.

"We'll come too."

As they trooped down the stairs toward the riverbank, it
occurred to Oesc that Artor, surrounded by old men who all
thought they knew what should be done better than he did,
was in a sense a prisoner too. There was something sad in
the thought that he had to turn to his own captives for company. It made Oesc uncomfortable to feel sorry for Artor,
and he thrust the thought away, but as the evening continued,
it kept coming back again.

The palace lay close to the river, but they had to follow
the path along the banks for a little ways before they came
to a landing where the bottom was shallow and firm enough
to wade in. Some of the men from the town were already

splashing happily, accompanied by shouting children. Someone looked up as they approached, saw they were strangers, and looked away.

Artor turned, his eyes alight, and held up one finger for silence. Oesc realized then that stripped down to thin tunics or breeches, with no mark of rank or royalty, they looked like any other group of young men out for a swim. He stepped out of his sandals, pulled off his tunic and laid it over a bush; in another moment his breechcloth had followed. Like all the children of the marshlands, he had learned to swim when he was small. He entered the water in a long, low dive that took him far out from shore. The current was stronger than he had expected, and cold. He had to swim hard to get back to the shallows once more.

Artor reached out and Oesc grasped his hand, a little surprised at the strength with which he pulled him in. Then he got his feet under him and stood, gasping.

"Don't go out too far—current will take you away," Oesc said in warning.

"I know . . . sometimes I wish it would. . . ."

There was a moment of strained silence. Then Artor saw Oesc staring at him, gave his head a little shake, and smiled. In the next moment he was splashing Betiver, and in the water-fight that followed the moment of understanding was gone.

But when the light of the long summer day faded at last and they reluctantly pulled on their clothing once more, Oesc still remembered that odd sense of equality.

The day might be ended, but they were young, and so was the night. A century earlier, Londinium had been the metropolis of Britannia, and for every one of the more utilitarian businesses there had been a wine shop or taberna. Most of them had disappeared with the Legions, but now that the high king was in residence, they seemed to be sprouting on every street corner once more.

Betiver, who was the sort of child who never forgot his hat or broke his shoe latchets, was the only one of them who had brought his belt-pouch. It held enough coins for them all to drink at the first taberna they stopped at, and the second. By the time they got to the third wine shop, Cunorix had won more money dicing with an Armorican sailor. At the fifth, Artor himself won them a round of drinks at ring-toss.

By this time, all of them were exceedingly merry. Oesc, a veteran of serious Saxon drinking bouts with ale and mead, discovered that he had no head for wine. But it didn't matter. Artor was a good fellow—Cai was a good fellow—and so were Cunorix and the boy. The serving girls with whom they flirted were all beautiful. The carters and tradesmen with whom they were drinking were good fellows too, seen through a vinous, rose-pink, haze.

"Got an idea—" He draped an arm across Artor's shoulder. "Take your people, my people, get 'em to drink together. Make 'em be friends!"

"You're drunk, Oesc." Artor hiccoughed, then laughed. "Guess I am too. Sounds good to me. Maybe that's how the Romans . . . got their empire!" They all laughed.

It was very late by the time they ran out of money again, and by then the tabernas were beginning to close. Betiver had fallen asleep with his head on the table, and Cai hoisted him over one shoulder as they staggered out the door. The damp night air was bracing after the boozy warmth of the wine shop, but their steps were still a little unsteady when they heard the first light footfalls behind them.

Oesc shook his head in an attempt to clear it, and saw the stars spin. If this was an ambush, he was going to have to fight drunk or not at all.

"My lord—" came Cai's voice from the darkness, the first time he had used the title all evening.

"I heard. Take the boy on ahead."

How, Oesc wondered, could he sound so cool?

"Artor! My place is here—"

"Get Betiver to safety. That's a command! Cunorix, Oesc, stand back to back with me!"

"I'll go for help!" Cai salved his conscience. He started to run, and at the sound of his footsteps, their attackers came out from the alleyway.

At least, thought Oesc as he braced himself against the others' shoulders, *this way I won't fall down.*

"We've drunk up all our money," Artor said clearly. "You'll get nothing but blows for your trouble."

"Yon black-headed lad has a silver buckle, and you are

wearing a ring. That's worth food and drink to starving men."

Oesc squinted at the approaching shadows. They didn't move like starving men.

"Go to the palace if you are hungry, and they will give you food. You are breaking the king's peace and will be punished if you harm us here."

As Artor was speaking, Cunorix whispered in Oesc's ear to watch out for the man on the right, who had a knife, while the others were armed with clubs or staves.

"Why should the king care what happens in the streets?"

"Believe me, he cares!" answered Artor. His laughter ceased as their assailants came on.

The robbers were five to three, and sober. Oesc drew a deep breath. "Woden!" he cried, as the first blow hit, and heard Artor calling out to Brigantia. The wine had blunted their reactions, but all three were warriors, trained to fight even when they could not see. With fists and feet they deflected the first rush and the second. When the third came they were gasping, but alarm and exertion had burned most of the alcohol away. What remained dulled the pain of the blows.

There were a few moments of furious action, followed by a pause while everyone stood gasping. One of their opponents lay on the ground, while another was holding his belly where Cunorix had kicked him. Oesc felt Artor straighten.

"Well, my friends, we have cleared the board a little. I think it is time for the king-piece to break out of the fortress!" Before they could object, Artor had sprung forward and scooped up a fallen club and was swinging it at the nearest foe.

Cunorix shrieked something in Irish, lowered his head and charged, and Oesc headed toward the third man. At last he was free to fight! The rage he had repressed during his captivity filled him with a new intoxication. He saw a stave whirr toward him, lifted his left arm to protect his head and heard a crack as it hit. The impact whirled him around, inside his opponent's guard, and his right fist drove toward the other man's throat. Something gave way with a sickening crunch and the man fell, gurgling.

Artor had felled his man, and Cunorix was grappling with

the other one. Oesc drew breath to speak and gasped as the numbness in his arm began to give way to a throbbing agony. Artor held up one hand, listening.

More men were coming. But what they were hearing now was the ring of hob-nailed sandals and the jingle of military harness, not a footpad's stealthy tread. Cai had rousted out the city guard at last.

Oesc's broken arm healed slowly, though the tongue-lashing Artor received from his advisors when they returned to the palace no doubt left deeper wounds. Only Merlin, who had returned from one of his journeys shortly after, seemed to understand. Rumor had it that the reaction of Artor's mother, arriving for one of her periodic visitations, was more vigorous.

To occupy Oesc's mind during his convalescence, a priest called Fastidius was sent to teach him the language of the Romans, and the others involved in their escapade were encouraged to study with him, whether as a punishment or to keep him company was not clear.

"*Arma virumque cano . . .* " The words were intoned with the sonority of a man who loved the language and a clarity of accent that Oesc was already learning to recognize as being of another order entirely than the camp Latin many of the soldiers used. "And what, my child, do those words say?"

"*Arma*—that means weapons," answered Oesc. This sounded much more interesting than the grammar the old man had been teaching them before. "Does *virumque* have anything to do with men?"

Through the open window he could hear the sounds of men and horses, and from farther off, a distant mutter of thunder. The heat wave had broken, and the air was cool and moist with the promise of rain.

"A man," Fastidius corrected. "The object of the verb. And the *que* at the end of it—what does that mean?" His watery gaze fixed on Cunorix, who stared as if an armed man had sprung from the ground before him. In fact, thought Oesc, he would probably have faced a warrior with less fear.

Artor took pity on him. "It means *and*, does it not? 'Of arms and the man I sing.' "

"Hmm," said the priest, "you have studied the language before."

"It was spoken in the home of Caius Turpilius, who fostered me," answered the king. "But I have not had much practice in reading."

"Ah . . . you will want to understand the messages you receive from foreign kings without depending on a scribe, and to make sure the messages written for you express what you want to say."

It had never occurred to Oesc that a king could be his own interpreter, but he could see now that it would be useful. Certainly the priest seemed to understand. Fastidius was an old man, trained in the golden days before the Saxon Revolt when his namesake the bishop wrote letters of civilized amusement at the idea that sensible men could ever accept Augustinus's harsh doctrine. Their sufferings at the hands of the Saxons had made a belief in predestination more credible, but the old priest still behaved as if the purity of one's Latin were as important as the purity of one's soul.

Cunorix cleared his throat. "But what does it mean?"

Fastidius smiled, and without looking at the scroll, began to chant once more—"*Troiae ui primus ab oris Italiam fato profugus Lavinaque venit litora* . . . Who from Troy by fate caused to flee came first to the shores of Italia and Lavinium . . . It is the story of Aeneas, who escaped the fall of the great city of Troy and became the founder of Rome."

"I have heard of him," Artor said slowly. "They say that the ancestors of the Britons came from there with Brutus, his great-grandson."

But to Oesc it seemed that the story of this Aeneas must be very much like that of his own people, driven by need to seek a new home on a foreign shore. He pointed to the scroll.

"How did this Aeneas get to Italia, and what happened to him there?"

Fastidius smiled. "I thought that you might like the story. It is full of battles. Some of my brethren would say that you should study texts of the Holy Fathers. But it seems to me that you will learn better with something you find interesting, and also, Vergilius wrote much better Latin."

"Even Cai, here, might learn something if it is about battles—" Artor punched his foster-brother playfully. "He was a very poor pupil to our housepriest at home!"

It did seem that with the *Aenied* for their text they made better progress, following the adventures of the Trojan hero around the Mediterranean in his search for a home. And when the frustration of untangling Latin declensions became too much for their patience, Fastidius could be tempted into regaling them with tales of British heroes, for he came from the isle of Mona, where memories were long.

When autumn arrived, the whole court followed the Tamesis upriver to the hills for a few weeks of hunting, and came back brown from sun and wind and pleasantly fatigued by hard riding, with enough wild meat to vary the menu for some time. It had been good to get out, but in some ways the city seemed even more stifling afterward, especially when the weather changed and the early winter rains set in.

"Do you know any stories about Londinium?" asked Betiver one day when the leaden skies wept steadily and damp draughts crept in under every door.

Fastidius set down the tablet on which he had been checking Betiver's lists of Latin verbs and smiled. "I have told you already how Brutus founded the city and called it Troia Nova, which was in the British tongue, Trinovantum, because the Trinovante tribe came to dwell there. They say that his descendent, Lud, built walls and towers and renamed the city after himself. But that was just before the great Julius Ceasar brought the Romans to these shores. The Latin histories tell us that Londinium was only a small river town which the Romans rebuilt in stone, so I do not know what the truth may be."

"Buildings are not very exciting," said Cunorix. "Are there no other tales?"

Fastidius's brows, which were white like his hair, and rather bushy, bent. "There is another story, that ends here. If you will take up your tablets and write out all the forms of *placare,* 'to soothe or calm,' *conloquor,* 'to negotiate,' and *agere,* 'to make a treaty,' then I will tell you a story from Pagensis, where the Ordovici ruled, about a king who was so great in stature that no building could hold him."

"You think that we are so averse to using words of peace that we must be bribed to learn them?" asked Artor, laughing.

"I think that you are all young men, who believe that glory can only be won in war . . ."

Betiver had already picked up his stylus and tablet and was busily making marks in the wax. Grinning, the others began to work as well.

When they had finished and been corrected, Fastidius kept his promise.

"A long time ago there was a ruler of the Britons called Brannos, so great a king that men called him Blessed, and that became part of his name—in British, Bendeigid Brannos. He gave his sister Branuen in marriage to the king of Hibernia, but one of her half-brothers was angry because he had not been consulted, and he disfigured the horses of the Hibernian king, which was a great insult. Brannos paid compensation, and the girl went over the sea with her new husband, but the Hibernians still brooded on the insult, and presently they forced the king to punish his wife by making her a servant at his court. But Branuen had some magic of her own, and she trained a starling to carry the news of her torment to her brother in Britannia."

Nobody looked at Cunorix, who had gotten rather red in the face, but Artor motioned to Fastidius to go on.

"So the princes of Britannia went to war, the warriors in ships, and Bendeigid Brannos wading across the water, and there were great battles, and greater treacheries, and in the end, the Hibernians were defeated, but of the Britons only seven remained beside the king, who had been wounded by a poisoned lance in the heel. When Brannos saw that the poison would overcome him, he gave certain orders. And then, as he had commanded, they struck the head from his body, and took it back with them to Britannia."

"What were his orders?" asked Artor.

"What happened to Branven?" asked Betiver. Cunorix only glowered.

"The princess, remembering that because of her, two great peoples had been destroyed, died of sorrow. But the seven companions feasted for seven years in one habitation, forgetting their sorrows, and in another for seven again, listening to the birds from the Otherworld, and the head of Brannos was with them, uncorrupted. And when that time was done, they opened the door that looked toward the south, and then, as he had prophesied, they remembered everything."

It was a strange tale indeed, as Fastidius had promised them. To Oesc it seemed as if for him and Cunorix it had more meaning, for their people still lived as the Britons had lived before the Romans came. Cai was staring out the window, bored, as usual, by anything that was not about fighting, and Betiver listened with a child's wonder. But what did Artor make of this story of an ancient king?

He was already taller than Oesc, who overtopped most men. But in the past year Artor's body had thickened to match the promise of the strong bones. *This is no longer a boy to be led about by old men,* thought Oesc, *I wonder when his advisors will realize that their bear cub has become a bear?* The cold illumination from the window lit one side of the king's face and left the other in darkness, eyelids half closed to hide his thoughts, mouth grim. *His father killed mine . . .* Oesc told himself, but some other part of his being wished only that Artor would smile.

He cleared his throat. "What did they do then?"

"They followed Brannos's orders. They carried the head to the White Mount, the sacred hill by the river in Londinium, and there they buried it, face set toward Gallia. The word of Bendeigid Brannos was this, that while his head remained there, so also would his spirit and his power, to ward Britannia from plague and destruction."

"So, even in death a king may still watch over his people . . ." said Artor. His mouth was still grim, but there was a light in his eyes.

"It is so in the old Jutish lands," said Oesc. "There, when a king's reign has been peaceful, with good harvests, they build a great mound over his bones and set out offerings, so that his name is remembered and he becomes one with the gods."

"It is the bones of the saints and the blood of the martyrs that protect Christian lands!" said Betiver.

"Neither saints' relics nor a severed head seem to have protected the empire from the heathens," growled Cai. "I prefer to trust to stout hearts and strong arms."

"Perhaps Brannos's protection depended on a different

kind of power," said Fastidius placatingly, and unrolled the scroll containing his grammatical notations once more.

The winter drew on, cold and wet. In the north and the midlands, it was a cruel season, with storms in which both men and cattle froze. But in Londinium, the sleet never quite seemed to turn into snow. The high king's household struggled with the old hypocaust system, but even when they got it working, the warmth that came up through the floors was never quite enough to offset the cold drafts that came in around the doors. There were many times when Oesc missed Saxon farmhouses. Dark and odorous though they might be, they were warm.

But presently the days began to lengthen, and occasionally they saw the sun. The skies echoed with the bitter music of the wild geese as they winged northward. Messengers went out to call the princes of Britannia to council. In the midlands, the snow that had fallen on hill and dale was melting, and the Tamesis began to rise.

"Am I or am I not the king?"

Oesc, who had been repairing his bow in hopes that they might soon get some hunting, opened his door and peered out. That had sounded like Artor's voice, but he had never heard it so angry.

Now he could hear a murmur of other voices, soothing or remonstrating.

"Be still—you prattle at me as if I were a fractious child!"

It *was* Artor. Oesc set down the bow and went out to see what was going on. He found Cai leaning against a pillar, watching the king stride back and forth across the cracked stones of the courtyard.

"He's always been like this, even when we were boys," said Cai. "He doesn't get mad often, but when he does, it's bad. He broke my nose and left me bruised for a week once when he thought I'd mistreated a horse, back when I was twelve and he was nine and I was a head taller than he."

Oesc didn't ask whether it was true. Cai was heavy handed with most things; he broke weapons and wore out his mounts faster than other men.

"He needs to crack someone's head or take a woman," Cai added, "but I don't suppose he will."

Oesc nodded. He knew that Cai sometimes went to the whores who served the soldiers, and Cunorix found comfort with the Irish serving girls. Oesc himself had always feared to be rejected because he was a Saxon. What Artor's reasons for continence might be he did not know.

"What's set him off now?" He asked.

"The old men on the council. They want someone to sit on the throne and look handsome, not a king. Artor got mad when they voted to exempt all Church lands from taxation."

"Does he want money?"

"Not for himself—for the troops up on the Wall. Your people have been quiet, but the Picts and the Scotti are always a threat, and all the regular army Britannia still has is up there. The landowners at least send men and supplies, but the Church expects to be protected for nothing."

Artor's long stride had slowed, and the high color was beginning to leave his cheeks. "Can't they understand? The time to build up your dikes is before it floods. We need to maintain a fighting force that can deter invasion, and that means money."

The placating murmur continued.

"I think God hears soldiers as well as priests. I have no quarrel with the Church, but its business is prayer, not politics, and not all in this land are Christian. Anyhow, that isn't the problem now. They wouldn't even listen to my reasoning! They as much as told me to run away and play, and I didn't—I couldn't—answer them!"

Oesc hid a smile. That's how it was for Saxon war-leaders most of the time. Except for the sword-thanes, vowed to stand by their chieftains till death, warriors served voluntarily, and felt free to argue. It amazed him sometimes that the Germans had been able to conquer as much as they had. But hunger was a powerful motivator. These Britons were too accustomed to safety. They had received a sharp lesson, but clearly it was easily forgotten. If they had been willing to pay the troops who protected them, Hengest would never have asked for land.

"If you could—if they would listen to you—how would you order Britannia?" he asked.

"With a strong government. Rome succeeded because there was strength at the center to make all the provinces help and defend each other. It failed because it got too big. Britannia is a good size for communications, with defined borders."

"You mean to rule all the island?" asked Betiver.

"What about the Picts? asked Cai.

"What about the Saxons?" Oesc echoed.

"It seems to me," Artor said slowly, "that when tribes or regions think too much about their own rights and practices and needs they fight their neighbors, and then they are easy prey for any better organized enemy who moves in. Julius Caesar conquered the British tribes because they could not work together. Your grandfather overran half the island because Vitalinus and Ambrosius would not make an alliance, and failed to keep it because your Saxon tribes would not accept a single high king. I know that rival emperors fought each other, but for most people, most of the time, within the empire there was peace."

"But at what price?" asked Cunorix. "Your Romans leveled peoples as they leveled the ground for their fortresses. Is peace worth losing everything that makes you who you are?"

"Did I say I thought it would be easy?" Artor said ruefully. "I would be king for the Romans and the British, the men of Eriu who have settled on these shores and the Picts and even the Saxons, if they would accept me, each with their own customs, living in peace with their neighbors."

"Foster-brother, you are crazy," Cai shook his head pityingly. "Even the Lord Jesus could not make them all agree."

"Jesus himself said his kingdom was not of this world, though some of our bishops seem to have trouble remembering it. What I am talking about requires an earthly king."

"You certainly seem to have spent some time thinking about it—" Betiver said admiringly.

Artor shrugged. "Sitting through all those meetings, what else do I have to do? I know that the king has to be strong enough to defend the borders and keep people within them from killing each other as well. He should encourage trade and sponsor public works. All this requires taxes, which people do not want to pay. He must keep local chieftains from oppressing their own people, but give them enough freedom so they will support him. Maybe it *is* impossible—but if they would stop treating me like a child, I would try!"

"You have a magic sword. Does not that give you the authority?" asked Oesc.

"That's an *old* miracle," Artor answered bitterly. "I need a new one to impress the princes—or maybe I am the one who needs a sign that this is what I am supposed to do. . . ."

Artor was still muttering when a workman appeared in the doorway, eyes bulging and muddy to the thighs.

"My lord, come quickly! They've found a head—some say it's a demon and some say it's a god. It was walled up, my lord, like a thing of power. They want to throw it into the river. I tried to tell them not to, but they wouldn't listen!"

"I know how you feel—" said the king. "Very well, I'll come. Perhaps the *people* will be willing to listen to me!"

"They call it the White Mount, my lord, but it's only just a little hill beside the water—"

Oesc saw Artor's step falter for a moment, and remembered suddenly where he had heard that name before. He hastened his own steps to catch up with them as the workman chattered on.

"The river's been rising, you see, and we was trying to drive in a few stakes to help hold the bank. And we hit something hard, though of course we didn't know that's what it was, and Marcellus says, 'That's funny—' and then the ground just sort of fell away and we could see the big slabs of stone with the water gurgling round."

Ahead a knot of people had gathered by the waterside. Someone saw the king coming, still dressed in the finery he had worn to the council, and shouted, and the crowd began to swirl toward them.

"I told them to leave it be, but Marcellus said that's good building stone, and he got a hook down the crack and pulled, and the whole slab came over, and then—"

But by then they were at the riverside, and Artor gestured for silence. As the workman had said, it was only a small hill, but it was crowned by three fine oak trees. Several ravens were sitting there, and as they approached, more came flying, calling as they circled the hill. Oesc felt a prickle of unease, and seeing Artor frown, knew that he too had felt the breath of the Otherworld. Cai stood with his arms folded, glaring back at the crowd.

People gave way before them. At the edge of the water the hill gaped open, the slab that had fallen revealing a small, square chamber, walled and roofed with stone. This was no Roman construction—the size of the stones reminded Oesc of etin-work he had seen. Water had seeped across the stone floor and around the stone block that stood in the midst of the chamber. On top of it was what appeared to be the head of a man of giant size, frozen in stone. Blank, almond eyes stared out from either side of a long straight nose, the whole surrounded by masses of undulant hair.

Artor gazed at it for a moment, then bent to peer in. "Look, Cai—" he called. "It's pottery, not stone at all."

"Don't touch it—" Cai began, but Artor was already entering the chamber.

"Nonsense," he said over his shoulder. "If we leave it here it will be destroyed." There was a general gasp as the king grasped the pot in both arms and turned to carry it outside.

As he brought it into the sunlight, the shouting subsided. "Bendeigid Brannos . . ." said someone, and the whispers became a murmur of awe.

Seen full on, the features reminded Oesc a little of Merlin, and yet, though the druid's brown mane had the same wildness, Oesc had never seen on his face such a look of majesty. But he did not have long to compare them. As the light fell full on the surface of the pot, a fine network of cracks began to ray out across it.

Artor fell to his knees in the mud, cradling the pot against his chest, but in moments the clay was crumbling. As it fell away, they saw that it held neither ashes nor treasure, but a single human skull. For a moment only they looked upon the great empty eye-sockets and the mighty jaws, and then the skull also began to crumble. Clay and bone fell in fragments through Artor's fingers into the water, and the current whirled them away.

The ravens came skirling down from the trees after them, lamenting, but above their cacophony rose a woman's scream—

"The Raven of Britannia is gone! Brannos the Blessed has

abandoned us and we are lost!" Now there was an edge of hysteria in the hubbub of the crowd.

Artor looked down at his hands, still white with clay and bone, then he stood up again, and there was something in his face that made Oesc go cold inside, for in that moment it held the same look he had seen in the statue's eyes. With a single easy movement Artor leaped up onto the grass.

"People of Britannia, do not despair . . ." The king's voice was not loud, but it carried. "The ancient king protected you for many years, but his task is done. His remains have been released to find rest with the sea, his father, but his spirit remains with me." He held out his arm, and the largest of the ravens, circling, alighted upon it.

"Do you see—the ravens recognize my right! Now it is I who shall be Brannos, and take upon me his duty. To the end of my life and beyond I will be your protector!"

"You are only a man, and one day your bones will be dust!" came a hoarse voice from the crowd.

Artor turned, and the people grew silent. "Keep this place holy, a sanctuary for the ravens, for I tell you now—so long as the ravens dwell on this hill, my spirit will ward Britannia!"

"Artor Brannos!" came the cry, "Artor the Blessed! Artor! Artor!" The echoes rang.

The people were all around Artor now, asking for his blessing, touching his hand. Oesc watched with wonder and pity in his heart. When he made his own dedication at the shrine it had only been for one lifetime. He sensed in this spontaneous avowal a commitment far more binding than whatever oath Artor had given to the Christian god when he was made king.

Eventually the people dispersed and the king was able to return to the palace. The raven flew back to the oak tree, but it was a long time before the strangeness left Artor's eyes.

"It was only a skull," said Cai very softly as they passed through the gates. "And Brannos was only a legend."

Oesc nodded. That might be true, but the moment during which that skull, whoever it belonged to, had been visible had been long enough for him to see that it was larger than the head of any ordinary man.

VI

The Feast of Lugus

Just after Beltain, in the eleventh year of Artor's kingship, Naitan Morbet, King of all the Provinces of the Picts, broke the peace that Leudonus had imposed upon him and came south in force. It was a year of barbarian victories. In Gallia, the new king, Chlodovechus, had led his Franks against Syagrius and defeated this last Roman at Augusta Suessionum. In Italia, the Ostrogoth, Theodoric, ruled as *magister militum* in the puppet emperor Zeno's name. And in Britannia, it seemed as if the time of the wild tribes had returned.

Before Leudonus could gather men to stop them, the Picts had swept around his eastern flank, across the tumbled stones where once the Romans had sought to establish a far northern frontier, and were swarming up the vale of the Cluta, burning everything in their path. King Ridarchus had warning enough to marshal his warband, but they were powerless against such a host and barely made it back to the safety of the Rock of Alta Cluta, where they took refuge, cursing. For this was no raid, but a carefully planned campaign. Leaving a swathe of destruction behind them, the Picts rolled up the old Roman road and through the passes, heading for the rich Selgovae lands and Luguvalium.

In Londinium, their first news came from a dust-covered courier whose horse fell dead beneath him as he pulled up before the palace. The scroll he bore was as clear a cry for help as anyone had ever heard from Leudonus. Indeed, commented Cai when he heard of it, ever since the British princes had chosen Artor over him as high king, the king of the Votadini had sent very few communications of any kind.

"Maybe so," Artor had replied, "but he has been sending his taxes, and even if he had not, this challenges the whole of Britannia."

Since the episode of Brannos's head, Artor had begun to assert himself. His counsellors protested, but they could not stop him from sending out messengers to speed past the fields of young grain, calling on the men of Eburacum and Deva and Bremetennacum and all the forts that were still manned along the Wall to gather to his banner at Luguvalium by Midsummer Day.

Oesc listened to the hubbub of preparation with mounting frustration. In the past, he had tried not to mind when Artor rode out against the Angles or the Saxons. But Artor and Cai and even young Betiver were already making names for themselves as fighters, while he, as young and strong as they were, practiced his Latin and his archery. Even if he were freed, why should his own people accept a man with no experience in war?

He was in the library of the palace, helping Fastidius to sort scrolls, when a sudden draft set the lamp flames to flickering and he turned and saw it was the king.

"It is your arms you should be sorting through, not these scrolls," said Artor, standing with arms folded in the doorway.

Oesc felt his cheeks grow red. He had never quite dared to think of the British king as his friend, but surely too much respect had grown between them for the other man to mock him.

"My lord, don't tease him—" said Betiver, appearing next to him. "Oesc, go get your gear—Artor wants you in his war-band when we go against Naitan!"

From red, Oesc knew he was becoming pale. Artor came

forward and grasped his arm. "I could not ask you to fight your own folk, but the Picts are no kin to you, and I will need every man. And indeed, I would be honored to have the grandson of Hengest at my side. . . ."

Oesc found his voice at last. "I have fought beside you once already, my lord." He rubbed the arm that had been broken in the fight, which still gave a twinge now and again when it was about to rain. "I will be glad to come."

Betiver looked up at the red sandstone walls of the great fortress called the Petriana with a grin of sheer pleasure. *This* was Rome, whose mighty works none of the new tribes would ever equal. The Petriana was still the headquarters for the senior officer of the Wall command, and it was better cared for than most of the forts the Legions had left behind them. When he surveyed the massive gatehouse and the strong walls that protected the city of Luguvalium, a few miles to the south, he was certain that the Empire of the West would be restored, with Artor as Imperator.

First, of course, they would have to do something about this troublesome Pictish king. But Betiver had grown from spindly youth to warrior in Artor's service, and it never really occurred to him that his king could fail.

Certainly, with the army that was gathering here to support him, Artor must have the victory. They had filled up all the empty barracks within the fortress, and more were camped along the banks of the river. And even as Betiver turned back toward the Principia, where Artor, following tradition, had made his headquarters, he heard a horn call from the eastern tower. Another band of warriors was coming in.

By the time Betiver reached the king, they all knew who it was. Leudonus of the Votadini, having come south by the eastern route and then along the Wall, was bringing all the men he could spare from the defense of his own lands to fight with them. Gualchmai, the eldest of his four sons and Artor's nephew, rode at his side.

That evening they feasted in the great hall of the Praetorium, where once Artor's grandfather had ruled with Caidiau, commander of the troops at the western end of the Wall. If there were a few more cracks in the tiled floor and a few more nicks in the pillars, still, it was a noble room, especially when the flower of Britannia filled it, glowing in their tunics of crimson and ochre and green, with gold at their necks and wrists and gleaming on the hilts of their swords. Artor himself had honored the occasion by putting on the Chalybe sword. It made some people uneasy, but there was no doubt it added to his majesty.

Artor had suggested that Betiver and Cunorix sit beside Leudonus's son, reasoning that he was the most likely to understand how a youngster new to the court might feel. Not that young Gualchmai had any problem with self-confidence—he was big for his age, with sandy hair and the promise of his father's burly build. One saw the resemblance to Artor only in the set of his eyes.

"My father is the greatest king in the north," he stated as the platters of boiled meat were being brought in. "Naitan Morbet is a sneak and a coward. If he had attacked Dun Eidyn instead of running around us, we would ourselves alone have been beating him already—"

"And saved the rest of us a very long ride," Cunorix responded pleasantly. "It was kind of you to let us share in the fun."

Gualchmai frowned, as if not quite sure how to take that. "I am hearing that my uncle Artor is a great warrior too," he said a little more politely. "It will be fine to see him fight."

"There are many fine warriors in your uncle's army," Betiver continued in the same tone. "There is Cai, who was his foster-brother, and Cyniarcus, son of the prince of Durnovaria. Beside them sits Cataur of Dumnonia, who is a very mighty man." He saw Oesc grimace at the name. Cataur had never ceased to hate the Saxons for killing his brother at Portus Adurni, and had made no secret of his opposition to Oesc's presence on the campaign.

"The men of the north are mighty too," Gualchmai said stoutly. "There is Peretur son of Eleutherius, come in from Eburacum, and Dumnoval of the southern Votadini over there by his side. But when myself and my brothers are grown we will be the greatest warriors in Britannia."

Betiver took a drink of ale to cover his smile. "How many brothers do you have?" he asked when he could control his face again.

"Gwyhir has thirteen winters, a year less than me, and wild

he was that he could not come with us. But my mother would not allow it. If she could, I think she would keep all of us by her, but my father insisted, which he does not do often anymore. Aggarban is only ten, which is far too young for war, and Goriat is four and just a baby. But they are all big and strong for the years they have, and I have given my promise that the first of them who can knock me down shall have my dagger!" He patted the weapon that hung at his belt, a handsome piece of work with a cairngorm set in the hilt.

Later that evening, when Leudonus had taken his heir off to bed, Betiver found himself with Oesc by the fire.

"I am sure that Artor set me there so that the boy might have a friend among all these warriors, but believe me, that young man needs no reassurance." He proceeded to summarize their conversation, hoping to get a smile. Oesc was a good fellow, but too often one saw sadness in his eyes.

"Where does it come from?" asked the Saxon. "Leudonus does not seem so overbearing a man."

"Not now, I suppose, though I hear he was very ambitious when he was younger. And then there is their mother, who was trained on the Holy Isle. If we get to Dun Eidyn, maybe we'll meet her."

Oesc nodded. "If we get that far."

"You will get there—" rumbled a deep voice behind them.

There's no reason to be nervous, Betiver told himself as he turned to face Merlin. But he came from a land where druids, if indeed Merlin was not something worse, were only a memory, and he never knew quite how he ought to react to the man. Oesc had stiffened, his face showing no expression at all, but then where *he* came from, every chieftain had a witch or wise man at his left hand.

"My lord Merlin—" he said politely. "Have you seen this in the stars?"

"I have dreamed of Artor standing on the Rock as the sun sets behind him." The druid leaned on his staff, frowning. "You will fight Naitan Morbet, and pursue him." The great beard, streaked with silver now, twitched as he smiled. "But I do not think I will ride with you. My bones grow too old for long marches with armies. Perhaps I will walk in the forest of Caledonia for a time, and refresh my soul."

Merlin trying to be pleasant was even more unnerving than Merlin being grim, thought Betiver.

"Do you wish me to tell you if you will survive the battle? That is what all the other warriors wish to know."

Betiver shook his head, suppressing a shiver. For a moment Merlin's eyes were unfocused, looking through him. Then the old man blinked, and that dark gaze fixed Betiver once more.

"What you do not ask, the spirits have answered," he gave a bark of harsh laughter. "You will live long, and serve your lord to the end." For a moment he looked at Oesc, frowning, then without another word turned and moved away through the crowd.

"How very odd!" said Betiver, trying to laugh.

"He is a dangerous man," answered Oesc, but he would say no more.

With the Votadini, Artor's muster was complete. They moved out in good order past the fields of ripening grain, fording the rivers that emptied into the Salmaes firth until they came to the Stone of Mabon, a finger of rock set there by men of a time so ancient no one remembered their names, and honored ever since as the phallus of the god. In happier times it had marked the border between the Novantae and Selgovae lands, and the tribes had met on the flats beyond it for trade and festival.

Betiver took a deep breath of the brisk air, rich with the scents of grass and tidal mud and the salt tang of the sea. He had fought with Artor before, but this was different. They were beyond the Wall, now, in a land which had only intermittently accepted the yoke of Rome. He tried to pray, but the Christian god seemed irrelevant in this wilderness; he understood why someone had cast a garland of flowers around the Mabon stone.

He wondered how long it would take for the enemy to get there.

Any force moving down from the north with designs on Luguvalium must pass this way or take to the water, and the Picts had never been seamen. To the north, smoke hung like a dark smudge across the sky. The enemy was coming, and Artor's army took position to meet them—in the center nearly a thousand light infantry who had ridden to the battle and left their horses in the rear, and almost as many cavalry, armed with lance and sword, arranged in two wings to either side.

Betiver's mare stamped nervously and he patted her neck beneath the mane. His sword was loose in the sheath, his shield slung across his shoulder. He unfastened the straps of his round topped helmet to cool his head, then tightened them once more and changed his grip on the lance that lay along his thigh.

When were the Picts going to come?

Artor had taken command of the right wing, spreading his horsemen out in a curve across the rising heathland above the meadows. The warriors of his household were with him, except for Oesc and Cunorix, who had never learned to fight on horseback and were stationed among the foot fighters, mostly men of the hill country to the south of Luguvalium. Cador of Dumnonia and his seasoned troops held the left, on horses accustomed to the ocean, who would not panic if the battle pushed them into the shallows of the firth. And in the middle, Peretur of Eburacum commanded, backed by the band of Alamanni warriors who formed his personal guard.

Betiver had been in battle against Saxons, using the weight of the cavalry charge to break their line. He had never fought other cavalry before. Neither had Artor, he thought unhappily. They had all done practice fighting, but it was never the same.

Every time he waited for the fighting to start he hoped that this would be the time he learned how not to be afraid. The child Gualchmai, sitting his horse behind his father, was watching the road with barely concealed impatience. But he didn't know how it was going to be. Artor's face, as always, was a little pale, his eyes intent and grim. Betiver had never yet dared to ask him if he felt fear.

Would the Picts never come?

And then between one moment and the next, the skyline changed. Suddenly, not only the road, but the meadows and the farther hillsides were covered with moving dots. Metal flashed and flickered in the watery sunlight. They didn't seem surprised to see the British force awaiting them, but then they must have had scouts out, and he had heard that a

Pictish scout could lie concealed in a clump of heather, and track a gull upon the breeze.

He felt hot and then cold. The dots were becoming tiny men on shaggy ponies. Most of the British had some kind of body armor—mail or scales of leather or metal or horn, as well as helms. The Pictish warriors rode with cinctured saddle cloths and only a few of them had helms. Many bore no more than a cloak or a sheepskin over their breeches; from a distance the tattooed beasts that spiraled all over their bodies made their skins look blue. But they carried stout shields, round or square and covered with bull hide, and long spears, and wicked looking swords. They seemed to be coming without order, but here and there a rider bore a wooden standard with a painted fish or bull or some other beast, so they must be riding in clan groups or bands.

Horns blared mockingly, answered by the bitter music of Artor's clarions. A shiver ran along the British line. Betiver picked up his reins and the mare bobbed her head, pulling at the bit. The clarions called again, and suddenly Artor's cavalry wing was moving, its line extending outward to hit the enemy on the flank and force them down upon the infantry's waiting spears. Ahead, he saw a larger standard with the elegantly executed image of a red stallion.

"Artor and Britannia!" cried the men. "Ar . . . tor . . ."

The shout tore through Betiver's throat. He dropped the rein on the mare's neck and shrugged his round shield down onto his arm; racing alongside the other horses, she needed little guidance. Without his will his arm lifted, lance poised.

And then the enemy horsemen were before him. A lance flew toward him and he knocked it aside with his shield, he stabbed, struck something and gripped the mare's barrel hard with his knees as he pulled it free.

"Ar . . . tor . . ."

Thought fled, and with it, fear, as Betiver was engulfed by the fray.

By afternoon, the battle was over. Oesc was glad to mount again, for what had been a fair meadow that morning was now a trampled wasteland, and blood ran in streams to redden the sea. He had come through the fight without much harm, though there was a slash on his thigh that made walking painful. The pony whuffed uneasily as he guided it back over the battlefield, calling the wagons to pick up British survivors and dispatching the more badly wounded of the enemy with a merciful thrust of his spear.

The fleeing survivors of Naitan Morbet's army were out of sight by now, closely pursued by Artor's cavalry. Perhaps he should learn to fight astride, Oesc thought grimly, so he could go with them. It was bad enough to fight a battle, but in the grisly work that came after there was neither excitement nor glory.

Where the land began to rise there was a heap of bodies, as if some desperate band of warriors had chosen it for their last stand. Most of them were Pictish, and all were quite dead. Among the corpses lay a wooden standard, carved and painted in the shape of a red stallion. Oesc frowned, remembering how it had threatened them in the morning light. He dismounted then, and began to pull aside the sprawled limbs of the warriors. Beneath them, as by now he was expecting, lay the body of a thick-bodied man with grizzled hair. Under the jutting beard a golden torque gleamed, and across the broad, naked chest was tattooed a horse and the double disc symbol of a king.

Oesc could see no mark upon him; perhaps the gods had struck him down in the midst of the battle. That happened sometimes with old men. But there was little doubt that this was Naitan Morbet, the lord of Pictland, who had set the lands from the Tava to the Salmaes ablaze. Oesc lifted his horn to his lips and blew, summoning the British captains to come and see.

Leaderless, the Picts fled northward like fallen leaves before the wind. Artor released his infantry and the men who lived farthest away to go home to their harvests while the British cavalry sped after the enemy, disposing of stragglers in a series of brief, bitter engagements that left the enemy dead, or less often, captive. The Picts were not destroyed entirely. Small groups of riders who knew the land could go where the larger, more heavily armed pursuers would never find them. Nonetheless, only a tithe of the great army that Naitan Morbet had led southward at Beltain ever returned to celebrate the feast of Lugus in the Caledonian hills and glens, and an unhappy line of prisoners followed when Artor's army at last reached Dun Eidyn.

From the high ridge of rock and the dun that crowned it to the flat meadow in the cleft below, the air pulsed with the sound of the drumming. From time to time a bitter skirling of pipes would gather the rhythm into their music, but when it ceased, the drums continued, the audible heartbeat of the land. The noise had continued since the beginning of the festival. By now, Betiver was aware of it only intermittently, when some shift in the wind amplified the volume, or when, for no reason that he understood, for a few moments it would stop. Sometimes, when the drums beat softly, he thought that pulsing might be the mead pounding in his brain, for during the past three days food and drink had flowed freely.

Those of Artor's men who had not gone home to help with the grain harvest camped in the meadow; it was a welcome opportunity to relax and recuperate from the long days on the trail. The hay had been cut, and the cattle brought down from the hills. The first fields of grain to ripen had been ceremonially harvested, and the clans of the Votadini, with the cattle they wanted to sell and the daughters they wanted to marry off, had come in. For the princes and lords of the king's household, it was a visit to a more ancient world that had never gone under the yoke of Rome.

"Is it so different?" asked Oesc, leaning back on the spread hides beside him. "My own people also make offerings at harvest time." Light from the bonfire reddened his fair hair.

Betiver shrugged. "At home in Gallia the priest offers prayers for the success of the harvest and the laborers feast when it is done. Maybe the country folk do other things, but I lived in towns and never saw them. There was never this great gathering." He sunk his teeth into the flesh that clung to the beef rib he was holding and worried it free.

"That is true. Among the Saxons, the next great feast will not be until autumn's ending, but that is for the family, like Yule. It is at Ostara and sometimes Midsummer that our tribes come together for the sacrifices."

"In Eriu, Lugos of the Long Arm is still honored," said Cunorix. "We hold a great festival for him at Taltiu, with a cattle fair."

Betiver nodded. For a moment it had seemed to him that the three of them, all born elsewhere and brought to Britannia, were equally foreigners. But he came from a land and a way of life long Christian, whereas Oesc and Cunorix were still as pagan as these Celts in their multicolored garments, dancing around the fires.

"Look there—" Oesc pointed. Gualchmai was moving among the feasters, his upper body swathed in a mantle of gold and brown and black checkered wool fastened with a silver penannular brooch. The skirts of a short saffron tunic showed beneath it, with black banding woven into the hem. In his hand he gripped a silver-mounted drinking horn.

He caught sight of the three Companions and made his way toward them, grinning widely.

"See—my father has given me this new horn! Tonight I have leave to stay and drink with the men."

"I am glad to see that you came through the battle unhurt," said Betiver. "Will you sit and drink with us, then, and tell us what is going on?"

"I will that—" Gualchmai said something in a dialect too thick for Betiver to follow to the wiry, red-headed tribesman who had been escorting him, and joined them on the cowhide. "Even my mother is agreeing that I am a warrior now I've seen battle. My brothers have to be staying up there with the women—" He pointed at the enclosure of loosely woven brush where the wives of the chieftains were holding their own festival. It was a flimsy barrier, but even a drunken man would not breach that sanctuary.

Not that the rest of them were without female companionship. The tribesmen had brought their families, and many of the girls had volunteered to help serve out the ale and mead. And when one of them, liking the looks of a southern warrior, settled down on the grass with him instead, no one seemed to think the worse of her. Betiver had noticed already that the women of the northern tribes had a freedom that would never have been permitted in a Christian land.

Gualchmai's red-headed servant returned with a pitcher full of mead and refilled their horns.

"Tell me, what is that platform with the fenced space in front of it?" asked Oesc.

"Oh, that is for the ceremony. Do you not have it in the

south?" he asked as the men looked inquiring. "When Lugus kills the Black Bull who has carried off the Goddess and is holding back the harvest."

"Nay," Betiver said gravely, "I have never seen such a thing."

"Well, the sun has set," answered Gualchmai. "You will see something soon."

Westward, the sky blazed with banners of gold, as if to honor the vanished sun. The last light glowed soft on the rough rock of the cliff and the timbers of the palisade above them, and the thatched roof of Leudonus's high hall. Even as they watched, a spark appeared on the ridge below the eastern gate; in the next moment there were more, a line of torches winding like a fiery serpent down from the dun.

Closer, one saw the white robes of the men who led the procession, ghostly in the half-light.

"Druids!" exclaimed Betiver. "I did not know so many of them remained."

"In the north they do—" Gualchmai said smugly.

"And in Eriu," added Cunorix.

"They call Merlin a druid," observed Oesc.

"Merlin . . ." Betiver shook his head, thinking of the stories. "He has the druid knowledge, but he is something different. Some say the Devil fathered him and gave him his powers."

"If I believed in your Devil I could believe that was so," said Oesc somberly. "But my grandfather's wisewoman calls him witega, which means an oracle."

"My father's druids prophesy, and read omens," put in Gualchmai. "But they also conduct sacrifices and ceremonies."

Betiver twitched. He had been raised a Christian and held to that faith. But so had Artor. Whatever was going to happen, they could not insult their hosts by refusing to participate. If there was sin in it, he would simply have to ask Father Fastidius to give him a penance once they were home again.

The druids drew closer, men of middle-age or older, with flowing hair and beards. Upon the breast of their leader gleamed a golden crescent, and he leaned on a staff. Then Oesc drew his breath in sharply, and Betiver saw that behind the druids walked a group of dark-clad women.

"Those are the she-druids, the priestesses—" said Gualchmai. "And my mother . . ."

But Betiver had already noticed that one of the women had covered her dark robe with a mantle of crimson. As she moved toward them, her ornaments cast back the torchlight in running sparks and flickers of red gold. He did not need to be told that this was the queen.

Margause walked as a woman certain of her beauty and secure in her power, shoulders braced against the drag of her trailing mantle, head high. Her hair fell in waves of dark fire across back and shoulders, bound with a golden band. More gold swung from her ears and lay across her breast and weighted her wrists. Men fell silent at her coming; some bent, foreheads touching the earth in reverence.

It seemed irrelevant to call her beautiful. Deep-breasted and wide-hipped, her body was made for bearing. But from her face all the girlish softness had been fined away to reveal the faultless sculpting of bone at cheek and brow. At the entrance to the women's enclosure she paused, gazing across the assembly beneath painted eyelids. Then she disappeared into the shadows within.

Only then did Betiver realize that behind the women marched the warriors escorting Leudonus and the high king. Leudonus wore a plaid of the same hues as his son's; Artor a linen robe the color of the ripening fields. It was the first time since he had first set eyes on Artor as a child of thirteen that he had not been immediately aware when his lord drew near. He blinked, wondering if it was the mead that had dizzied him. Artor and his host were still talking. While the chieftains feasted, the kings had spent the afternoon hearing reports from the couriers sent to Caledonia to arrange for the ransom of prisoners. Men said that Drest Guithinmoch was the Picts' new king.

"And there is my father," said Gualchmai. "With the lord Artor. When you ride south again, I will be going with you. My mother was against it, but my father thinks it will be good for me to learn about the southern lands."

Betiver and Oesc exchanged glances, but managed not to smile. Until Artor married and begot a son, this boy had a good claim to be considered his heir.

The royal party ascended the platform and took their places on the benches there. The druids formed a line across the front and one of them lifted a bronze horn with a curious long shaft and blew. The sound did not seem loud, but it echoed from cliff to cliff and vibrated in the bones. When it finished, Betiver realized that every drum in the valley had stilled.

> *"The host of heaven, the summer stars,*
> *Upon the sky fields they are gathered,*
> *Upon the earth, fair Alba's children . . ."*

The voice of the druid was thin and clear; Oesc felt the fine hairs on his neck and arms lifting at the sound. The northern intonation made it hard for him to understand some of the words, but it hardly mattered. The dark earth was sown with fire, and the cliffs framed a sky of luminous dark blue, blazing with a harvest of stars. The meaning of the words blossomed in his awareness without need for understanding as the ceremony went on. Woden had given the god-men of the Saxons this power, but until now he had not found its like in the British lands.

> *"Behold, Midsummer has passed,*
> *the moon's sickle harvests summer stars;*
> *The womb of the Mother swells:*
> *Cattle grow fat, grain grows high.*
> *Her children arise and flourish in the land.*

The line of druids divided, revealing a throne set at the back of the stage, and upon it the shape of a woman, swathed in dark veils.

> *"The Mother has given birth, and her Son is grown;*
> *Lord of the Spear of Light, the god of the*
> *clever hands,*
> *Let the Son of the Mother arise and come forth to*
> *bless his people—"*

The hides nailed across the base of the platform shivered, and a new figure emerged, costumed in golden straw. Plaited and sewn, it formed a helm that covered head and face. Two tiers of straw flared out in a cape and a skirt below it. But his shield was of new wood with a gilded boss, and the head of his spear flashed gold.

For a moment he stood, staring around the circle, then, his voice slightly muffled through the mask, he began to sing.

> "Well have you worked and long have you labored,
> Now comes the time to receive your reward.
> Rest and rejoice now, all uncertainty ended;
> Laugh, make music, feast and frolic—
> My love is the heat that warms you;
> My light is the radiance that shows you the world."

"That is Lugus," said Gualchmai. "He is the bright god who can do everything. The ravens teach him wisdom."

"In my country they say that his spear is so powerful its head must be kept in a cauldron full of water or it would burn up the world," Cunorix said then.

Startled from his trance, Oesc stared at him.

"The god of my people, Woden, sends his ravens out to bring him knowledge, and claims the battle-doomed with his spear . . ." he whispered.

"My old tutor once told me that the mother of Apollo came from the land of the Hyperboreans in the far north, and that once he guided the people of Thera in the form of a raven," said Betiver. For a moment his eyes met Oesc's, then he crossed himself and looked away.

The god is here, thought Oesc. *Maybe this is the name he bears in the British lands.* After being for so long cut off from his own rites and his own people, he trembled, opened suddenly to awareness that the mummery before him was raising and focusing power. And even as this thought came to him he realized that the energy was shifting. The hides moved once more as a huge, dark figure shouldered between them, swathed in a cloak of some black stuff, helmed in leather that supported a pair of bull's horns.

"*Lord of the Lightning, canst Thou deny me?*" His voice was a deep rasp that raised the hackles. He lumbered back and forth, head lowered, while the bright god turned continually to face him. The druids moved back, and torchlight glittered from brooch and torque as the princes seated on the benches leaned forward to see. Artor's eyes followed the mock-combat, bright with interest.

> *"I am the Shadow at Thy shoulder,*
> *The darkness Thy light casts.*
> *I come from the depths of earth*
> *To devour the children of the day.*
> *All that the Mother bears is meat for me—*
> *The harvest and the cattle that eat it*
> *And the men whose life the cattle are.*
> *The Lady of Life I will hold prisoner—"*

He made a rush toward the platform, feinting with his club, and the veiled woman who sat there flinched. He stopped then, club upraised, and the valley rumbled with his deep laughter.

> *"I am the Black Bull.*
> *I am the plague that kills your young men,*
> *the flood that drowns your fields,*
> *the fire that burns your homes.*
> *I am the Destroyer*
> *Who shall trample your lives to dust!"*

At the words, Lugus straightened, brandishing his spear.

> *"And I am the Defender!*
> *I fight for all that the Mother has made!*
> *I will stop the floods and free the Lady,*
> *I will bring back the sunshine and win*
> *   the harvest."*

The veiled Goddess rose and came to watch from the front of the platform as weapon poised, he advanced upon his foe.

Once, twice, thrice, they circled, feinting back and forth in mimetic combat. But though their movements were stylized, the energy they were raising was real. With the third exchange, the Black God struck, and a sudden billowing of dust obscured the scene. When it thinned, in place of the human opponent stood a black bull.

It was, Oesc realized in astonishment, quite real. Like the men, it must have come from beneath the platform, but how they had kept it quiet there he could not imagine, for the beast was clearly in good health and full possession of its senses. Its dark gaze fixed on the glittering figure and it snorted, head lowering. A little shiver of tension ran through the crowd; there was hardly a man among them who had not at some point in his life been chased by a bull, and they recognized the warning signs.

The priest of Lugus shook his spear and began to sidestep around the bull, getting into position for a fatal blow. But the bull, shaking its head, turned with him. The priest extended his shield arm, shaking it a little to get the beast's attention. The massive head lowered, and suddenly the animal was in motion. If the priest had intended to strike as the bull went by, the beast was too fast for him. Even as his arm moved the bull was passing; the spearhead scored a long gouge in the animal's flank just as it hooked one horn into the shield and jerked it away.

The shield soared like a sunwheel, slapped against the fence and fell to the ground. The priest's gaze followed it, but the bull, with a better sense of priorities, was already wheeling toward the brightness of his cape and helm. The man was brave enough. He stood his ground as the bull surged forward, leaping aside at the last moment to stab.

But his courage was better than his timing. As he leaped, the bull swerved with a vicious sidewise swipe of the horns that hooked through straw and leather and grazed the priest's side. As the impact knocked him backward, the spear flew from his hand and slid rattling across the ground.

The torches flickered as a collective gasp of horror passed through the crowd. There was always this chance, that the Black Bull might win, and a murrain on the cattle and storms that spoiled the remainder of the harvest, would bring them a starving winter and death in the spring.

The bull turned, pawing, as the priest struggled to his feet, eyeing the distance between himself, the bull, and his spear. At almost the same moment it became clear to both the man and the beast that he could not reach it in time. With pre-

ternatural intelligence, the bull moved, tail twitching, not toward the man, but toward the weapon that lay on the ground.

And then there was another movement, another figure that
dropped, as if from the heavens, into the ring. For a moment
Oesc thought it was one of the druids; then he recognized
the barley-gold tunic and his blood chilled.

"Sacrilege!" cried someone. "He must not interfere!"

"Nay—he has the right," said another, "he is the king!"

A memory of his grandfather filled Oesc's vision, the body
swinging from the old oak tree. *It is the right of the king to
give his life for the people . . .* he told himself. Without willing it he leaped to his feet; his muscles locked with the effort
it took to keep from rushing to Artor's aid. Betiver stood
swaying beside him. Others had risen as well. But for each
British warrior there were two Votadini, ready to seize him
if he should try to intervene.

The bull hesitated, for a moment uncertain as to what this
new foe might be. It was long enough for Artor to pick up
the spear. Muscles rippled along the dark flanks as the black
bull charged. The king made no attempt to evade him. Still
on one knee, he braced the spear and held it steady as the
bull came on.

"Sweet Jesus," exclaimed Betiver, "does he think he's facing a boar?"

But a boar-spear had a cross piece to prevent the animal
from running all the way up the shaft, and hunters could be
killed trying that trick even so.

Then the bull was upon him. Dust swirled madly as the
bull's own weight impaled him upon the spear. The wicked
horns jerked savagely—was the man under them?

The thrashing figure changed shape suddenly; somehow
Artor had evaded horns and hoofs and got astride the bull's
massive shoulders. One hand gripped a horn; a dagger
flashed in the other as Artor bent, reached, and ripped the
sharp steel through the throat of the bull.

One last time the mighty body convulsed, nearly unseating
him. Then the black bull collapsed, blood pumping onto the
ground.

For a long moment nobody moved. Then Artor freed himself from the body and the druids, frantic lest the sacrifice

be wasted, rushed forward with bronze basins in which to catch the blood.

Oesc remembered how the life of the bull he offered before the battle of Portus Adurni had ebbed away beneath his hands. But it seemed to him that the energy that flowed out of this bull was pouring into Artor, who stood wide-eyed in the torchlight, with a crimson stain across his golden robe.

Drums began to pound, a soft insistent rhythm that transformed shock and confusion into a mounting excitement. "Behold!" cried the chief of the druids, his voice steadying as he went on—

> "... the Goddess is freed and the monster is slain.
> Now shall the sun return to those lands that
>   need it.
> To each power there is a proper season—
> A time for the light to shine and a time
>   for darkness,
> A time for death and a time for life to flourish.
> But now it is the time for harvest!
> Therefore let there be no shadow on our celebration;
> The Bull's blood buys your lives!"

The druids moved among the people with their blessing bowls, and Oesc pressed forward with the others, and felt, for a little while, as if he were no longer a stranger.

The priestess of the Goddess still stood on the platform, swaying to the drum beat. As she moved, her draperies swirled around her, and it became clear that, although she was masked, beneath the veils she wore nothing at all.

The druids finished cutting off the head of the bull and hoisted it onto a pole. On the platform before the Goddess they placed some of its flesh, along with bread baked from the first grain of the harvest. Some of the others pulled Artor back up onto the platform and set his hand in that of the priestess.

Lifting their linked hands, she cried out in a great voice—

> "The grain feeds on the earth,
> The folk feed on the grain,
> Earth feeds on the folk;

> *So it is, so it was, so it will be—*
> *Eater and eaten, feeder and fed,*
> *All that dwell on earth must become.*
> *Receive now the blessing of the harvest*
> *the grain that is cut down,*
> *the blood that is shed.*
> *From these things, my children,*
>   *your life shall spring."*

Men moved through the crowd carrying platters of meat and bread. Girls followed them with skins of mead and ale. The drums grew louder and the pipes began to skirl above their beat in ecstatic melody. The rhythm pulsed through Oesc's veins like fire.

On the platform, the priestess had begun to dance—if it was the priestess, for to Oesc's altered vision she seemed suddenly taller. Beneath the half-revealing veils, her pale flesh glowed. Someone handed him a horn of mead and he swallowed. He heard laughter, saw a red-haired girl grab Betiver around the neck to kiss him. For a moment he resisted, then his arms went around her. After a moment she pulled back, laughing, took his hand and drew him after her. Vaguely he remembered Cunorix following another girl a little earlier; Gualchmai had disappeared as well.

Oesc looked back at the platform. Some of the priestess's veils had come off; he glimpsed bobbing breasts, a long, rounded thigh, and felt his flesh spring to agonized attention. *Frige . . .* he thought, *Desired One . . .* then he remembered that the Lady was called Brigantia here. But whoever She was, she had the kind of beauty a man sees in dreams. Artor still stood before her, swaying in a tranced echo of her movements, his eyes wide and dazed.

A soft hand closed on his and Oesc looked down, glimpsed dark eyes and a merry grin and wildly springing black hair. But it hardly mattered what the girl looked like. He grabbed for her, groaning as soft breasts were crushed against him, a supple waist flexed beneath his hands. Over her head he saw the veiled Goddess take Artor's hand and lead him toward the back of the platform. In another moment they had disappeared into the darkness.

Then the girl's arms locked around his neck. Groaning, he let her draw him down to the hide, and after a brief struggle with their clothing sank between her welcoming thighs and came home.

vii

The High Seat of Hengest

A.D. 488

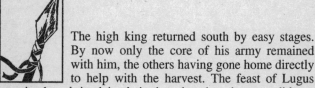 The high king returned south by easy stages. By now only the core of his army remained with him, the others having gone home directly to help with the harvest. The feast of Lugus remained enshrined in their thoughts, but the men did not speak of it, neither to boast of their conquests, nor to wonder if some of the laughing girls with whom they had lain that night might come away from the festival with something more than a memory.

That winter they stayed with Peretur in Eburacum. The Saxons of the north remained quiet, for which Oesc was grateful. He was finding it hard enough to remember the brief time he had spent in this country with his father, without having to face in battle men who had given him his first lessons with the sword.

For he knew that if Artor asked, he would ride with him. The other men had accepted him as one of the high king's chosen Companions. At night he dreamed in the British tongue and by day found his memories of Cantuware growing dim. Even if he returned there, would the people accept him? He had become some curious hybrid, neither fully British nor truly Saxon anymore.

From Eburacum they moved south and west. For a time they stayed with Bishop Dubricius in Isca. There was some fighting as well, for Cunorix's kin in Demetia had been reinforced from Eriu, and were seeking to extend their territory. They proved more troublesome than expected, and the campaign lasted through the summer. And so it was not until early in the following year that the high king returned to Londinium.

Just after the feast of Candlemas, a rumor came to them that Hengest had died. Oesc knew of it first when men began to look at him oddly, whispering. An overheard remark revealed the cause, but he continued to behave as if he had not heard, grateful for time to try to understand his own feelings before he was forced to some public acknowledgment.

Oesc had at that time been among the Britons for nearly nine years. If this had come in the first years of his captivity, he thought, his grief would have been overwhelming. But for too long his memories of Cantuware had brought only pain, and so he had walled them away where even he could not reach them anymore. And that, he told himself, was probably for the best. No doubt Hengest's empty high seat would soon be filled by some ambitious Jute, or perhaps it would be seized by one of Aelle's sons.

By the time a month had passed, he had well-nigh persuaded himself that he believed this. And so when Artor summoned him it was, at least to his conscious mind, a surprise.

"Let us walk along the river—it is too fine a day to stay indoors." Artor reached for the crimson cloak that lay across the chair.

Oesc raised one eyebrow, for the wind had been brisk as he crossed the courtyard, and Artor flushed.

"Well, maybe it is a bit chilly, but I refuse to stay cooped up here. You can wear a cloak of mine—"

And so they fared out, wrapped alike in royal crimson and very much of a height. From a distance, the only difference between them would be his fair hair against Artor's brown.

But Artor was lord of most of Britannia, and Oesc was, despite all the marks of consideration, his prisoner.

A brisk wind was blowing up the Tamesis, ruffling the ripples into little wavelets as it scoured the smoke of Londinium's hearthfires from the sky. They had both been right, thought Oesc, wrapping the crimson mantle more securely. It was cold, and it was a beautiful day. With the air so clear, he felt he ought to be able to see downriver all the way to the sea. A sudden memory came to him of sunlight on the water of the estuary below Durobrivae, and he turned swiftly away.

"Was there no one else to keep you company, or did you have something to say to me?" He realized too late how ungracious that had sounded and tried to soften it with a smile.

Artor, who had been gazing southward at the scattering of farms and fields and the distant blue line of the downs, turned back to him, frowning. Oesc felt himself being assessed and examined; it was a look he had learned to recognize when they were on campaign. Then the king released his gaze with a little smile. But there was still trouble in his eyes.

"What is it, my lord?"

"A messenger has come from Cantium. Your grandfather is dead."

Oesc felt a muscle jump in his cheek, but he kept his gaze steady. "He was very old. Many people think he died years ago." *When the Britons captured me. . . .*

Artor cleared his throat. "The message is from your witena-gemot, a formal request from the elders of your people to send you back to them to be their king."

Oesc felt all the blood leave his face and then flood back again. For a moment, staying on his feet took all his strength of will. Then he felt Artor's hand on his arm and his vision cleared.

"And what . . ." he swallowed and tried again, "what was your reply?"

"I have not yet given it. I have to ask you—do you want to go?"

Oesc stared at him. "I have a *choice?*"

"I cannot hold prisoner a man who has guarded my back and fought at my side," said Artor impatiently. "I blame myself now for keeping you by me. It was selfishness on my part. I should have given you this choice a year ago. I suppose it's time to let Cunorix go as well."

Thoughts and emotions suppressed so long Oesc had forgotten them battered against his awareness. Seeing his trouble, Artor went on—

"Oesc, you have earned a place among my Companions. You would be accepted. My own grandfather was a German in the service of Rome. As a man I would ask you to stay— there are many who fight for me because it is their duty, but few who do so because, if I dare assume so much, they are my friends."

There was a short silence. Oesc watched a gull soar toward the sun, then swoop earthward once more. He cleared his throat.

"And what do you ask . . . as a king?"

"If you stay with me, someone else will seize power in Cantium. I cannot afford to have an active enemy on my doorstep. As a king, I want a man in Durovernum who will at worst be neutral, and at best, perhaps, a friend." It was his turn, now to look away.

Gazing at that bent head, Oesc understood two things. The first was that what he felt for Artor was a love which he could never give to any other overlord, and the second was that he had to go home.

"Your grandfather was a Germanic Roman officer. Mine was the man who killed him, as your father killed mine," he said painfully. "If I were not who I am, I would serve you my life long. But if I were not Hengest's grandchild I would not be here at all. And there is another thing. Before ever I saw you I had made my dedication to the goddess who rules the land of Cantuware. I must go back to be her king."

"The Lady . . ." Artor turned back to him, his eyes clouded by memory. "I understand. I will miss you—" He reached out to grip Oesc's hand. "Because of you, even those Saxons whom I must fight will never be a faceless enemy, and to those who live in the lands I hold I will be a fair and honest lord."

Oesc nodded. Surely it was the wind that was making his eyes sting with tears.

"And one more thing, in thanks for the service you have

done me. I will have a treaty drawn up between us, confirming you in the rights granted to Hengest by the Vor-Tigernus. It has been three generations since Cantium became Cantuware—even if we were to take it back tomorrow, the Britons who used to live there are scattered and gone. To you and your heirs I grant it, Oesc; it is Saxon soil."

The night of Oesc's farewell feast Artor got drunk for the first time since the rite to Lugus at Dun Eidyn. At least Betiver believed that the king had been drunk that night, certainly everyone else had been, and he did remember that Artor had been as red-eyed and dazed the next morning as the rest of them.

The feast was formal, the menu heavy on the Roman side, with spiced beets and wild spring greens dressed with oils, boiled grains with sauces, and chickens delicately seasoned as well as a suckling pig stewed in wine. For certain Oesc was not going to get a meal like this in his Saxon hut, thought Betiver, trying to decide whether he had room for just one more morsel of elderberry pie. But though his mouth still watered, his belly had another opinion, and he had let his belt out one notch already. With a sigh he pushed his plate away.

"Are you not wanting that?" Gualchmai reached across the table and scraped the remains from Betiver's plate to his own. Gualchmai had grown at least a foot since coming south with Artor, and was always hungry. He was going to be a big man.

Servants cleared the plates away and began to serve more wine. Oesc proposed a toast to the king; the king responded in kind, his cropped brown hair rumpled and his eyes very bright. Cai toasted the armies of Brittania; Artor drank to their commanders. It should have been Cataur, but the Dumnnonian, who had barely tolerated Oesc's presence with the army, had refused to attend. No one missed him. Indeed, by this time everyone was beginning to feel quite mellow, though Oesc looked depressed, except when he was forcing a smile.

The gifts that Artor was sending with his former hostage were brought in. Oesc went red and pale again as he accepted them. There was a lorica hamata of mail with punched and riveted rings and an officer's helmet with decorations in gold. But except for their quality, they would not make him stand out at home—half the Saxon fighting force was outfitted in looted Roman gear. Betiver did wonder, though, where Artor expected the Saxon to wear them. Perhaps he intended to raise auxiliaries from Cantium when the Picts made trouble again.

There were tunics of Byzantine silk, an officer's belt with gold fittings, a pair of arm rings, and a fine woolen cloak of deep blue that was the mate of Artor's crimson, with a great round brooch of gold. There was a table service of figured red ceramic ware and a silver ewer with goblets. Taken together with Oesc's share of the loot from the Pictish campaign, it was an impressive dowry to be taking home to Cantium.

Then the gifts were carried away again and the king called for more wine. Artor stood up and began to make a speech about how brave they had all been during the Pictish war. Betiver felt his eyes closing and surrendered to a dream in which he was dancing around the festival fire with a girl whose body he could still picture in arousing detail, though he had never learned her name.

He came abruptly awake again to find Gualchmai poking him.

"There's a man come from home to bring me messages, and he's asking for you as well. He has a young woman with him who says she's brought your child. . . ."

He had not spoken softly, and Betiver's progress toward the door was followed by a chorus of advice and comment that made him redden, though he pretended not to hear.

He went, determined to see the girl off in short order. There was a widow in the city whom he visited sometimes, but he knew that she was not with child. He was not like Gualchmai, who had progressed from kitchen maids to married ladies and was reputed to have one bastard already, though he was barely sixteen.

He was starting to question the messenger, a ginger-haired fellow wrapped in the yellowish checkered stuff Leudonus' people wore, when he heard a cry. A red-headed woman came forward into the light with a yearling child in her arms, and it was the girl he had just seen in his dream.

For a long moment Betiver stared at her. "What is your name?"

"Roud—" She took a deep breath. "Do you know me, then? I was fearing you might not remember after all."

"I remember."

"Well, that's a start—" Her words tumbled out as if she were afraid that she might not have the courage to say them all. "I know you are great among the princes of the south, and I don't ask you to marry me. But the boy deserves better than I can give him, out in the hills. There was no other man for a moon before or after the festival, my lord, so I am certain he's yours. If you will swear to do right by him, I'll trouble you no more."

Betiver lifted the blanket and saw a frowning, pug-nosed face topped by a tangle of dark hair that looked so much like his own father's that he blinked in surprise. *A boy child . . . I have a son. . . .*

"A child needs his mother," he said softly. "It would be better if you stayed."

Roud stared at him, then her eyes filled with tears. "We'll be no trouble to you, I promise—"

"Nay—you had the trouble of bearing him. If I had known of this, I would have provided for you before. Tonight you may sleep in my rooms here, and tomorrow we'll see about finding a house for you in the town."

By the time Betiver had settled Roud and the boy in his own bed and returned to the feasting hall, everyone had gone but Cai and young Gualchmai, who was pouring more wine for the king.

"You never knew you were planting a field, but it seems you got a fine crop all the same!" commented Gualchmai with rude good humor.

"I remember the girl," said Betiver, "and I'm satisfied that the boy is mine."

"You have a son?" asked Artor, his eyes dark with the wine.

"It would seem so. He wrinkles his forehead just the way my father does when he's annoyed. My memory of the festival in Dun Eidyn is somewhat confused, but I would guess mine was not the only seed to sprout from that sowing."

"Ah, indeed," said Gualchmai, "it was generous of you to replace the men we lost on that campaign."

"You are an unregenerate heathen!" exclaimed Cai.

"Maybe so, but in the north, festival babes are held to be a blessing from the gods."

"A man needs to know that his son is his own," Cai replied.

"Then get married and breed them!" exclaimed Gualchmai. "When will you be taking a wife, uncle? I'm heir to my father's lands already—I've no need for yours!"

His mother would be irritated to hear him say it, thought Betiver. By all accounts Morgause was ambitious for her sons. She had a fifth boy now to follow the others, he had heard.

Artor shook his head. "Kings don't make marriages, they make alliances. So long as I'm unmarried, any man of good blood can hope to make his daughter queen."

"I suppose that Oesc will settle down now and raise a troop of flaxen-haired brats," said Betiver.

"I suppose he will—" Artor sighed. Clearly the wine was wearing off. The sadness had returned to his eyes.

"Are you so sorry to lose him?" asked Cai gruffly. "Oesc is a good fellow, for all his moody ways, and I suppose we'll miss him. But *we're* still here!"

"That's true—" Artor reached out to grip their hands. "But I value each one of you in a different way. I'm afraid that when I see Oesc again he'll be a stranger, and then he might as well be dead to me—"

Betiver felt the king's hand strong and warm in his own, but in spirit Artor was far away. He tightened his grip, trying to draw him back again. *My dear lord, are we not enough for you?*

Oesc rode across the bridge into Durovernum on a fine spring evening just before Ostara, wearing a British tunic and riding a fine British horse that Artor had given him, and still thinking, despite a week of journeying with his Saxon escort, in the British tongue. The remains of the theatre still stood like a monument in the center of the walled town, but the walls themselves seemed lower, and several of the other Roman buildings he remembered had been scavenged for building stone. The long Saxon houses huddled under their weight of thatching like sheep in fleece, and everything he looked on seemed small, and poor, and old.

As they reined in before the hall, a figure appeared in the doorway, shading his eyes with his hand against the westering light. He shouted something, and in another moment Hæthwæge appeared, Hengest's silver-mounted meadhorn in her hands. There was more silver in her hair than he remembered, but otherwise she hadn't changed.

"Oesc son of Octha, waes hal—be welcome to your hall!" She came down the steps, and he took the horn. The mead was yeasty and dry, with an aftertaste of sweetness and fire. The taste of it brought a sudden flood of memories. He drank again, dizzied by the conflict of old knowledge and new, uncertain for a moment who he was or where.

"Thank you . . ." he mumbled, clinging to the formalities. A thrall came up to take the horse's head and he swung a leg across the high front of the saddle and slid to the ground. His escort were dismounting behind him. More thralls led their horses away. A horn blew and he heard people shouting.

For so long, he thought, he had dreamed of this moment, longed for it. And now, it seemed the capacity to respond was dead in him. *What am I doing here? How can I be a king to these people? Would Artor take me back again?*

Hæthwæge was saying something. He forced himself to attend.

"You are tired. Come into the hall."

He nodded gratefully and followed her.

Inside it was cool and dim. As his vision adjusted, light from the opened smoke vents beneath the eaves at either end of the hall showed him the carved and painted pillars that upheld the peaked roof and the curtained compartments to either side. But he had become accustomed to separate sleeping chambers and columns of stone. Then the scent, composite of woodsmoke and ale, dog and old leather and the sweat of men, caught at his throat, and for a moment he was thirteen years old once more. Someone opened a side door, and a rush of fresh air brought him back to the present.

"There are only half a dozen men now in the houseguard, and most of those are old," Hæthwæge was saying. "He gave the younger men land to farm. And there is only one cook and three kitchen thralls, but I have asked some of the women to come and help us."

Oesc nodded, thinking he would have to use much of the treasure Artor had given him just to set things in order here. Compared to the crowded, noisy place he remembered, this was like a hall of ghosts.

His footsteps echoed on the planking as he passed the boards and trestles for the tables that leaned in stacks against the walls, and he thought of colored mosaic floors. The raised stone hearth nearer the doorway was cold, but a little blue smoke rose from smoldering coals in the one before the high seat at the end of the hall. He remembered the clear light that fell through windows of nubbled glass, and Artor's marble throne.

The wisewoman paused as if she expected him to sit there. Oesc looked up at the serpentine carving on the posts, worn where Hengest had leaned against them, and at the cushion that still bore the impress of his body, and shook his head.

"Not yet. It has been a long time, and my soul is still stretched like a drying hide between here and Londinium. Build up the fire and let me sit on a bench beside it. I'll take the high seat when we drink Hengest's funeral ale."

She frowned at him thoughtfully and handed him the meadhorn once more. From outside came the sound of many voices. The light from the door flickered as if someone were hovering there.

"The people are gathering, wanting to see you. Two lambs are already roasting, and tonight you will feast. When you are ready, come to me and I will tell you how your grandfather died."

It was late before the shouting and the singing died away in the hall. But when the last of the revelers set off for his home or rolled up in his cloak beside the hearth, as Hæthwæge had known he would, Oesc came to her.

He had still been a boy when he left them, with the soft flesh of youth covering his bones. Now the strong structure of his face made the resemblance to his grandfather clear, all the more so because he looked so tired.

"Was it too bad?" He would have had more than enough

ale in the hall. She dipped some of the mint tea that had been steeping on the hearth into a beaker and offered it.

Oesc sighed. "The skin of the boy who lived here nine years ago no longer fits, and the man he became is some sort of Saxon-British hybrid who doesn't fit anywhere. I told them I was tired from the journey, and they made allowances, but I am afraid my grandfather's thanes will think they have got a bad bargain in me."

"You have half a moon until the feast of Ostara when the æthelings and freemen will gather to drink Hengest's funeral ale. It will be better by then."

"I hope so! Otherwise I might as well lay myself in his mound . . ." He took a long drink of the tea and settled back on his stool. "This place is as I remember, and so are you. Talk to me, bind me back into this world again. . . ."

At least he knew what he needed, she thought, watching him. She would have to shape the man as she had shaped the boy, but it would be harder now because he was not so much scarred as armored by his time in the British lands.

"When one has a slow illness, or is very old, there comes a time when the spirit turns inward. Mostly our folk go quickly, in battle or sudden sickness, but I have seen this often enough so that when Hengest began to drift away from us I understood what it was. His health was no worse, nor was he in pain. He ate less and slept more, and delegated most of the household decisions to Guthlaf or to me. When he sat in his high seat he spoke of the battles of his youth sometimes, or of you, but as time went on, he mostly stayed in his bed."

Oesc frowned unhappily. "I should have been here for him. I knew how old he was—I should have begged Artor to let me visit him."

"It would have made no difference. It was that boy whose skin is too small for you that he remembered, not the man you are now."

"Whoever *he* is . . ." muttered Oesc, and refilled his cup. Then he straightened, obviously trying to lift himself out of the mood. "It is hard to picture Hengest, the conqueror of Britannia, dying in his bed like a woman or a thrall."

Hæthwæge shook her head. "He did not. There came a day when the hills echoed with the cries of new lambs, and the sky with the calls of returning waterfowl. There was a wind, and we opened all the doors to air out the hall." She shut her eyes for a moment, remembering the brilliance of the sky, and how life had tingled in that air. "The kitchen thrall who used to bring Hengest his porridge called me. The king was sitting up, asking for a basin to wash in and the Frankish lapped tunic with the gold borders to wear. The folk here rejoiced, thinking that he was getting well at last."

"Where did he want to go?"

"He asked me to take him to the god-grove, and to bring the Spear."

Oesc's eyes widened, and his gaze went to the shrouded shape by the door. Hæthwæge knew he was remembering how his other grandfather had died. In the same, measured tone, she went on.

They had brought a lamb, and the old king cut its throat and splashed its blood on the god-posts and the stones. She remembered how the air around them grew heavy, as if something had awakened and was watching as Hengest set his back against the ash tree and pulled open his tunic to bare his breast. The green shadows had given his old skin a sickly pallor, as if he were dead already.

And then, as he had commanded, she scratched Woden's knot into his belly just below the ribs, and tied the rags with which she stanched the bleeding onto the branches of the ash tree. And at that a great wind had shivered the new leaves.

"The god was there," she said softly. "The offering was accepted. But Hengest said that as the god had made him live so long already he would let him choose his own moment to claim him. And so he closed up his tunic and we went back to the hall."

"He sat down in his high seat and told them to build up the fire, but he would take neither food nor drink. Some of the men wanted me to force him to lie down, but the warriors of the houseguard backed me. They understood very well."

"How long did it take him to die?" asked Oesc in a still voice.

Hæthwæge drew a deep breath, remembering the old king sitting like a carven image in his bloodstained tunic, listening to Andulf sing of Sigfrid and Hagano, of Offa of Angeln and Scyld Sceafing, one of the few heroes who lived to be old.

He had sung of Eormanaric. He sang until even his trained voice grew hoarse and Hengest told him to be still. That was the sixth night. Three days longer the king stayed, without eating or sleeping. By then he had stopped speaking as well, and only the occasional movement of his breast told them that he lived still.

"Nine days and nights altogether Hengest sat there, and when the tenth morning dawned, although he had not moved, we saw that his breath no longer stirred his beard. The god had come for him at last."

"And *that* is the high seat you want me to sit in?" Oesc said unsteadily.

"You will sit there, and Hengest's spirit will guide you," said Hæthwæge with the certainty of prophecy.

"I drink to Hengest, wisest of warriors, first to be king in the British lands—" Aelle lifted his drinking horn, and the others followed his example with a roar of approval.

Oesc, sitting on a bench before the high seat, gazed around him at the men crammed into the hall. They had begun to arrive just after the Ostara offerings, when by custom kings feasted with their chieftains, to celebrate Hengest's funeral ale.

He had expected Aelle to bring his son Cymen, and Ceretic to come over from Venta, and he knew that Hengest's thanes, Hrofe Guthereson and Hæsta and the others, would be there. But he was surprised by how many others made the journey—old men who had fought in Hengest's battles, and young men to whom they were legends. There was even a small party from Gallia, bearing the condolences of Chlodovechus, the Frankish king.

Each day more tents went up in the field beyond the hall as new groups settled in. It was just as well that Artor had gifted him with so much treasure, he thought ruefully, for this feast would exhaust their stores. He did not delude himself that all these folk had come for his sake. Hengest had been the father of the Saxon migration. With his death an era was ended.

Many times that night the meadhorn had gone round. Men laughed and said it was time the hall had a queen to honor the warriors. Hengest had been an old wolf, who had rather embrace his sword than a woman, but Oesc still had juice in his loins. He should take a wife—the talk grew ribald with speculation. Aelle had granddaughters, girls of good Saxon stock who would give him strong sons. Ceretic had a little daughter, but it would be a dozen winters before she was husband-high. The lords from the Anglian lands suggested that one of the Icelinga girls could bring him a useful alliance. Even Chlodovechus's representative joined the discussion, pointing out that his master also had marriageable daughters, and Cantuware possessed fine harbors that could benefit from Frankish trade.

Oesc shook his head, laughing. "Nay, I must see how my grandfather's high seat fits me before I seek someone to share it. Give me a year or three to settle into my kingship. I promise you I will consider an alliance then."

Hrofe began to talk of how Hengest had married his daughter Reginwynna to the Vor-Tigernus, and Oesc sat back with a sigh. For so long, even the idea of marriage had been out of the question; the thought of a connection more meaningful than his brief encounters with whores or serving-maids took some getting used to. More important still, any marriage he made would commit him to an alliance. If Artor had had another sister—his lips twitched as he remembered the overwhelming beauty of Leudonus's queen. Even if Morgause had been free, it would take a brave man to husband her. She was fertile, though. It was said that nine months after the feast of Lugus she too had been brought to bed of a fine boy that her husband accepted as his own.

Lost in his own thoughts, he did not realize that Andulf had begun to sing

> "... Where once he had held
> most bliss in the world, war swept away
> all Finn's thanes, save few alone
> that he might not at that meeting place
> with war against Hengest finish the fight
> nor the survivors with warfare wrest free
> from the king's thane...."

It was the tale of the fight at Finnesburgh, the first of Hengest's great deeds, though Hengest himself had never boasted about it. That was a hard and bitter story, of the time when Hengest had led the war-band of the Dane-king Hnaef on visit to his brother-in-law the Frisian Finn, and when enmity between Finn's men and Hnaef's had become warfare, first forced the Frisian king to divide the steading between the two sides and keep them through the winter, and when the Danes insisted on revenge, broken the peace-troth pledged with Finn in order to avenge his lord.

> "... But they bid him take terms,
> that the king another hall should clear,
> hall and high seat, that they half would hold
> of all the Jutes' sons might possess,
> and at wealth-giving, Folkwalda's son
> every day the Danes would honor,
> and Hengest's riders, with rings as was right
> even as well with treasured wealth
> and golden cups, the Frisian kin
> in the beer-hall he bolstered in spirit."

Hengest had done the same thing again, he thought, when for the sake of his people he turned against the Vor-Tigernus and attacked the British princes. Oesc looked up at the empty high seat, contemplating once more the stature of the man who had occupied it. *What would I do, faced with such a decision?* he wondered then. *If I am ever forced to choose between my own folk and Artor, what will I do?*

Andulf ended the story of the slaying of the Frisians, and once more the meadhorn went round. The tales of Hengest's deeds had inspired his mourners to vows of emulation, most of them, as might have been expected, at the expense of their British neighbors.

"This is my oath, in Woden's name—" Ceretic lifted the horn. "To push the borders of the West Saxon lands outward until Dumnonia is ours, to found a line of kings who shall rule in this island for a hundred generations, to leave a name that shall be remembered as that of the father of this island's kings!"

That did not leave much scope for the other dynasties, and there were a few raised eyebrows, but neither was it much of a threat to the present balance of power. Oesc waited with growing apprehension for the horn to come round to him. Even when he took it in his hand he did not know what he was going to say.

For a long moment he stared at the empty high seat, then he turned to face his guests once more.

"I have fought in battles and killed enemies," he said slowly, "but all my great deeds are still in the future. I am too new in my lordship to make great boasts for my people. I was not here at Hengest's death to take his blessing. To sit in his seat without having performed some great exploit would be overweening pride. This therefore, is my boast. I will go from this place now, at night's high noon, and sit out upon my grandfather's grave mound. If I can sit in that high seat without scathe until dawn, I will claim his place as king."

As he finished, men began to nod and pound the tables in approval. Oesc's vow was unexpected, but not unworthy. It was true that Hengest had met his death in good heart as befitted a warrior and had no reason to hate the living, but the ghosts of the mighty dead could be unchancy, especially when disturbed in their howes.

At first the chill of the night air was welcome after the heat of the hall. But as Oesc approached the mound that had been raised for Hengest just inside the southeastern wall he began to feel the cold, and was glad of the heavy cloak he had brought along. Mist lay heavy on the fields, beyond the tumbled stones, luminous in the light of the waning moon. A dog howled in the town behind him and he suppressed a shiver, hoping that the two warriors who were escorting him had not seen. His shadow lengthened before him in the light of their torches, as if his fetch were hastening toward the mound.

The hill they had raised above the box containing his father's head was as he remembered, flattened a little by time and covered with green grass. Hengest's mound rose stark and black beside it, the colors of the white stallion carved on his grave-post still bright.

"Hengest son of Wihtgils, it is I, Oesc, blood of your blood, who come to your howe seeking counsel. Accept this food and drink, grandfather, and allow me to sit with you in safety until dawn." He unstoppered the flask of mead and poured its contents into the ditch that surrounded the grave mound, then crumbled the barley cake between his fingers and scattered it there.

He waited in silence, and presently it seemed to him that the night had grown a little warmer. "Woden, lord of the slain, be with me now . . ." he whispered, then he gathered up the folds of his cloak and leaped across the ditch onto the mound. He lifted one hand in salute to his men. Then they turned and left him alone.

Oesc's first awareness was of stillness without silence. From the woods beyond the fields he heard the bark of a fox and from the town a dog answering it. From time to time some unusually exuberant burst of shouting echoed faint from the hall.

He patted the earth beside him. "I am glad that you can hear the celebration, grandfather, and that you are not completely alone out here in your mound . . ."

The Christian priests would say that Hengest burned now in their Gehenna, and that it was superstition to talk to him as if he were alive in the mound. But that did not stop them from praying at the graves of their saints, who were said to dwell with their god in bliss. Hæthwæge had always taught him that a man was a vastly more complex creation than the Christian duality of body and soul, and that while part of the being that had been Hengest feasted in Woden's hall, another part might still cling to the ashes buried in this mound, while the clan-soul which he had inherited from his forebears waited to take flesh again in some future child of his line.

He had seen how they buried Octha's head, and he supposed that after they burned Hengest's body, the bronze urn containing his ashes had been treated likewise, set within a wooden chamber with his shield and seax and spear, his helmet and arm rings, bronze-bound buckets and bowls with food and drink and all such other gear as he might need. Oesc tried to imagine what it was like down there in the heart of the mound.

"I have no wish to disturb your rest, grandfather, but I need your wisdom," Oesc said softly. "Give me your mind, teach me what you have learned from your deeds; and give me your luck, the might and main that carried you across the sea to claim this land, and that will help me to hold it. It is not your treasure that I need from you, Hengest, but this ghostly inheritance."

Once more the wind blew, ruffling the guard-hairs on the fur that lined his cloak. Oesc pulled it more tightly around him and settled himself to wait, breathing in and out in a steady rhythm as Hæthwæge had taught him. Time seemed to move slowly, but when a night bird's cry brought him briefly to awareness, he saw that the moon had moved a quarter of the way across the sky.

It was in the dead of the out-tide, when even the singing from the mead-hall had stilled, that Oesc became conscious in a way that was different from before. He saw the moon low in the west, but he saw also the grey shape that sat beside him on the mound. It was Hengest, the metal-woven braid on his Frankish tunic glinting in the moonlight, but though the wind bent the grass, it did not stir a hair of his flowing beard.

His lips did not move, and yet Oesc felt knowledge precipitating in his awareness like the dew on the grass. He knew the snarling faces of men now fifty years in their graves, the white cliffs of Dubris above the heaving grey waves of the sea, the clamor of a thousand fights, and the long slow years in Cantuware, growing into the land. Everything that had made Hengest a king was now his, if he had the might to use it.

"I see now what you have done . . ." he sent his own thought to that powerful presence, *"but not what I must do . . ."*

There was amusement in the answer that returned to him. *"That is your Wyrd, not mine. But this I will say—land-right belongs to those who give themselves to the land. Seek the Lady, and offer Her your seed and your soul. . . ."*

In the sky the stars were fading. Hengest's form dimmed— for a moment Oesc could see the shapes of field and tree through it, then it was gone.

He took a deep breath, returning sensation rushing tingling through hands and feet. Stiffened muscles did not want to move, but he got upright, and going carefully, for his balance was still unsure, descended the mound. On the other side of the ditch he fell to his knees and plunged his fingers through the new grass and into the soil.

"Earth, my mother, my life is yours. In return I take this kingdom into my hand."

As the first light of the new day scattered gold across the softly flowing waters of the Stur and glowed on the grass, Oesc son of Octha son of Hengest returned to his grandfather's mead-hall and ascended the high seat that was waiting for him there.

VIII

BATTLES IN THE MIST

A.D. 493

"Can there be any Angles left in Germania?" Artor slapped the table so hard that the map shivered and the inkwell skipped dangerously. "For fifteen years every spring has brought more of them flocking northward like wild geese across the sea. But these geese don't fly home again. The Iceni and Trinovante lands have long been lost to us, and now the Angles are spreading into the Coritani country. If they link up with their countrymen above the Abus, King Icel will have a stranglehold on half the island!"

The flicker of a hanging lamp added an uncertain illumination to the grey light coming in through the thick panes of the window, further distorted by the rain that was streaming down them. It had been raining for some time.

"To answer your first question," answered Betiver, "in Gallia they say that the Anglian homeland has become a wilderness. There are no more reinforcements left to come. To answer your second question, the last messengers we had say that Lindum is surrounded. Even if he does not take it, eastern Britannia already lies in Icel's grasp. . . ."

"You are such a comforter," commented Gualchmai, lounging against the doorframe. He had grown taller even than Artor, and had to duck these days to go through. His brother Gwyhir, who had joined Artor's household two years after his brother, was almost as tall, and no doubt young Aggarban, the third of Artor's nephews to come to them, would be a big man too.

"Lindum was badly hit last time the Saxons attacked, and the walls were never repaired." Betiver traced the line of the Roman road northward. "By now it may have fallen. We should have reinforced it long ago."

"Gualchmai is right," muttered the king. "You *are* depressing."

"You would not thank me for lying to you . . ."

Artor looked up with that quick smile that took the sting from his words. "You are right, of course, but this is horrible weather for doing anything with cavalry. Do the Angles have webbed feet? I'm told that Anglia is all fenland—they must feel right at home."

Gualchmai guffawed. "I'll wager they do! I ought to have looked at old Oesc's feet when he was here. But he is a Jute of some kind, is he not?"

"His mother was Myrging, but Hengest was Anglian. Fortunately Oesc is rooted in Cantium, and content to keep to his own borders, thank God," added Betiver.

"But he is oathed to Artor—surely you could call—"

The king shook his head. "I raised a wild gosling once that followed me as if I were its mother. All through one summer it fed with the white farm geese and seemed content. But when the wild geese passed overhead in the autumn, my gosling opened her wings and flew away. I tried to call her back, and she circled thrice, but she could not deny her nature and so I lost her."

Gualchmai met his gaze blankly.

"I believe I have won Oesc's friendship, and I have his word," Artor said then, "but even though Hengest's line and Icel's were rivals, I know better than to overstrain Oesc's loyalty. There is more to kingship than giving orders—you must understand the nature of those you rule."

Gualchmai's ruddy skin grew redder. "Your orders are enough for me . . ."

"Because that is *your* nature," answered Artor softly.

"No doubt Cataur will send men, but it will take some time for them to get here," Betiver said into the silence that followed. "He loves killing Saxons, whoever they may be. There will be a troop from Glevum, and one from Deva—" He began to reckon the forces at their command.

"And we'll need some infantry. I wonder . . ." Suddenly Artor smiled. "Perhaps Cunorix would like to bring me a band of his wild Irishmen. They should have no objection to fighting Icel if they get a good share of the spoils."

Outside, it continued to rain.

It was raining in Cantuware as well. Oesc made passing travelers welcome in his hall and listened to their news. Sitting snug by his fire, he told himself that he pitied men who had to march across the soggy soil of the Coritani lands, that there was no glory in that kind of fighting anyway.

The weather that had delayed the royal messengers also slowed the men who were responding to Artor's call. But the Angles, accustomed to muddy footing, pushed onward, and shortly after Beltain, word came that Lindum had fallen. Icel now possessed a base, if he could keep it, from which he might control everything between Eburacum and Durolipons.

Oesc tossed a coin to the pack-man who had brought the news and strode out of the hall. The fine drizzle beaded the blue wool of his cloak with tiny crystals, but he scarcely noticed the damp. He was seeing not the mud of the yard, but the bloody earth of a battlefield, and instead of Wulfhere and Guthlac and the other men of his household, Betiver and Gualchmai and Artor himself, riding against the foe. He should have been with them—but he understood why the king had not called him. Did Artor really fear that Oesc would have been tempted to fight on the other side?

He had faced Artor in battle once before, when he did not know him. His gut twisted unpleasantly at the thought of doing so again. But his body cried out for action, he wanted to fight. At that moment he scarcely cared who, and the folk of the steading scattered before him.

Presently he found himself in front of the barn.

He called for his horse. Someone asked a question about

hunting, and he nodded, and a few minutes later he was trotting toward the southeastern gate of the town. The road cut straight across the flats to the east of the river for several miles. To their right the river gleamed among marshy islets. Beyond it the skirts of the North Downs were clad in forest. But Oesc made no move to get to the other side—these woods, so close to the town, held no game capable of challenging him now.

It was nightfall before they crossed the river and came to the ancient trackway that climbed to the tops of the Downs. There they made camp, and before the sun was high they were taking the path into the hills. A night in the open had muted Oesc's sense of urgency. As riding warmed him, stiff muscles began to ease. He drew a deep breath of the morning air, heavy with the scents of leaf mold and new grass, and felt something that had been drawn tight within him grow easier as well. He actually *saw* the scenery he was looking at for the first time since leaving his hall. And when, just after noon, they crossed the track of a stag, awareness of all else fell away and he gave himself entirely to the joy of the chase.

By the depth of the prints, the stag was old enough to have learned all the tricks by which a hunted beast can elude its foes. But Oesc's tracker was a lad whose folk had lived on the Downs since before the Romans came, and he knew the beasts of his native woods as well as his own kin. A little past noon, they caught sight of the quarry and kicked their horses into all-out pursuit. Oesc's mount was the swiftest, and so he was out of sight of the others when, swinging wide to avoid a fallen tree, his horse put a foot into a hole. Oesc felt the beast lurch beneath him, but before he could get clear the horse went down. He was aware of trees blurring past, and then a resounding impact, and then, for quite some time, of nothing at all.

When Oesc came to himself again the clouds had wrapped the hillside in a damp embrace; everything beyond a few feet was dissolving into featureless grey. His horse stood a few feet away, one foreleg barely touching the ground. With a groan Oesc got upright, made his way over to the animal and gently felt the limb. It did not seem to be broken, thank the gods, though it was clearly a bad sprain. When he tugged on the rein, the horse followed, on three legs only, after him.

Their progress was painfully slow. It hardly mattered, thought Oesc grimly, since it was becoming increasingly apparent that he was lost. Even if he had known this countryside, the mists would have made everything seem strange. And yet to keep moving, even with no goal, was better than bleating like a lost sheep in hopes that someone would find him.

He could see nothing but the shadows of tree trunks in the mist, but downhill, he knew, the forest grew thicker still. His only hope was to struggle up to the bare open slopes that crowned the Downs, where he might strike the ancient track that crossed them. Local legend held that these hills had been well-peopled in ancient days, when the world was warmer and there were no iron ploughs to turn the heavier lowland soils. One still sometimes found the marks of ancient round houses in the soil. Even today, Oesc might hope to encounter a shepherd, or a pack-man trudging across the hills.

Once he found the track he could follow it back to the river, and have a good laugh at his escort, who must be quite frantic by now. But he had his bow, and had learned which of the spring greens could be eaten. He might be separated from his friends, but at least there were no foes hunting him. He was still better off than he would have been in Artor's army.

The same storms that pounded Cantuware had drenched the north as well, saturating the soil and exposing Artor's army to attack by the elements as well as the enemy. Rising waters lapped the raised Roman causeways, wagons bogged down in the sticky mud and animals went lame. Rain spoiled the rations they carried, and though water surrounded them, it was thick and foul. The fact that these hazards had been anticipated did not make them easier to bear. More than once men wished for Merlin to magic the clouds away, but the sorcerer was in the north on some errand of his own.

The Anglians, well aware of their danger, made good use of the country's natural defenses. And yet, though bowstrings stretched and leather rotted, still the Britons came on. In a battle near the ruins of Lactodorum they faced the Eslinga Saxons and had their first victory. Artor took oaths and hos-

tages from their leaders and sent them eastward to Durolipons to garrison the fens against their former allies. Two
more muddy skirmishes, hardly worth dignifying with the
name of battle, could be counted as victories, since it was
the Anglians who retreated when they were done.

Artor led his army along the old legionary road beside the
Blackwater. By the feast of Pentecost the royal forces could
see the smoke of Anglian cookfires in Lindum across the
marshes to the northwest, where the Blackwater, curving into
the lowlands, had breached its banks and made a lake of the
land. Even in high summer the country of the Lindenses was
largely water meadow and marsh. In a wet spring, it seemed
an inland sea, in which the scattered bits of higher ground
stood like islands. To beseige the city, surrounded by marsh
in the midst of hostile territory, was not an attractive prospect, given the problems the Britons had already experienced
with supply. But perhaps Icel, unfamiliar with both cities and
seiges, would not be aware of Artor's difficulties.

Two days after Pentecost, the king sent one of his captured
Saxon chieftains with a challenge. If the Anglians would wager all upon one battle, the Britons would abide by its outcome—to take back all the Lindenses lands if they won, and
to abandon the campaign and cede the territory to Icel if their
foes had the victory. When the delegation had gone, Artor
ordered his army to make camp. The cooks began preparing
the first hot meal they had had for a fortnight, and every
warrior was set to repairing and preparing weapons and gear.

For three days they remained in camp, waiting for an answer. Then, leaving the baggage train on the high ground,
they set out once more upon the road to Lindum.

"Be thankful, man—it could still be raining!" Gualchmai's beard and mustache glittered with fine droplets as he
grinned. The clouds still hung low, but the weather had
warmed, and the earth was giving back its excess moisture
in the form of patchy mists that drifted among the trees.

"What's this, then? Liquid sunshine?" growled Betiver,
shifting uncomfortably in the saddle. His thighs were chafed
from riding in wet breeches and his nose was stuffy. But he
was luckier than some, for the flux, plague of armies, was
beginning to thin their line.

"Man, it would be counted a fine day in my own country!"

Betiver shook his head, wishing they had stayed in camp a day longer. But they might stay for a week and still be plagued by bad weather, while in the meantime the Anglians could be filling Lindum with supplies and men. Here, the Blackwater ran to their right, more or less paralleling the road. But soon, as he recalled, it would make a bend to the westward, where it flowed through the marshy valley. The Romans had made a ford there, so that the road could continue straight along the narrow neck of higher ground that led toward the town.

"Soon we'll be over the river, and then a straight march to Lindum it will be!" said Gwyhir, peering ahead. The mist had thickened. Only the ring of hooves on stone assured them they were still on the road.

"If the floods haven't washed the ford away," grumbled Betiver. Artor's companions headed the column, though the king himself had stayed near the middle to hearten the men. There were scouts out ahead somewhere. He hoped they hadn't gotten lost in this gloom. His stuffed nose was turning into a headache, and his back and shoulders hurt as well.

"Nay, they went out to look last night, remember, and reported that it was still whole," Gwyhir replied. He was, like his brother, exasperatingly cheerful in weather that made everyone else complain.

"If I were Icel, I would set stakes in it, or tear out the stones. He knows we must pass this way . . ."

"What's that?" Gualchmai checked his mount, peering ahead. Betiver strained to see, wishing he were taller. A touch of damp air on one cheek was echoed by a shift in the intensity of the greyness before them.

"The fog is lifting—" he began. A flicker of light rippled through the mist. He stiffened as the wind strengthened, rolling back the mist to unveil the road before them, where morning sunlight gleamed from the well-honed points of a host of spears. With each moment the size of the army that faced them grew clearer. A British horn bugled alarm.

Betiver let out his breath on a long sigh. "It would seem that Icel has given us his answer, after all."

Hooves clattered, and Artor pulled his big black horse to a halt beside them.

"Well. Now I know why our scouts did not return." He was scanning the foe, calculating numbers and dispositions. The Anglians had formed up on the other side of the ford, on the last broad piece of solid ground before the land narrowed. "They've chosen well. The ground's too soft for our heavy cavalry to flank them. Icel wants to force us into a slugging match. . . . we need some way to improve the odds."

The king's tone was detached, as if he were considering a board game. Could he really be that calm?

"Use your archers to soften them up, then," suggested Gualchmai. "They're mostly unarmored."

"Not yet—" Artor frowned. "First, let's try a parley."

"Do you think it will do any good?" Gwyhir asked.

"No, but I need a better estimate of their numbers, and a check on the state of the ford."

"I'll go—" offered Gwyhir.

"Nay, that you will not! You've not the experience—" retorted his brother. The king shook his head.

"The task is for neither. Your eloquence is all in your sword arm, Gualchmai—" Artor grinned. "This requires sweet talk and flattery, so Icel won't realize I'm playing for time." He looked at Betiver, who sighed.

"I understand. Let me wear that white cloak of yours with all the gold embroidery and I'll flatter him like an emperor."

It was amazing, thought Betiver as he splashed through the ford, how the imminent expectation of a spear in the gut put other pains in perspective. He could hardly feel the aches with which he had begun the day.

At least the ford had not been damaged. Perhaps, he thought as he looked around him, the Anglians had considered that precaution superfluous. There were certainly a lot of them, drawn up in groups surrounding their chieftains. Icel sat his white stallion in the middle of the line. He was a big man with a fair mustache, glittering in a shirt of ringmail and a spangenhelm inlaid with figures of gods and heroes in gold.

Meeting that cold grey gaze, Betiver found that respect came easily. Icel's homeland might be small compared to the empire, and poor, but he traced his descent, father to son, through a line of kings that went back to the god Woden, and that was an older lineage than either Artor or the emperor in Byzantium could claim.

"The king of the Britons has good warriors, but they are wet and weary. My men are fresh and strong," said the Anglian king when Betiver had stated Artor's terms. "It is not for him to demand surrender. This is our land now, and we will defend it. Eight hundred spears stand ready to prove my words—" He gestured. "We have heard much of Artor's battles and are eager to fight him. Go tell him so—"

As Betiver rode back toward the British lines it occurred to him that the Eslingas and Middle Saxons had been eager too, and Artor had beaten them, but Icel had spoken truly, and his own side, battered and muddy, seemed a rag-tag excuse for an army next to the barbaric splendor of the warriors surrounding the Anglian king.

But though Betiver's embassy had been fruitless, Artor had made good use of the delay. The British were armed and ready, their heavy cavalry in the middle, the archers positioned in the wings. The king was cantering along the lines, his red cloak bright against the black horse's flanks, his armor gleaming dully in the sun. He listened to Betiver's report with a smile that did not reach his eyes.

Then he wheeled the horse and came to a halt before the first line.

"Men of Britannia—" His voice was pitched to carry. "You have marched a weary way. But Lindum is in sight, and the Anglians have come out to make us welcome!" He waited for their answering laughter. "We have faced their kin three times already and beaten them. But Icel's own warriors have not encountered our like before. We are the heirs of Rome and the children of this island. Draw up strength from this sacred soil, and we will prevail. One more battle, lads, and we will break them. The way to Lindum lies before us—win this one, and tonight we'll lie in soft beds with roofs to keep out the rain!"

After the past few weeks, thought Betiver, dry beds sounded better than gold. He jerked the chin-strap of his helmet tight, wondering wistfully if the baths of Lindum were still usable. Artor was right. He would kill for the chance at a hot soak at the end of the day.

Artor lifted his hand and the air rang to the bitter calling of the horns. The enemy ran to meet them, intending to close the distance so there would be no room for a charge. A ripple of movement swept through the ranks of mounted men, and then the column was moving forward and Betiver's awareness narrowed to the area above his horse's ears through which he could see a glittering line of spearpoints that grew more distinct with every stride.

The air darkened as the archers let fly. The riders splashed through the ford. A horse went down on the right, where the bottom was treacherous, but the others kept their feet and labored up the far bank. An Anglian, outstripping his companions, cast a spear that sped past Artor's shoulder and gashed the flank of the horse behind him. The animal squealed and lurched, but its rider kept it going. Gualchmai plucked a javelin from its loop and cast, and the Anglian went down.

First blood to us— thought Betiver, but now all his vision was filled with grimacing enemy faces. He dug his heels into the horse's sides, striving for the momentum they would need to smash the Anglian line. More spears flew and he heard cries. One after another he reached for his own lances and threw. Then they were crashing into the first group of enemy warriors; for a moment the charge faltered, then they drove onward.

A spear jabbed up at him. Betiver swung his shield around to deflect it and pulled his sword from the sheath. It was all blade-work now, as their pace was slowed by crowding foes. But still they pushed onward, and then they were through. Artor called to them to form up again and hit the enemy from the rear. Light flared from his sword. In that moment of freedom Betiver heard shouting from the flanks. He blinked in confusion as figures rose up like ghosts from the misty waters. Then a familiar war cry shrilled above the clamor of battle and he laughed as Cunorix and his wild Irishmen emerged from the marshes and fell upon the foe.

Artor yelled again, and Betiver's mount, catching the excitement, lurched into motion after the others. His sword arm swung up, and screaming, he charged back into the fray.

The bay horse lifted its head, ears flicking nervously, and Oesc stilled, listening. In another moment his duller ears caught the bleating of sheep. He let out his breath in a long sigh, only then admitting his fear that he might have wandered somehow into Nebhelheim, and would never find his way back to Middle-Earth again. Through the thinning mists a ewe gazed at him with a flat, disapproving stare that could only belong to the sheep kept by humankind. Then the herd dog caught his scent and dashed forward, barking.

"There, boy, down—I mean no harm—"

The dog, a brisk black-and-white beast with a plume of a tail, did not seem convinced. It continued to advance, growling, and he looked around for the shepherd.

He was waving his hands to repel the dog when something moved on the hill. He looked up, saw a blur in the air, and threw up his arm. There was a crack. He reeled, then gasped as pain flared through his arm like white fire. Someone was running toward him, whirling a slingshot in one hand and brandishing a staff in the other; Oesc stepped back, caught his heel in a root and went down.

The stick whistled through the air where his head had been. He rolled as it thwacked downward, and made a grab for his assailant. His good hand closed on a slim ankle and he pulled. The staff went flying and they grappled, rolling over and over in the wet grass.

His foe was wiry as a wildcat, but Oesc was a trained fighting man, and despite his useless arm, in a few moments his size and strength began to tell. It was only when he had got his opponent's arm in a twist and the thrashing legs locked between his own long limbs that he realized his attacker was a girl.

For several moments neither could do more than gasp. He stared down into a heart-shaped face, flushed now with fury and surrounded by a Medusa-tangle of nut-brown hair. Her eyes were a gold-flecked brown, like amber, he thought, gazing into them, or honey-mead.

"A fine welcome you give to strangers here on the Downs," he said finally.

"I thought you were a robber." Her gaze fixed on the fine embroidery at the neck of his tunic, and the golden arm ring. "They've taken two sheep in the past week. I thought they'd come back again." She tensed, trying to free herself, and he was abruptly aware that it was a female body that lay crushed beneath his own.

"It's not mutton I would have from you—" He muttered, and kissed her, at first a light brush of the lips that held her still with surprise, and then hungrily, until she began to struggle once more beneath him and he came up for air, his heart beating hard in his breast.

"How *dare* you!" She got a hand free and tried to box his ear. He pinned her with his body, since he could not use his arm.

"You owe me some weregild—I think you've broken my arm—" he began, and felt her stiffen.

"You're a Saxon!"

He stared at her, and realized they had been speaking in the British tongue.

"A Myrging, to be more precise, and your master—" he said then.

"Then you *are* a robber, after all! My grandfather was lord of this land!"

"You're Prince Gorangonus's kin? We're well matched then, for *my* grandfather took Cantium away from him." He grinned down as her face flushed with angry color once more. His body was urging him to take her, but this was no thrall to be tumbled on a hillside, even if at the moment she looked more like a troll-maid than the daughter of a royal house.

"Hengest's brat—" On her lips it was a curse.

"Hengest's heir," he corrected softly, "and Cantium's king . . ."

"How can you be the king, when you were born across the sea?" She had stopped struggling, and sorrow was extinguishing the fire in her eyes.

"So were the Romans, when they came here—" He released her and sat up, wincing as the movement jarred his arm. "And it was they who put your father's fathers on that throne."

"Perhaps, but it was my mother's mothers who gave them the right to rule. That's why I came back—" She gestured toward the misty sweep of the Downs. "Folk of my blood have dwelt here since before the Romans, even before the Cantiaci came. This land belongs to me!"

For a moment Oesc felt the moist chill of the shrine on the Meduwege once more and remembered how its spirit had spoken to him there. There was a sense in which her claim was true. Men ruled by right of conquest, but sovereignty came from the Goddess and the queens who were her priestesses. Still, he knew better than to admit that, or to point out that without the power to defend it, she might as well have been the wild child she appeared.

"What is your name, granddaughter of Gorangonus?" He winced as an unwary movement jarred his arm, the same that had been broken in Londinium.

"I am called Rigana, for my mother said I should have the name of a queen even if I spent my days keeping sheep upon the hills."

"Very well, then," said Oesc. "I will treat with you as a king does with a queen. Give me shelter. Bind up my arm and tend my horse, which has gone lame, and when my men come to find me you shall have gold."

In a single supple movement she was on her feet, looking down at him.

"That is not the way you treat a queen, but an inn-wife. It is as a queen I will shelter you, for you are the suppliant. But the boy who helps us will go for your men as fast as he may, for I would not have the sight and smell of you in my house for one hour longer than hospitality compels."

Clean, warm, and dry at last, Betiver considered the captive Anglian lords. It made him shiver even now to remember what a near thing the battle had been. A score of times during that dreadful morning he had been sure they were beaten. But whenever he could stop to draw breath long enough to consider surrender he had seen that Artor was still fighting, and gritted his teeth, and kept on. He was not ashamed at his own grim satisfaction—now it was he who was dressed like a prince, and the Anglians who were gashed and grimy. However the reversal of fortune did not seem to have daunted their pride.

"Look at Icel!" exclaimed Gualchmai. "Lounging at his ease, as if he still held this hall! You would think he'd be showing a wee bit of apprehension. Did he never hear about the Night of the Long Knives?"

"He trusts to Artor's honor, and besides, that atrocity was the work of Hengest's Saxons. They may all look like the same kind of barbarian to us, but to Icel, his folk are as different from the other tribes as, say, your Votadini are from the Picts who are their neighbors."

"Hmph. Well, I won't deny the Picts have come to us at times for husbands for their princesses. But their sons are raised by their uncles, and mother's milk is stronger than father's blood."

Betiver lifted a hand to silence him. Artor stood in the doorway, drawing men's eyes and stilling their tongues. He too had taken advantage of Lindum's baths, and had dressed in a Roman tunic of saffron-dyed linen with bands of purple silk coming down over the shoulders to the hem and patches bearing eagles worked in gold. His mantle, also edged in goldwork, was of a red so deep it was almost purple, and he wore a Roman diadem upon his brow. Cai, behind him, was actually wearing a toga. Gualchmai whistled softly and grinned.

"Is it the emperor himself who's come to call on us? I hope Icel is impressed."

There had been a flicker of appreciation in Icel's grey eyes, but his face showed no emotion at all. That clothing had certainly never made the muddy journey from Londinium. Betiver, wondering which rich merchant had provided it, fought to keep his own face still. Icel had sought to impress them as a folk-king, lord of a mighty people, but Artor was meeting him as the heir of Rome.

Moving with conscious dignity, Artor seated himself on the carved chair on the dais, and Betiver and Gualchmai took their places with Cai behind him. Icel and two of his surviving chieftains, still in the grubby tunics they had worn beneath their mail, had been given low benches on the floor.

"You fought well, " said Artor, "but your gods have given you into my hand."

"Woden betrayed us," muttered one of the chieftains. "Nine stallions we gave him, and yet he did not give victory."

"But many of your warriors earned a place in his house-guard," said Artor, who had learned something of the

German religion when Oesc was his captive. Icel responded with a rather wintry smile.

"Woden will take care of his own. My care is for the living. What is your will for those who are your prisoners?"

"Kill them," muttered Cataur, "as they slaughtered our men."

Most of those who had survived the battle, thought Betiver, belonged to Icel's houseguard, who had made a fortress of flesh around their king. If he had fallen, they would not have survived him, and only Icel's order could have made them lay down their arms. He leaned close to Gualchmai. "He doesn't ask about himself—"

Gualchmai snorted derisively. "He knows the high king cannot afford to let him go."

But Artor was leaning on the acanthus-carved arm of his chair, resting his chin on his hand, and frowning.

"What would you have me do?"

The question disturbed Icel's composure at last. "What do you mean?"

"You are their king—what did your people seek on these shores?"

"Land! Land that will not wash away in the winter rains!"

Artor raised one eyebrow, indicating with a turn of the head the flooded wastes outside the town, and someone laughed. But Icel was shaking his head.

"Oh yes, this land floods, but the water will go away again and leave it all the richer. We can ditch and dam and make good fields. The river is not so greedy as the sea."

"The Romans did not have that craft—"

Icel's lips twitched again. "The Romans built like etins, great works of pride and power that forced earth to their will. Our farmers are content to work with willow wands and mud and coax our Mother to be kind."

Artor's gaze moved slowly around the faded frescoes of the old basilica, and the worn mosaics on the floor, and he sighed.

"The Romans were mighty indeed, but they are gone, and the land remains," he said then. "And save for your folk, there are now none left to till that soil."

Something flickered in Icel's gaze at the words, but he

kept his features still. Cataur's face began to darken dangerously.

"Many men of my blood have died," Artor went on, "but
my duty is to the living also. To leave this place a wasteland
and its shores desolate will serve no one. But I *am* high king,
and any who would dwell here must go under my yoke." He
frowned at Icel. "If I give you your lives, will you and your
folk take oath to me, to hold these coasts and defend them
in my name? As the Romans gave districts to the Franks and
Burgunds and Visigoths, I will give the Lindenses lands to
you, saving only Lindum itself, which I judge my own people better able to garrison."

As the Vor-Tigernus gave land to Hengest . . . thought Betiver grimly, *and look what that led to!* But Hengest's men
had been a rag-tag of mercenaries and masterless men, not
a nation. It was the same agreement Artor had made with
Oesc, in the end, and that seemed to be working well.

There was a short silence. "What guarantees . . . would
you require?" the Anglian king said then.

"That you shall swear never again to take arms against me
or my heirs, to defend these lands against all others, and to
send a levy of warriors at my call. You shall pay a yearly
tribute, its size contingent upon the size of your harvest, and
in cases affecting men not of your people, be judged by my
laws. I further require that you give up all looted goods and
treasure, that one son from each of your noble families shall
be sent as hostage to dwell among the youths of my household, and that all warriors who are not of your tribe shall
remain my prisoners."

Cataur surged forward, and Gualchmai moved to stand between him and the dais. "My lord, you cannot do this! He's
a *Saxon* . . ."

"An Anglian," Artor corrected coldly, "and I am your
king—"

"Not if you betray us!" Cataur exclaimed, his hands
twitching as if he reached for someone's throat. But Gwyhir
and Aggarban had come to stand beside their brother, and
Morgause's three sons made a formidable barrier. "You'll
regret this day!" Still sputtering, Cataur whirled and strode
from the room. Gualchmai started after him, but Artor waved
him back.

It took a few minutes for the murmur of comment to die down. But despite the fact that there were those on both sides who like Cataur would obviously rather have kept on fighting, it was a fair offer. Indeed, it was more than generous, especially when the alternative was to be slaughtered like a sheep, without even a sword in one's hand. Icel must have hoped for something like this, even if he had not dared to expect it.

Icel got to his feet, his eyes still fixed on Artor. "I am the folk-lord, and I stand for my people before the gods. But for all things that belong to this land and the Britons I will give my oath to you."

Artor gestured to one of the guards. "Unloose his bonds." He looked back at Icel. "As you keep faith with me, so shall I with you, for the sake of Britannia."

A little past sunset three weeks after Oesc returned from his ill-fated hunting trip, the hounds who ran loose around his hall began barking furiously. Oesc, who had been drinking to ease the ache in his arm and trying not to think about Rigana, sat up, and Wulfhere rose to his feet, reaching for the spear that leaned against the door.

"Who comes to the hall of Oesc the king?"

"One who carried him on his saddlebow when he was a boy," came the gruff answer, "and I have not made my way across half Britannia, beset by enemies, to be challenged in Hengest's hall!" Taking advantage of Wulfhere's astonishment, the newcomer shouldered past him and into the light of the fire. Two other men came after him, looking about them nervously.

Oesc leaned forward, striving to see behind the dirt and the dried blood and the wild grey-streaked hair.

"Is it Baldulf?" he asked, coming down from his high seat and opening his arms. "It must be! You stink too badly to be aught but a mortal man! Old friend, what has happened to bring you to my door like—" He shook his head, seeking words.

"Like a fugitive?" Baldulf sank down upon a bench, took the horn of ale the thrall-woman offered and drank it down. "That's what I am, boy—fleeing a lost battlefield and the wrath of your young high king."

"You were in the north—" Oesc said, "were you with Icel?"

Baldulf grunted. "I was safe enough in my dale, until that smooth-talking Anglian sent messages around seeking allies in his campaign against Lindum. All went well for a time, but Artor came at last, and brought Icel to battle. Lad, I was lucky to survive that day, and luckier still not to be captured. The Anglians have taken oath to Artor, but the other prisoners were killed. If I never see another marsh I shall count myself happy!" He shuddered reminiscently and held out his horn to be refilled with ale.

"I won't give you up to him, if that's what you were wondering," said Oesc, "but I can't keep you here."

"Nor would I stay—help me to a ship and I'll be over the water to the Frisian lands." He took another drink and reached out for a hunk of the bread which had been set before him. "There may be no Anglians left to replace those Icel lost, but there are still fighters on the coast who might be willing to try their luck in Britannia. Two men only survived from my warband—" He gestured toward his followers, who were being fed at a table by the door. "But I'll soon raise another. The Britons have not heard the last of me!"

Oesc nodded bemusedly. Listening to Baldulf was like stepping back into another time, to the days when Hengest and his father tore at Britannia like wolves. Things were different now. He understood why Icel had accepted Artor's peace. Now Britannia was his land, too. After a moment he realized that Baldulf had asked him a question.

"Come with you? No—all that I want is here—" He shook his head, smiling.

"All? What about a plump wife to warm your bed, and fair-haired children about your knee? Shall I look for the daughter of a Frisian chieftain, or maybe a Frankish princess, to be your queen?"

Oesc stared at him, all his frustration focusing suddenly into a single need. "I do need a wife," he said then, "but not a woman from across the sea. I must marry into this land if my heirs are to hold it. . . ."

Suddenly Rigana's face filled his vision. Tomorrow, he thought, he would ride to the hut on the Downs. After that first encounter he had not touched her, but one way or another, he knew that she would be his queen.

IX

ALLIANCES

Torches had been set into the crumbling city wall and upon the green height of Hengest's mound. They flickered with pale fire in the last light of the soft summer day. The space before the mound had been cleared and spread with rushes to accommodate the tables for the wedding feast. The King's Hall had not room enough for so many, and in any case, this close to Midsummer it was far too warm to huddle indoors.

The sound of Andulf's chanting floated on the wind. He was old now, and his voice no longer as resonant as it once had been, but he still had the trick of pitching it to carry across the field.

> *"Hail the heir of high-born heroes—*
> *Son of the Saxons who first to these shores;*
> *West over whale-road, borne by the wind,*
> *The old land left, new lives to fashion—"*

Oesc, who had gone to consult with his steward about serving more mead, surveyed the scene and smiled. Two

dozen tables rayed out in a semicircle from his own, where
Rigana, draped in crimson silk and hung with gold, awaited
him. Her features were half-hidden by the fall of her veil,
but his pulse leaped at the sight of her all the same. In the
month since he had brought her home to Cantuwaraburh, he
had discovered that he could always sense her presence, and
his pulse quickened at the mere brush of her hand.

But he had, in addition, a very different reason for feeling
satisfaction. The Cantuware chieftains, nodding approvingly
as Andulf began to recite Oesc's ancestry, had all turned out
with their sworn men, but that, he had expected. It was their
duty to witness the wedding of their lord to the woman who
would give him his heir. But Ceretic had brought his West
Saxons, and Aelle, his hair now entirely white but his frame
still well-muscled, had journeyed up from the south coast to
attend the celebration, and that was an honor on which Oesc
had not dared to depend.

And beside Rigana, where her father, had he been living,
would have had his place, sat Artor the High King, who had
made time between campaigning against the Anglians and
dealing with the new threat from Irish raiders in Demetia to
come. He almost looked the part of a father, thought Oesc,
watching them. In the past year or so Artor had broadened
out—not with fat, but with the muscle that comes from wearing armor for long hours over an extended campaign. In
Artor's eyes Oesc could still recognize the boy he had first
faced across a battlefield sixteen years before, but the body
was now emphatically that of a man, and a king.

It was with enthusiasm that Artor had accepted Oesc's
invitation to stand for the family of the bride at the wedding.
More eagerness, to tell the truth, than Rigana had shown
when she heard about it. To be sure, it was Vitalinus the
Vor-Tigernus who had given away her grandfather's princedom, not Uthir, but even though there was now no man of
that line fit to hold Cantium, Rigana blamed the House of
Ambrosius for not having won it back to British rule, and
Artor for confirming Oesc as its lord.

It was no use to point out that if the Saxons had never
come, she would most likely have been married off young
to some lord living elsewhere in Britannia, whereas now she
would be queen in her own country. Oesc was coming to

understand the bride he had brought home from the hills. Courageous she was, as well as passionate, but logic was not one of her virtues.

> *"In wisdom he weds a noble woman,"*
>   sang Andulf.
> *"Daughter of drightens, radiant as day.*
> *Bold is her heart, as bright her beauty,*
> *Lady who links the lord to the land."*

Surely that must please her, thought Oesc. Artor had signed the marriage contract on her behalf, and now he was slicing meat from the joint that had been set before them, and as he transferred slices to her platter, she smiled. Should that make him uneasy, wondered Oesc?

Watching them, he saw in Rigana's face no coquetry, but it seemed to him that there was something wistful in Artor's eyes. The question of the high king's marriage had been often discussed, but although many maidens had been proposed for the honor, there had never been time, it seemed, for him to court one of them. But if Artor had found love of a more casual kind, no one had heard about it.

Oesc did not think the high king could have had a mistress in secret, but he was not a cold man. When he came to love, it would be deeply.

It is not my bride I should fear for, Oesc thought then, *but my king.*

He saw Ceretic's daughter Alfgifu approaching, bearing the great silver-mounted aurochs horn filled with mead. Andulf struck a last chord and finished his song.

Oesc strode quickly back to take his place at Rigana's side as Artor accepted the horn.

"It is my honor to be the first to offer a toast for the couple who sit before you. Any marriage is a harbinger of hope, for thus the race is renewed. But this wedding, more than most, gives me hope for the future, for the groom, who was once my enemy, has become a friend and ally, and the bride, a woman of my own people, is a living link between the old royal line and the new. It is always something of a miracle that two creatures so different as male and female can live in harmony—" He paused for the murmur of laughter. "But if Oesc and Rigana can do so, then there is hope that Britons and Saxons can live in peace as well.

"This, then, is my wish for the bridal couple—that as they join their lives, our peoples may be linked as well, and if they do not always manage to live in perfect accord—" again, he waited for the laughter "—then I wish that their differences may be quickly resolved, and that from their union new life shall spring!"

He turned the horn carefully so that its tip pointed down, and raised it to his lips, taking a long draught without spilling a drop. Then he handed it back to Alfgifu, who bore it to Aelle, and then to Ceretic and the other chieftains.

The other blessings were more conventional, with a heavy emphasis on the breeding of strong sons. Oesc scarcely heard them. His beating pulse reminded him that soon the feast would be finished, and it would be time to make Rigana his wife in fact as well as name.

When the toasts were completed, the women led Rigana off to the hall to be prepared for bed. As their singing faded, the sound of men's laughter grew louder as the male guests were released from such bonds of propriety as they had observed so far.

"Drink deep, my lord," said Wulfhere, refilling his horn.

Oesc took it and drank, fighting not to cough as he realized that this was not the mild ale mead they had been drinking, but a brew whose heavy sweetness did not quite hide its strength. He swallowed, feeling his head swim as the fire began to burn in his belly, and handed the horn back to the other man.

"That's fine stuff, but I'd best go easy or I'll be no use to my bride—"

"You'll be no use either if you cannot relax," said Ceretic with a grin, offering his own horn. "Drink up, man!"

"That's true," answered Oesc. He reached for the horn.

Ceretic moved closer, bending as if to continue his teasing. "At your wedding feast, the high king of Britannia himself sits down with his Saxon enemies. Are you not honored?" He was still smiling, but there was something unexpectedly sardonic in his tone.

Oesc raised an eyebrow. "Shouldn't I be?"

Ceretic shrugged. "Artor sings a sweet song about peace

between Briton and Saxon, but it is like trying to build an alliance between dogs and wolves."

"You yourself are half Briton—" Oesc began.

Ceretic grunted. "But my heart is Saxon. The blood may mix, but the spirit must be singular. The Britons lick their wounds now, but they hate us still, especially Cataur, who has never forgiven us his brother's death at Portus Adurni. They say he protested making peace with Icel and left the army immediately afterward with all his men, nor will he take them to Artor's aid in Demetia. That man wants blood, and he'll not care where he gets it. I would put a guard upon your borders if I were you."

"Artor will keep him leashed—"

Ceretic shook his head. "Artor may desire peace, but one day his princes will force him to turn against us. When he summons you to war against your own people, which will you choose?"

For a long moment Oesc frowned back at him, the mead growing cold in his belly. "I will choose my own land," he said finally. "I will fight for Cantuware."

Ceretic opened his mouth as if he would say more, then closed it without speaking. The torches flared suddenly in a gust of wind, and Oesc turned. Hæthwæge had come into the circle of light. Silence spread as men saw her standing there, and one or two made a surreptitious gesture of warding where they thought no one could see. It occurred to Oesc that Hæthwæge must be in her sixth decade by now, but as always when she put on the regalia of a priestess, she seemed beyond age.

The wisewoman looked around the circle, smiling slightly, then turned to Oesc. "This is a time of change, when the spindle twirls and new strands are woven into the web of Wyrd. Would you know, my king, what fates shall fall as a result of this marriage of yours?"

The men who stood nearest backed away uneasily. Oesc found himself abruptly sober once more.

"Are you afraid?" she asked then.

He shook his head. This was Hæthwæge, who had guided and guarded him since he was a child.

"I fear neither my fate nor you. Whether my Wyrd be good or bad, foreknowledge will enable me to face it well."

The guests drew back to leave a space around them. Hæthwæge spread a square of linen on the ground and drew the bundle of runestaves from her pouch.

"Say, then, what it is you wish to know—"

For a moment Oesc stood in thought, choosing his words. "Tell me if this marriage will prosper, and whether my queen will bear a son to follow me in this land."

Hæthwæge nodded. Her eyes closed, and she whispered a prayer he could not hear. Then she bent, and with a practiced flick of the wrist, scattered the runestaves across the cloth.

The yew wood sticks rattled faintly as they fell, bounced against one another, and then lay still. Oesc leaned forward, trying to make out the symbols incised and painted where the sides of the sticks had been planed smooth. It was quite dark now. In the flicker of torchlight the rune signs seemed to twist and bend.

Like any man of good blood he knew something of the runes, but their deeper meanings, especially in combination, were a mystery. The sticks the old woman had cast lay scattered across the cloth. Most of them had fallen near the edges; it was the ones that lay within the circle painted in the center that would provide the prophecy.

"*Ing,* the rune of the king who comes over the sea, the god in the royal mound—" Hæthwæge pointed to a rune of crossed angles that lay in the middle of the cloth. "Your seed will take root in the ground." There was a murmur of appreciation from the other men.

"And there, near to it, are *Ethel,* for heritage and homeland, and *Ger,* the rune of good harvests. It means that you will bring luck to your land. But *Hægl,* the hailstone, lies close by them. Some violent upset threatens as well."

"What is the rune that lies across the other, just to the right of the middle of the cloth?" asked Oesc.

For a moment Hæthwæge stared at them, swaying back and forth and muttering softly. Then she sighed.

"*Gyfu* is crossed by *Nyd*—the rune of gifts and exchange cut by Necessity. You see how similar they are—one equal-armed, the other showing the firedrill crossed by its bow. *Gyfu* is a rune that wins great gains, but it is also a sign of self-sacrifice. Some say that *Nyd* represents the slash of a sword, or the spindle of the Norns. Whichever is true, these two crossed runes intersect." The wisewoman looked up at Oesc, and his heart chilled at the sorrow he saw in her eyes.

The wisewoman sighed, then spoke again. "This is the Wyrd that these runes show to me. Your reign will be fruitful, my king, and your son will rule long in this land. But there is a price to pay. Always. Only if you are willing to give all will all you have wished for come to pass."

"All?" he echoed softly, remembering how his grandfather's body had swung from the tree. Since childhood he had understood what might be required of a king. "I made that offering before I ever ascended Hengest's high seat, when I sat out upon his mound."

"You have answered well." Leaning on her staff, the wicce straightened. "Your bride awaits you. Go now, and fulfill your destiny."

The light around them brightened. Oesc turned and saw that four of the women who had escorted Rigana to the hall had returned, bearing fresh torches whose flames were whipped out into ribbons of fire by the rising wind.

"To your destiny!" echoed Ceretic, grinning, "and a fair one it is!" He gave Oesc a push, and fell in with the other men behind him, cheering, as the women lit his way toward the bridal bower.

To satisfy his bride's Roman preference for privacy, Oesc had built a partition to wall off the end of the hall that held the king's boxbed from the rest. Four pillars still supported the framework, stuffed with straw and featherbeds. But instead of closing the space between them with wooden slats, it now was hung with lengths of heavy woolen woven in bands of crimson and gold. A wooden floor had been laid and a wolfskin rug cast over it. Terracotta lamps hung from brackets on the wall, and the women had garlanded the bed with greenery and early summer flowers.

More important still, the bower had a door. As he shut it firmly behind him, Oesc was suddenly extremely glad he had taken the trouble to build it. This moment would have been even more difficult if there had been no more than a single bedcurtain between him and the raucous encouragement he was being given by the men outside. He cleared his throat.

"Rigana?"

From the other side of the curtain came a noise that sounded suspiciously like laughter.

She answered, "The sooner you come to bed, the sooner those louts outside will shut up and go away."

Oesc fumbled with the clasp of his belt, dragged his tunic over his head and dropped it, and pulled off his breeches. As he pulled aside the curtain and climbed into the bed he could feel his heart beating as it did when he was going to war.

Light filtered through the rough weave of the curtains, glowing on the pale flesh of the woman who sat cross-legged on the coverlet. Oesc's breath caught as he looked at her small, uptilted breasts and rounded thighs, confirming with his eyes what his hands had learned about her body when they struggled on the grass. Since that day, she had scarcely let him touch her. But she did not seem to be afraid.

"Are you drunk?" she asked suddenly.

He blinked, then shook his head. "Did you think I would have to be drunk to lie with you?"

"I only wondered what was keeping you so long." She settled back among the pillows, looking at him with the same frank interest with which he had eyed her.

Hoping that the dim light would not show his blush, Oesc climbed the rest of the way into the bed.

"Hæthwæge read the runes. She says we will have a fine son to be king of this land."

"Does she? Then we had better get started on making him—"

Oesc could not decide whether her smile held eagerness or defiance.

He had meant to be tender, to take her slowly. He had dreamed of this moment in exquisite detail—how he would stroke first her cheek, and then work his way carefully down until her breast lay like a tender fruit in his hand. He had not anticipated the way that lust would flame in his blood in response to the challenge in her smile. *Frige be with me!* he thought desperately as he pulled Rigana into his arms.

The wiry, whipcord strength was as he remembered, but the feel of her smooth skin against his own as they wrestled together made his mind reel. His fingers tightened in her hair as he kissed her, his body straining against hers until she lay still. She cried out as he thrust through her maidenhead, and began to fight him again, but imperceptibly their struggles became harmony, their breath coming together in harsh gasps as they rode the storm. He felt her convulse in his arms, and her final frenzy swept his own awareness away.

An eternity later, they became aware of each other as separate beings again. Wind was whispering in the thatching, and from the feasting ground they could hear men's voices lifted in song. Oesc raised himself up on one elbow, looking down at his bride.

"Don't think it will be this easy every time . . ." she said shakily.

"Easy?" Oesc winced as bites and scratches began to sting. "I feel like a ship that has barely survived the storm. If this coupling has made a son, he will be a warrior!"

"A typical Saxon!"

"As fierce as his mother!" Oesc replied. He shook his head in exasperation. "If you hate us so, why did you marry me?"

"You carried me off—" she retorted, "what choice did I have?"

"You know very well I would not have forced you. And at the end there, your body seemed very eager for mine! Rigana—the same wind buffeted us both, and brought us in the end to safe harbor. Even now will you not give truth to me?"

"The truth is . . . that my body may have surrendered, but my mind still tells me that you are my enemy."

"And your heart?" he asked softly.

Rigana sighed. "My heart is a slow learner—you must give it time to understand."

In the weeks that followed, Oesc remembered those words. Marriage with Rigana was like sailing the sea at the mercy of conflicting winds. At times they blew as balmy as some fabled southern isle, and Oesc, half-drunk on his new wife's kisses, would swear that he had won her at last. But then some clash of culture or concept, or even the sight of the ruins over which her grandfather had ruled, would set the wind wheeling round to the north again, with a chill that could freeze his soul. But the body had its own imperatives. Their lovemaking, when Rigana would submit to it, was a force that shook them both to the core. And soon it became apparent that Oesc's seed had taken root in fertile ground.

Pregnancy, of course, gave the queen a whole new source of invective, especially during the early months, when she was often ill. Nonetheless, as the result of their lovemaking became increasingly apparent, Rigana began to turn to her husband more and more. It was a golden year, with a bountiful harvest and a mild winter, and Oesc tasted his new happiness with astonished joy.

Just after the spring equinox, when the rain storms followed each other in stately succession across the land, Rigana's pangs came upon her. The bed in the bower was spread with clean cloths and fresh straw for her lying in, and Oesc was banished from the room to wait beside the fire in the hall with the other men.

"Women!" exclaimed Wulfhere, "they act as if all men were monsters when one of them is in the straw!"

"Not all men—" said Oesc, wincing as he heard Rigana swearing from the other side of the wall. "Just me. . . ." He rubbed his left arm, where Rigana's slingstone had cracked the old break in the bone. He had still not gotten back full use of that hand.

"She has a good vocabulary," observed Wulfhere, running a hand through his thinning ash-brown hair.

Oesc managed to smile back at him. Wulfhere was a good friend, he thought, straightforward and steady, as good a man as one might find in the Saxon lands. But he had been born in Cantium, son to a man who had come over in Hengest's first warband. He understood Oesc's love for this land. More to the point, he was also the father of four children, and understood what his lord was going through.

Oesc looked up suddenly, realizing that he could hear nothing from the bower. He started to get to his feet, but Wulfhere shook his head.

"Someone will come out if there's news." He pushed the beer jug across the table.

"No. I don't want to be drunk when—if—she's been at it since morning and it is past midnight! I'd rather fight a battle than wait here. At least I could *do* something there!"

"This is a woman's battlefield. But life, not death, is the victory."

"I hope so—" Oesc sat down once more.

From the bower came a grunt, and then something very like a battle cry. The two men stared, scarcely daring to breathe, until they heard, like an echo, a thin, protesting wail.

Women's voices murmured busily as the door opened and Hæthwæge beckoned. Two steps brought Oesc to her side.

"Is Rigana—is the baby—" He could not find words. Beyond the wicce he saw his wife lying in the bed in which the child had been begotten. A pile of bloodstained cloths lay on the floor. She looked pale, but her eyes were very bright. Walking carefully, as if his footfalls might break something, he came to her side and took her hand.

"My dear, I'm so sorry—" he stammered, "I didn't know!"

"Sorry! When I've given you a fine son? Look at him!" She flipped back a piece of linen and he realized that what he had taken for tumbled bedclothes beside her were the cloths that swaddled a tiny being who mewed at the disturbance and rooted against his mother's breast.

"You're all right?" he asked.

"Of course. I've helped too many ewes bring their lambs into the world to make a fuss—though I must say the sheep seem to have an easier time! Pick him up—is he not beautiful?"

Oesc realized that the women were all watching him expectantly, and someone had summoned his sword-thanes, who were crowding into the room.

"Beautiful—" he muttered, although the crumpled red features looked more like those of a tiny troll than of a man. Carefully he got his hands under the small bundle and lifted it, and caught his breath as the slitted eyes opened and for a moment he saw his grandfather Eadguth's face overlaid on that of the child.

"Beautiful—" he said again, knowing what they were waiting for. "And I claim him as my son! Is there water?" He looked at Hæthwæge.

"Here—I brought it from the sacred spring . . ." She held out a bowl of dark brown earthenware incised with a zigzag design around the rim.

Oesc dipped his fingers into the water and sprinkled the cool droplets on the baby's brow. "Eormenric son of Oesc I name you, grandson of Octha and Gorangonus of Cantium, great grandson of Hengest of the royal Anglians, and Eadguth the Myrging king. I dedicate you to Woden, who has given you breath, and to the Lady of this land, who has given you flesh. Live long, my son, for Cantuware is your heritage!"

"I think I never knew what it was to simply feel happy before . . ." said Oesc. Wulfhere, who was riding beside him, laughed.

"Well, lord, you have reason."

Oesc found that he was grinning. The movement of the horse beneath him, the way the summer sunlight glowed through the whispering leaves above the track that led north through the Weald toward Aegelesford, even the sweetness of the air he drew in—today, everything gave him joy. But he had ridden through fine summer days before and never noticed their beauty. It was the happiness he had found in the great things of his life that allowed him to value the little ones as well.

"To the fortunate man, all things are golden—" he repeated the old saying. "It is true, I have been greatly blessed."

Still smiling, he silently enumerated the gifts that the gods had given him: Rigana had recovered well from the birthing, and Eormenric had outgrown the first fragility of babyhood and was now as fine and lusty a child as any man might wish for. The first, disturbing resemblance to his grandfathers had faded as he put on flesh. At three months, he was all plump cheeks and bright eyes, reaching out to grasp the world with chubby pink hands.

In his delight with the baby, Oesc did not forget the wife who had produced him. Rigana would never be an easy woman to live with, but after a year of marriage, she had lost the abrasive edge that had at first turned every conversation into a battle. Now they only fought once or twice a week, and since their battles more often than not ended in bed, Oesc could hardly regret them.

And Hengest's old hall had never been so bright. Rigana had the manner of a princess, but her life on the farm in the hills had given her a realistic understanding of the labor needed to maintain a hall. She asked nothing of her maids that she could not do better, and though at times they felt the lash of her tongue, they respected her.

His marriage had won him new respect among the men of Cantuware as well, especially the eorls and elders. *They no longer have to fear I will lead their sons off on wild adventures,* he thought. *I am becoming a land-king now.*

Certainly Hæsta seemed to think so. At this last lawgiving, the southern eorl had praised his judgments. Even Hengest, he said, had not understood the land and its needs so well.

And Oesc was still young, and save for that lingering weakness in his left arm, in robust health. There was no reason he should not live as long as his grandfather and see his own grandchildren root themselves in this land. He had taken Rigana and the baby to Aegele's ford so that they could get the blessing of the goddess of the sacred spring.

Suddenly his joy demanded action. The ford was barely an hour away, and then he would see his wife and child, but he did not want to wait so long. The horse's ears twitched as he lifted the rein.

"Wulfhere, that nag of yours is plodding like a plowhorse. I have a mind to reach Aegele's ford by noon. Do you think you can match me?"

"I'll come there before you!" Wulfhere's eyes kindled.

"Do it and I'll give you the Frankish swordmount that Hæsta gifted me."

"And you shall have your pick of Prick-Ear's next litter if you win—" Wulfhere returned. The other men shook their heads indulgently, but they reined their mounts out of the way as with a shout their young king and his friend set their horses careering up the path.

Bent over the grey mare's neck, gulping in air strained through her flying mane, it was not until Oesc began to cough that he realized the air smelled of smoke—not the smoke of a hearthfire, or soapmaking or the burning of brush or any of the other uses of fire about a farm, but the acrid reek of a big fire, of burning timbers and smoldering straw. He had smelled it too often to mistake, when he was at war.

He straightened, shifting his weight back and hauling on the reins. For a moment the mare fought him, then she pulled up, plunging, just as Wulfhere thundered around the bend behind him.

"What is it? Is your horse—" he began. Then he too caught the scent the wind was bringing and his face changed.

"Go back and bring up the warriors," Oesc said softly. "Leave the baggage ponies to follow as best they can."

"But my lord—"

"I've done scouting. I'll go slowly and take care not to be seen."

Oesc waited until the clatter of Wulfhere's departure faded and the forest grew quiet around him. He could hear neither shouting nor hoofbeats, but the burning must be close for the reek to be so strong. Perhaps Aegele was only burning brush, he told himself, and the men would get a good laugh at his fear. Then a shift in the wind brought him a whiff of roasting flesh, and the mare lurched forward at the touch of his heel.

He slowed again as he started down the slope toward the ford, but now he could hear ravens calling to their kindred. They would not do so unless the fighting was done.

It was strange, some odd, detached part of his mind observed as he rode into the farmyard, how clearly he could still read the signs, though it was nearly ten years since last he had ridden to war.

The attackers had hit the farm without warning. The women had been dyeing cloth. Two squares of blue flapped damply from the rack, but the pot had been overthrown, its contents mixing with the blood on the ground. One of the thrall women lay beside it, her head crushed, her hand still gripping the wooden bat she had been using to stir the pot. But her skirts modestly covered her thighs.

Where is Rigana? Oesc forced the yammering voice within him to be still.

The raiders had not raped or even pillaged—cattle still lowed from the byre. But the hoofprints had already told him that these folk were riding good Roman-bred horses, not the shaggy hill ponies that outlaws would use. He found two more thralls by the byre, and then one of Aegele's men with a sword still in his hand. Outlaws would not have left the weapon, and the strokes that had killed the man had a military precision. This was not robbery, but a raid, conducted by trained warriors with a military objective in mind.

My wife and my son! Dead, or hostages? Once more he shut the voice away.

Methodically Oesc worked his way around the buildings. More men lay with their throats cut in addition to their wounds. The attackers had left no one living to tell the tale. Aegele himself lay just inside the ruins of his house, with his wife beside him. His body was partly burned, but the golden band that marked him as a thane was still on his arm.

Hæthwæge was with them. Could her magic have hidden Rigana and the child?

He left the mare standing and made his way up the path to the shrine. The devastation that had hit the farm had not touched it—more reason for that cold, evaluating part of his mind that kept his rage at bay to conclude British warriors had done this thing. He saw signs of a scuffle in the dirt before the shrine. Blood had been drawn—dark drops speckled the ground.

A breath of wind lifted his hair and chilled the sweat on his brow. He went inside.

The lamps were cold, but a bunch of summer asters, barely wilted, still lay on the stone, and beside it, a baby's teething bone.

"Lady—" he whispered, "they came to serve you. Could you not have protected them?"

Water murmured musically from below, the same song as it had sung for Celt and Roman, and for those who came before. *I am here as I have always been . . .* it whispered, *be still, and know . . .*

But Oesc could not listen. In his ears a furious wind was rising, sweeping both patience and reason away. A swift step took him back to the doorway and the devastated farm below. Wulfhere and his men were just riding in. But he scarcely saw them.

"Rigana . . ." he whispered. The roar of the wind grew louder, though no leaf stirred. "*Rigana. . . .*" Reason was reft away in a great shout that shattered the silence as her name became a berserker's wordless cry. Still shouting, Oesc ran down the hill.

* * *

For the next four days they followed the raiders. Messengers galloped off to raise the fyrd while Oesc and his best trackers kept on the trail. It was not difficult. The British had hit other steadings on their way into Cantuware, but in Rigana, they realized they had a prize beyond all booty and were losing no time in getting her away from the Saxon lands. North to Durobrivae led the trail, and then straight west along the old Roman road.

To those they passed, the attackers were no more than an echo of hoofbeats, a rumor in the night. But as word spread through the countryside, folk came from the places they had hit on their way in. By the time Oesc reached the borders of his own lands, his fyrd was over a hundred strong. But the British were a day ahead of them. They had left the road before it reached Londinium and headed cross-country, following minor paths that the Saxons did not know.

Clearly they meant to avoid Venta Belgarum as they had Londinium, but still their way led westward.

A week after Rigana had been taken, Oesc halted his warband at the edge of the British border. Their quarry had gone west and south into Dumnonia, where Oesc had not the force to follow them. But by then he knew whom he was chasing. The warriors who had captured his wife and child belonged to Cataur, prince of the Cornovii and enemy of the Saxon kind.

"What will you do?" asked Wulfhere, his face gaunted by a week of hard riding.

Oesc looked around him. "Beric—" he gestured to a red-headed lad on a roan pony. "Your mother was British, and you speak the tongue well. I will write a message in the Latin tongue, which you must take to Artor. I believe he is in Demetia—the Irish have been raiding again. It is time to hold him to his oath. Rigana and the baby are only valuable as hostages if they are alive. I have to believe that Cataur will take care of her. But he will have to give her up to his king."

"And if he does not?"

Oesc could feel his own features stiffening into a mask of rage. "If Artor does not get her back for me, then my own oaths to him are also void. I will go to my own kind, to Ceretic and Aelle, and together we shall make such a war of vengeance as will drive the British into the sea!"

X

Mons Badonicus

A.D. 495

 A brisk wind was blowing up from the Channel, bringing with it the scent of the sea. Oesc took a deep breath, and for a moment he was sixteen years old and on his way to the battle of Portus Adurni once more. *And at the end of it I was Artor's prisoner,* he fought down rage as that old sorrow amplified the new. Cataur still held Rigana and his son.

Struggling for calm, he told himself that this was the same war that his grandfather had begun, the war to make Britannia Angle-land. His alliance with Artor had been an interruption, that was all. The thought should have given him comfort, but the angry knot in his belly still throbbed.

"My lord, you must eat—" said Hæsta, pushing the wooden platter of swine-flesh toward him. Around the table of the kings were others for the eorls and the thanes and lesser warriors, and behind them the rush mats where their warriors were sitting, chunks of meat and bread before them and drinking horns in their hands.

Oesc ignored it. "Has there been any word from Beric?"

The thane shook his head. For a moon they had waited,

while the news of Rigana's abduction spread as though carried by the wind. Had Beric found the high king? Had he even gotten through?

Artor—Artor— his heart called. *Why did you never answer me?*

Perhaps the king was unwilling to go against one of his greatest princes. Perhaps he had not the power to force Cataur to give up his prize.

I would have held to my oath to life's end! It is you who have broken faith with me....

The wind shifted, and Oesc smelled the sweetness of curing grass. It was a moon past midsummer, and all over Britannia men were getting in the hay. The cornfields were ripening, the barley hanging down its head and the green emmer wheat turning gold. Who would harvest them, he wondered, once the Saxons had set the south aflame with war? The men they had sent directly to Cataur had returned with the message that Rigana was his guest, and would remain safe and comfortable so long as Oesc prevented his neighbors from attacking the Dumnonian lands. But if Cataur wanted peace, his own action had destroyed it. Wherever men spoke the Saxon tongue they were calling for revenge.

If Artor, who was acknowledged high king of the Britons, could not rule his princes, it was certain that Oesc could not control the Saxons, over whom he had no lordship at all. It was Ceretic, scenting the excuse that he had been seeking since Portus Adurni, who had summoned the tribes to gather here.

"Oesc, what are you doing?" Hæsta grasped his arm and Oesc realized that he had risen to his feet, his hand on his sword. He looked around him, blinking.

This army was already greater than the one that had challenged Artor eighteen years ago; each day more were coming in. A new generation of warriors had come to manhood, born in this land. They laughed as they ate, boasting of new conquests. His own men of Cantuware, with the West Saxons led by Ceretic and the South Saxons of Aelle, made a formidable alliance. In addition to the kingsmen, from the lands to the east of Londinium had come the Sunnings and the Mennings, the Geddings and Gillings, and more—warriors from a gaggle of clans who were oathsworn to no overlord.

Once more the wind changed. Now the scents were of horses and leather and roasted meat. Two thralls came past, pulling a cart with a vat of ale. Oesc held out his horn to be refilled and sat down. He took a long swallow, willing his racing heart to slow. For the others, avenging Oesc's loss was only the excuse for a campaign. Their beds were not empty, their children's first words would not be in the British tongue.

Gradually the muted roar of men's voices stilled and he realized that Ceretic was standing. His voice rang across the field as he spoke to the kings and chieftains, chanting names and lineage, bidding them welcome. He knew them all, and their exploits as well. Even as Oesc twitched with impatience, he realized how long Ceretic had been preparing for this day.

"And so, we are come together—" he cried. "Against this army, the Britons will never be able to stand. All that remains is to say who will lead us against this foe!"

"Ceretic! Ceretic hail!" shouted his thanes.

But Hæsta had jumped to his feet as well. "Oesc son of Octha should be our leader! It is his wife who was taken, and he's the heir of Hengest, who brought us to this land!"

"He has not led men in battle—" came the rejoinder.

"But will Ceretic give up his lordship when the war is over? He wants to rule us all!"

"Oesc will be too rash against Cataur and too weak against Artor—"

The meadow erupted in disputation. The British had grown powerful because they all obeyed one high king. Who, Oesc wondered, could command the allegiance of the proud-stomached, hot-headed, independent-minded warriors who were gathered here?

Oesc kept silent as the arguments went on. He wanted his wife back, but did he want to rule? *Artor won his kingship at the age of fifteen by pulling a God-Sword out of a stone. Shall I attempt the same trick with the Spear?*

He smiled grimly, remembering how even his own house-guard had grown pale when they realized just what the long, swaddled bundle he had taken from Hæthwæge's hut contained. At the time it had seemed right to bring it, but he knew that the Spear was not a token of sovereignty, even though it belonged to the god of kings. Whatever use he might make of it on this campaign, it would not make him Drighten of all the Saxon kind.

Oesc was not sure that anyone could claim that title here. The British were accustomed to overkings and emperors, but no Caesar had ever united the peoples of Germania. It seemed to him sometimes that to do so would be to pervert their very nature. German war-leaders who developed Imperial ambitions always seemed to come to a bad end.

Voices grew louder as tempers frayed. At this rate, the Saxon alliance would not last long enough to bring the Britons to battle. At the other end of the table Aelle was frowning, as if he had heard it all before.

Curse them all! thought Oesc. Rage roared in his ears. Suddenly he was on his feet; when no one seemed to notice, he leaped to the tabletop. Platters danced and food flew, but he kept his footing. Pitching his voice as Andulf had taught him, he cried out—"*Hold!*

"You are squabbling like dogs while another hound takes the bitch away. I want my wife back, and I want Cataur's head—it doesn't matter to me who leads us so long as we win. We need someone with experience, with an authority that all can see. I will pledge myself and my warriors to Aelle of the South Saxons until this war is done!"

A murmur spread through the assembly like wind in the trees. Aelle's head came up and he frowned as if uncertain whether to be grateful. Oesc grimaced back at him. *If you don't want it, all the better! You will be less likely to cling to power.*

"He is right," said Hæsta. "It is the ancient way of our people to choose a war-leader. Aelle is an old wolf and will lead us well."

Everyone looked at Ceretic, whose face had gone dangerously red. But he was a wolf himself, and he could see that the temper of the gathering was against him. He shot Oesc a look of mingled amusement and fury and nodded.

"I agree." He lifted his horn. "In Woden's name I swear it—I and all who are sworn to me will follow Aelle for the duration of this war!"

"Aelle!" came the shout as more horns were raised. "Aelle!"

For a time Aelle listened, then he stood, and gradually the shouting ceased.

"As you have chosen me your leader, I accept the call." His deep voice rumbled through the air like distant thunder. "The Britons have given us fair words, but they cannot uphold them. There is no safety in oaths or treaties. Not until all of Britannia is Saxon will our wives and our homes be secure. Let us go forth in Woden's name, and fight until we have the victory!"

"Look, my lord—from here you can see the Isle of Glass. Beautiful, is it not?" Merlin pointed across the vale, where a scattering of hills rose from a sea of cloud. But only one of them compelled attention. The king reined in abruptly, and Merlin knew he had seen the Tor, its pointed cone dark against a sky flushed rose with morning light, its line pure as some Grecian vase.

"Very beautiful, had I seen it at any other time." Artor's lips tightened and he kicked his mount into motion down the hill. "Does Cataur think that because this is a holy place I will hold my hand? This war is his doing!" His horse broke into a trot.

Merlin held back a little, gazing across the vale. *You will not be stopped by coming to the holy Tor, but perhaps you will be changed.*

The druid had been in Isca when word of the Saxon outbreak arrived. For one terrible moment the events of the first Saxon Revolt had played themselves out in memory. Even before the messenger appeared his dreams had been filled with images of blood and fire. Was it because of them that he felt as if he were repeating actions performed long ago? Or was it only because this was the old enemy, the White Dragon, that had come forth to do battle with the Red once more?

Hengest was dead. This was his grandson, and his foe was not an old king worn out with wars, but Artor. Still, it seemed to Merlin that this campaign was only the culmination of the wars he had fought so long ago, and it was right that one more time he should ride to battle behind a king.

At this season the marshlands were mostly dry. As they reached the bottom of the hill and clattered across the logs of the causeway, cattle grazing in the water meadows looked up with incurious gaze. But mist still hung in the hollows and dimmed the copses, as if they were moving through a series of veils between the worlds.

Artor's face was grim. His control, thought the druid, was no doubt too rigid just now for him to sense any changes in the atmosphere. But the other men, less preoccupied, were looking around them with mingled distrust and wonder. As the Isle grew closer, its rounded slopes rising up to hide the Tor, Merlin felt its power growing steadily stronger, like the vibration of a great river, or the heat of a fire. It had been a long time since he had come here. He had forgotten how, to those with inner sight, the Tor could become in truth an isle of glass through which the light of the Otherworld shone clear.

Open your heart and your eyes, boy, he thought, fighting to control the intoxication of that radiance. The Christian wizard who had brought his followers to this place and built the first church at its base had known what he was doing. The Tor was a place of power.

By the time they reached the Isle, the sun was high. The mists had burned away, and with them, some of the visible mystery. The round church and beehive huts of the monks nestled at the base of the hill, with the community of nuns beside the sacred well beyond them. The lower meadows had sprouted a new crop of tents of hide and canvas, and men and horses were everywhere. The pressure of so many minds buzzed in Merlin's brain.

"Speak with Cataur," he told the king, "and when you are done, however it goes, come to me on the top of the Tor. You will not wish to take the time, but you must do so. From the summit you will be able to see more than the road across the vale—you will see your way." He held Artor's gaze until the angry light in the king's eyes faded and he knew that the younger man was sensing, at least a little, the ancient power that would outlast all of them and their fears.

"Look at that arrogant son of a swine, parading in here as if he had won a victory instead of plunging the land into war!" exclaimed Cai. "I know how I'd reward him if I were high king!" He frowned as Cataur approached the awning that had been set up to shade the meeting, escorted by Leo-degranus, the prince of Lindinis who was in a sense their host here. His hand drifted toward the pommel of his sword.

"Just as well you are not—" answered Betiver. "Artor will have to handle him like a man carrying coals through a hay-field, or we'll have all the west and south aflame. This deed of Cataur's has united the Saxons, but it could break the British alliance."

"And Artor knows it—" Gualchmai shook his head. "He's got a frown on him that would curdle new milk. Still, 'tis not entirely a bad thing. With every year the Saxons have been getting stronger. Do we smash them now, we'll not risk being too weak to do it in a few years' time. . . ."

His younger brother Gwyhir bared his teeth in a grin. He was pale of hair and combative, like his brother only in his height. The third brother, Aggarban, was short and darker. Men said that after the first son, all of Morgause's children had been festival got, of fathers unknown. In the north, where they held to the old ways, no one thought the worse of her. In the south they remembered that she was the king's sister, and if they spoke of it, did so in whispers.

"I hope we will fight—" said Aggarban. "You have had your shares of glory, but I still have to make my name!"

"You sound as if we should thank Cataur for starting this war!" Betiver said bitterly.

Gualchmai shrugged. "I will not blame him. I do admit it has all been a bit unexpected, but ye must bring a boil to a head before ye can lance it. Cataur is only forcing the king to do what one way or another had to come."

Even as Betiver frowned he had to admit that there was a certain hard logic in his words. But he remembered Oesc's fair head next to Artor's brown as they bent over the tabula board or stood at the butts for archery. Oesc had begun as Artor's prisoner, but in the end it seemed to him that they had found a kind of peace in each other's company that Artor had with no one else. The breaking of that bond must surely be hurting both of them now.

There was a little murmur of anticipation as Artor pushed through the crowd. For a moment he hesitated, glaring at the canopy beneath which Cataur waited. Then, without looking to see if his escort followed, he marched toward him. The

Dumnonian prince stood up as Artor neared. His sandy hair had grown thinner, noticed Betiver. But the flush on his fair skin was probably from the heat, not shame.

The king's warriors stepped back out of earshot, facing the men of Cataur's houseguard. They could not make out words, but the rise and fall of the two voices came clearly, Artor's deep and tightly controlled and Cataur's higher, with the hint of a whine. But perhaps that was only Betiver's interpretation. Certainly the Dumnonian's face was getting even redder as the discussion went on.

"Say what you will!" Cataur's voice rose. "Giving the woman back now won't stop the war!"

"The war you wanted!" came Artor's shout in reply. The escorts moved closer as he went on. "Send the woman to my stronghold at Dun Tagell. The chieftains of Demetia are still gathering their men. I must go north to join them. Take your own men east and hold Aelle's forces for as long as you can. If you fail me I promise that when I have dealt with the Saxons I will come after you myself!"

He stood, and Cataur got to his feet as well, grinning tightly.

"My lord, we will do all that men can."

The afternoon was far advanced when Merlin felt the energy that pulsed around the summit change and came back from the aery realms in which he had been wandering. Looking down, he saw the pattern of the encampment dislimning as the Dumnonians moved out. Then he became aware of a subtler alteration and knew that Artor was climbing the hill. No other would dare. Even the monks came here only on feast days to make prayers to the Archangel Michael, whom they hoped would bind the old powers that lived in the Tor.

The strengthening breeze set dust whirling in a spiral, and he smiled. Could one bind the waters that flowed through the earth, or the wind that stirred his hair? Perhaps the monks' prayers kept them from feeling the power of the Tor, but even with his eyes open, Merlin could see the lines of power radiating out from the holy hill.

He turned as the high king appeared at the edge of the flattened oval of the summit, his hair blown, a sheen of perspiration on his brow. But the haze of anger that had pulsed around him that morning was gone. Perhaps he had worked off his fury on the climb.

"Have you brought me here to show me all the kingdoms of the world and the glory thereof?" Artor asked wryly when he had his breath again. To the north and south, hills edged the vale. To the west one could guess at the blue shimmer of the sea. Eastward the land fell away to dim distances veiled by the smoke of burning fields.

Merlin shook his head. "Glory you shall see, but not of this world. Take a deep breath—this air comes pure from the heights of heaven."

"Cataur and Oesc are in *this* world—" Artor said angrily.

"Breathe!" Merlin's voice compelled obedience. The air the king had drawn in to argue with was expelled without words. He breathed in again, more slowly, and his eyes widened.

"What is it? I feel a tingling, and there are little sparkles in the air!"

"Look at me . . ." said the druid.

"There is a haze of brightness around you," whispered Artor after a moment had passed.

"Now, look at the land. . . ."

This time, the silence was longer. The king stood still, trembling, his eyes wide and unfocused.

"What do you see?"

"Light—" came the answer. "With every breath, light flows through the grass and stone and trees. . . ."

"Life," corrected the druid. "It is the Spirit that you are perceiving, that moves like a wind through all that is."

"Even the Saxons?"

"Even through them, though they do not perceive it. He who understands this mystery is part of the land. This is the power that will carry you to victory."

Nearby, someone was groaning. Oesc roused, smelled horses and old blood and the smoke of a watch fire, and knew he was encamped with Aelle's army. The groaning man must be Guthlaf, one of his houseguard who had taken an arrow through the thigh. But he would live, and they had won the battle. He turned over, wincing as the movement jarred stiff muscles, and gazed upward, where stars winked through a high haze of cloud. The gods had favored them with good weather for campaigning, and barring a few scratches, he had come through the fighting unscathed.

But he was tired to the bone. He tried to remember what it was like to sleep in a real bed with the soft warmth of a woman beside him. He had had Rigana for little more than a year—it was not long enough to offset a lifetime of loneliness. *Is she even alive? Is the child?* By day he could assure himself that Cataur would have no reason to kill her. But in the dark hours he imagined a lifetime spent grieving for her loss.

Even if Cataur had offered to give her back tomorrow, Oesc could not break the oaths that bound him to the war. That was the doom that haunted his nightmares. Living or dying, how could Rigana forgive him for not rescuing her? He had meant their marriage to join their two peoples in harmony, and instead it had led to a new and more devastating war.

It was small consolation to reflect that Cataur must be regretting his action as well. One of Ceretic's warriors was boasting that he had struck the Dumnonian prince from his saddle. The Britons had got their leader safely away, but it would be long before Cataur could fight again. After several preliminary skirmishes, the main forces had met near Sorviodunum, and the Dumnonians, if not quite defeated, had been prevented from retreating westward. Now the larger Saxon army was pursuing them across the plain.

Burdened with wounded, the British would go slowly. Aelle hoped to cut them off before they could join with the forces Artor was raising in Demetia.

Oesc felt a new set of muscles complain as he turned onto his side and closed his eyes once more. But the deep slumber he so badly needed eluded him. Instead he fell into a state halfway between sleep and waking in which he wandered through a landscape of warring ghosts.

At first he thought of the old story of Hild, whose curse set her father and lover to repeat their final battle throughout eternity. But this was a battle of Saxon against Briton, and it was Rigana who walked among them, shrieking imprecations. It seemed to him then that he followed after, begging her to forgive so that peace might come. And then she turned, and her face was that of a wælcyrige, one of the battle hags who choose the slain for Woden's hall.

Oesc halted, shaking his fists at the heavens. *"What do you want? When will you bring this slaughter to an end?"*

And it seemed to him then that a great wind swept across the battlefield, swirling up the bodies of men like fallen leaves and flinging them across the sky. And like the roar of that wind, came the answer—

"When you choose wisdom over war. . . . When you learn how to use the Spear!"

The Britons were retreating. Cataur's appeal had brought Artor's forces down from Demetia to his aid, but the Saxon army was larger than anyone had expected. In the open field, the Britons could not stand against them. Several skirmishes and one pitched battle had proved that in numbers at least, the Saxons had superiority. Every villa in their path had been looted, and the ruins of Cunetio still smoked behind them. But if the defenders were being forced to fall back, at least they were doing so in good order. Their losses had been relatively light—to some, that made their retreat all the more ignominious. Only Artor seemed unconcerned.

When the murmurs became too bitter to ignore, he called his chieftains to council.

They had made camp just outside the hamlet of Verlucio, a staging post on the main road that led from Calleva and the Midlands toward Aquae Sulis. The inhabitants, recognizing that any supplies they did not share with their own side would soon be taken by the Saxons, had been generous with food and drink, and the men were in a more mellow mood than they had been when the day began.

Even Gualchmai, who had been growling like a chained hound, seemed to have been pacified by a skin of wine. But Betiver, gazing at the circle of flushed or frowning faces, still felt a hard knot of anxiety in his gut.

"What is the matter, old friend?" came a voice at his elbow. "You are looking around you like a sheep that has just heard the first wolf howl." It was the king.

Betiver sighed. "It is not the wolves I fear just now, but the sheepdogs. They do not like to be beaten, and they do not like to run."

"And you fear the shepherd will not be able to command them?" Artor's eyes were as bright as if he were going into battle.

Betiver flushed. *He understands what is at stake here, despite his soft words.*

"Have faith. No man can guarantee victory always, but I do have a plan."

"My lord," Betiver answered softly, "I have believed in you since I was thirteen years old."

It was Artor's turn to color then. He turned away rather quickly and took his place in the folding camp chair with the crimson leather seat and back that he used as a portable throne. Gualchmai moved into position behind his right shoulder and Betiver took the left. Gradually, the men gathered before him grew still.

"Let me tell you a story—" the high king said into the silence. "Once I hunted a stag. He was an old beast, and wily, but I was confident that my dogs could run him down. But he knew the ground better than I did, and the chase went on and on. By afternoon, I was far from my own hunting runs. I had no food, and the trail was leading into the hills. But my prey was so close, I could not give up. And then, the ground rose suddenly and I looked up and saw the stag above me on a rock that jutted out from the cliff. Three dogs were killed as they tried to leap up at him. I lifted my spear, but before I could throw, the stag charged. His horns took out two more dogs as he crashed through the circle, and my horse reared and threw me. By the time I sorted myself out, he was long gone, and the dogs that remained to me were quite happy to head home. . . ."

For a long moment there was silence, then Agricola of Demetia let out a guffaw. "Is that why we've been bolting for the hills for the past ten-day?"

"You are trying to draw the Saxons into hostile territory?" asked Cunorix, whose Irish had, in the face of this new threat, been transformed into allies once more.

Artor let the babble of speculation run its course before raising his hand. "Aelle's army is too great for him to carry sufficient supplies. He must live off the land, but if he splits his forces to forage they risk coming upon a larger body of our own men. The farther he gets from his own lands the worse his problem becomes."

"And where do you propose to stand at bay?" a new voice put in.

"Aquae Sulis nestles among hills. In such broken country, the Saxons will find it hard to bring their numbers to bear. There is a hill that overlooks the Abona across the river from the town, above the place where the Calleva road joins the road to Corinium. It stands alone, and its summit is flat, big enough for our mounts but not too big to defend. That is where I propose we make our stand. We have enough in our saddlebags to hold out for some days, and we can bring river water in barrels from the town. I have sent orders already to the people of Aquae Sulis to flee, to leave what food they cannot carry on the hill, and to take with them every scrap of food they can."

For a moment longer the issue was in doubt. Then Cunorix grinned. " 'Tis a trap, then, that we'll be setting for our foes."

"It is, and we the bait and the jaws of it both!"

Cunorix half drew his sword. "Then I'd best get busy sharpening mine—" More laughter followed, and Betiver relaxed. He should never have doubted, he thought then, that Artor could handle his men.

The hill bristled against the pale blue of the sky.

At first Oesc thought the uneven line was brush or treetops, but as they drew closer he could see the stubble of cut tree trunks and bushes on the slopes above. The sides of the hill had once been covered with foliage that might have hidden ascending enemies, but now they were denuded, trunks and branches woven into a spiky rampart around the summit.

He swore softly. "Ceretic was so sure we had them on the run! But if Artor was running, this was his goal—he *meant* to lead us here."

Hæsta, who was marching beside him, grunted agreement. "You may know less about leading armies, but you know Artor. Aelle should have listened to you. On the other hand, Artor may not have expected quite so many of us—" He squinted up at the hill. "They're safe for the moment, but where can they go?"

By nightfall, the hill was surrounded, and the Saxon war-

songs drifted upward on the wind. On the next morning the
first assault was mounted on the southern, and least precip-
itous, side of the hill. It was also the best defended, and the
picked force that had ascended was soon retreating once
more.

That afternoon they tried again with a general assault from
all sides at once. In the process they discovered the hard way
that the Britons had a good supply of arrows and retired with
significant, though not crippling, losses. That night they
tended their wounds, and in the chill hour just before dawn,
sent warriors creeping silently up the western side of the hill.
Just as the burning rim of the sun edged the eastern hills a
second force charged the eastern side, screaming war cries,
and the defenders, springing to the breastworks, were dazzled
by the first light of day.

The western force made good use of their distraction,
swarming over the piled logs and taking out the sentries, then
pulling as much of the breastwork down as they could manage to give those who followed easier entry.

It should have worked. The Britons, waking dazed from
sleep, thronged toward the eastern side of the hill, and the
Saxons who were infiltrating from the west fell upon them
from the rear with silent ferocity. Oesc, who was leading
them, was the first to see the figure that reared up before
them, glowing with pale light and crying out words of power
in a voice that paralyzed the soul.

His warriors, not knowing what had come against them,
froze in terror. Oesc recognized Merlin, but for the few cru-
cial moments it took for the Britons to realize where the real
threat lay, his knowledge of the druid's powers incapacitated
him as completely as it had his men. Then the brightness
faded, to be replaced by yelling shapes silhouetted against
the rising sun. Now it was the Saxons who were blinded.
They turned and ran.

For a moment Oesc glimpsed Artor, clad only in breeches,
the dawnlight flaming from his sword. He cried out in challenge, but caught in the midst of his fleeing warriors, he was
carried back to the gap in the breastwork and down the hill.

By the end of that day, the disadvantages of maintaining
a seige with a large army in hostile territory were becoming
clear. Artor and his warriors were surrounded by Saxons, but

the Saxons were surrounded by trackless hills from which all sources of food seemed to have disappeared.

"If we are getting hungry, then they must be too," said Ceretic grimly. "And even if they have food, they must run out of water soon. They have horses up there, lads—tomorrow morning we'll attack again, and keep coming until we overrun the hill. Then we'll feast on horseflesh and offer the king's stallion to the gods."

They were fine words, thought Oesc, binding up a gash on his thigh, but if the Saxons did not succeed in bringing the Britons to battle, they would be eating each other soon. His gaze moved to the long, shrouded shape that lay with the rest of his gear. Until now he had not unwrapped it, for Artor had left his Sword in Londinium, safely sheathed in stone. But Merlin had used magic against them that morning. The next time the Saxons attacked, Oesc would use the Spear.

At sunset it was the high king's custom to make the rounds of the breastworks unescorted, stopping at each guard post to hearten the men on duty there. On the evening of the second day of the seige, Merlin fell into step beside him. He had been waiting for the right moment, when the king, driven to the limit of his resources, would be willing to hear his words.

"Have you come to point out my foolishness, as you used to do when I was a boy? I gambled that if I took refuge here, Aelle would be forced to raise the seige, and my pride may have lost not only the war, but Britannia," Artor said bitterly as they moved along the breastwork. "Tomorrow we must try to break free."

"You did not choose so badly. This hilltop has been a fortress before—" Merlin replied.

"What do you mean?" asked Artor. He paused to greet the men who were leaning against the tangle of logs at the post on the eastern side. Torches on tall poles cast an uncertain light down the slope, a garland of fire that was matched by the larger necklace of watchfires below. Between them, dark shapes lay among the stumps; bodies that neither side had dared to retrieve for fear of arrows from above or below.

"Did you think the gods had leveled this summit in foreknowledge that one day you would need a refuge?" Merlin said as they moved on. "Men lived here before the Romans came. That is why the top is flat and the edges so sheer. Your breastworks are built on the remains of the ramparts they raised to protect their village."

"I wish they were here! I speak words of cheer, but this morning we lost men we could not spare."

"What makes you think that they are not?" said the druid. "Now, in the hour between dark and daylight, all times are one. Open your ears and listen—open your eyes and see. . . ."

As Artor turned, frowning, Merlin touched his forefinger to the spot on his brow just between his eyes. The king staggered, blinking, and the druid held him, his own sight shifting. Overlaid upon the shapes of hide campaign tents he saw round houses of daub and wattle with conical roofs of thatch. The ghostly images of earthen ramparts crowned by a palisade veiled the breastwork of piled logs. And among the warriors of Artor's army moved the figures of men and women and children dressed in the striped and checkered garments of ancient days.

"I see . . ." whispered the king, his voice shaking. "But these are only memories."

"By my arts I can give such substance to these wraiths as will send the Saxons shrieking. But you must call them—"

"In whose name? To what power that they would recognize can I appeal?"

Merlin drew from his pouch a bronze disc with a woman's face in bas-relief. "This is an image of the Goddess—one of those they used to sell to folk who came to bathe in the waters of Sulis. The ancient ones will know it. Fix it to your shield and summon them in the name of the Lady of this land."

The time for tricks and surprises was over. Today must see an ending—both sides knew it, thought Oesc, tightening his grip on the Spear. Before the sun rose the Saxons had taken up their arms; the first rays glittered on ranks of helmets and spearpoints and shields. The toll was likely to be terrible, but by the end of it the Britons would be broken. He would be avenged.

He wondered why that knowledge brought no triumph. *I will weep for you, my king, but I will not hold my hand. . . .*

Saxon cowhorns blared in challenge, and from behind the ramparts, British trumpets shrilled a reply. On the southern side, where once had stood the gateway to the fortress, he glimpsed a shiver of movement. The tree trunks and brush were being pulled away. Of course, he thought then, this was the only slope on which the horses could hope to keep their footing. The momentum of the hill would aid that of the British charge.

Aelle had given Oesc the right flank. His thanes had formed the shieldwall in front of him, but all around him men edged back as they saw him fumbling with the wrappings that covered the Spear. The dawn wind was rising, tugging at the bindings, whipping back the hair that flowed from beneath his helm.

Are you so eager, lord of the slain? Soon, you shall have your prey!

The last knot came free and the transclucent stone of the spearhead glowed in the light of the rising sun. A tremor ran through the rune-carved shaft. Oesc tried to convince himself it was the wind.

Wood cracked above and a horse whinnied shrilly. Wind gusted, flattening the grass, and suddenly the whole world was in movement, logs bouncing and clattering downward, bowling over the first rank of Aelle's houseguard. The first of the horses followed.

Oesc tensed, balancing the Spear. In a single moment he glimpsed Artor's big black horse with the white blaze among them, and felt his arm swinging back of its own accord.

"To Woden I give you!" he cried. The god-power rushed through him as light flared from the boss of Artor's shield. That same power brought his arm forward, plucked the Spear from his hand and sent it arcing through the air, higher and higher. Surely the wind was lifting it, carrying it where the god required it to go.

Oesc followed it with his eyes, over the horsemen who were cascading down the hill through the opening in the breastwork and straight for the man who had sprung onto the logs beside it, his grey beard flying in the wind. He stared, ignoring the tumult around him, as that white-robed figure seemed to expand, reaching, and impossibly, caught the Spear.

To Merlin, it was a streak of incandescent power. He reached out with body and spirit, knowing only that he must keep it from plunging into the mass of men behind him. And then, like a striking eagle, it came to his hand, and agony flared through every nerve and limb. He wheezed as the air was squeezed from his lungs, breathed again in a great gasp and felt the pain replaced by ecstasy.

Consciousness whirled upward as through the gateway thundered wave after wave of men and horses. With awareness at once precisely focused and impossibly extended, Merlin heard each battle cry and knew the name of the man who uttered it. He heard the silent yelling of the wraiths who rose from the earth as Artor called them, felt them flow down the hill, and heard the terrified babble of the men who fell before them. He heard, as once before at Verulamium, the battle-shriek of Cathubodva's raven that weakened the sinews and fettered the will, as Artor swept back and forth across the field, scything down men as a reaper cuts grain.

He knew all words in all languages, and the language of the earth itself, the song of every blade of grass and leaf on tree.

And he heard, with a clarity beyond mortal hearing, a Voice that whispered, *"All those who battle on this field I claim—my speech will fill the mouths of their children's children; my law will rule this land. But today, to your king I give the victory. . . . "*

Oesc fought an army of shadows, with shadow-warriors at his side. Some of them had faces he knew—men he had led to battle, and men he had known as a child. It was when he saw Octha his father among them that he understood that this battlefield was not the British hill he had left, but the plain before Wælhall. He stopped then, and put down his sword. His father saw, and turned to him, gesturing toward the foe.

"Is this all," Oesc cried, *"Is there no other way but war?"* As he spoke the shadows faded, and he fell down a long tunnel and back into his body once more.

At least he assumed it was so, for he was very cold. With an effort he drew a breath, and felt the first tinglings of pain. With sensation came hearing—the cries of wounded men, and someone speaking nearby.

"Oesc, can you hear me?"

With another effort of will, Oesc made his eyes open. Artor was bending over him, his hair matted by the pressure of his helmet and the smudges of fatigue shadowing his eyes.

"My lord. . . ." It was barely a whisper. "He took Rigana. Why didn't you answer me?"

"I didn't know!" Artor's face contorted. "By our Lady I swear that you were on the march before I knew." He reached out to take Oesc's hand.

Oesc tried to return the grip, but nothing seemed to be happening. "I can't . . . feel . . ."

He sensed movement and saw that Artor was cradling his hand against his breast, but he felt nothing at all.

"A horse fell on him," said another voice. He could not turn his head to see. "I think his back is broken."

There was a moment of shock, and a rush of bitterness as Oesc understood that he would never hold Rigana in his arms, never see his son grow to be a man, never again watch the rich grasslands of Cantuware rippling in the wind from the sea. All his hopes, his ambitions . . . whirled away like dust on the breeze. . . . He fought for control.

This, then, was the Wyrd that the runes had foretold for him, the outcome of all the choices he had made. It was the gift of a hero to know when the time had come to cease fighting. To choose whether his spirit should dwell with the gods or stay to guard his people was the gift of a king.

"I don't remember that . . . only the fighting. . . ." With difficulty, he drew breath once more. The cold had increased; he didn't have much time. "My lord . . . find Rigana and my son. . . ."

"They are safe—" Artor said quickly. "I will bring them back to Cantium. And you—" His words failed.

Oesc remembered the shrine at Ægele's ford and the promise he had given there. "Make my mound next to Hengest's, and I will guard the land. I am . . . its king. But you . . . are different. You belong to all . . . Britannia."

A sudden flush of color came into Artor's face, as if only

now was he realizing that with the Anglians tamed and the southern Saxons broken, for the first time in his reign he was truly the high king. He cleared his throat.

"Eormenric shall have your high seat, and while I live no one will dare to challenge him!"

Oesc managed a smile, and after another moment, the breath to speak again. "Only one last gift . . . to ask. . . ." Sudden anguish filled Artor's eyes, but Oesc held his gaze until he nodded acceptance. "Now. . . ."

Light glinted from the king's dagger. Still smiling, Oesc closed his eyes. There was a swift pressure, but no pain, only the sweetness of release as his heart's blood flowed out to feed the earth and he gave his breath back to the god.

PEOPLE AND PLACES

†

PEOPLE IN THE STORY
CAPITALS = major character
* = historical personnage
( ) = dead before story begins
[ ] = name as given in later literature
Italics = deity or mythological personnage

Ægele—thane holding Ægele's ford for Hengest
*AELLE—king of the South Saxons;
Æthelhere—one of Eadguth's thanes
Aggarban [Agravaine]—third son of Morgause
Alfgifu—daughter to Ceretic
(*Ambrosius Aurelianus—emperor of Britannia and Vitalinus's rival)
(Amlodius—Artor's grandfather)
Andulf—a Burgund bard in the service of Hengest
(Artoria Argantel—Artor's grandmother)
ARTORIUS/ARTOR [Arthur] son of Uthir and Igierne, high king of Britannia
(*Augustinus of Hippo—St. Augustine, originator of the doctrine of predestination)
Baldulf—a Jutish warrior settled in the North
Belinus—prince of Demetia

BETIVER [Bedivere]—nephew to Riothamus, one of Artor's companions

Brigantia [Brigid]—British goddess of inspiration, healing, and the land

Byrhtwold—a thane in the service of Eadguth and Hengest

CAI—son of Caius Turpilius, Artor's foster-brother and companion

Caidiau—commander of the western forts on the Wall

Caius Turpilius—Artor's foster-father

CATAUR [Cador]—prince of Dumnonia

Cathubodva—Lady of Ravens, a British war goddess

*Catraut—prince of Verulamium

*CERETIC [Cerdic]—son of Maglos of Verulamium, king of the West Saxons

*Chlodovechus—king of the Franks in Gallia

*Constantine—son of Cataur

*Cunorix—a hostage from the Irish of Demetia, later leader of Artor's Irish allies

*Cymen—Aelle's eldest son

Cyniarchus—son of Matauc of Durnovaria

*Cynric—son of Ceretic

*Dumnoval [Dyfnwal]—daughter's son of Germanianus and Ridarchus's brother, lord of the southern Votadini

Docomaglos [Docco]—prince of Dumnonia, second son of Gerontius the elder

*Dubricius—bishop of Isca and primate of Britannia

Eadguth—king of the Myrgings, Oesc's maternal grandfather

Eadric—one of Hengest's thanes

Ebrdila—an old priestess on the Isle of Maidens

Eldaul [Eldol]—prince of Glevum

Eldaul the Younger—his son, one of Artor's ministers

Eleutherius—old lord of Eboracum

(*Eormenaric [Ermanaric]—king of the Goths at time of Hun invasion)

*Eormenric—son of Oesc, heir to Cantuware

Fastidius—a priest in Artor's service

Freo [Freyja, the Frowe]—Germanic goddess of love and prosperity

Frige [Frigga]—Germanic goddess of marriage, queen of the gods

Ganeda [Ganiedda]—Merlin's half-sister, wife of Ridarchus

Geflaf—chief of Eadguth's sword-thanes

*Germanianus—prince of the South Votadini

*Gerontius the Younger—son of Docomaglos

Godwulf—oldest of the Saxon priests, formerly one of Merlin's teachers

(Gorangonus—prince of Durovernum, grandfather of Rigana)

(Gorlosius—elder son of Docomaglos, father of Morgause)

(*Gundohar [Gunther]—king of the Burgunds, killed by Attila)

Goriat [Gareth]—fourth son of Morgause

Guthlaf—a warrior in Hengest's hall

GUALCHMAI [Gawain]—first son of Morgause

Gwyhir [Gaheris]—second son of Margause

Hæsta—a Jutish chieftain who settles in Cantuware

HÆTHWÆGE—a wisewoman in the service of Hengest

*HENGEST—mercenary warrior, later king of Cantuware

(Hildeguth—Oesc's mother)

Hrofe Guthereson—eorl holding Durobrivae

Hyge and Mynd [Huginn and Muninn]—Woden's ravens

*ICEL—king of the Anglians in Britannia

IGIERNE—Artor's mother, Lady of the Lake

Ing [Yngvi]—Germanic god of peace and plenty

Johannes Rutilius—count of Lugdunensis, father of Betiver

Leodagranus [Leodegrance]—prince of Lindinis

LEUDONUS [Lot]—king of the Votadini

Matauc [Madoc]—king of the Durotriges, lord of Durnovaria

Maglos Leonorus—king of the Belgae, Ceretic's father

Mannus—mythic ancestor of the Ingvaeones

MORGAUSE—daughter of Igierne and Gorlosius, queen of the Votadini

MERLIN—druid and wizard, Artor's advisor

*NAITAN MORBET—king of all the provinces of the Picts

Norns—Germanic goddesses of fate

*OCTHA—son of Hengest, Oesc's father

*OESC—son of Octha and king of Cantuware

(*Offa—king of Angeln, enemy of the Myrgings)

(*Pelagius—fourth-century British theologian who believed in salvation through good deeds)

Peretur [Peredur]—son of Eleutherius, lord of Eboracum

*Ridarchus—king at Alta Cluta

RIGANA—granddaughter of Gorangonus, wife of Oesc

*Riothamus—duke of the Britons of Armorica

(Sigfrid Fafnarsbane [Siegfried]—hero)

Thunor [Thor]—Germanic god of thunder

Tir [Tyr]—Germanic god of war and justice

(*Vitalinus, the VOR-TIGERNUS, over-king of Britannia)

(Uthir [Uther Pendragon]—high king of Britannia, Artor's father)

(Wihtgils, Witta, Wehta—Anglian kings in Hengest's line)

Woden (and Willa and Weoh) [Odin, Vili, Ve]—Germanic god of magic, war, and wisdom

Wulfhere—one of Oesc's sword-thanes

†
PLACES

Aegele's ford—Aylesford, Kent
Abus—Humber
Afallon [Avalon]—Glastonbury
Alta Cluta—Dumbarton Rock
Ambrosiacum—Amesbury
Anderida—Pevensey, Kent
Anglia—Angeln in northern Germany
Blackwater—River Dubglas, probably the Witham
  in Lincoln
Calleva—Silchester
Camulodunum—Colchester
Cantium/Cantuware—Kent
Cantuwaraburh—Canterbury
Cluta Fluvius—the Clyde
Cornovia/Kernow—Cornwall
Demetia—modern Pembrokeshire
Deva—Chester
Dubris—Dover
Dumnonia—the Cornish peninsula
Dun Breatann—Dumbarton
Dun Eidyn—Edinborough
Dun Tagell/Durocornovium—Tintagel
Durobrivae—Rochester
Durolipons—Cambridge
Durovernum Cantiacorum—Canterbury
Durnovaria—Dorchester, Dorset
Eburacum—York
Fifeldor—"Monster Gate," the mouth of the Eider, Germany
Giant's Dance—Stonehenge
Glevum—Gloucester
Guenet—Gwynedd
Icene—River Ictis

Isca Dumnoniorum—Exeter

Isca Silurum—Caerleon

Isle of Glass—Glastonbury, Somerset

Jute-land—northern Denmark

Liger—River Loire

Lemanis—Lympne, Kent

Lindum—Lincoln; Lindensis—the country around it

Londinium—London

Luguvalium—Carlisle

Lugdunensis—Lyons, France

Maridunum—Carmarthen

Meduwege—the Medway River

Mona—the isle of Anglesey

Myrging lands—between the Eider and the Elbe

Novantae lands—Dumfriesshire and Galloway

Portus Adurni—Portsmouth

Regnum—Chichester

Rutupiae—Richborough, Kent

Rhenus—River Rhine

Salmaes—the Solway

Saxon lands—between the Ems and the Elbe

Sorviodunum—Old Sarum (Salisbury)

Stratcluta—Strathclyde

Tamesis Fluvius—Thames River

Tanatus Insula—Isle of Thanet, Kent

Tava Fluvius—the Tay

Treonte, Trisantona—the Trent

Vecta Insula—Isle of Wight

Venta—later Gwent, modern Monmouthshire

Votadini lands—southeast Scotland, from the firth of Forth
to the Wall

Venta Belgarum—Winchester

Venta Icenorum—Caistor St. Edmunds

Venta Silurum—Caerwent

Verulamium—St. Albans

AVON EOS PRESENTS
MASTERS OF FANTASY AND ADVENTURE

LORD DEMON
by Roger Zelazny and Jane Lindskold
77023-7/$6.99 US/$9.99 CAN

CARTHAGE ASCENDANT
The Book of Ash, #2
by Mary Gentle
79912-X/$6.99 US/$9.99 CAN

THE HALLOWED ISLE
The Book of the Sword and The Book of the Spear
by Diana L. Paxson
81367-X/$6.50 US/$8.99 CAN

THE WILD HUNT: CHILD OF FIRE
by Jocelin Foxe
80550-2/$5.99 US/$7.99 CAN

LEGENDS WALKING
A Novel of the Athanor
by Jane Lindskold
78850-0/$6.99 US/$9.99 CAN

OCTOBERLAND
Book Three of the Dominions of Irth
by Adam Lee
80628-2/$6.50 US/$8.99 CAN

THE GARDEN OF THE STONE
by Victoria Strauss
79752-6/$6.99 US/$9.99 CAN
